One Night on Ice

ALSO BY MANDY BAGGOT

One Last Greek Summer
One Christmas Star

ONE NIGHT ON ICE

Mandy Baggot

An Aria Book

This edition first published in the United Kingdom in 2019 by Aria, an imprint of Head of Zeus Ltd

Copyright © Mandy Baggot, 2019

The moral right of Mandy Baggot to be identified as the author of this work has been asserted in accordance with the Copyright, Designs and Patents Act of 1988.

All rights reserved. No part of this publication may be reproduced, stored in a retrieval system, or transmitted, in any form or by any means, electronic, mechanical, photocopying, recording, or otherwise, without the prior permission of both the copyright owner and the above publisher of this book.

This is a work of fiction. All characters, organizations, and events portrayed in this novel are either products of the author's imagination or are used fictitiously.

A CIP catalogue record for this book is available from the British Library.

ISBN 9781789546316

Cover design © Charlotte Abrams-Simpson

Aria
c/o Head of Zeus
First Floor East
5–8 Hardwick Street
London EC1R 4RG

www.ariafiction.com

For Joff – who I love very much and who tirelessly printed the manuscript out! x

I

'Oh my goodness!' Samantha shrieked.

Two boxes, one from either side, toppled down onto her and in seconds she was knee-deep in tubs. The coldness spread up her legs and she began to dive her hands into the pile, shovelling them upwards and back into boxes as rapidly as she could.

Four thousand tubs of ice cream, all Berry Fruits. How could this have happened? She had been staring at the boxes, piled high in the walk-in freezer, for more than five minutes wondering what to do and then they'd attacked, jumped on her and made a break for freedom.

She wanted to scream. Dave the manager had done this. She had been on her lunch break when the ice cream company called last week, randomly, out of the blue and not on their usual day. Dave had placed the order. Her systems interfered with, stock control blown.

Now she was squeezed into the ever-decreasing space desperately hoping that the audiences to come would have an uncontrollable desire for iced Berry Fruits and that her colleagues Jane and Felicity would be able to navigate their way past all the boxes to access the vanilla and chocolate.

She picked up the ice creams in a frenzy, slinging them

back into boxes to restore order and trying to make an access pathway as she went along.

'Miaow!'

The sound of a cat screeching loudly and then hissing had Samantha reeling back into the boxes. She scuffed her foot against a tub and banged her head against the shelf. She clutched at her chest recovering from the fright and then, seeing what had made the noise, she bent down to the tabby cat as it started to scratch at anything accessible.

'Gobby, what are you doing in here? I've told you before about going places you shouldn't. Going places you shouldn't only leads to trouble,' Samantha spoke, picking up the scruffy animal and stroking it under the chin.

Glad of the attention, Gobby looked up at Samantha, his wide blue eyes staring at her affectionately as he began to purr. She put the cat down and began to straighten up the boxes. They had to fit. They had to be straight or the door wouldn't shut and then they would defrost, and it would be hundreds of pounds of wastage.

Her fingers were numb by the time she had finished, and she was sure her hair had got frost bite. She surveyed the ends and then pushed it back behind both ears. Catching sight of her reflection, she let out another irritated sigh and began to pick at her jumper. It was covered in bits of ice. She started to try and pick them off and then gave up and just poked them until they melted. So much for West End glamour!

Although it wasn't really West End, that was just what Dave told the paying public and mentioned on the telephone as often as any conversation would allow. 'In the heart of the West End' he would tell customers, 'in the West End's historic centre'.

Three Tube stops from the glitz and sparkle of any of the illustrious theatres was not, as far as Samantha or anyone else on the planet was concerned, 'within a whisker of Theatreland'.

Her uniform covered in flakes of frost and her fingers tingling with cold, she scooped up Gobby and headed towards the front doors.

'Now, I don't know where you hang out during the day, but you can't stay here. Dave wouldn't like it and Jane sneezes when you're around.'

The stray mewed and looked up at Samantha sadly, its shoulders hunched. She had given Gobby his name. When she was a child, she had loved the story *Gobbolino the Witch's Cat* and the name somehow suited him. He didn't look much like the main character in the book, but he was so scruffy he could easily have belonged to a witch at some time. A witch with a grooming aversion. Gobby walked with a limp, had a damaged eye (that confused you as to which way it was looking) and he was the scrawniest animal she had ever seen. He had just appeared one day at the back door of the hall scrounging for food in the bins and she had taken pity on him. He had rubbed up against her, mewed sweetly and then ravenously devoured the ham she gave him. Ever since that first day when he had gone on to polish off a piece of chocolate cheesecake, he had kept coming back. Mostly at lunchtime, especially if fish was on the menu.

'Looking like that is blackmail, now shoo,' Samantha ordered, waving an arm towards the street in front of them.

Gobby didn't move but continued to fix Samantha with

a timid, downtrodden expression.

'Alright, come back later and I'll see what's left over.'

Happy with the response, as if he understood, Gobby turned his back on Samantha and sprinted off down the street in the direction of Andre's kebab shop. Samantha hoped he found some scraps and didn't end up skewered and on the menu.

Pulling at her cold, ice-ridden hair she went back behind the brick façade to sit down at the front desk.

Woolston Civic Hall wasn't exactly The Prince of Wales theatre. It was an old, rather dilapidated building just far enough away from the bright lights and buzz of the West End to be completely missed by anyone who didn't know it was there. Samantha's parents had been regular visitors to the hall, attending shows ranging from slapstick comedy to opera and everything in between. It had been popular then, a centre for variety – it was a lot less popular now. Variety had taken a nosedive and now people either wanted celebrity, lovey-darling musical theatre, or Shakespeare. The Civic Hall didn't attract that type of performance and if it ever tried to, it would be putting itself in direct competition with the West End theatres, with little hope of winning.

Samantha hadn't ever envisaged working in a box office. She had dropped into the hall during her lunch break, when she worked for Simpkin's Shoes, on a mission to buy tickets for the ABBA tribute band. ABBA wasn't really her thing, but her elder sister Cleo loved anything that embraced the Seventies. She loved all the big hair, shiny flares and glitter balls.

When Samantha arrived at the hall the whole place was deserted. She'd waited for a while, just to see if anyone appeared, passing the time by looking at a poster of Dual Eclipse, an illusionist act scheduled for the following week. And then the telephones had started ringing. No one appeared to take ownership of the situation and when the incessant ringing got too much, Samantha decided to act.

She had answered the first call and given someone directions and on the second call, managing to navigate the computer system, she had sold six tickets to Puppetry of the Penis. After her timely intervention, Dave hadn't been able to get a name badge on her fast enough.

She had started work at the hall two weeks later and that was five years ago. Five years of booking tickets for almost forgotten Eighties pop stars and five years of selling programmes and ice creams. Nothing had changed, well apart from a lick of paint in the foyer. It was called Wheat Dream. Cleo thought that had sounded well dodgy.

In the five years Samantha had been at the hall, Cleo had had seven jobs and twice as many boyfriends. At first Samantha tried her best to remember their names as she caught fleeting glances of them when their paths crossed, usually on their way from Cleo's bedroom to the bathroom. Then, after she mistook a Simon for a Steve, she decided enough was enough and all any of them got now was a mumbled 'hello'. Besides, she was quite sure none of them knew her name – or even Cleo's.

Living with Cleo was an experience in itself. Her sister was as outgoing as Samantha was introvert. Everything about her shouted. Her clothes were bright and up to the minute and she changed her appearance as often as she changed her men. Their mother called Cleo 'flighty'. Samantha had always thought that was a bit of a putdown but Cleo treated it almost as a compliment. 'Flighty' to Cleo meant exciting and mysterious, someone who experienced all things with passion and pizzazz. In contrast, Samantha didn't know the first thing about being flighty and she wasn't entirely sure she wanted to. Cleo lived her life at a hundred miles an hour whereas Samantha was content chugging along in first gear. That way you always knew where you were. It was comforting to know where you were in life.

'Good afternoon Woolston Civic Hall, Samantha speaking.'

Her headset was itching today. She didn't know why but it was definitely more uncomfortable than usual, and it was making her want to scratch. Or perhaps it was Gobby's fault, maybe he had fleas again and was sharing. That wouldn't be good, that would probably mean a rash. Itching wasn't good either when you needed both hands for navigating your way around the booking system.

The woman on the other end of the telephone wanted tickets to *Skating on Broadway* the following evening. Eight tickets. There was nothing like leaving booking to the last minute.

Skating on Broadway was a first for the Woolston Civic Hall and a bit of a coup. The Apollo Arena (the biggest entertainment venue in the capital) had a month-long run of Mickey Mouse – Magical Party that meant the Civic Hall was the London venue of the skating show's nationwide tour. For the next few weeks the main auditorium would be transformed into an ice rink where former skating champions would whizz around the ice to the sounds of *Phantom of the Opera* and other musicals, performing hair-raising jumps and lifts in brightly coloured Lycra. She had got Cleo six tickets for a couple of performances (using her discount) as she knew her sister was trying to impress some colleagues at her new job at the estate agents.

'I'm afraid we don't have any tickets left in the first ten rows, Madam. The closest to the ice I can get you are rows K and L, four seats in each row, directly behind each other,' Samantha bargained, looking at the plan of the seating chart on her screen.

She had devised the seating plan herself as Dave was more into management in a PR capacity. He was good with the customers and the acts, but rather lacking when it came to actually managing. It had been a difficult job, it was the first time they had had the performance taking place in the centre of the auditorium instead of on the stage.

The seats she had offered were not doing it for the woman on the phone and as she was suggesting eight seats all sat together in row R, she noticed someone loitering by the entrance. The man had caught her attention because he was carrying the largest bag she had ever seen. She saw him look at the poster outside advertising *Ballet for All Seasons* and then, with his free hand, he pushed open the double doors at the entrance and came into the hall.

'I realise you'd like to be nearer the ice, Madam, but tomorrow night is almost sold out and there are only so many seats I can offer due to fire regulations,' Samantha spoke, tapping on her keyboard and wishing the woman would just hurry up and book something. If she was honest, she could think of nothing else but the ice cream. She didn't know what to do for the best. What she wanted to do was buy it all herself and eat it, just so she didn't have to worry about it anymore, but even she knew that was a bit mad.

The man was walking across the room now and heading towards her. He was tall, almost six foot and slim. He had light brown hair that was fashionably spiked up, and he was wearing sunglasses. As well as the huge bag in his hand, he had a rucksack on his back.

Samantha smiled politely as he approached her desk and he removed his sunglasses and smiled back at her. Immediately she noticed his deep brown eyes. They were like dark chocolate. Chocolate. Vanilla. *Ice cream*. She was back to fretting about the excess supply of Berry Fruits.

'I can offer you another date, perhaps Friday?' Samantha bargained.

Dave should have been back from lunch by now. He'd been gone almost an hour and a half, and he was supposed to be manning reception while Samantha took her break.

The man put his bag down on the floor and picked up a leaflet about the ice show from the rack on the counter.

'No, I'm sorry, nothing nearer the front for tomorrow night's show. No, absolutely nothing, not even if you've been patronising us for a decade, Madam,' Samantha spoke, her patience wearing thin.

She couldn't tell Felicity about the ice cream, she would laugh and find it all highly amusing, she wouldn't understand Samantha's concern. She had a system in that freezer, cones on one side, tubs on another, ice poles on the top shelf. At the moment all you could see was the Berry Fruits logo as soon as you opened the door, Billy Blackberry leapfrogging Sally Strawberry.

The man raised his head to look at her, a smirk appearing on his face in appreciation of her comment to the customer.

Samantha mouthed an apology to him and then, seeing

writing implements in reach, she took a pen and a piece of paper and quickly wrote:

How can I help?

She pushed the paper and the pen across the desk towards him.

'Do I have any tickets for *Ballet for All Seasons?* Yes, of course, that performance isn't until later in the year,' Samantha spoke to her customer on the telephone.

She watched as the man wrote something on the paper and passed it back to her, together with the pen.

Samantha picked it up and read it:

Which way are the dressing rooms?

Samantha hurriedly scrawled on the paper, this time two lines' worth, and pushed it back across the counter.

He looked at the message:

The dressing rooms are for performers only if you are entourage you need the door at the back of the building

'I can book you tickets for the ballet now, but did you want tickets for *Skating on Broadway?*' Samantha asked, truly getting fed up with the caller. Perhaps she should ask her preferred ice cream flavour though, as a bit of market research.

She watched as the man began to draw on the *Skating on Broadway* leaflet, a large round circle and an arrow, and then he wrote something on the bottom of the paper. He passed both things to her with a smile.

Samantha looked down at the leaflet and then at the note.

I'm Jimmy and that's me in the red Lycra

Samantha looked at the picture of the skaters on the front of the pamphlet and saw that he was indeed the principal skater, Jimmy Lloyd.

She could feel her face redden and the Woolston Civic Hall jumper turn into inappropriate warm wear as the embarrassment threatened to engulf her. Now all she wanted to do was hold on to her irritating caller. She was her only reason for not having to talk to the ice star she hadn't recognised.

She hurriedly scribbled on the paper and, not daring to look at him again, she passed it over.

First door on the left, follow the corridor – sorry

Jimmy smiled and wrote a hasty reply. He passed the paper back to Samantha, picked up his bag and made his way down the room.

'No, Madam, the ballet's only here for one night,' Samantha spoke, turning the paper towards herself so she could read it.

Thank you, Samantha

The name badges had a lot to answer for. Dave called them a useful tool that made the customers feel they were 'getting to know you each time you interact'. Samantha only enjoyed having her name emblazoned on her chest when it meant people wrote cards or telephoned Dave to praise her on the wonderful service she had given them, which didn't really happen that often. Other than that, it was a nuisance, particularly when customers started bandying it around in conversation, like the ability to see your name suddenly made you best friends. 'Will there be any flashing lights during the performance, *Samantha*?' or 'Oh it's *Samantha*, isn't it? I wonder if you could tell me, *Samantha*, what time the show is due to finish'. And if someone had cause to complain, *Samantha*, who was exposing her name so brazenly, was in the firing line immediately. She hadn't had a complaint since the guide dog incident, but failing to recognise one of the main stars of *Skating on Broadway*, that was unforgiveable.

What was the matter with her? She studied the What's On guide in detail, she should have been expecting the performers to start turning up, she should have paid more attention.

She didn't notice Dave's reappearance until it was too late and he leaned over her, resting a plump hand on the desk and breathing deeply so she got the full benefit of the beer and pork scratching fumes. Real ale was obviously on special offer at the pub again. It wasn't pleasant and Samantha immediately removed her headset and rose from her chair to avoid any further wafts that might be directed her way.

'Alright, Duck? How were sales while I was out?' Dave questioned, sitting his large body down on the chair that immediately depressed a few inches under the weight.

'Good. *Humpty Dumpty and Friends* is almost sold out, I've sold about fifty tickets for various nights of *Skating on Broadway* and *Ballet for All Seasons* is also doing well,' Samantha informed him, taking her bag down from the peg behind the desks.

'Well done, Duck. Keep this up and you could be in line for a BOB,' Dave informed her, smiling just enough for Samantha to catch a glimpse of his gold tooth.

She smiled back and picked up her bag. A BOB (Box Office Bonus) was a night out with Dave at his favourite pizzeria where he ate too much garlic, drank too much wine and tried to make you do the same. Then you had to try and do or say anything to avoid sharing a taxi with him or letting him walk you anywhere. She had been on a BOB night once, when she had first started working at the hall. Now, although she was the highest selling assistant every month, she made sure she assigned a large proportion of her ticket sales against Felicity's code. Never again was she going to experience the humiliation of a fat, balding, forty-something trying to hit on her.

'Oh, one thing that happened – Jimmy Lloyd turned up. But the show doesn't start until tomorrow night and I didn't think we were expecting anyone today,' Samantha spoke as she paused by the door that led away from the front desk.

'Prior arrangements, Samantha, I should've mentioned it. Did he ask for me? I expect he asked for me, didn't he?' Dave spoke, leaning back in the chair and cracking his knuckles loudly as he put his hands together.

'Well no, but...' Samantha started, the noise setting her teeth on edge.

'I let the boys in earlier, the technical crew who are setting up the rink. Nice lads, down to earth, you know – *au natural* as we say. Jimmy Lloyd wanted to get in some extra rehearsal time,' Dave informed Samantha.

'Oh,' Samantha responded.

She was doing her best not to become irritated as she watched Dave slick his hands through his hair before putting on the headset she had just been wearing. No wonder it was making her itch. It wasn't Gobby's fur or fleas, it was two tonne of hair products. He went on to put his Brylcreamed fingers all over the keyboard. Sanitising wipes, she needed to order some, she was down to her last packet.

'OK, Duck, you get off to your break. The manager's here to manage,' Dave told her with another gold-toothed grin.

Samantha gave him a weak smile and headed out of the office and into the main lobby.

She never went out at lunchtimes. She wasn't a shopper or one for fancy wraps or expensive pasta lunches, and sitting on a bench in the nearby park did nothing for her. The park was usually full of single mothers with kids who screamed and chased swans with sticks, or tramps lying on the best benches away from the bins. There was usually bird shit on any benches that weren't taken up by tramps or single mothers and if you didn't get an over-friendly dog wanting to hump your leg while you were eating your sandwich you were lucky. And then there were the joggers who gave you a death stare as you bit into your tuna mayo and made you feel like you should be eating nothing but Nimble bread and watercress or eating nothing at all and racing round the park supping Evian like it was going out of fashion.

So, lunchtimes for Samantha involved a short trip up two flights of stairs to the light and sound booth. Although it was only a small room predominately filled with a mixing desk that controlled the in-house speakers and lights, she had made it her haven. She had some favourite books there, a radio and magazines Cleo had given her (the usual celebrity and fashion trash but it passed the time) and she had a bird's eye view of the arena of the Civic Hall. Most importantly it was quiet, there were no telephones, no customers, and no Dave, meaning she could sit and relax for an hour.

Cleo had no understanding of what it was like to be quiet and alone with just your thoughts for company. When she'd asked Samantha what she did for her lunch hour she felt compelled to lie. She told her she walked up West most days mentioning Primark and H&M a good few times.

She wasn't sure Cleo believed her, but it was better than admitting she hardly ever left the Civic Hall in the daytime and was back there again most evenings.

It wasn't that she didn't have friends, she had been out with Felicity and Karen for drinks after work at least twice, she just preferred her own company. What was wrong with that? Plus she had Cleo to fill any void she might have with her endless chatter and racy lifestyle. It was like sharing a flat with a principal actress in a continuing drama, there was just no need for Samantha to assert herself towards excitement, Cleo provided it all with no effort required.

She was just about to start flicking through *Star Life* magazine when she suddenly realised there appeared to be more light coming from the main arena than usual. She moved her seat forward, so she was closer to the window that overlooked the floor. She pressed her nose against the glass and the scene that greeted her almost took her breath away. A large proportion of the floor space had been turned into an ice rink and the bright whiteness was shining up into the arena like a reflection from a giant mirror.

She was just beginning to marvel at her seating arrangement around the rink when she saw someone step onto the ice and start to skate round it. She put *Star Life* magazine down on top of the mixing desk and watched the skater moving around the ice, getting faster and faster as he warmed up his blades.

She could see it was Jimmy Lloyd, but he'd changed from what he'd been wearing earlier and was now dressed in a deep blue long-sleeved polo neck and black tracksuit bottoms with thick socks tapering the trousers in at the top of his skates.

Samantha was transfixed, watching him gather speed across the ice and then jump. He made two turns in the air and landed on one foot, elegantly moving off again as if it had been the simplest manoeuvre in the world.

Her knowledge of ice skating could be summed up in three words. Torvill & Dean. But she had skated herself, years ago. When she was a teenager, she and Cleo had been regulars at an ice disco near to where they'd lived. She had enjoyed the music and the exercise while Cleo had enjoyed teetering around the café in her blades chatting up boys who used to speed around the ice for five minutes, not caring what or who was in their path, and then decamp to the café and decant Martini Rosso into their coffee. The ice rink had long since been turned into a housing estate.

She watched Jimmy moving around the ice, changing direction and speed, jumping and twisting and turning. She didn't know much about the technicalities of what he was doing, but even someone with her limited knowledge could tell he was good.

And then abruptly he stopped, in the middle of the ice, and raised his head to look up towards the sound booth. Immediately Samantha launched her chair backwards away from the window, wheeling herself up against the back wall and dipping her head. She had to make sure she wasn't seen. No one knew this was her place and she wanted to keep it that way. If she lost the sanctuary of sitting alone in her hideaway at lunchtimes, she might be forced to sit in the restaurant that, even though it was rarely busy, was not a place to collect your thoughts. She would end up being befriended by Mrs Nelmes, the lady who came in every day smelling of wee, made a cup of tea last three hours and picked the sultanas out of her scone. Or even worse, she might have to start walking up West and pretending to be interested in boutiques.

She was such an idiot. She shouldn't have been staring out of the window watching what was going on. It would be her own fault if she'd been seen. She flipped open *Star Life* magazine and went back to reading about anorexic footballers' wives. How did it feel to be that thin? She didn't really want to be that thin because it looked like some of them had quite a lot of difficulty just standing up, or maybe that was just the mad, sometimes multi-storey shoes they wore and nothing to do with their lack of waistline. If she was honest though, she wouldn't mind being slightly slimmer, like Cleo. Perhaps that was why Cleo enjoyed shopping so much. Cleo's figure was such she could walk into any shop, pick something off the rail and it would fit. Samantha, although only a size fourteen, never seemed to fit into anything properly. It was either too long in the leg or too tight round the waist and that was the main reason why there was no joy in shopping for her. She had had a bad experience in one of the large chain stores once, involving a 'helpful' sales assistant, a size fourteen dress and a jammed zip. The incident had scarred her. She didn't really do clothes anyway, so it didn't matter. She was in uniform most of the time and there was always her wardrobe full of Cleo's cast offs if she was desperate.

She also wasn't blonde. Everyone who was anyone was blonde. Samantha had inherited her mother's mousey brown hair which never seemed to respond to any shape it was cut into, unlike Cleo's hair that was blonde and wavy like their father's. Cleo's hair could be fashioned into any style, given some curlers or tongs and imagination. Currently Samantha's hair was in a sort of chin length bob. It was supposed to resemble Victoria Beckham's latest transformation, as suggested by Cleo, but it was starting to annoy her because it flopped over her face at really inappropriate moments. Cleo was also always trying to persuade her to dye it. A number of times she'd brought home some Superdrug own brand colorant she had bought on a BOGOF and insisted that they both turn Lightest Light Ash Blonde together over a Chinese and a box set of *Friends*. So far Samantha had managed to wriggle out of it. Twenty-four years old and she had never dyed her hair. Apparently, that was weird.

Samantha turned the page of the magazine and saw to her dismay that the problem page had been torn out. The problem page was one of her favourite features as, as hopeless as the stories were, it reminded her of the fact that her life was uncomplicated in comparison. She knew she didn't have hairy nipples, gonorrhoea or a boyfriend who called her 'lard-arse' and those facts were comforting.

She closed the magazine and slowly inched her chair back towards the window. Very carefully she lifted her head up to look out of the glass and down onto the ice. She took a deep breath and moved so she could see the whole of the rink. She was glad to see it empty. Jimmy Lloyd had gone.

She breathed a sigh of relief and retrieved her lunchbox from her bag. She opened it up and very quickly realised it wasn't hers, it was Cleo's. This meant it housed cream cheese and Worcester sauce. Samantha made a face, she couldn't stand Worcester sauce. It had been a lifelong hatred ever since her mother had added it to the gravy to pep up the family roast one Sunday. The mixture had been the vilest substance imaginable and had spawned her detestation of anything made by Lea & Perrins. Cleo, in contrast, had to have Worcester sauce with everything, so much so she carried a bottle of it in her handbag. Samantha had once investigated whether you could actually buy the sauce in sachets hoping they would be more discreet to use in restaurants than a two hundred and fifty millilitre bottle.

She hastily put the lid back on the lunchbox to stop the smell escaping even more and put it down on the sound desk. Cleo would be mad when she noticed. She wouldn't eat tuna, she would have to buy something from the deli and then liberally splash it with the smelly brown stuff. Gobby hated Worcester sauce too, that and cottage pie.

2

It was 6.00 pm before Samantha got home. Home was the two-bedroom house she shared with Cleo, ten minute walk (one Tube stop) from the Civic Hall. They had used to live in the outskirts of the city in a large, somewhat spooky house, their father had inherited from his grandmother. Then, when their parents decided to retire to the coast, the spooky house was sold for a small fortune and this enabled the purchase of Samantha and Cleo's home, as well as their parents' bungalow by the sea. Cleo had chosen the house. It was at the top end of their parents' budget in a smart area of the city, and it had been close to Cleo's work at the time (an assistant at the jewellers where she lasted three weeks before getting caught in the safe snogging a customer). Samantha knew their parents were feeling guilty about moving away, even though their daughters were nineteen and twenty-two at the time, and she knew that her mother would be fretting and raising her blood pressure unless she knew they were settled and happy. As long as it had four walls and the essentials, Samantha didn't mind what it was like, as long it wasn't too far away from the Civic Hall. There had been no question of her and Cleo going their separate ways. Who would turn down the offer of a property with no mortgage just because it meant living with your sister? They complemented each other anyway, well kind of, and Samantha would never have forgiven herself if Cleo had gone to live alone and been burnt to a crisp one day drying a much-needed top over the hob.

Samantha let herself in and knew at once Cleo was already home. She could smell incense and that meant one of two things. Cleo was either trying to create an ambiance for a boyfriend she was entertaining later, or she'd overcooked something and was trying to mask the smell of burnt saucepan. Or it could be both, that had happened before.

Cleo was in the kitchen, sat at the table, when Samantha entered. She had one foot on a chair with, what looked like, newly painted nail varnish on her toes. In one hand she was holding a copy of this week's *Star Life* magazine and in the other was a fork she was using to eat from the plate in front of her.

'Hi, Sis,' Cleo greeted cheerfully, without looking up from her reading material.

'What are you eating? It looks gross,' Samantha remarked, leaning over the plate and taking a sniff.

'Urgh, don't sniff at my plate. It's a new recipe,' Cleo responded, pulling the plate towards her defensively.

'Throwing a mixture of items from the fridge into a pan doesn't make it a recipe,' Samantha told her as she crossed the room and put the kettle on to boil.

'I think if you look the definition of "recipe" up on Wikipedia that's exactly what it does make,' Cleo spoke.

'OK, let's see. There's onion in there, ham, maybe a little cheese, and potato, oh and Worcester sauce, naturally,' Samantha told her, getting two mugs out of the cupboard.

'If you're trying to make me believe you can smell all those things, I won't have it,' Cleo remarked, staring at her sister.

'My sense of smell may be a strong talent but no, I just ran through the things I knew had been hanging round in the fridge for a while,' Samantha told her.

'You're sad, Sam, you know that?' Cleo said, dipping her head back into the magazine.

'Yes, I know. So, how was the estate agents? Were you busy? Did you get to go to any cool houses?' Samantha asked her, putting a normal tea bag in her cup and a herbal bag into Cleo's.

'It was boring. I spent half the day answering the telephone. I thought that was what they paid a receptionist to do! The other half I spent checking through house details, not very nice house details either, I mean some of these places I wouldn't put a dog in,' Cleo responded.

Samantha smiled to herself. Cleo did love to exaggerate. She expected that the homes not fit for a mongrel were fine, but probably located on an estate or in a less illustrious postcode than theirs. Cleo was a little bit of a snob really.

'So, you don't like it,' Samantha said as she made the drinks.

'Oh, I wouldn't say that. There are a couple of cute guys that work there,' Cleo said, spooning another forkful of food into her mouth.

'Does that mean you'll stick it out for a while – at least until you've laid them both?' Samantha questioned, dunking Cleo's herbal teabag up and down in the mug.

'Sam!' Cleo exclaimed in horror at her sister's statement.

'What?' Samantha asked, turning to face her sister.

'You don't say things like that! Not you! Not my little sister! Mum would have a fit if she heard you,' Cleo continued, putting her fork down on her plate as if Samantha's comment had put her off her food.

'Well Mum isn't here, and I am twenty-four years old. Just because I haven't acted the act out yet doesn't mean I can't use the word in conversation. Being a virgin doesn't make you completely oblivious to sex you know,' Samantha answered, bringing the drinks over to the table.

'Oh, stop it, you know I don't like you talking about that,' Cleo responded, and she refused to take her tea and clamped her hands down over her ears.

Samantha smiled in amusement again. Cleo hated the fact she was still a virgin. She was sure she found it almost embarrassing, that was why she hated her mentioning it. If she was truthful though she was a bit embarrassed by it herself. It should have been something she was proud of, but as time went on it just became more of a hurdle she wondered whether she would ever get to jump, so to speak.

It wasn't that she didn't want to do it, she did, for lots of reasons, like to get it over with and to stop herself feeling like an outsider in a worldwide club. She also wanted to find out what was so wonderful about it that Cleo wanted to do it all the time with practically every guy she met.

She had come close to doing it. The first time was at Cleo's eighteenth birthday party when she was just sixteen. Cleo had invited Thomas Clancy, one of their neighbours when they had lived in the spooky house. Samantha had thought he was the most gorgeous man she was ever likely to set eyes on. He was tall and lean with thick, dark hair and blue eyes like Martin Kemp from Spandau Ballet. She knew

Cleo had already slept with him but that hadn't mattered because Cleo had slept with most of their neighbours under thirty at the time and on this occasion Cleo's heart was set on laying Miles Jones, the manager at the Post Office.

She remembered vividly the moment when Thomas had asked her to go upstairs with him. Her heart had felt like it was going to burst right out of her chest it was hammering so hard. He had held her hand and pulled her towards him to kiss her and then, just as she started to think the moment had arrived, just as she could almost taste the sweetness of his lips, Cleo burst out of her bedroom, shirt undone, tears streaming down her face with Miles Jones hurrying after her.

And so had ended her moment with Thomas Clancy. The rest of the night was spent consoling her sister about Miles Jones' wife and two children. His family at home hadn't bothered Cleo, it never did, she wasn't looking for commitment, but when it came down to it something had pricked Miles' conscience and Cleo's birthday hadn't gone with the bang she had hoped for.

The only other time was a slightly closer brush with sex when she actually managed to get down to her underwear. The object of her affection had been Joe Phillips who used to work at one of the nearby independent bookshops. Bookshops did more for Samantha than boutiques, so if she did have to venture up West for groceries or something Cleo couldn't possibly live without, she would inevitably end up browsing in a bookshop. Joe had ordered her a copy of a book she'd been waiting for that she believed to have gone out of print.

She had returned to the bookshop a week after Joe had

placed the order and it was then, as he was putting the book into a bag that he asked her on a date. She hadn't known what to say at first. She was thrown at the suggestion as she didn't look her best. Her hair hadn't been washed in two days (thanks to Cleo's inability to let her know that she had pinched her shampoo and used it all) and she was wearing a pastel pink tracksuit (Cleo having hand washed a scarf with the last liquitab). But Joe had been clever, he hadn't worded the invite like he was asking her out, he had said it more like they were going to casually bump into one another at one of the nearby pizzerias. So, before she really knew it, she found herself accepting and meeting him for a meal.

Cleo leant her the freshly washed scarf and helped her choose what to wear. She washed her hair, put on some perfume and felt excited about the prospect of going on a date. And to begin with it had gone well. Joe was interesting and amusing. He talked, but not too much, he asked her questions but she didn't feel like she was being interrogated, and he made her laugh. He also paid her compliments. That usually would have embarrassed her, but he had such an easy way about him she accepted what he said without thinking too hard about it.

The evening went well, and she invited him back for coffee. They listened to some music and talked some more and then he had kissed her. It had been nice, much nicer than most of the kisses she had had and without needing too much consideration, she let him lead her to her bedroom. And that was when it had all gone wrong.

She had let him undress her, right down to her underwear, bought especially for the occasion (M&S, but the nice stuff, sexy with a bit of class but also sturdy and durable). And then she had helped him to unbutton his shirt. It was at that moment, in the half light, she had seen it. He had a pierced nipple.

The breath had caught in her throat and it was all she could do to stop herself screaming. Instead she froze, for what seemed like forever, unable to take her eyes from the glittering, gold ring that was proudly protruding from Joe's chest. And then, thawing from the momentary freeze, she fled. She leapt up from the bed, grabbed her clothes and ran for the sanctuary of the bathroom without saying a word.

And there she stayed, sat on the toilet, clutching her clothes to her, the image of the piercing stuck in her mind. It wasn't nice, it scared her, it reminded her of pirates and Peter Andre. She listened for a sound, some indication of Joe moving, or hopefully, leaving and eventually he knocked lightly on the bathroom door inquiring as to whether she was OK. She had muttered something hurriedly about food poisoning and quickly cited the pepperoni as the culprit. But predominantly she had made it clear she would not be coming out of the bathroom any time soon.

Joe went and when she felt it was safe to return to her room, she discovered he'd left her a note, suggesting another date and leaving his mobile number. She hadn't called or been in the bookshop since. It was a shame because the bookshop had been one of her favourites.

She knew, if she was honest, that the nipple ring wasn't really the problem. It had just been a trigger. It was something in her subconscious that called a halt to proceedings. The trigger could have been too much body hair or not enough, a Celtic tattoo, gaily patterned underwear or bad breath. Something shocked her into realising the significance of the event and made her call time on the moment. She could only assume it meant she wasn't ready but if she wasn't ready at *her* age, when would she be?

'I could always set you up with one of them. The blonde haired one, he's called Connor, he's about your age and he drives a Jaguar,' Cleo informed her sister.

'I remember the last time you set me up with someone,' Samantha replied, sitting down at the table.

'It was ages ago,' Cleo responded.

'His name was Gary and he took me to the speedway,' Samantha reminded her.

'I get your point, but Connor's different. I mean he drives a Jaguar,' Cleo repeated.

'So did Inspector Morse,' Samantha answered.

'What are you doing tonight anyway? I thought we might go up West, you know the classy bit. There's a new wine bar opening, half price drinks all night,' Cleo spoke.

'I'm working,' Samantha informed her.

'Again! How come? There's no show tonight is there? I thought the skating didn't start 'til tomorrow. By the way I've invited Connor to the show, along with Jeremy. He's really hot, and a couple of the girls whose names I don't know yet, so you can see what you think of him,' Cleo spoke.

'One look at me in my Civic Hall sweater should scupper any ideas you might have of a beautiful romance. Tonight's the committee meeting for the Pigeon Association, I'm working the bar,' Samantha informed her.

'Thrilling, I'm sure you'll meet Mr Right there,' Cleo responded.

'Unlike you, I don't treat every second of my day as an

opportunity to meet a man,' Samantha told her sister.

'Well, perhaps you should. Well maybe not a pigeon fancier, but there's no harm in giving Connor a chance,' Cleo suggested.

'I don't think you realise how much hard work it is selling programmes. I doubt I'll have a second to even look in his direction, let alone give him a chance,' Samantha replied, sipping her tea.

'Well the only person I'm going to be looking at is Jimmy Lloyd,' Cleo announced, a smile spreading across her face.

'Jimmy Lloyd. You've heard of him?' Samantha said, unable to hide the surprise in her voice.

'Are you kidding? Don't you read those magazines I give you? He's had more than his fair share of exposure in *Star Life* magazine,' Cleo informed her.

'He's an ice skater. Ice skaters aren't in magazines like *Star Life*,' Samantha replied.

'Ordinarily no, but let's just say he isn't just renowned for his skating abilities. He's dated anyone who's anyone,' Cleo elaborated.

'Really? Well he looked quite ordinary to me. I'm sure I haven't seen him in any of your magazines, perhaps you're getting him mixed up with someone else,' Samantha suggested.

'You've *met* him! My God, you've been in the house for over half an hour and you've held back this important information from me! What's he like? What did he say? What was he wearing? Did he look cool?' Cleo babbled excitedly.

'I notice you've temporarily forgotten all about the boys in your office with the smart cars,' Samantha remarked.

'Come on, Sam, Jimmy Lloyd has to be the biggest celebrity Woolston Civic Hall's ever had appear there. If you've had a conversation with him then your sister deserves to know all the details,' Cleo continued, her voice still retaining its excitement.

'Actually, the lead singer of the Queen tribute band won *Stars in Their Eyes* and there's a rumour that Jane McDonald might be coming to the hall next year.'

'Sam, what is wrong with you?!'

'Nothing's wrong with me. I'm not the one sounding like a groupie. He was very ordinary, and we didn't speak. I was on the phone and gave him brief written directions to the dressing rooms. The whole thing lasted less than a minute,' Samantha explained, and she picked Cleo's abandoned plate from the table and sniffed at it.

'My God, there are very few occasions in my life when I wish I was you, but this is one of them. I would have killed to have been across a desk from him,' Cleo remarked, her eyes glazing over as she daydreamed.

'Don't you mean across a desk *with* him! Is my corned beef in here?' Samantha questioned, eyeing the leftover meal with suspicion.

'You are unbelievable,' Cleo replied, snatching the plate from her sister and standing up from her seat.

3

That evening the bar was deathly quiet. There were no shows, there was no passing trade to speak of and the pigeon fanciers were ensconced in their meeting. Samantha had already polished all the glasses, rewashed those with hardened, seemingly irremovable lipstick marks and now she was reorganising the shelves. Still, it was almost 10.30 pm and the meeting would soon be over which meant the members of the Pigeon Association would shortly be flocking to the bar for a nightcap before heading home.

She was just about to move the crisps boxes into alphabetical order when the doors to the conference room swung open and people began to head towards the bar area. Samantha put down the crisps and hurriedly washed her hands. Any moment now she would have to attempt to make at least twenty coffees using the completely unreliable coffee machine.

But no one seemed to be coming up to the bar at all. Then she saw Arnold Forester, dark hair, thick Brian Blessed beard, and her hopes were raised. He always had a whisky and lemonade after a meeting. However, he hurriedly headed for the exit without even looking in her direction. Hot on Arnold's heels was Michael Knowles, grey hair, moustache like Hercule Poirot, usually a double brandy. What was wrong with them tonight? Where were they going?

As more and more people left the hall without so much as a glance her way, Samantha lost heart and again picked up the box of crisps. She bent down to put it back under the bar and when she stood up, she jumped. Jimmy Lloyd was sat on one of the bar stools in front of her.

'Hello again,' he greeted.

'Hello, sorry, I didn't see you there,' Samantha replied, hurriedly picking up a packet of filter coffee and crinkling it noisily in her hands.

She then shook the box containing more packets of coffee, in the hope the sound would attract the pigeon fanciers to the bar facility.

'Would you recommend the coffee?' Jimmy enquired, watching her shaking the box up and down.

'Sorry?' Samantha asked, still looking at the exit and wondering why all her potential customers were going home.

'The coffee you're shaking up there, would you recommend it?' Jimmy repeated.

Mrs Danvers, the treasurer of the Pigeon Association caught Samantha's attention. The buxom lady, Fern Britton before the gastric band, had her trademark, Millets tent-style dress on, in fuchsia. Samantha offered a smile but tonight she wasn't acknowledged. Mrs Danvers swished towards the door. She was a sweet sherry and a packet of pistachios. Now all hope of significant takings was truly gone.

Jimmy cleared his throat. This brought home the fact she had practically ignored him, and he was a customer she could do with.

'Oh, I'm sorry. What can I get you?' Samantha asked him, putting down the coffee she had been drumming against her hand.

'Coffee seems like a good choice,' Jimmy responded, smiling at her.

He had white teeth. Very white teeth. The kind of teeth that could advertise the after effects of Pearl Drops.

'Well, you're very welcome to have a coffee, but I have to admit the machine is temperamental and they had the training course for the temperamental machine when I was on holiday so...' Samantha began to babble.

'Instant coffee will be fine, or tea. Black, no sugar,' Jimmy responded, again smiling at her.

He had a small scar, no more than half an inch long, leading from his bottom lip. It was barely noticeable, probably because of the beautiful teeth.

'Which would you prefer? Coffee or tea? I mean we have a choice of teas. There's fruit tea, green tea, Earl Grey,' Samantha spoke, digging into the box of bags under the bar and producing several different packets.

'Which would you recommend?' Jimmy enquired, resting one elbow on the bar and looking directly at her, a smile still on his lips.

'Well, I wouldn't say I was a tea connoisseur or anything, but I quite like the blackberry. Although the mint tea is our best seller,' Samantha responded, holding up the appropriate bags.

'Then I'll go with your recommendation and have the blackberry,' Jimmy answered.

'OK,' Samantha replied, and she hurried along the bar to

where the kettle was kept.

'You were expecting it to be busy tonight,' Jimmy commented as he watched her prepare a cup and saucer.

'No, no, not really,' Samantha answered.

'So you were going to fill up the temperamental coffee machine and risk using it just for yourself? You should've said, if you were going to take a chance I might have been persuaded to try it,' Jimmy told her.

Samantha felt her cheeks turning crimson and she looked at him out of the corner of her eye. She saw a grin play on his lips. She wished she had paid attention to more than the agony aunt columns of *Star Life* magazine, perhaps there would have been an article about his cosmetic teeth whitening.

'Pigeon fanciers,' Samantha blurted out, the words tumbling forth before she had gained control of her mouth.

'I'm sorry?'

'The Woolston Pigeon Fanciers Association meets here on a monthly basis. We were expecting them to want some drinks after their meeting,' Samantha elaborated.

'I see. So, you don't work the bar every night?' Jimmy enquired.

'No! Goodness no! I mean I *do* have a life you know! I wouldn't want to spend all day and all night here,' Samantha exclaimed with a nervous laugh.

What was the matter with her? She was starting to perspire, and she had goose bumps on her arms. She didn't feel at all well. Could you catch viruses from Brylcream?

'Well, that's what I'll be doing for the next few weeks,' Jimmy replied.

The kettle came to the boil and Samantha was able to

hide her blushes in the steam. She poured in the water and put the tea bag into the cup to infuse.

'I didn't mean that spending all day and night here was awful, just that it isn't for me,' Samantha told him as she came back along the bar and placed the tea in front of him.

'I'm glad for you. I was beginning to think you didn't have a home, seeing that you eat your lunch in the sound booth,' Jimmy spoke, toying with the tea bag and looking up at her.

Samantha let out a loud nervous laugh. It was something she always did when she felt backed into a corner. It was an affliction she had had since childhood when Mary Kennedy once suggested in maths class that Samantha didn't know how to do long division. Of course, Samantha had had no idea how to do long division at the time, but she couldn't let Mary Kennedy know that. So she had done the only thing she could do, she had let out the loudest laugh she could manage and shook her head at Mary Kennedy as if the very idea of her being unable to accomplish anything was utterly ridiculous.

Jimmy was just looking at her, watching her laugh, seeing her hold her sides and bend forward onto the bar in a fit of hysterics. After what seemed like an age Samantha took a deep breath, wheezed, and raised her head, facing him.

'Eat my lunch in the sound booth! I'm sorry, that's just so funny. It's ninety-five pence for the tea by the way,' Samantha replied, still smiling with laughter.

'I have to say I've told much better jokes and had less of a reaction,' Jimmy responded as he reached into his jacket for his wallet.

'Oh, if only you knew how amusing that was. I mean if

I ate my lunch in the sound booth that would imply I have nothing better to do with my lunch hour than sit in the sound booth and goodness that is so not true. I mean who would want to sit in a dark, dingy, sound booth on their own?' Samantha exclaimed, rolling her eyes.

'I don't know, I presumed it was a quiet place away from everything. I don't think there's anything wrong in wanting a little quiet now and then,' Jimmy told her.

'No, for some people that's just fine, but not me. I'm not one for quiet,' Samantha stated, the words almost catching in her throat as she spoke them.

'No? So, does that mean you're a woman who knows how to party?' Jimmy enquired, taking a sip of his tea.

'Party was going to be my middle name until my dad suggested Margaret. Not that my middle name is Margaret, it was just his suggestion, at the time,' Samantha said, wishing she had never started this conversation.

'I see,' Jimmy replied with a nod.

Samantha had never felt so much of a fool as she did now. What was she saying? It was like some horrid Harry Potter style goblin had taken control of her mouth and planted random things in it. Any second now she would be talking about owls and broomsticks.

'I don't have a middle name,' she blurted out, still having no control over her voice.

'No? That seems a shame, since your dad had his heart set on Margaret,' Jimmy enquired.

'My sister has a middle name, it's Charlotte. Cleo Charlotte Smith. She had a spate of making people call her CC for a while, when she was younger, but now it's just Cleo,' Samantha continued to talk.

'Why don't you join me and have some tea? You were right, it's very good,' Jimmy suggested, amused by the conversation.

'I can't really, I've got all this tidying up to do,' Samantha answered, and she waved the tea towel she was holding behind her.

This only emphasised the sparklingly clean mirror and brass work, the freshly cleaned glasses, all arranged in size order and the neat rows of snacks all stacked identically.

'I insist, let me buy you a tea,' Jimmy spoke, getting a note out of his wallet.

'No, no, that's OK, I'll just have a glass of water. It's quite warm in here, must get the heating looked at,' Samantha remarked, still perspiring due to embarrassment.

She picked up a glass and filled it with water from the mixer tap. She took a large gulp and then brushed away some imaginary dust from the bar top.

'So, is there anywhere else you work in this building? I'm beginning to think you run this place single-handed,' Jimmy said, looking at Samantha as she drank some more water, tipped the rest away and began to wash up the glass.

'I sell ice creams,' she blurted out.

Goodness! The ice cream, she really did need to do something more permanent with those boxes.

'Really?'

'And programmes – you know, I'm one of those women who walks up and down the aisles holding a programme above her head. And in the interval I hold the programme over my head and have an ice cream tray round my neck, until it gets really busy and then I have to lose the programme because you can't really serve ice cream one handed, not when you have to take lids off tubs and dispense the little wooden spoons,' Samantha babbled on.

'I can imagine,' Jimmy answered, looking at her with interest.

'I couldn't run this place, that's Dave's job. He has years of experience in managing,' Samantha told him.

'D'you want to know something about Dave?' Jimmy asked her in a hushed voice, leaning over the bar slightly to bring himself nearer to her.

'Oh, I don't like to listen to gossip, and it isn't really ethical to talk about people behind their back, particularly your boss. I don't think you should tell me,' Samantha said immediately.

'Personally, I think Dave comes across as being a good manager because he's got a strong team around him. Obviously, I can't comment on your colleagues, but from what I've seen today, I think you might just be holding him up,' Jimmy told her.

'Well that's very nice of you to say, Mr Lloyd, but that really isn't the case. I just do my job and that's that. Would you like any snacks?' Samantha offered, grabbing hold of one of the newly arranged trays and placing it on the bar in front of him.

'Call me Jimmy, won't you? And what about you? Are you a Samantha or a Sam?' Jimmy wanted to know.

'Erm, I don't know, I...' Samantha began, having never been asked the question before by anyone at the hall.

Her pondering on the answer to his question was interrupted by Jimmy's mobile ringing. He excused himself, got down from his stool and went across to the corner of the bar area to take the call.

Samantha was glad he'd gone, she felt terrible. Her heart was hammering, her face felt like it had been under a sun bed for twenty-four hours and she had an awful headache. She was obviously going down with a bug. She hated being ill, unlike Cleo, who positively embraced sickness because it meant she could lie in bed all day and have Samantha bring home comfort food and Lemsip.

Was she a Samantha or a Sam? What sort of question was that? She had a name badge, didn't she? Why couldn't he just use it like everyone else did? And what was with all the small talk? Worst of all he knew she ate her lunch in the sound booth. Or should that be he knew she *used* to eat her lunch there, she couldn't eat it there ever again, not now someone knew. Her privacy had been violated.

She was still polishing the glass she'd just washed up when Jimmy returned to the bar and gulped back the remainder of his herbal tea.

'Thanks for the tea and the chat, see you tomorrow. Save me an ice cream for the interval,' he said with a smile.

'I can't guarantee it. I mean they go quite quickly, and I couldn't reserve one, it wouldn't be fair,' Samantha informed him.

Four thousand Berry Fruits could theoretically go in one night if everyone in the hall bought two point five each.

'That's OK, I'll send someone out to queue for me,' Jimmy responded, preparing to leave the bar area.

'Well, I suppose…' Samantha replied.

She watched him walk towards the exit. He was very tall and lean with it. He reminded her of Patrick Swayze. A young Patrick Swayze. Patrick Swayze in his prime, with shorter, more fashionable hair. Samantha was just reminding herself to share this comparison with Cleo when she got home when Jimmy stopped walking and turned back round to face her. He looked at her and smiled, as if something was crossing his mind and Samantha froze, afraid that her thoughts were suddenly transparent. She knew she was grimacing, but she couldn't change her expression now he was looking at her. It felt like she was gurning.

'By the way, in my opinion – I think there's a Sam lurking under that Samantha,' Jimmy told her.

'Thank you,' Samantha blurted out and then she felt herself blush violently.

Thank you?! Thank you?! What on Earth was she saying thank you for?! It wasn't a compliment, it was a statement, his opinion. She was a complete idiot.

'By the way, apparently there's a new wine bar opening tonight – might be where your customers have gone.'

'Thank you,' Samantha repeated, unable to say anything else.

Goodness she really needed him to leave.

'See you,' he replied, still smiling at her. Then he left the building.

She felt completely faint now, like she was going to collapse at any moment. She took the freshly polished glass and refilled it with water, guzzling it down greedily in the hope of stabilising herself. What was the matter with her? If Cleo had brought home an infection from the estate agents, she would not be happy, she had a lot to prepare for tomorrow night's show and as good as Dave was at talking the management talk, she had to admit he didn't have a clue when it came to detail. Detail was Samantha's forte. Small talk with ice skaters was not.

ONE NIGHT ON ICE

★

It was close to midnight when Samantha arrived home. The second she opened the front door she knew Cleo had company. She could smell a mixture of incense and essential oils and she could hear Luther Vandross. The ultimate giveaway was the pair of size ten brogues sitting by the front door. Brogues! Samantha thought the only person who wore brogues any more was her father and the odd accountant or estate agent. As her mind offered the last occupation it all clicked into place and she assumed Cleo, having been turned down in favour of the Pigeon Association, was now entertaining one of her colleagues. She was certainly a fast worker!

Samantha smiled to herself and headed upstairs. She paused outside Cleo's bedroom door and listened. She could hear hushed talking, so she knocked.

'Go away! Can't you read?' Cleo shrilled back immediately.

Samantha looked down at the door handle, on which was hanging a black coloured crystal. After Samantha had once burst into the room unannounced to be greeted by the sight of Cleo and a man old enough to be their father engaged in removing each other's clothes, Cleo had designed a traffic light system in the form of coloured crystals. The green crystal meant you could come in without knocking, the amber coloured crystal meant knock once and proceed with caution, the red crystal meant knock, stop and wait for instructions and the black crystal meant do not enter, knock or even breathe too heavily on walking past the door or your life wouldn't be worth living. Samantha had named that particular crystal The Bonk.

'Sorry, it's just I'm going to bed and you said it would be a crime if I didn't keep you informed about things,' Samantha called through the door.

'I'm not interested in anything any of those pigeon fanciers had to say – now piss off!' Cleo called back and Samantha heard the music being turned up.

'He's got dark brown eyes and a small scar under his lip!' Samantha shouted above the music.

It was barely seconds before the door was hurriedly open and Cleo, loosely dressed in her robe, her hair all over the place appeared. She stepped out onto the landing, pulling the door to behind her.

'You spoke to Jimmy Lloyd again? My God he wasn't with the Pigeon Association, was he?' Cleo exclaimed.

'No, he was just having a drink at the bar,' Samantha informed matter of factly.

She liked having something happening in her life that her older sister was interested in. It was unusual for Samantha to feel that she was in possession of something Cleo was envious of. It didn't happen often, the last time had been when Samantha unknowingly got a Prada handbag for ten pounds in the January sales. Cleo couldn't have been more jealous then. She had practically looked green for a week.

'What did he have and how many? Jack Daniels? Vodka? Beer? I thought he hadn't long come out of one of those expensive rehab clinics in America. Did he look cool? I bet he looked cool, what was he wearing?' Cleo enquired her eyes wide.

'Rehab?' Samantha spoke, shocked by her sister's statement.

'Of course he's been to rehab! I told you what he's like,

women, sex, booze, recreational drugs, it's part and parcel of the celebrity lifestyle. So how did he look? Was he with anyone?' Cleo continued.

'He's been in rehab,' Samantha stated again.

'Sam! Are you going to tell me what he said or are you just going to repeat "rehab" over and over again like a poor Amy Winehouse tribute? What's the matter with you? Almost everyone in *Star Life* magazine has been to rehab at some time during their career, most of them have been twice,' Cleo spoke.

'But he didn't look like someone who would do that. He had herbal tea and he liked it,' Samantha informed her, still mulling over in her mind the information Cleo had given her.

'Herbal tea! God, perhaps the deep breathing and exploration of his inner self worked this time. So, what else did he say?' Cleo asked her.

'Oh, you know, nothing much,' Samantha responded with a shrug.

Suddenly she didn't feel like talking anymore.

'Are you OK? You look a bit pale. Are you coming down with something?' Cleo asked, staring into Samantha's eyes and scrutinising her pallor.

'I think I'm going to go to bed now. Sorry I interrupted humping the brogue wearer. Which one is it? The hot one? Jeremy wasn't it?' Samantha said hurriedly and she turned away from Cleo and headed towards her bedroom.

'Hey, wait a minute, Sam! You didn't say what he was wearing! Sam! Was it something cool from GAP?' Cleo called as Samantha retreated.

Samantha went into her room and shut the door behind

her. She leaned heavily against it, her head throbbing. Jimmy Lloyd had been to rehab and she felt disappointed. Someone who skated so beautifully and had such perfect white teeth took drugs. That just wasn't right.

4

They were white and a size five. Some of the laces were fraying and the blades had seen better days. Samantha picked up the ice skates that were lying on the front desk and was just about to study them in more detail when Dave arrived through the front door, half a Cornish pasty in his hand and the remainder close to spilling out of his mouth.

'Ah, good, you're here, Duck. Like the footwear?' Dave enquired, leaning on the desk and breathing out meat and potato fumes in Samantha's direction.

'Are these for lost property? Or do they belong to one of the skaters from the show?' Samantha enquired, holding the skates up by their laces and letting them dangle dangerously close to Dave's face.

'*Non, ma cherie*, those are yours – well, for the duration of the ice show anyway,' Dave responded, poking the remainder of the pasty into his mouth and grinning widely.

'I don't understand,' Samantha answered, looking again at the boots as if she expected them to contain a hidden message she had overlooked.

'Well, I thought as sales for *Skating on Broadway* have proved so popular, the least we could do for our audience is provide them with the full, unadulterated skating experience

– from the grass roots up so to speak,' Dave replied.

'What are the boots for, Dave?' Samantha asked him bluntly.

'They're for you, size five. And there's a pair for Felicity, Jane and Karen too, you are going to be my Ice Maidens. Just picture the scene – the interval arrives and there you are, an armful of programmes, gliding round the edge of the ice to some well-chosen intermission music, exchanging pleasantries and selling brochures,' Dave spoke, his eyes glazing over as he imagined.

'Oh my goodness, you're not serious!' Samantha exclaimed, immediately filled with horror at Dave's suggestion.

'*Tres bon*, of course I'm serious. What could be better than coming to watch an ice dancing show and having the programme and refreshment sellers coordinating with the theme of the evening? Is Jane really a size ten shoe? I found it quite hard to get ladies skates that big,' Dave spoke, putting his greasy hands onto some paperwork on the desk and picking it up to read.

'Dave, it's a great idea and I'm sure it would enhance the ambiance of the evening, but I haven't skated for ages and I can't skate well enough to be able to hold programmes and ice creams and not break my neck. And what about Felicity's ankle? She was off work for three weeks last year. Ice skating won't be conducive to a joint injury,' Samantha said, looking at the skates and then pleadingly at Dave.

'Ah, now that's where I've done my homework. Felicity's been given the all clear by the doc, Jane used to do roller-skating, Karen's brother used to work at an ice rink and as for you, Duck, you put ice skating as one of your hobbies on your CV,' Dave spoke triumphantly.

'Dave, I did that CV when I was fifteen and it was a vague hobby then at best,' Samantha exclaimed.

'I'm sure it's like riding a bike – once learnt, never forgotten. Anyway, you and the girls have some ice time around eleven to get accustomed to it,' Dave announced, looking at his watch.

'Dave, this isn't going to work. Perhaps if we'd had more time then...' Samantha started, as the telephone began to ring.

'Don't be defeatist, Samantha, remember Dave's motto? "Negativity will always cost ya..."' Dave began, a smug grin appearing on his face.

Samantha just looked at him, cringing as she recalled the slogan. She knew he wouldn't need any encouragement from her to finish his own sentence.

'"Persevere and you will prosper!"' he announced and then let out a loud belly laugh which reverberated around the foyer.

She had learnt there was no point trying to have a discussion with Dave when he was in this sort of mood. Once his mind was made up there was nothing you could say to change it. It wasn't that he was stubborn, just blinkered, with complete tunnel vision. Once he was set on an idea, any other suggestion or challenge to it just flew over his head.

Samantha looked at the skates again. The blades were very blunt, they were probably one of the actual pairs she had hired at the ice discos. She wasn't relishing putting them on and getting on the rink. She hadn't skated since she was a teenager and she had serious concerns about her colleagues' abilities to skate and sell merchandise at the same time. It was all shaping up to be an unmitigated disaster. But Dave was the manager, and it was his call. Although Samantha noted he hadn't mentioned any skating intentions for himself.

Her attention was drawn away from the boots by the arrival of dozens of people through the main doors.

'Oh, here they are, our skating stars. I'll show them to their dressing rooms. Don't forget to distribute the skates, Duck and all on the ice at eleven. You have a twenty-minute slot while I man the desk – hello one and all! Dave Gordon, manager, let me lead the way. *Allez!*' Dave boomed, bounding across to the group as they entered the foyer area.

As she watched Dave sharing his greasy hand with as many of the skaters as he could, Samantha dropped the skates to the floor, hurriedly put on her headset and answered the ringing telephone.

'Good morning, Woolston Civic Hall, Samantha speaking.'

It was another person wanting tickets for the performance that evening. She'd had one after another the previous day even though there were now 'sold out' stickers across the date on all the posters in town and she knew it had been announced on local radio.

As she attempted to sell the caller tickets for an alternative night, she saw Jimmy and a woman with long red hair appear in the foyer. Jimmy was carrying two boot bags and something in a plastic cover over his shoulder. She recognised the woman immediately as being Dana Williams, the principal female skater in the show. In the flyers for *Skating on Broadway* she was dressed in a black cat suit that showed off her amazing figure to perfection. Samantha was sure some of the city's male population had bought tickets for the show on that visual recommendation alone. It was like using Cheryl used-to-be-Cole in a leotard as advertisement. Now she was wearing tight jeans, an emerald green, sleeveless crop top and very high shoes. There was no denying her beauty. In fact, she looked like she had just stepped off the pages of *Star Life* magazine. At nine in the morning it was almost criminal to look that perfect.

'Yes, we have tickets for next week but there's definitely more choice on weekdays. Weekends are almost sold out,' Samantha spoke to her caller, as she watched the skaters' entrance.

Jimmy and Dana were talking together. He with the perfect teeth and well styled hair, her with the catwalk model body and tight clothes. It was like watching a scene from an American drama full of attractive people with beautiful accessories.

But then the mood suddenly changed, and Samantha watched as Dana snatched one of the boot bags from Jimmy's hands and began to raise the volume of her voice. It was a loud voice, a voice that didn't fit the beautiful face or the petite frame. In fact, she sounded a lot like Ruby Wax at full throttle. Samantha strained to hear what Jimmy was saying in reply, but he was quieter and more controlled. Despite her best efforts all that was audible was Mrs George's voice in her headset trying to work out which row she and her husband would be best suited to, given his arthritic hip.

Then Jimmy was raising his voice too and some of the

other skaters had stopped their entrance and were joining the couple and interjecting into the conversation as if to bring it to an end. Dana was screeching and throwing her arms about, like a gesticulating football manager – all hair flying and red lips mashing, and one of the other female skaters began to pat her shoulder and tried to draw her away from Jimmy.

'Sorry, Madam, what did you say?' Samantha asked Mrs George, as her concentration was interrupted by the scene being played out.

Jimmy then said something loudly to Dana and suddenly she lashed out and struck him across the face with a manicured hand. Samantha gasped out loud before she could stop herself, prompting her telephone customer to query whether she was actually listening to her.

'Oh, Mrs George, I do apologise, of course I'm listening to you. Yes, I can do tickets near the exits on the first row for that date,' Samantha spoke, her eyes still on the commotion in front of her.

Jimmy had his hand to his face and Dana was being dragged, kicking and screaming away from him, across the foyer towards the entrance to the dressing rooms.

Mrs George finally managed to purchase two tickets to one of the ice shows and Samantha was still watching as Jimmy was left alone by his skating comrades. He picked the boot bag up from the floor and turned in her direction.

Embarrassed that she had been staring, Samantha immediately turned her head towards her computer screen and began frantically tapping at the keyboard, any button would do, trying to mask the fact she'd been paying attention to what had occurred. Although it was her job to be concerned, particularly if there had been an altercation in the middle of a public area. And it was only natural to be curious, especially when Dana Williams had seemed so furious. Perhaps she was on drugs too.

She let a few more seconds elapse before she felt brave enough to shift her gaze back to the foyer, putting a biro to paper for effect. Another group of people carrying bags and costumes were entering and she saw that Jimmy had gone.

*

It was almost 10.30 am before Samantha plucked up the courage to mention Dave's ice-skating plans to her colleagues. It came as a complete shock to all of them that firstly, Dave somehow knew their shoe size and secondly that he expected them to sell programmes, refreshments and souvenirs from the ice, on thin metal blades, like kitchen knives attached to shoes. On hearing the plan Karen had merely nodded, but Jane had burst into tears and fled to the toilets. Felicity, well aware of Dave's hair brained ideas, had just given Samantha a look of despair mixed with begrudging acceptance and folded her arms across her chest. It had taken all three of them to get Jane out of a cubicle and into her boots, but they'd been unable to stop her from shaking like a leaf.

Now, all four of them were at the edge of the temporary rink in the large arena, wondering what to do next. There were groups of people dotted around in the seats, talking, bending, stretching, some rooting through rucksacks. Some were eating and drinking, others were tending to their skates. Samantha felt self-conscious and stupid. Were they really expected to skate around this rink in front of everyone without any assistance?

Next to her, Jane began to whimper like a small dog that'd had his paw caught in a heavy door. Jane wasn't the most capable of people. Life had dealt her a bit of a raw deal in so far as she lived with her infirm, chain-smoking mother. Hence her inability to cope with anything that strayed from her basic routine of answering phones. Samantha remembered her weeping hysterically when Dave had asked her to help in the restaurant one particularly busy day. She had been signed off for a week with stress after that episode. He hadn't asked her again.

Felicity was more stable. She was efficient, organised and reasonable. Her only downfall was that she picked unsuitable men and moaned to Samantha about them constantly. The last one had been called Tariq. He had remained interested for six months and then proposed. Before she had time to consider her answer, she found airline tickets from Delhi to London Heathrow for his mother, father and eight brothers. There was only one option left to her then, turn him down flat and move on, or say yes and have his family getting cosy in her two bedroomed apartment, drafting their applications for citizenship and fattening up her house rabbit for their giant *karahi*.

Felicity was looking less and less impressed with the whole skating situation now and Karen had already sat down. The whole scenario was starting to become depressing. But it had to be done and she was second-in-command.

'Look, I don't like the idea of this any more than any of you do but it's Dave's decision. The least we can do is humour him. He is the boss. Besides, if we all fall on our arses on the first night and trash the entire stock of ice creams, I'm sure he won't be asking us to skate again,' Samantha spoke bravely, and she smiled encouragingly at Jane who was beginning to cry again. They'd be doing well to trash the entire stock of ice creams as things stood at the moment, but they didn't know that.

'Remember I told you I would poison his tea after he tried to get me into a chicken suit to advertise *Mother Goose*? Well I still have the medication,' Felicity snarled, her arms still folded across her chest.

'Hey, coming to skate?'

The four women hadn't noticed anyone approaching their group and now Jimmy was stood on the ice just in front of them.

'Unfortunately. Do you have a first aid kit?' Felicity asked him.

Samantha suddenly felt very hot. She couldn't understand it as she was stood just a few metres away from a whole rink's worth of cold ice. It was the same feeling she'd had the night before while working the bar. She'd had two paracetamol before getting into bed to rid her of her headache and she now wished she'd packed some in her bag this morning. Although she wasn't sure it was wise to take painkillers so often, particularly when your fever came and went so rapidly. Perhaps it was Gobby. He'd been in already this morning, pissed in the foyer and gnawed at a frozen cod fillet. He was most likely riddled with fleas and she didn't react well to bites. Last time she'd been bitten she'd been on antihistamines for a fortnight.

Jane began to snivel and wiped her nose with the back of her hand while Karen attempted to console her. Samantha couldn't help but notice that Jimmy was dressed in one of his costumes for the show. Very tight black trousers and a turquoise coloured vest covered in diamantes. The vest was as snug as the trousers and showed off his impeccable torso and well-defined arm muscles. She didn't know where to look – muscular chest, tight thighs. Her head felt like it was spinning.

'Come on, come onto the ice. I'll take you all round,' Jimmy spoke kindly, and he took hold of Jane's tear-soaked hand and helped her to walk gingerly from the safety of the floor of the arena and onto the ice rink.

'You don't have to do that. In fact, I'm sure it's against the insurance regulations. I mean if you were to injure yourself assisting us then…' Samantha began as Karen and Felicity followed Jane's lead and teetered onto the rink, their fears forgotten at the mere appearance of a handsome man.

'Come on, Sam, you're going to be the last one out here. That's OK, Jane, you can hold the side or you can hold my hand on the first go round and then we'll have you going round on your own before you know it,' Jimmy encouraged as he helped Jane coordinate putting one skate in front of the other.

Samantha watched as he spoke to all three women, advising them on what to do and how best to start off, while effortlessly gliding around the ice with Jane holding onto his hand. Jane was beginning to calm down, in fact she was almost smiling. Samantha didn't think she had ever seen Jane smile before, certainly not like she was now.

'Remember, knees bent and body weight forward,' Jimmy instructed.

Samantha stepped onto the ice, tried to remember what to do and then took a deep breath and launched herself forward in the hope that it would all come flooding back to her. She hurriedly skated across the rink to join the others, very aware that the performers were now looking at the action on the ice and not concentrating on their warmup routines.

'Hey Sam, check you out. You've done this before, you can skate quite well,' Jimmy remarked as she joined Felicity and Karen in scooting along the edge of the ice area.

'She used to skate when she was younger. She went to ice discos,' Felicity informed him as she wobbled sideways and had to catch hold of Samantha's arm for support.

'It was a long time ago, I didn't go all that much,' Samantha responded, her cheeks flushing with embarrassment.

How did Felicity know that? Damn her CV. Who else had read it?

'Well, you have good movement,' Jimmy complimented as he skated backwards, facing her.

'I bet he says that to all the girls,' Felicity remarked with a wide smile and a wink in Samantha's direction.

'I think we should just try and concentrate on the task in hand. After all, we'll want to be able to stay on our feet tonight, won't we?' Samantha spoke, feeling nauseous.

'Well I think Jane is doing great now. And Felicity I think you can take her round the next turn. Karen, you can put on some speed on the next circuit. Sam, you can come with me,' Jimmy told the women and he took Samantha by the hand and set off skating, pulling her towards him.

'I can't skate away from everyone, I'm supposed to be supervising them,' Samantha blurted out, as a hot flush engulfed her whole body.

'I'll supervise them. Show me what you've got,' Jimmy

encouraged, smiling as he held her hands and increased his speed across the ice.

What was going on? She couldn't hold his hand. She didn't do handholding with anyone – ever. She had never done handholding. She even remembered being ostracised at infant school because she wouldn't take part in 'Ring o' Ring o' Roses'. It wasn't her. It displayed too much emotion towards people you barely knew, and it spread germs. She was handholding with someone in a turquoise Lycra vest, that wasn't right at all.

'I beg your pardon,' Samantha responded in horror at his question.

'Show me some crossovers,' Jimmy replied.

'How about *you* show *me* a triple Axel,' Samantha snapped as he continued to move her forward at speed across the rink.

Jimmy smiled and let go of her hands. She stopped herself and watched as he powered around the ice gaining terrific speed and momentum. Then he took off from the left forward outside edge of his blade, turned three and a half rotations in the air and landed perfectly on one leg, coming out of the jump to gasps and applause from his fellow skaters.

He skated back to Samantha and stopped neatly in front of her.

'Now, I've shown you mine, you show me yours,' Jimmy spoke with a smile.

'I haven't skated since I was fifteen,' Samantha responded.

'Then this is the perfect opportunity to revisit it – come on,' Jimmy urged, and he took hold of her left hand and pushed off, urging her to do the same.

Samantha was left with no choice but to allow herself to be pulled along by the skater, trying desperately to keep up with him.

'So, having you serve your tubs of ice cream and little spoons from the rink is Dave's latest brainwave is it?' Jimmy asked as they skated.

'It wouldn't have been such a bad idea if he'd given us the appropriate notice. At least one, if not all of us, are going to end up flat on our faces at some point during the evening,' Samantha replied, concentrating on keeping her feet moving.

'I don't mind spending a bit of time with you all if you want to get more confident with it,' Jimmy told her.

'That's very nice of you but it isn't your concern. You're one of the performers and we're staff, the two don't usually interact in that way,' Samantha spoke, performing almost perfect crossovers without noticing what she was doing.

Jimmy laughed out loud both because she had performed the manoeuvre without noticing it and because of how she'd phrased her reply.

'What's funny?' Samantha asked him.

'Do you always talk like that?'

'Talk like what?' Samantha enquired, as they gathered speed over the ice and Jimmy took hold of both her hands and skated backwards in front of her.

'Like you're quoting from some Civic Hall employment manual,' Jimmy told her.

'I don't know what you mean,' Samantha answered, feeling herself reddening even more than she had reddened already.

'I think you work here too much. You never seem very

relaxed,' Jimmy continued.

Samantha could feel the urge coming and she was powerless to stop it. It was almost like a tic, overwhelming and unhaltable. She laughed out loud. She stopped skating, let go of Jimmy's hands and held her ribs, doubling up with laughter. The noise was so loud it reverberated around the arena and everyone there turned their attention to her. She soon realised they were all watching her, and the laughter began to catch in her throat until she could barely breathe. She started to cough, over and over, unable to catch air. Before she knew it, she was wheezing violently, and Jimmy had put an arm around her and escorted her to the side of the ice.

'Just take deep breaths and stay calm,' he urged, his arm around her shoulders as she hunched over herself.

Despite trying to keep herself from fainting or throwing up, Samantha was distinctly aware of his bare arm around her shoulders and the feeling of it, resting comfortingly upon her was making her feel even more ill. It was the closest she had been to a man since Joe and his nipple ring and that thought alone made her cough again.

'I'm OK,' Samantha insisted as she coughed and covered her hand with her mouth.

'Sure,' Jimmy responded with a nod, unconvinced.

'It's a bug I'm coming down with. I think Cleo's passed something on from the estate agents. She says some of the houses are very dirty,' Samantha babbled, taking a deep breath and standing up straight.

'Seemed more like a panic attack to me,' Jimmy told her bluntly.

Her stomach was turning over again, the fear was

engulfing her, the laughter was on the verge of coming out. She fought to control it and began coughing violently again, so much so, she almost fell down onto the ice. Jimmy caught her, steadied her and then held her up as Felicity, Jane and Karen hurried, as best they could on skates, over to the side of the rink.

'Is she OK?' Felicity asked Jimmy as the group watched Samantha attempt to recover from another bout of coughing.

'I *am* here you know, I'm not deaf or dying,' Samantha snapped between coughs as she removed herself from Jimmy's grasp and clutched at the barrier at the side of the ice.

'What's the matter with her?' Jane enquired, looking concerned for her colleague.

'There's a virus going around the skating guys, could be the same sort of thing. Perhaps one of you could get her a drink or something while I take her to sit down,' Jimmy suggested, taking hold of Samantha's shoulders and shepherding her off the ice.

'I'm fine! Please... just – stop touching me!' Samantha hissed, her chest burning.

Jimmy ignored her request and helped her walk to the first row of seats. He flipped one of the seats down and helped lower her onto it.

'I'm fine. Thank you for your help, but I need to get back to the front desk. Dave only gave us twenty minutes and I hate to think what he'll have done to my systems if I leave him any longer,' Samantha spoke, attempting to rise to her feet.

'You're not going anywhere until you've sat down and had some water,' Jimmy said as an order.

'You don't understand. We don't get breaks you know, just lunch and that's no more than an hour,' Samantha said, clearing her throat.

'Will you quit quoting that employment manual,' Jimmy replied.

'Rules are rules and...' Samantha started, putting her hand to her chest to try and stop the aching.

'Sam, come on, it's five minutes.'

She was trying not to look at him. Bare arms, tight clothes, very close to her, it was uncomfortable.

'So, do you get the panic attacks a lot?' Jimmy wanted to know.

'I don't get panic attacks,' Samantha exclaimed, her voice starting to squeak.

Jimmy didn't reply.

'And what was with all that making me skate business? I can't skate, I'm a box office assistant. This is Dave's madcap idea and I hate it,' Samantha spoke, looking up at Jimmy.

He had amazing eyes, deep, dark brown. The colour of Galaxy Minstrels. His face was just perfect in every way, except for the small scar under his lip, but even that was straight. He had well defined cheek bones and a firm jaw. Samantha suddenly realised she was just staring at him, like he was a piece of real-life art in a gallery she couldn't draw her eyes from. The sick feeling returned to her throat. She could almost taste that morning's toast.

'I think you're a natural skater. Some people have that raw ability and some of us have to work at it. I think you could be good if you put in some practice,' Jimmy told her.

The Minstrel eyes were looking at her, it was off putting when she didn't feel very well and she was no good at conversation, particularly with men. This was by no means the first time she had had trouble stringing sentences together when it came to the opposite sex. How dissimilar she and Cleo were.

She could feel words coming to her mouth and she tried to clamp her lips shut before they spilled out involuntarily. It was to no avail.

'Cleo says you've been to rehab.'

The chocolate brown eyes dimmed slightly, but only for a moment, and Jimmy's expression remained unchanged.

'Yes, I have. So, tell me, is the sister I've heard so much about coming to one of the shows? I can't wait to meet her. I feel like I know her intimately already,' he responded with a smile.

'She's not like me, at all. She's bubbly, you know, the type of person that walks into a room and makes everyone aware of her – in a good way though,' Samantha spoke hurriedly.

'She sounds great,' Jimmy replied.

'I'm sorry we took up your time on the ice, I…' Samantha started, scratching around in her brain for something sensible to say.

'Not at all. Look, here are the girls with your water. Just take five and drink it slowly,' Jimmy told her, rising to his feet and preparing to leave.

'I will and I apologise for – you know, for…' Samantha started, feeling a complete idiot for a hundred different reasons all at once.

'I'll catch you later,' Jimmy replied.

Felicity, Jane and Karen joined her, and Felicity handed her a polystyrene cup of water as Jimmy skated back onto the ice.

'Are you alright now? You looked really white for a minute back there. Thought we were going to have to perform Airway, Breathing, Circulation,' Jane commented, her fear and tears temporarily taking a back seat.

'Of course I'm alright. We must get back to work, goodness it's almost half eleven and Dave wanted an early lunch. Pie shop has steak and kidney on offer for the first twenty customers,' Samantha spoke hurriedly as she swallowed all the water in one go.

What had she been thinking of? Damn Cleo for mentioning rehab and damn her stupid subconscious for allowing her thoughts to filter out. She was convinced there was a flaw in her brain, she didn't know anyone else who had the same problem in as severe a degree as she did. The moment she thought something it was usually at her lips and out before she had a chance to process the 'Stop! You cannot say that' thought. How could she have asked him about rehab? She barely knew him. He was a performer at the Civic Hall. There were boundaries you did not cross, there was respect to be paid, there was distance to be kept. Cleo would have died if she had been witness to it. *She* would have known exactly what to say. *She* never got tongue-tied – well at least not with words.

5

Cleo was very much tongue-tied later that evening. Jeremy, the hot brogue wearer, (glossy black hair and film star looks) could hardly keep his tongue away from her. He and Cleo were sat in the second row, together with two bottle blondes from the estate agents. One was called Chantelle, the other was called Harmony. Sat with them was the much talked about Connor. Why Cleo thought that Connor would be a good match for her Samantha didn't know. He was short, no more than five foot four inches and little in every way. He had a thin chest and narrow hips and he was wearing tight beige trousers and a white shirt that just made him look shorter and narrower. He wasn't unattractive in the face, in fact he had quite a pleasant look about him and had managed quite a nice smile when they had been introduced. But all the time, while Cleo was bigging him up, Samantha couldn't help looking at his tiny feet thinking that they could probably share shoes.

The Civic Hall auditorium looked resplendent, almost like a wintry film set courtesy of the lights and smoke on the rink. Every seat was occupied, and the audience chatted excitedly amongst themselves waiting for the performance to begin.

Samantha's ice skates were already hurting her feet. She had a chafe on her shin where the tongue wasn't positioned properly, and her ankles were aching. She had skated round the rink too many times to count, selling programmes and souvenirs. It had deteriorated into a double act of her and Felicity as, to no one's surprise, Jane and Karen had both called in sick.

It was a few moments before the show was due to start so Samantha left the ice and hopped up the steps next to Cleo in order to change into shoes and man the fire exits.

'So, Sam, you've seen the costumes. How much tight Lycra round nice firm arses can we expect tonight?' Cleo asked loudly for Chantelle and Harmony's benefit.

'I believe the costumes are made to a very precise measurement if that's what you're asking,' Samantha replied as she removed the skates and put on her trainers.

'My sister! She's so innocent. Honestly Chantelle, Samantha will actually be admiring the skating!' Cleo exclaimed with a loud laugh that prompted a smirk from the two bottle blonde women.

'I didn't know you could skate, Samantha. It's very impressive,' Connor spoke, leaning his thin chest forward so he could see past Jeremy and Cleo.

'It might not be so impressive once she has the ice cream tray round her neck at the interval – I think there may be some balance issues,' Cleo told her new acquaintances.

'By the way we're out of Worcester sauce crisps at the bar,' Samantha told her sister as she got to her feet and tucked the ice skates under the seat.

'What?! Sam! Product control! You knew I was coming tonight!' Cleo wailed as if a crime had been committed.

Samantha hurried down the steps and walked around the arena to take up her position at one of the rear exits. She hadn't told Cleo about the incident with Jimmy that morning. She had tried hard not to think about it at all. The inappropriate laughter problem she had been aware of, the feeling like her chest was going to burst open, like a cadaver having its rib cage cracked on an episode of *Silent Witness*, she had not. It had been hideous, she had been so embarrassed, and she had felt vulnerable. And people had *watched* her being vulnerable. She hated that more than anything. And then, after all that had happened, she topped it off by asking Jimmy about something personal, something only a brainless tabloid reporter would ask. She cringed as she remembered her stupidity.

But if she had told Cleo she would have focussed on the hand holding and the consoling arm. She could hear her now 'Jimmy Lloyd held your hand, he actually touched you! You skated with him!' Cleo would have screamed and made a fuss and probably wanted to smell her to see if she could smell him. No, she couldn't tell Cleo. All her questions would be too much to bear, and she would have to relive the coughing fit and the insane question about rehab. She only hoped Jimmy didn't mention that to Dave. Although from what she remembered about their conversation at the bar the previous night, he didn't seem to be a big fan of Dave.

'Ladies and Gentlemen, welcome to *Skating on Broadway* a show that combines the sounds of the stage with the moves of the world's most renowned ice skaters. On the ice, please welcome former Olympic gold medallists, Dana Williams and Jimmy Lloyd!' the compere announced.

Samantha heard Cleo scream out loud and saw her, the

peroxide blondes and two other women in the second row, jump to their feet and begin clapping wildly as Jimmy and Dana skated onto the ice.

The couple wore pale blue outfits and Samantha knew from the running order they were skating to 'Memory' from *Cats*. As they took their positions the crowd silenced, and the music began.

Dana looked like a Cinderella doll. Her hair was swept back into a tight bun, her dress was a beautiful mix of lace, Lycra and diamantes and her skin positively shone under the spotlights. Samantha watched her effortlessly move across the ice in synch with both Jimmy and the music. She was so graceful, so in control, so not like her. Self-consciously she smoothed her bobbed hair behind her ears and pulled her Woolston Civic Hall jumper lower down over her waist.

There was no denying that both Jimmy and Dana were fantastic skaters who complemented each other perfectly. Jimmy was the power and the strength and Dana was the grace and the elegance. There was an entourage of over thirty other skaters in the show, but it was Jimmy and Dana who truly wowed the crowd during their many varied routines.

Just before the interval, Samantha had confided in Felicity about the four thousand tubs of ice cream in the freezer and, after laughing hard for a minute or so, she had confirmed her agreement to Samantha's plan to put twice as many Berry Fruits in each serving tray in the hope that less alternative would increase sales. There was brief disappointment when the vanilla and chocolate ran out but a vast quantity of the four thousand were sold and Samantha was looking forward to being able to fit into the freezer again without having to breathe in.

By the end of the show the crowd were all on their feet, screaming, cheering, clapping and insisting on an encore of the final group performance. Samantha had never seen the audience so animated after a show and some had even brought flowers to throw onto the ice for the performers.

As the lights went up Samantha opened the set of double doors she was manning in order for people to leave the arena. She thanked people for coming and then saw Cleo and her guests preparing to leave, no doubt for the bar. However, just as she was starting to wonder where the slimline Connor had gone, she felt a tap on her shoulder.

'Hi, Samantha,' he spoke with a smile.

'Oh hello,' Samantha responded.

'It was a great show, I'm glad Cleo invited me. I didn't really think ice dance would be my thing, but it was really very enjoyable,' Connor told her.

'Yes,' Samantha answered, not knowing what else to say.

'So, are you going to be finished soon?' Connor enquired.

'Finished?' Samantha queried.

'Working. I mean I've seen you escort people to seats, check tickets, skate around selling programmes and ice creams, now you're seeing people out of the building. There can't be anything else for you to do surely,' Connor remarked.

'Oh, there's plenty to do. I have to help pick up all the empty tubs of ice cream, the used ticket stubs and other general rubbish the audience leave behind and I'm in charge of locking up,' Samantha informed him.

'Well, maybe I could stay behind and help you. Cleo and Jeremy are going for an Indian, I said we might join them a bit later,' Connor spoke.

Oh no, he had done it. He had asked her out and he had done it in such a way that she was convinced Cleo had almost put the words into his mouth. Cleo had also probably told him that she hadn't had a date in over a year and made her sound like the most desperate twenty-four-year-old in the whole borough of Woolston. Samantha knew her sister meant well but she also knew she thought the only way to be happy was to be bedding men on a regular basis. Oh, what a complete disappointment Samantha must be to her.

'No, I'm allergic,' Samantha blurted out and she moved away from Connor, pulling the exit doors out wider and standing with her back against one of them.

'Allergic?' he queried.

'To Indian food. It brings me out in a rash,' Samantha explained.

'Oh, Cleo didn't say. Indian was her idea and I thought...' Connor began, his thin face looking puzzled.

'Oh, that's typical Cleo. She loves Indian food, she wouldn't want any of my allergies getting in the way of her having a good vindaloo,' Samantha answered.

'*Any* of your allergies?'

'I'm allergic to most food served in restaurant environments. Pizza, burgers, kebabs, pasta, Chinese, Cantonese, Thai, Pan Asian...' Samantha started, desperate not to leave anything out.

'Fish and chips?' Connor offered.

'I have a potato intolerance and an adverse reaction to omegas three and six,' Samantha spoke quickly.

Connor nodded and smiled at her.

'And, I won't be finished until gone midnight probably,'

Samantha added.

'It's OK, I get the message. It's a shame though. I think we might have had a lot in common,' Connor said putting his hands in his pockets, a signal that he was admitting defeat.

'It was nice to meet you,' Samantha replied politely, glad he wasn't being too persistent.

'If you do change your mind about how you feel about dating, Cleo has my number,' Connor told her.

'How I feel about dating? What do you mean "how I feel about dating"? I date,' Samantha exclaimed immediately.

'It's OK. Cleo told me you're a bit apprehensive about the whole dating thing,' Connor answered.

'Oh, did she? And what else did my sister tell you?' Samantha wanted to know.

'I think she was just being protective you know, the big sister act,' Connor responded.

'Well perhaps it should have occurred to Cleo that her taste in men might not be mine and that if I wanted a date I would just go out and get one,' Samantha snapped at him, surprised by her own fury.

The tone and volume of her voice was enough to make some of the audience leaving the show look at her and Connor. Samantha felt her cheeks going red and she just shut her eyes, indicating that their conversation was over. She didn't know what else to say to him. She closed her eyes tighter and almost wished him away. Be gone, be gone. When she had the courage to open them again, he had left.

Cleo really *did* think she was a charity case. Now, in a desperate attempt to see Samantha with a man, Cleo was even telling the potential mates that she had dating issues. She didn't have dating issues, she'd been on dates, granted not recently, but she had done it. Although, thinking about it she hadn't really enjoyed any of the dates she'd been on. Well, the date with Joe was OK, until they'd got back to the house, gone into the bedroom and the piercing was revealed. Perhaps Cleo was right, perhaps she was kidding herself. Maybe she *did* have dating issues. The more she thought about it the more it became clear. Goodness, she did have dating issues. She never went on dates anymore. In fact, lately, after Joe and the body jewellery, she would do anything to avoid the opposite sex. She wouldn't walk down any street with scaffolding erected on it in case there were workmen waiting to whistle or comment on her or enter into flirtatious banter. She had been caught out once by a wolf-whistle, fallen into the road and put a hole in her Civic Hall trousers. She also always chose a checkout at the supermarket with a female cashier. She told herself it was because the women were generally quicker at checking out, but really it was because she didn't want a man giving her her pasta twists and accidentally touching her hand. She even blushed every time the teenaged boy in the newsagents made conversation with her about Cleo's *Star Life* magazine. In fact, the only man she interacted with was Dave. That couldn't be healthy.

She was still thinking about her failed dates while she finished picking up litter. She'd sent Felicity and Aaron home half an hour ago and all that was left to do was lock up when Milo had finished with the bar. Although, as it took him longer and longer each night, she was coming to the conclusion that he spent more time helping himself to drinks than he did tidying up.

She tied the last black bag of rubbish and set it down with

the others she'd congregated at the front of the hall. The lights of the arena were low, and the ice rink looked eerily empty. It was a stark contrast to its appearance earlier, when it had become a plateau for bright lights, glittery costumes and fantastic skating. The skaters had been wonderful, so skilful and in perfect unison with each other. They really put her capabilities to shame. She picked up her skates from underneath the seat and looked at them. She turned around and looked about the arena. There was no one there, the crowds had gone almost two hours ago. All the performers had headed back to the hotel and only Milo was left in the building and he was probably busy knocking back vodka and Red Bull. As quickly as she could Samantha pulled off her shoes, put on the skates and made her way onto the ice.

The air was cold, but it felt refreshing as it hit her. She skated round, trying to emulate some of the moves she had seen performed earlier. The women had spun and twisted and turned without putting a foot out of place and when they'd been lifted high in the air, they had held themselves with such poise. They'd been dainty and coordinated, things Samantha didn't know the first thing about.

She skated on, gaining speed and relishing the feeling. She lifted one foot off the ice and straightened her leg behind her, copying a move from the *Miss Saigon* routine. She smiled to herself. She was shaky but she had tried it, and no one had seen her. She felt like a naughty schoolgirl doing something she shouldn't. It was unlike her, she didn't do anything she shouldn't, but this felt fun.

She was so busy racing back round the rink to try the move again she didn't see Jimmy taking to the ice behind her. She pushed off, gained momentum and gingerly lifted her leg up behind her again.

'Nice work,' Jimmy announced, appearing at the side of her.

Samantha panicked, shocked at the sound of a voice so close to her. Her leg came down, she slipped in her desperation to stop herself and she landed with a bump on the hard, cold floor, jarring her back. Dainty and coordinated, hmm.

'God, I'm sorry. I thought you heard me come on the ice, I didn't mean to scare you. Are you OK?' Jimmy asked, bending down beside her.

'I'm fine. I was just being stupid. I'm sorry I was on the ice, I didn't think anyone else was here,' Samantha responded, quickly getting to her feet.

'Just me and some guy on the bar. He let me back in. What are you still doing here?' Jimmy wanted to know.

'Cleaning up, health and safety regulations. It all has to be properly disposed of,' Samantha informed him.

'I can imagine. So, are you going to keep me company? Skate a while?' Jimmy asked her.

'No. No, I should get going. Cleo will be wondering where I am,' Samantha spoke, skating across the rink towards the exit.

'I don't think she will. She seemed rather attached to Jeremy. Said they were going for an Indian and then on to a club,' Jimmy responded, following her to the edge of the ice.

'You met Cleo! Oh, I'm glad. She'll be so pleased, she thinks you're fantastic,' Samantha gushed, happy for her sister.

'I didn't have a lot of choice. She burst into my dressing room with two other women with really blonde hair. They screamed a lot and wanted photos,' Jimmy told her with a smile.

'That was Chantelle and Harmony. They work with her,' Samantha answered, preparing to get off the rink.

'Come on, don't go. Skate with me a bit, tell me what you thought of the show,' Jimmy asked her.

He had put his hand out and touched her bare arm. Her arm wouldn't usually be bare, but she'd got awfully hot sweeping up and had to remove her Civic Hall jumper. Now she was wearing the short-sleeved Civic Hall polo shirt and he'd touched skin. Her stomach turned over and she felt sick. Then the words were tumbling to her lips again, threatening to gush.

'I'm sorry about earlier, about the coughing and the laughing and for what I said – you know – the rehab thing,' Samantha blurted out, her temperature rising and the headache returning.

'Come and skate with me,' Jimmy urged her, and he took hold of her hand.

His hand was firm and warm and not unpleasant to hold. He was coaxing her back onto the ice, smiling. She didn't want to offend him, it would be rude and she kind of knew him. It wouldn't be like touching the fingers of an acne-faced Tesco employee.

She stepped back onto the ice and let him lead her back into skating around the rink.

'So, did you enjoy the show?' Jimmy enquired as he let go of her hand and they skated alongside each other.

'Well obviously, for the most part, I had to pay attention to the audience – to ensure there were no breaches of Civic Hall regulations. But what I did see was very entertaining,'

Samantha replied.

Jimmy laughed out loud at her response. It was a nice laugh, warm and deep and it made his eyes wrinkle at the edges.

'What?' Samantha queried, unaware she had said anything to provoke laughter.

'I really don't know whether you're being serious or not,' Jimmy told her.

Samantha didn't reply, she didn't like being laughed at, even if it was a nice laugh. And she really didn't know what she was doing skating round a temporary ice rink after midnight with a man.

'Hey, I didn't mean that the way it came out. I understand, your job means a lot to you,' Jimmy spoke, reaching out to catch her hand as they turned a corner.

'I think I ought to see if Milo's finished clearing up the bar. He might need some help,' Samantha said, pulling her arm away, ensuring her hand was well out of his reach.

'Don't go. Come on, let me teach you some stuff. I meant it this morning when I said you were a natural skater,' Jimmy insisted, moving in front of her and blocking her path to the exit.

'I really don't have time and I have to lock up. You can't stay here either. We have to close by a certain time or we're contravening our contract with the council,' Samantha informed him in a serious voice.

'Blame it on me. I'm Canadian, what would I know about local council regulations?' Jimmy responded.

'I know about them and I know you're here. Milo shouldn't have let you in, I'll have to speak to him about that,' Samantha continued, feeling herself getting more and more flustered as she attempted to skate around him to the safety of solid, un-slippery ground.

'I did almost have to beg. I left my hotel key card in the dressing room. But then I saw the lights were still on and I thought it wouldn't hurt to put in some extra practice, so I laced up and came out here,' Jimmy spoke, spinning around in front of her so she was unable to get past.

'I really have to go, Cleo will be…' Samantha started, her head thumping and her heart racing.

'Tucking into a chicken vindaloo about now,' Jimmy answered.

'She'll worry if I'm not there when she gets home,' Samantha insisted.

'Half an hour's skating and I'll drive you home. Come on, humour me,' Jimmy bargained, moving to block her exit again.

'No, I've got to go. Milo will be expecting me to be through soon to set the alarm system,' Samantha babbled, trying desperately not to look at him.

All she could see were the chocolate eyes and the warm smile, the chiselled cheekbones and the firm jaw. And it was then it hit her, full on, like an out of control train she hadn't seen coming. The truth was she found him undeniably attractive. She couldn't stop looking at him because she thought he was the most handsome man she had ever seen. Incomparable with Thomas Clancy, at least a thousand leagues above. This famous skater, someone who Cleo fancied, someone who had bedded an array of women, someone who'd been to rehab, she found him attractive too, just like everyone else. It was the most outrageous suggestion, but she couldn't deny it. That was the cause of her headaches and the sweats and the panic. She had a crush on Jimmy Lloyd.

The jolt of this realisation made her physically reel backwards on her skates. She wobbled and Jimmy swiftly reached out and grabbed both her arms to stop her from falling down.

'Whoa! You OK?' Jimmy asked as he held her arms and steadied her.

'I'm fine, I have to go. I need to secure the building,' Samantha spoke hurriedly as the lightheaded feeling returned.

She pushed off swiftly on her skates, made it to the side of the rink and hopped off the ice. She tottered over to where she'd left her shoes and the rubbish bags, and began hastily unlacing her boots. She had to go home, she had to get out of the arena and away from him. She'd have to leave Milo to drink himself into a stupor and hope he remembered to lock up. She couldn't stay behind a second longer, not one second.

'OK, listen, we don't start rehearsals until ten tomorrow. If you want to learn some moves, I'll be here from eight,' Jimmy called to her as he watched her remove her boots.

'Oh, I won't be here that early tomorrow. I have – I have stuff to do first thing,' Samantha responded, not daring to raise her face to look at him.

'Well, if you change your mind, I'll be here,' Jimmy repeated.

'Goodnight,' Samantha answered briefly, and she practically ran along the front of the seats, trailing the three full bin bags behind her.

6

Samantha heard Cleo scream out loud at just after 7.30 am. Cleo didn't have an alarm clock. Ordinarily, Samantha was up as soon as it was light outside. She usually showered, went downstairs, made a drink and had some breakfast. Then she made the packed lunches. At just after 7.00 am she always took a cup of herbal tea to Cleo, unless the crystals on the door handle told her not to. But today was different, today Samantha hadn't woken up at dawn because she hadn't actually been to sleep. She was led on her bed, still dressed in her Civic Hall uniform. Her eyes felt gritty from lack of sleep and she still had a horrendous headache.

She'd got home at 12.45 am, feeling like her head was going to burst. She'd hurried up to her room and started rifling through the pile of *Star Life* magazines she kept on the bottom of her bookcase. She was looking for evidence of her insanity. She was looking for any articles she could find on Jimmy to prove his complete unsuitability as an object of her affection. She found three.

One was an article about him attending a film premiere a year ago. In the picture he was dressed in a tuxedo, accompanied by well-known actress and complete floozy, Hilary Polar. She was barely wearing anything in the photo and seemed to have a vice like clamp on Jimmy's arm. They were both smiling, their matching perfect, white teeth gleaming like ice caps. The article attached listed almost fifteen women that Jimmy had been 'connected' with over the last two years. Reason one for unsuitability – he was nothing but a gigolo.

The second report she'd found was nine months old. It was a montage of photos of Jimmy falling out of various nightclubs and bars in the US. The article with the pictures commented on his excessive drinking and general bad behaviour. Reason two for unsuitability – nothing more than a drunken thug.

The third report, only six months old, stated that he had spent two months in a rehab clinic for alcohol addiction. The picture tagged to the article was of Jimmy leaving the Freedom Vale Rehabilitation Centre, looking how he looked now. Toned in body, fresh faced, handsome and chocolate eyed. Reason three for unsuitability – good enough to eat, makes your heart leap when he touches you. No, that wasn't right! That was a pro not a con. Well, unless you didn't like your heart leaping. She was undecided.

She didn't know why she didn't remember seeing the articles the first time she looked at Cleo's magazines. Except that she never would have considered that someone in *Star Life* magazine would appear at the Civic Hall or that their character would matter to her as much as it seemed to matter now. But the articles were exactly what she needed to see, all in all he was unsuitable, completely not her type. He was the archetypal celebrity indulging in all the excesses that life offered him. He had slept with more people than Cleo and he was an alcoholic. So why did she feel warm all over the minute she saw him?

Cleo burst into Samantha's room, her hair tied up in a dotty scarf, and last night's mascara heavy round her eyes.

'Have you seen the time?! Why aren't you up? Where's my tea?' Cleo shrieked at her sister.

'Sorry,' Samantha responded, hurriedly sitting up and pushing the magazines under the bed with her foot.

Cleo marched into the room and peered at Samantha suspiciously, putting her face right up close to her sister's.

'Are you ill?' Cleo wanted to know.

'Yes, maybe, I'm not sure. Sorry about your tea, I…' Samantha started, not wanting Cleo to ask her too many questions.

'Something's happened. I can tell when you're keeping things from me. Something's happened hasn't it?' Cleo said with a nod, still not taking her eyes from her sister.

'No, nothing's happened. I just overslept that's all,' Samantha replied.

'Argh! Oh my God!' Cleo shrieked, and she grabbed a fistful of Samantha's Civic Hall polo shirt.

'What's the matter? What are you doing?' Samantha demanded to know, trying to pull herself out of Cleo's clutches.

'This! This is why something has happened! This is last night's uniform!' Cleo exclaimed, her eyes wide in horror.

'It isn't,' Samantha lied.

'Yes, it is. Yesterday was a jumper and polo shirt day and today is a Civic Hall sweatshirt day. I live with you, Sam, I know all your completely annoying routines, and this is yesterday's uniform. So, spill, what happened last night? Because I know you didn't go out with Connor. He phoned

Jeremy, right in the middle of the main course I might add. Said you rattled on about allergies and fish oils,' Cleo spoke.

'Nothing happened. The hall was a mess after everyone left. I stayed behind to clean up, I got home late and just got into bed. I didn't even clean my teeth,' Samantha informed her, trying to kick a wayward protruding *Star Life* magazine back under her bed.

'You didn't clean your teeth? You didn't gargle with that awful mouthwash stuff you use? Now I know something's going on. Come on, out with it. You might be making me late, but this is serious. You're not being normal,' Cleo answered, and she sat herself down on the edge of Samantha's bed.

'I don't always do the same thing every day,' Samantha responded, moving a little away from her sister, hoping she hadn't taken up mind reading.

'Yes, you do,' Cleo insisted.

'I told you. I cleaned up the hall and it was late so I just – you know – crashed,' Samantha told her, knowing how ridiculous she sounded.

'Oh God, it's a man! This is man behaviour. This is how you behaved the last time you were interested in someone. This was what you were like when you met that guy from the bookshop, the one with the…' Cleo began as she became animated.

'Don't say it!' Samantha begged, cringing at the thought of the body piercing.

'When you met him, you went all weird and started acting out of character and that was when you did a wash without separating the whites. You never do that, ever!' Cleo reminded her.

'You're making me sound like some sort of freak,'

Samantha answered, not enjoying hearing her personality analysed.

'So, it's a man. And that's why you turned down Connor. Why didn't you tell me you had your eye on someone? Poor Connor, I actually think he was quite interested in you – despite your best attempts to ruin it,' Cleo continued.

'Connor was very nice but very small. For future reference I really don't go for men who could jockey greyhounds,' Samantha told her.

'So, who have you gone for then? Who is this mystery man that's made you throw caution to the wind, go to bed with your clothes on and forget your sisterly duties?' Cleo demanded to know, jumping up and down on the bed.

'There isn't any man. I told you, I was just tired. I *had* worked all day and most of the night,' Samantha reminded, swallowing as she lied.

'You swallowed, you're lying. Sam, I know you. You not only have major routines, but you have major habits too, ones you can't control. Swallowing when you're lying is one of them. Now let's not spend all morning playing cat and mouse, just get it over with and tell me,' Cleo ordered, her eyes wide.

Samantha let out a sigh. There was no use lying to Cleo. She knew her too well and she was like a dog with a bone. Once she latched onto something there was no stopping her.

'OK, there's a man,' Samantha admitted bravely, sitting up straight and taking a deep breath.

'Argh! I knew it! Who is it? Do I know him? Tell me! What happened last night?' Cleo blurted out, pulling the scarf from her hair and twirling it round her hand excitedly.

'Nothing happened last night, and you don't know him,'

Samantha informed, putting her hand up to her throat so Cleo couldn't see her swallowing.

'So, who is he? I want name and vital statistics,' Cleo carried on.

At that moment Darren Jacobs was invented. Samantha made him six foot, with blonde hair and blue eyes. Average looking, a nice pleasant face but not someone Cleo would call 'drop dead horny'. Even though she was thinking of Jimmy she was trying to depict a handsomed down version of Jason Donovan – although she didn't really know why. She told Cleo he'd been in the audience and had stayed behind to talk to her after getting chatting while buying a Berry Fruits ice cream in the interval. If only! He worked in the financial sector and lived in the smart area a couple of Tube stops away, in one of the expensive apartments that Samantha knew Cleo loved. She embellished the story with details of what he'd been wearing, what car he drove and the fact he'd been accompanied to the show by his seventy-five-year-old mother who was hard of hearing but a big ice-skating fan.

'Wow Sam, he sounds fantastic! So, when are you seeing him again?' Cleo asked excitedly.

'Today, maybe. I have his number and he wants me to call,' Samantha responded with half a smile.

She almost believed the story herself. Although she wished she'd dressed him in something less bright – a red shirt and chinos made him sound a bit camp.

'Well, I would leave it until lunchtime at least before you ring. You mustn't seem too keen. That's the art of seduction, you have to keep them guessing,' Cleo spoke with a nod of authority.

'Oh, I don't know whether to ring or not. I'm not sure he's really my type,' Samantha answered.

'He's six foot, nice looking and has money – of course he's your type! Get with the program!' Cleo ordered her.

'Yeah of course, silly me,' Samantha said with a nervous laugh.

'Now, now that we've got it all out in the open, you'd better change into the sweatshirt and go and make me a cup of tea, because otherwise I'm going to be really late and probably lose this job. Do you want to be responsible for me having to go into that horribly dowdy job centre with all the benefit cheats again?' Cleo spoke, standing up and moving towards the door of Samantha's room.

'No of course not. I'm getting on to it right now,' Samantha replied with a false smile, standing up from the bed as well.

'Good and I want an introduction to Darren as soon as the first date is over. And I want all the gory details if you – well you know – if you…' Cleo spoke, referring to Samantha's pure status.

'Complete rundown if we go all the way, of course,' Samantha answered, smiling so much her face was aching.

Cleo giggled excitedly and then disappeared as swiftly as she had appeared, banging the door loudly behind her.

Samantha was just about to let out a sigh of relief when Cleo reopened the door and screamed loudly again.

'I almost forgot to tell you! I met Jimmy Lloyd last night! Oh my God, he is so gorgeous and so nice. Chantelle took photos, I almost died!' Cleo exclaimed, her eyes glazing over as if she was reliving the moment.

'That's nice,' Samantha responded.

'It was more than nice it was fantastic. The funniest thing though, he knew who I was, and he knew your name. Obviously because of that silly name badge you wear, but he remembered it nonetheless. Actually though, I think he called you Sam,' Cleo exclaimed, pondering on the fact.

'Well that's just typical. Can't even read a name badge properly,' Samantha remarked quickly with a smile.

'Right, well, I'd better get ready. Any chance of tea in ten minutes?' Cleo asked, smiling at her sister and leaving the room.

Once the door was finally closed and she could hear Cleo running the shower Samantha slumped back down on the bed. She was crazy, why had she made up a fictional boyfriend? Nothing had happened last night with anyone. All that had happened was she had come to the devastating realisation she was no different to Cleo and had developed some insane crush on Jimmy Lloyd. She hated herself, she was pathetic. The chocolate eyes and the athletic frame affected her.

But no more. Now she had spent the entire night reading about his questionable character, no amount of sex appeal was going to make her resolve weaken.

*

It was after 9.00 am when Samantha arrived at the hall. Gobby was parading up and down outside the front doors, as if waiting for her and when he saw her approach, he trotted up to her, clawed at her trousers and began weaving in and out of her legs.

'It's too early, Gobby, there's no food yet,' Samantha told the cat, bending down to stroke his back.

He mewed and nuzzled his mouth against her hand.

'Samantha! What time d'you call this? It's well after nine. I do trust you'll be working through your lunch hour to make up the time.'

Samantha was completely taken aback at the tone of Dave's voice and the way he was tapping his fat finger to his watch as he came to the front doors. She was also a little surprised to see him dressed in a clean white shirt, a brand-new Civic Hall waistcoat and a Dickie bow tie. He looked ridiculous, like a circus ringmaster with a gut like a Swiss gym ball.

'Sorry I'm late, Dave, but...' Samantha began, moving towards him and trying to detach Gobby from her trousers.

'It's Mr Gordon to you and I won't have any excuses about your grandmother being ill or your dog being run over. We run a tight ship here and punctuality is the key to our success,' Dave boomed loudly.

Samantha looked at him, almost waiting for a punch line to the mad sketch he had just performed. Nothing happened. Dave just stood staring back at her. Gobby let out a loud miaow and hissed at Dave, arching his back in disapproval.

'Get that matted thing away from the hall. The scrounging beast probably has worms,' Dave snarled.

Samantha gave Gobby a pat and urged him to leave. Sensing he was going to achieve nothing by staying the cat turned tail and hot footed it up the street.

As they entered the foyer the telephone rang, and Dave practically leapt to answer it.

'Good morning, Woolston Civic Hall, Dave Gordon speaking, the manager. How can I assist you?'

Before Samantha's jaw could drop open at Dave's keenness to answer the phone and his jovial, if somewhat elongated introduction, she was aware of someone standing in the doorway of Dave's office.

A tall, thin man dressed in a grey pinstriped suit was positioned behind the counter, picking up paperwork and studying the charts on the wall. He was carrying a clipboard and marked the piece of paper attached to it as Samantha caught his eye. His expression was unchanged, and he reminded her of a pall bearer.

'Hello,' Samantha said, looking at the solemn man who continued looking sombre.

'Good morning. You must be Miss Smith, Samantha Smith. Am I correct?' the man enquired, peering down at Samantha from above his tiny, gold-rimmed glasses.

'Yes, I'm Samantha Smith,' Samantha responded, feeling a little like she was back at school.

'Good. I'm Radcliffe, Nigel Radcliffe from the borough council – amenities division,' the man introduced himself.

'Oh,' was the only reply Samantha could manage.

'Your appointment is at twelve, in Mr Gordon's office,' Mr Radcliffe informed her, and he made another pencil mark on his clipboard.

'Appointment?' Samantha queried.

'Everyone's being interviewed. We need as much information as possible to report our findings,' Mr Radcliffe informed her cryptically.

'Findings?' Samantha asked again.

'All will become clear at twelve. Don't let me keep you any longer, I can hear you're busy,' Mr Radcliffe said as the other telephone line began to ring.

He moved away from her and drifted like a ghostly apparition towards Dave.

At least the presence of someone from the council explained Dave's attempt to look smart and his attitude towards her being late. He was obviously worried about making a good impression. Though Samantha was surprised Dave hadn't given her a warning about a visit from the council. For all his failings it was unlike him not to want all the stops pulled out.

★

When 12.00 pm arrived, she was in the middle of dealing with an awkward customer on the phone. It hadn't been a good day. Mabel had slipped up on a stray piece of cauliflower cheese in the kitchen and had needed Rest, Ice, Compression and Elevation, Gobby had sicked up something that resembled curry just outside the main doors and they had had a drunk come in repetitively singing 'We are Sailing' and wanting to kiss all the female diners in the restaurant.

She knew Nigel Radcliffe was stood behind her now, the clipboard tight in his hands, waiting. The customer had bought tickets to the pantomime and wanted a refund. Samantha was trying her best to persuade them to exchange the tickets for a different show or take a gift voucher. She could feel Mr Radcliffe's eyes boring into the back of her neck. She really didn't need this pressure today, not with everything else that was on her mind, like three thousand five hundred and one iced Berry Fruits and her ridiculous infatuation with Jimmy Lloyd.

Just as she thought she was going to get a result from the

caller and they were going to accept tickets for Jethro, she saw Jimmy and Dana come through the doors that led from the arena floor into the foyer.

'I've told you time and time over I'm not doing it! When's it gonna start sinking in?!' Samantha heard Dana yell as Jimmy walked swiftly towards the exit.

Samantha turned her head slightly to watch.

'For God's sake stop shrieking and go away. I've got nothing else to say to you,' Jimmy responded firmly, stopping in his tracks to turn and face his skating partner.

'You can't just walk out! We've gotta practice, you know we weren't one hundred per cent last night,' Dana carried on, dramatically sweeping back her long red hair.

'No, we weren't,' Jimmy replied in an accusing tone.

'And what the Hell is that supposed to mean?! It isn't me who has the problem Jimmy – remember that,' Dana screamed hysterically.

Samantha watched intently, half expecting a director to shout 'cut' and a make-up artist to appear and put shine control powder on both their faces.

Jimmy took a deep breath and then a step back.

'I can't be around you when you're like this, Dana,' he told her coolly.

He turned away from her and proceeded to leave the hall.

Dana let out a frustrated sigh and then turned in Samantha's direction, looking straight at her. Samantha felt her cheeks flushing and her headset suddenly slipped off her head and fell onto the desk with a loud crash as the cable caught her elbow. Dave's Brylcream made it prone to slipping and it was even worse if you had conditioned your hair.

She hurriedly picked up the headset but to her dismay the caller was no longer on the other end of the line.

'Miss Smith, it's past twelve. I think it might be best if Mr Gordon telephoned that particular caller back, don't you?' Mr Radcliffe's headmasterly voice spoke from behind her.

Samantha turned round in her chair and gave the man from the council a sober nod of agreement.

'Please go through,' Mr Radcliffe spoke, putting out his arm and indicating towards Dave's office.

Samantha, somewhat reluctantly, left her seat and walked into the manager's office. He had certainly made an effort to tidy it up. The in-tray was almost empty, the pen pot was neat, the 'Tits & Arse' calendar had been taken down and there was no sign of any leftover food. There were no half-eaten pastries or open packets of biscuits in sight. This meant Dave had been well aware of the visit from Mr Radcliffe. She had never seen Dave's office this tidy – not since his assignation with the confectionary saleswoman. It was surprising that Dave hadn't mentioned the visit though. She could have bought some flowers, brightened the place up a bit.

'Please sit down, Miss Smith,' Mr Radcliffe spoke as he entered the room behind her and shut the door.

Samantha quickly sat down in the chair opposite Dave's desk and watched Mr Radcliffe almost get swallowed up in Dave's huge executive leather seat as he eased his small, wiry frame down into it. It was like Tom Thumb trying to sit down on a bouncy castle.

'Now, I don't know if you've heard the rumours about the changes the council are going to have to make, but I'm here today to carry out an official appraisal. I'd like to try and glean some information from you and your colleagues about the Civic Hall and the service it provides to the community. I've also been taking a look at the figures to establish if it's still a viable entity,' Mr Radcliffe spoke, looking straight at Samantha.

'Rumours?' Samantha queried, trying desperately to take in what he was telling her.

'There was an article in one newspaper about the action we might be forced to take, due to a drop in budget for leisure and amenities, and about the possible closure of some facilities. But I want to assure you, as I have assured Mr Gordon and your colleagues, that nothing will be decided until we've carried out a full and thorough audit of the situation,' Mr Radcliffe said.

'Closure,' Samantha muttered in no more than a whisper, a feeling of dread overwhelming her.

Closure! Closure meant the end of something, shutting of doors, boards going up.

'Nothing's been decided yet. As I said, I just need to see which of the amenities is the most cash consuming and which establishment is going to prosper with the revised budget we've been allocated in the new ten-year vision plan,' Mr Radcliffe told her.

Samantha felt like she had been stabbed. She could feel the colour draining from her face, her energy ebbing away and a state of paralysis hurriedly creeping over her. Was this what anaphylactic shock was? She'd always wondered. What was next? The inability to breathe? The windpipe closing up? Unconsciousness?

'I've been looking at your sales records, they're most commendable. But that said, is there anything else, in your opinion that could be done to boost these sales further? Or is there anything here that's stopping the hall from fulfilling its potential?' Mr Radcliffe questioned, picking up a pen and preparing to scribble Samantha's response onto his clipboard.

She hadn't heard what he said. She hadn't been able to listen to anything after he had said 'closure'. The fear was building. The laughter was rising in her stomach, her stomach was rising in her throat and her heart rate had sped up. She could no longer see Mr Radcliffe's gold-rimmed glasses, nor his face, or his pin striped suit. In fact, the whole room was starting to blur. She felt dizzy, sick, and faint, like someone who had spent too long in a hot tub drinking copious amounts of wine.

She laughed out loud and gripped her sides and then she coughed and gasped and tried to stand up. She flapped her arms like an aroused ostrich batting its wings and Mr Radcliffe, shocked and alarmed by her reaction, pushed his chair away from the desk and stood up to assist her.

'Close the Civic Hall? Are you mad?! You can't close the Civic Hall! That's the most ridiculous idea I've ever heard!' Samantha screamed, as she gasped for breath and clutched at the handle of the door to Dave's office. Her windpipe was tightening, she was sure of it.

'Miss Smith, please sit down. You don't look at all well, perhaps if you just...' Mr Radcliffe suggested, coming round the desk to reach her.

With all the effort she had left, she opened the door of Dave's office and struggled out into her workspace. She needed some fresh air. She felt like she was going to vomit, if the vomit could make it past her ever decreasing windpipe space and the breath catching in her throat. Perhaps she could make it outside and puke in the patch Gobby had made, at least that would mean less clearing up to do later.

'Miss Smith, please come and sit down. I can see I've shocked you and I...' Mr Radcliffe began, following Samantha as she made it out from behind the counter and into the foyer.

'You can't close the Civic Hall – you can't close it because it's... it's my life,' Samantha told him, her face now the colour of beetroot and her breathing erratic.

She felt the foyer spin and her eyes begin to close. The final thing she saw before she lost consciousness was Jimmy coming back through the main door.

7

She had nightmares about it. The fear stemmed from sitting all day on the front desk seeing countless elderly people collapse in front of her. It was either because it was too hot or too cold or they had stumbled or their friend had stumbled, causing a domino effect. Now *she* was going to be the casualty. Now people would be standing around her looking concerned, some hoping she wasn't going to die in front of them, others hoping she was so they could post a video on You Tube. She didn't want to open her eyes, she couldn't. There would be the shame, the embarrassment, Jane in tears and Dave's awful breath.

'You missed our date this morning,' a familiar voice spoke.

She was dreaming! Thank goodness! But no, she didn't want to dream about him, it was against her rules. If she let the dream carry on, she would see the Minstrel eyes and the nice hair, and she would smell the mixture of musky eau de toilette and testosterone. She had to wake up.

Samantha slowly opened one eye and caught sight of the nice hair.

'No!' she exclaimed out loud.

The volume of her voice convinced her that it was far

too loud to be in any dream and that meant the nice hair was really attached to the object of her affection and his presence wasn't imagined.

'Hey, are you OK?' Jimmy asked as Samantha opened both eyes and hurriedly tried to move.

One of her arms was behind her back and the other was propping up her head. As she tried to move all she succeeded in doing was raising her chest slightly and bucking her top half like a break dancer attempting the Caterpillar.

'Here, let me help you up,' Jimmy urged, taking hold of her arms and assisting her in getting to her feet.

Everyone was staring. There were a group of people stood around her and she could see the customers dining in the restaurant had all put down their cutlery and were looking in her direction. She had never felt so embarrassed. She couldn't stay there a moment longer being looked at and pitied.

Without saying another word Samantha hurriedly shook herself from Jimmy's grasp, turned towards the exit and began to make her escape. She almost got as far as the door. She caught her foot on the matting and fell nose first onto the rough carpeting.

The ice skater was again the first person to reach her and offer assistance.

'I think you need to slow down. Come and sit,' Jimmy ordered, helping her to her feet and attempting to guide her back to a seat.

'No! Look at all those people, looking at me. I can't stay here, with them, like that – all looking,' Samantha blurted out, tears welling up in her eyes as she saw customers begin to whisper amongst themselves about her. The pensioners, usually doddery and a concern of hers were now looking over their toasted tea cakes at her, pity in their cataract ridden eyes.

'Then let's go sit outside,' Jimmy suggested quickly. He put an arm around her shoulders and hurried her away from the prying eyes.

'I don't need you to help me, I'm fine,' Samantha said, shrugging his arm away from her shoulders.

'Your nose is bleeding,' Jimmy announced.

'What?' Samantha queried, immediately putting a hand to her face.

She touched her nose and then let out a scream as she saw her fingers were covered in bright, red blood. And then she felt it on her lips and in her mouth. The taste made her gag. Where was that closed up windpipe when she needed it?

'Here, sit down and use this. Pinch your nostrils together,' Jimmy ordered, directing her quickly to the nearest bench.

Samantha took the material that was offered and began mopping up her face. She hated blood, particularly her own. It all stemmed from playschool when Daniel Murphy had played an over enthusiastic game of Doctors and Nurses with a pair of scissors, some fishing line and one of his Action Man's military bandages. The cross stitch had to be removed at A&E.

'Pinch your nostrils together hard and keep it like that for ten minutes,' Jimmy informed her, taking the material from her and holding her hand in place.

Samantha turned her head slightly to look at him and saw, to her horror, he was bare-chested. She couldn't help but gasp out loud and her hand came away from her nose, letting more blood escape.

'What are you doing? You've got to keep holding it for ten minutes and make it stop or you'll be going to the emergency room,' Jimmy ordered her.

'Where's your shirt?! You can't sit here like that! This is a main street!' Samantha exclaimed in horror.

'What did you think was mopping up your blood? Come on Sam, keep it pinched,' Jimmy told her, again using his top to mop the blood from her face.

'Please, go and get another shirt. There are shops, just there,' Samantha told him, pointing and again taking her hands away from her nose.

'Will you stop worrying about what I'm wearing and keep still?' Jimmy spoke and he put his hands over hers and pinched her nose together tightly.

With her nostrils held together so tightly she could no longer speak. That meant there was nothing else to focus on but Jimmy's torso. It was perfection. Not a hair in sight, well defined pecs and abdominal muscles. The combination was certainly an advertisement for ice skating as a form of exercise. And even better, there was no sign of a tattoo or nipple ring. It was the longest ten minutes of her life, sat next to a gorgeous man with no top on, in the middle of the high street, blood stains on her face, mute.

Finally, Jimmy let go of her hands and allowed Samantha to stop pinching. He closely scrutinised her nose.

'I think it's stopped. Just don't touch it or sneeze or cough or anything – not for a while at least,' Jimmy instructed.

'Well for how long? I mean you don't always know when you're going to need to cough or sneeze. What if it happens and I can't stop it?' Samantha queried, studying her bloodied fingers.

'I have a car. How close is the nearest hospital?' Jimmy asked her, putting on a serious expression.

'I can't go to a hospital, I can't...' Samantha began, feeling panicked once more.

'Will you relax? It was a joke. Jeez, is there anything you aren't scared of?' Jimmy queried.

'I'm not scared of hospitals, I just wouldn't want to waste their time. I had a nosebleed that's all. Thanks for your help and for your shirt, I can arrange to replace it and...' Samantha began as she rose to her feet and tried not to look any more at Jimmy's bare chest.

It was like a Greek Adonis meets the Chippendales.

'There won't be any need for that. I never really liked it anyway – unwanted gift. OK, the nosebleed I get, you hit your face on the floor, but the panic attacks are becoming a real issue,' Jimmy told her, his tone serious.

'How many more times? I don't have panic attacks! I just fainted a bit, it was hot that's all. I overheat when it's hot, ask anyone. No air conditioning in the foyer, a design flaw but it's an old building. I've got to get back to work,' Samantha spoke, looking at her watch and nervously shifting her weight from one foot to the other.

'Before they close the Civic Hall down?' Jimmy responded.

He watched the colour disappear from her face and her eyes widen. Straight away she swayed on her feet and Jimmy quickly stood up, took her firmly by the arm and made her sit back down on the bench next to him.

'What do you know about that?' Samantha spoke in no more than a whisper.

She was scared if she talked any louder it would make

her worst fear closer to becoming the truth.

'I know that guy from the council was talking to you about their audit of the hall. While you were unconscious, he told us he thought he'd upset you with the news. He didn't say too much more because Dave had to escort him to his office when he started to have an angina attack,' Jimmy informed her.

'They're just looking into the finances that's all. It'll be fine, we're very profitable. I mean stock control can sometimes be a concern but we're getting through the worst of that and action will be taken,' Samantha responded. Three thousand five hundred and one iced Berry Fruits was better than four thousand.

'I'm sure he'll be OK. He had medication with him,' Jimmy answered her, referring back to Mr Radcliffe.

'Who did?' Samantha answered, her mind unable to focus on anything but the plight of her beloved Civic Hall.

'Mr Radcliffe? His angina?' Jimmy reminded.

'Angina is very common in a man of his age, perfectly treatable. D'you think he had a chance to look at Dave's awful pie chart projections? Because I don't think a pie chart is the best way to display the figures and I know Dave only does that because he has some sort of affinity with pies but...' Samantha gabbled.

'What will you do if the hall closes?' Jimmy asked her bluntly.

'The hall isn't going to close! There's been a hall here since 1947. It's tradition, it's our heritage, it...' Samantha started enthusiastically.

'It doesn't have a website where people can book online. It has a larger capacity than other venues round here, but it doesn't attract big named acts. The menu in the restaurant needs updating, and so does the décor,' Jimmy spoke.

Samantha just stared at him, her mouth almost hanging open. What was he saying? Wheat Dream had only been on the walls a year or so.

'And it isn't in a great area, I mean the West End is where people want to be. That's where the real nostalgia is, that's the place to be seen.'

'The West End is overrated, the tickets are overpriced, and people don't always want to watch tired musicals and plays, they want variety and the Civic Hall gives them that,' Samantha spoke passionately.

'It needs updating, revamping and reinventing. All those things I said, the website, the menu – I've just thought of those off the top of my head and I know nothing about running a venue. But you do. I think you could manage the hall a whole lot better than Dave. I suspect a great deal of the finances go on his wages, when the staff around him are actually doing the hard work. Maybe it's time for a change of leadership,' Jimmy suggested to her.

'I don't know where all this is coming from, I mean Mr Radcliffe said they were just doing a preliminary look into the running of this hall and the other council run hall in the district, the Presbook Centre. Preliminary means there's no need to panic doesn't it? I mean preliminary means the beginning of a long drawn out, well considered investigation, with lots of meetings and public consultation,' Samantha spoke quickly as her mind whirred with thoughts.

'I guess it could mean that, but if I were you, I'd want to start acting now. You need to ensure whatever he does find leaves him in no doubt which hall he should save,' Jimmy told her.

'It isn't my place, Dave's…' Samantha began.

'From what I've seen, the only person Dave cares about is himself. He doesn't care about the heritage or the history and I don't think he could save the hall even if he wanted to,' Jimmy spoke sincerely.

'I can't start implementing new ideas over Dave's head, he's the manager and…' Samantha responded, her mind actually aching with all the thoughts bubbling around inside it.

'Well it's up to you. I'm just shooting my mouth off, but I think the hall could have a great future. It just needs some time and effort to be invested in it by someone who has real enthusiasm,' Jimmy said.

'It won't come to anything. No, there's no need to panic. This isn't the first time the council's had to juggle their amenities budget. They always make it work out in the end,' Samantha spoke, sounding less than convinced in her own words.

'Yeah of course and what would I know anyway? All I know is ice skating. Listen, I'd better get back or Dana will eat me for breakfast – again,' Jimmy said, standing up and giving Samantha a full-length view of his torso.

'OK,' Samantha responded, hurriedly averting her gaze to the floor.

'See you at the show tonight,' Jimmy spoke.

'Yeah, the show,' Samantha responded, without lifting her gaze from the concrete paving.

What was she going to do? Why was this happening? All she had to worry about for the last few years was ticket sales and preview guides. OK, so the hall was dated, but it was also familiar and comfortable. It was like a well-worn baggy jumper you'd had since you were fifteen and just couldn't bear to part with. It was *her* comfortable baggy jumper. And it ticked along. But Jimmy was right, ticking along wasn't enough. She was always saying herself about the acts being tired and repetitive, perhaps if they attracted a different type of show they would bring in a whole different kind of audience. Out with the Blue Rinse Brigade singing 'Roll out the Barrel' when *Wartime Warbles* came to visit and in with the twenty first century and psychological illusionists like Derren Brown. They could get more bands, something Cleo would approve of, more original acts instead of cover groups and the conference rooms were never fully utilised, perhaps they could advertise. And they definitely needed a better website. But what if the council had already made up its mind? What if, on today's visit alone, Mr Radcliffe had decided the Civic Hall was not worthy of the lion's share of the amenities budget? Even if he hadn't made a decision yet, how was she going to convince the council where best to invest its funds? After her dramatic hyperventilating and collapsing, he was probably wondering what sort of lunatic was working the box office of the hall. Her word wouldn't count for anything. She had no authority, the only thing to do would be to try to convince Dave of what needed to be done. She would do what she usually did, she would steer Dave towards her conclusions and make it seem like it was all his idea in the first place. He liked that.

Samantha raised her head from the floor and caught sight of her blood-stained hands. The first thing she needed to do was have a wash.

8

Samantha couldn't get the blood out from under her fingernails, no matter how hard she rubbed. She had never been convinced about the performance of the brand of hand soap in the ladies' toilets and now the inadequacy was confirmed. It would usually have been something she would report immediately to Dave, but in the light of today's events, it probably wouldn't be on the top of the manager's agenda.

What was she going to do? In little more than an hour, her whole world had come crashing down. She couldn't possibly imagine her life without the Civic Hall. She barely remembered what her life was like before the Civic Hall, except that she had been a victim of the Witches of Woolston, the catty girls who'd worked alongside her at the shoe shop. They had giggled and laughed to themselves over the kitten heels and wedges, looking Samantha up and down and undermining her confidence at every turn. They'd talked loudly about who they had shagged, who they would like to shag and who they were definitely going to shag at the weekend. Somehow, they knew about her virgin status like it was tattooed on her forehead.

The job at the Civic Hall had saved her. She felt like she

had a place there and a purpose. There was a feeling of belonging as she walked through the door each day. OK, Dave was a pain and her colleagues weren't as dedicated to the job as she was, but they didn't laugh at her (at least she didn't think they did) and they kept their private lives to themselves, well apart from Felicity filling her in about her latest disastrous relationship and Jane updating her on her disabled mother's varicose veins. If the hall closed, what were the chances of finding somewhere else that made her feel like she fitted?

Samantha took a deep breath and splashed her face with water. She looked at herself in the mirror. She was beginning to look like her mother when she frowned. In a few decades it could be her in a retirement bungalow by the sea, knitting for other people's grandchildren, probably still virginal.

She swept her hair back behind her ears and swallowed. She needed to compose herself and get the full story on the council's plans from Dave.

*

When she opened the door to his office without knocking, he almost fell out of his chair. He had a half consumed Ginsters pasty in one hand and his other hand was concealed inside a family sized packet of ready salted crisps.

'Ah, Samantha! I was just going to come and look for you,' Dave spoke, hurriedly opening a drawer to hide the pasty.

Samantha sat down in the chair opposite his desk.

'Don't worry, the front desk is manned. I passed Felicity on the way here and she's happy to have a late lunch. I'll relieve her as soon as we've spoken,' Samantha said.

'No matter, Duck, I was concerned about you. Are you feeling OK? You took a nasty tumble,' Dave said, spraying crisps across the desk as he tried to remove the packet from the workspace.

'Dave, did you know Mr Radcliffe was coming today? Did you know about the council's plan?' Samantha asked bluntly, looking at her boss with wide, frightened eyes.

'Well, I knew he was coming but I wasn't fully aware of the reasons. I'm sure it's nothing to worry your little head about. We're very prosperous at the moment, very prosperous indeed. The ice show is really getting bums on seats,' Dave responded, shifting about in his chair like a man feeling uncomfortable at being questioned.

'What's going on? I mean I see the figures, things didn't seem that bad. I'm sure we've had worse years. The hall can't close. What's your plan? I'll do anything I can to help,' Samantha told him, leaning on the desk and looking straight at him almost pleadingly.

'Calm down *mon petit souris*. There's no use getting in a two and eight. Sometimes you just have to let things run their course. I'm sure all this will blow over,' Dave spoke, and he began leafing aimlessly through a pile of papers on his desk.

'But Mr Radcliffe said only one hall can survive, there's us and the Presbook Centre, oh and the playhouse. Do you think he's counting the playhouse? We need to shake things up a bit, have a real drive at selling more tickets, some special offers perhaps. And we need a web page, perhaps online booking, everyone has that and…' Samantha began, the words coming out at a hundred miles an hour.

'Well actually, Duck, that will be something to discuss

with the new manager,' Dave responded.

'We could do meal deals in the restaurant and perhaps spruce up the menu – what did you say?' Samantha asked, stopping abruptly and just staring blankly at her superior.

'I have had a calling,' Dave continued, a smile spreading across his podgy face.

'What? I don't understand,' Samantha replied, her voice weakening, her conviction drifting away.

'I am joining the auspicious Herald Cruises as the Director of Entertainments. Me! A director! I start next week, and the first cruise is round the Aegean,' Dave boasted, puffing out his chest as he always did when he thought he had said something earth shattering.

'No,' Samantha said, her bottom lip beginning to tremble as tears welled up in her eyes.

She could feel everything slipping away, the hall, her life. Where would she go? What would she do? Who would feed Gobby?

'Yes, isn't it a wonderful opportunity for me? I'll get to show my true potential at last. There will be no restrictions, no council budgets, no boundaries. I can be a maker or breaker of careers,' Dave carried on, the inane smile not leaving his face.

'But you can't leave – we're in crisis,' Samantha managed to speak as the tears began to roll down her face.

'There's no such thing as a crisis in entertainment Samantha, you should know that. The show will always go on,' Dave spoke, still smiling.

Samantha couldn't believe what she was hearing. Her life was turning into something that resembled a *Twin Peaks* episode. All it needed was a procession of dwarves. The world had gone mad, that was the only explanation. She needed to restore some sanity, somehow, reality needed to be gripped.

And then she was weeping. Her eyes had glazed over and all she could see was Dave's fat, doughy face, still smiling. He didn't care about the hall, perhaps he never had.

She stood up, using his desk for support and without saying another word she turned towards the door of his office.

'Cheer up eh, Duck? Still time for one more BOB before I leave,' Dave told her.

And then he let out a hearty guffaw that turned her stomach.

With his laughter echoing in her ears Samantha ran. She ran out of his office, through the foyer and out of the hall. She felt upset, scared and betrayed. She needed familiarity. She usually found that at the hall but not today, perhaps never again. She had to get home.

She ran down the main street, past commuters, past joggers, past women pushing buggies, past tramps and over friendly dogs, not noticing any of them. A million thoughts were spinning around in her brain. What was happening? What was she going to do?

*

She didn't stop running until she was outside her front door. She quickly let herself in with shaking hands, her heart racing and her forehead clammy. She needed to sit down, her head was aching. She walked through the hallway towards the kitchen and was just contemplating how her life couldn't get any worse when she looked up. The sight before her stopped her in her tracks.

Cleo shrieked at the top of her voice, Samantha gasped and hurriedly turned away. Jeremy practically vaulted from the kitchen table picking up his trousers from the chair.

'What are you doing home?! It's only two!' Cleo exclaimed as she hurriedly put her blouse over her head and tried to cover up her nakedness.

'Since when did I have set times to come in and out of our house?' Samantha questioned, still not daring to look back at the scene.

'Since always. What's happened? Has the Civic Hall burnt down or something? No, if it had you'd be there, in the thick of things, coordinating the recovery operation,' Cleo spoke, trying to cover up her embarrassment.

'Is that supposed to be a joke? What do you know? Who have you spoken to? Goodness, how long does it take you to put a pair of trousers on? I bet it didn't take that long to get them off,' Samantha said to Jeremy as she briefly turned back and caught sight of him in just his underwear.

'Come on, Jeremy, let's go up to my bedroom,' Cleo said, doing up the zip on her skirt and looking defiantly at Samantha.

'Actually, Cleo, I'd better get back to the office,' Jeremy responded, his cheeks reddening as he caught Samantha's eye.

'What? I thought we were being rebellious and not going back this afternoon. You aren't going to let my usually routine driven little sister ruin our plans, are you?' Cleo demanded to know.

'No, don't mind me. You carry on – hope I haven't spoiled the mood,' Samantha spoke sarcastically.

'I'll call you later – sorry,' Jeremy said as he moved past Samantha and headed for the front door as fast as he could.

The front door closed, and Cleo glared at Samantha. Samantha ignored the look and walked into the kitchen. Cleo had a death stare akin to Darth Vader and Samantha knew better than to join in the game. She began to fill the kettle with water.

'Well thank you very much! Do you know how much persuading it took to get him to skive for an afternoon?' Cleo told her.

'No, but I can imagine you had a lot of fun getting him to agree,' Samantha responded, putting the kettle on to boil.

'If you were coming home early you could have rung or something,' Cleo continued, watching Samantha get two cups ready for tea.

'It wasn't anticipated, nor was it anticipated that you would be shagging on the kitchen table at two o' clock in the afternoon. I mean Cleo, we have to eat off this. And anyway… you should be… you should be… at work too!' Samantha replied.

And then she burst into tears. All the emotions of the day overwhelming her and making her break down again. She felt like a wreck. She had spent practically the whole day crying. Her face was beginning to feel damp, crumpled and prune like, like a grieving *Casualty* extra. She bawled, sobbed and shook and Cleo rushed over to her, enveloping her in a perfumey hug.

'What's the matter? It isn't Darren is it? If he gave you his number with no intention of taking you out on a date then I will kill him,' Cleo spoke sternly as she hugged her sister.

Samantha just continued to cry, unable to stop herself.

'Sam, tell me what's wrong. I'm imagining the worst here. Has something happened to Mum or Dad? Are you OK? Are you ill? God, look at your nose, is it something to do with that? It doesn't look right at all,' Cleo said, making a face as she stared at the swelling.

'It's the worst, the very worst,' Samantha managed to mumble into Cleo's shoulder as she held her.

'Oh God, Sam just tell me. I'm freaking out here,' Cleo exclaimed in fright.

'The Civic Hall might close. I just found out today. Oh God, what am I going to do?' Samantha spoke, lifting her head and stepping slightly away from her sister's embrace.

Cleo looked at her momentarily and then she pushed her away with a hiss.

'What?! Is that all?! I thought you had some terminal disease or something, or that Mum and Dad had died in some horrific motorway pile up or that Darren had dumped you before you've even been out with him. I suppose I should've guessed it was something to do with that flaming place. You don't go anywhere else or do anything else,' Cleo blasted, furious at her sibling.

'This is serious! We had a visit from the council today and there might only be room for one entertainments centre. One! What if they close us down?' Samantha questioned, her eyes wide, hoping for support from her sister.

'Oh, so what if they do? I only go there because you get staff discount and let's be honest – it doesn't really attract the greatest acts – the ice show and that hotty Jimmy Lloyd are the only exception,' Cleo responded bluntly.

'Cleo, we went there as kids to see all the pantomimes. Mum and Dad used to go to all the shows there, you had your thirteenth birthday party in one of the conference rooms. Doesn't that mean anything to you?' Samantha asked her.

'Things change and time and people move on. The place is outdated and the people that go there are past their best. It's stuck in a time warp in acts and furnishings and the food in the restaurant sucks. I'd say it was an open and shut case that it needs tearing down. Maybe they'll put something decent in its place, like a big Primark,' Cleo told her, making herself a cup of tea.

'How can you say that?' Samantha asked, her heart bursting with fear and panic.

'Because it's the truth and I think you should start looking for another job and try getting a life, because when the hall closes, gone are all your excuses for avoiding the real world,' Cleo told her.

Samantha stood stunned. Her sister had never been so harsh with her before. She was unable to respond, her voice choked. She just stood and watched, like she was having an out of body experience, as Cleo calmly made herself a cup of tea. Without uttering another word her sister turned and left Samantha alone in the kitchen, with the table soiled in bodily fluids.

9

Her uniform was creased. It was the only time in all the years she had worked at the Civic Hall that she had ever gone to work with an un-ironed uniform. What was worse still was that she didn't actually care. Imagine, going to work at your favourite place and not caring that you looked like a vagrant.

What's more, Samantha's nose had now turned a reddish purple. It had started to ache when the water hit it in the shower but now it was bruised and swollen and twice its normal size. Gobby had also ambushed her on the way in, covered her in hair and dribbled on her un-ironed trousers. Those things and the agony she felt at the possible closure of her beloved Civic Hall, made the evening ahead seem practically unbearable. She didn't want to be there, everything felt insecure and uncertain. She had forced a smile on her face when selling programmes, but her heart just wasn't in it like it should be. Now she was stood in her position at one of the rear fire doors as the ice show played out before her.

Two skaters had just performed to a piece from *Guys & Dolls* and now it was Jimmy and Dana taking to the ice to perform to 'All that Jazz' from *Chicago*. It was one of Samantha's favourite routines because it was fast paced and full of lifts and difficult moves. She couldn't deny that Dana was an excellent skater and she was envious of her ability.

She was so graceful, and Jimmy held her above his head like she weighed nothing. She probably would if she didn't have so much hair. She was the same build as Posh Spice but with Ginger's colouring.

And then suddenly, as they turned immediately in front of her, Jimmy went to lift Dana above his head, and she seemed to hesitate. As she was elevated, she fell forward and came crashing down onto the ice. There was a thud, sequins were shed and the whole audience gasped.

Samantha put her hands to her mouth in shock. But then, as quickly as she had fallen, she was back up on her feet to continue the routine. Samantha watched as they caught up with the timing of the music and ended the performance as smoothly as if the fall had never occurred.

The audience applauded graciously, and the partnering smiled and waved as usual, but as they turned to leave the ice Samantha could see that Dana's expression was thunderous.

None of the crowd seemed to be concerned by the mishap and they began applauding the next group of ice skaters which was an ensemble, doing a song from *Riverdance*.

Samantha was thankful the rest of the performances went without a hitch. The last thing the Civic Hall needed was for people to stop coming to the ice show, it was its popularity that was holding the hall together.

But it was obvious that Dana's confidence had been knocked by her fall. Her other skates were hesitant and not as assured as usual. The audience hadn't seemed to notice though, in fact all the comments Samantha received when showing people out of the hall were complimentary.

It was well after midnight when everyone had finally left the building and Samantha and Felicity were left to shut everything down. Felicity was tending to the upstairs of the building and the bar area, while Samantha dealt with the main auditorium.

As she walked back into the hall, picking up sweet wrappers and discarded drink cartons on the way, she could see Jimmy was back on the ice. He was skating furiously round the rink at almost breakneck pace.

Samantha watched him. He was out of breath, sweating and he didn't look in a good mood. She took her skates out from under the seat and looked at them. She wanted to skate, she wanted to lace up her boots and get out onto the ice. She wanted to do something to help her forget about everything. But Jimmy was there, she was supposed to be staying away from him. She was meant to be keeping him at arm's length, remembering he was a performer and she was staff – forgetting he was hot.

But the rink was calling to her. She needed to skate. She needed to do something other than worry about the fate of the Civic Hall and what it could all mean for her. She took a deep breath, sat down and began to tie up her boots.

By the time she got down to the edge of the rink Jimmy was doubled over in the middle of the ice taking deep breaths to restore his natural rhythm.

She skated over to him and, hearing another pair of blades on the ice, he looked up.

'Hey,' he greeted still out of breath.

'Hello,' Samantha replied, stopping herself opposite him. 'You good?'

'Yes, I just wanted to thank you again for – you know – helping me out with the whole nosebleed thing earlier.'

'No problem.'

'And I appreciated your ideas about the hall,' Samantha spoke in a business-like manner.

'You're welcome.'

'Well, I…'

'See the show tonight? Hey, what am I saying? Of course, you saw the show tonight – you and thousands of other people all watched me mess up,' Jimmy responded frustration in his voice as he kicked at the ice.

'*You* mess up? I thought Dana hesitated and she ended up in the wrong position when you lifted her. Well, not that I know anything about skating, but well – you know – I thought that was what did it,' Samantha mumbled.

'You really think that? Thank God, I thought I was going out of my mind. You should have heard her after the show. She was telling anyone who would listen that I dropped her, how it's because I haven't put enough hours in – how it's because I'm drunk,' Jimmy exploded angrily.

Samantha didn't respond, not knowing what to say. She swallowed and looked at her feet. What was she doing here? This wasn't giving him a wide berth. He was unsuitable and unobtainable, she knew better. Jimmy took a deep breath and tried to compose himself.

'I don't drink any more by the way. I did go to rehab, for alcohol rehabilitation – not drugs. I don't take drugs, never have. Alcohol does enough for me – well, too much actually,' he said.

Samantha still didn't reply. She felt such an idiot. She didn't know what to say to him. She wished she did know what to say to him.

'I'm sorry, I shouldn't be laying all this on you. It just hasn't been the best day you know. Did you want to skate?' Jimmy asked her, running a hand through his hair.

'Dave's leaving,' Samantha blurted out.

'Shit, when did that happen?' Jimmy asked her as he set off skating and encouraged her to follow.

'I went back to work after the nosebleed, I meant it about reimbursing you for the shirt by the way, or getting it laundered or something...' Samantha babbled as she skated alongside him.

'Forget the shirt, it's fine. You went to see Dave and...' Jimmy spoke, wanting her to continue.

'And I asked him about the inspection, about Mr Radcliffe visiting and he tells me he's leaving next week for some job with a fancy title on a cruise ship. Just like that, no warning, no build up to it, just like that. I mean how can he do that? The hall is in jeopardy, how can he just abandon it? Doesn't he care?' Samantha questioned desperately.

'No, I'm quite sure he doesn't,' Jimmy replied.

'But he's been the manager here for years, it must mean something to him, it just must,' Samantha continued.

'Well, I don't think it's important whether Dave's committed to his job or not. Someone like him is always going to be out for himself and someone like him isn't going to be interested in safeguarding the future of the hall. I mean how can you trust a man who speaks bad French and thinks it's clever and funny?' Jimmy told her.

'No one seems to understand that the hall isn't just a building, it's vital and it's a lifeline to some – the OAPs in particular. I mean I know the bingo evenings and the special half price lunches aren't money makers, but no other amenity provides that. I know there's room for improvement, I know things need updating and we need new acts and more people through the door, but I want to maintain the hall as a centre for the borough's community – that's what it's always been,' Samantha blurted out passionately.

'That sounds like fighting talk to me and you need to say all that to Mr Radcliffe and his council buddies,' Jimmy answered as they skated alongside each other.

'I can't do that! I can't tell anyone, that's the problem. I don't know whether you've noticed but I'm a little orally challenged. I have all these things in my head that I want to say and then when I go to say them I either laugh or throw up or want to pass out. Why am I telling you this?' Samantha said as she desperately tried to suppress the nausea.

'I hate to tell you this, but I had noticed,' Jimmy replied.

He skated in front of her and took hold of her hands, forcing her to skate backwards. His hands were warm and the feeling of his fingers in hers only served to make her feel even more ill and a little giddy.

'When I tried to speak to Dave none of it came out properly and he just talked over me about his stupid new job. I get home and my sister is having it off on the kitchen table right in front of me and, once she's clothed herself, I tell her about it, hoping for a bit of support, and she just says she's glad the hall might close and she thinks I need a new life, with Darren and...' Samantha began practically hyperventilating.

'Who's Darren?' Jimmy queried.

'You don't know him. *I* don't even know him! Goodness, what am I going to do?' Samantha exclaimed as panic crept up on her, wrapping itself around her whole body until she was physically shaking.

'You're going to take on the role of managing this place and ensure its survival,' Jimmy told her firmly, squeezing her hands supportively.

'I'm not up to that job. It'll be stressful and I'm not good with stress. In fact, I'm not good with anything. But I do feel immense responsibility for it, I just don't know if I'm strong enough to do anything about it,' Samantha continued.

'I believe you're up to the job,' Jimmy answered.

'I'm terrified. I'm scared of trying to do something about it, I'm scared of not doing something about it. And why are you being so nice to me and caring? Why do you care anyway? I mean it's just another venue on your tour to you and why should it be anything else? It isn't where you live, you don't know the history, you...' Samantha spoke, getting herself into an emotional state.

She knew she was going on and on now, like a mental patient, but she couldn't stop it.

'Hey, I care. There aren't enough facilities like this the whole world over. It isn't easy to find places to stage a big ice show you know, not now half the original rinks have been closed,' he replied.

He put a halt to their skating but carried on firmly holding her hands. It felt nice but it was torture. She liked it and she shouldn't. It was a bit like trying not to find Mick Hucknall ever so slightly sexy. As hard as you tried you just couldn't stop yourself.

'As far as being scared goes, well these days I'm terrified every time I set foot on the ice. Dana's just about stripped away every shred of confidence I have and that isn't much when you're a recovering alcoholic, but I was just about hanging on to some. And most days now she makes me feel about two inches tall and she tries to force her opinion of me on to other people. Anyway, you shouldn't be scared, you've been given this great opportunity to save the hall and really come into your own here. I haven't ever met anyone who believes so passionately about anything like you believe in this hall and you should have confidence in that passion,' Jimmy told her.

He was holding her hands tightly and looking at her. All thoughts of the Civic Hall were evaporating second by second as Samantha was unable to concentrate on anything but his face.

'I'll help you,' Jimmy spoke, breaking the silence that hung in the air.

'What?' Samantha questioned, trying to direct her gaze away from the Minstrel eyes.

'I'll help you save the hall. We'll come up with an action plan. I have friends in this industry, I can call them, and we can put together a proposal to the council that will knock their socks off,' Jimmy carried on almost excitedly.

'No, no I couldn't. I mean that isn't why I told you. I don't know why I told you, I was just venting, and I shouldn't have. I…' Samantha gabbled, trying to gain control of her speech.

'There would be conditions. I actually have my own selfish agenda for offering assistance,' Jimmy admitted as he made them recommence their skating.

'It's OK, thank you for the offer and everything but you've so much to do with the show and everything and I don't really know you and I wouldn't want to burden you with…' Samantha started again.

'Just hear me out. I'll help you try and save the hall if you let me teach you to improve your skating,' Jimmy suggested to her.

'That doesn't sound right. I mean I'd be getting all the benefit,' Samantha spoke as she thought about his idea. More time with him, looking into the gorgeous face, lots of handholding. It sounded great and completely perilous at the same time.

'Not true. I think teaching is kind of what I'd like to do long term. I get amazing satisfaction out of seeing the progression people can make. I hoped you might agree to be my guinea pig,' Jimmy said with a smile.

'Oh, I don't know,' Samantha spoke nervously, still feeling the warmth of his hands in hers and enjoying the sensation a little too much for her liking.

She tried to think of something gross – Worcester sauce, the late Bruce Forsyth, licking Worcester sauce off the late Bruce Forsyth.

'Come on, Sam, what have you got to lose? I help you keep this place open and you help me develop my coaching skills,' Jimmy stated, and he pulled her arms hard making her fall forward and bang into his chest.

It made Samantha gasp and when she raised her head, he was smiling down at her.

'First lesson, always keep your head up,' Jimmy spoke with a laugh.

Samantha smiled but inside her stomach was churning with a plethora of emotions. Concern about losing the Civic Hall and fear about accepting assistance from someone who could make her feel physically weak just by being in the same room.

10

Before she knew it, she'd agreed. What was she thinking? She couldn't let him teach her to ice skate! It meant spending more time with him. Him touching her and her touching him. She must be out of her mind! But he did have knowledge of the entertainment industry, he had a lot of influential friends and that could be absolutely key if she wanted to ensure the Civic Hall stayed open.

She'd left him half an hour ago and now it was almost 1.00 am. The place was in a state, Milo hadn't tidied up properly, not to her standard anyway, and there were three cans of Red Bull suspiciously hidden away at the bottom of one of the bins. She'd hoovered and emptied the bins in the foyer and now she was sorting out the bar.

She was enjoying skating again. It was so long since she had done it properly, she had forgotten how much fun it was. It was like being set free from who she was off the ice. She could forget about everything and concentrate on the moment. It wasn't often she got to do that.

She bent down to restack the crisp boxes in order.

'Hey, I know it's late, but can I get a tea?'

Jimmy's voice in such close proximity shocked her. She got up too quickly and banged her head on the edge of the bar.

She took a sharp breath inwards and put her hand to her head, holding the injury.

'You OK?'

'Yes, I thought you'd gone. You said you were going back to the hotel.'

'I am, but the tea's not all that. Can I have one?'

'Well we're not really open and...'

'Come on, Sam, it's just a tea. Have one with me, then we can share the guilt of contravening the council regulations?'

Samantha knew she had started to sweat. On the ice when there was skating to practice, she could pay attention to her feet and half ignore the gorgeous being dancing with her. But here there was nothing else. Just her and him and conversation.

'What flavour?' Samantha asked, willing away the pain in her head.

'Well it's gonna have to be the blackberry, really enjoyed that last time,' Jimmy spoke.

'Would you like anything with that? Nuts?'

'No thanks.'

'Or ice cream? I'd highly recommend the Berry Fruits,' Samantha babbled.

'Just the tea for now, thanks.'

'Well, you can always change your mind,' Samantha said as she filled the kettle.

She was feeling very hot and considered taking her sweatshirt off. No, she couldn't do that, not in front of him. Her polo shirt might ride up and she would probably get her head caught in the neck hole and wouldn't be able to get it off. Then she'd be stuck underneath it, unable to get it off and he would help, and the polo shirt might come off with it. No, she would leave it on and sweat, it was safer.

'So, you're still here too, I thought you had chores,' Jimmy spoke.

'Just clearing up.'

'You do *have* a home to go to, don't you?'

'Of course! But things have to be done,' Samantha spoke, feeling criticised.

'Do you ever stray from your routines?' Jimmy questioned, looking at her full of intrigue.

'They aren't *my* routines, they're Civic Hall routines.'

'Yeah but you're running the hall now, you've got to have some input.'

'Don't be ridiculous, *I'm* not running the hall,' Samantha exclaimed.

Jimmy let out a laugh.

'Just a matter of time,' he said.

'One blackberry tea. That will be 95p.'

'Thanks,' Jimmy said, passing her the money and taking the tea.

'You can't stay long, I'll have to close soon,' Samantha made clear.

'So, what's there to do round here? I know the place to be is the West End, but I'm not a traditionalist and I like to explore. Where are all the happening places round here?'

'Happening places?'

'Yeah, the "in" places to go. Where do *you* go?'

Samantha was prevented from having to say anything by some vigorous thumping on the front doors.

'Sorry, I'll have to see who that is.'

Samantha excused herself and made her way to the

front door where she found Cleo banging furiously on the glass, hair flying everywhere in the wind. Her lipstick was smeared, and she was wearing neon pink sunglasses.

Samantha opened the door and let her sister in.

'What are you doing here?'

'We went to the pub, sshh,' Cleo spoke, putting her finger to her lips and laughing.

She was swaying on her feet and was very obviously drunk. She was wearing a tiny yellow and white spotted Ra-Ra-style skirt and stiletto heels. It wasn't a good combination when she could barely stand up.

'Where's Jeremy?'

'Don't know. Sshh, someone will hear,' Cleo replied and laughed hysterically again.

'How much have you had to drink?'

'Not enough. Is the bar still open?'

Cleo didn't wait for a reply but headed in the direction of the bar where, to her delight, she saw Jimmy sat on a bar stool. Cleo squealed out loud and grabbed hold of the skater's arm.

'Jimmy! What are you doing here? Shouldn't you be back at your hotel or tucked up in someone's bed?' Cleo questioned, wriggling herself onto the stool next to him and taking off her sunglasses to leer at him.

'The bar's closed and you need to go home,' Samantha said, taking her sister's arm.

'He's got a drink. I'll have what he's drinking, what is it? Vodka?' Cleo asked, peering into Jimmy's teacup.

'It's blackberry tea, but I think I'll have a coffee now. How about you Cleo? Coffee for you?'

'We're closed,' Samantha spoke desperate to get her sister

home.

'Come on, two coffees, I'll pay. Don't bother with the machine, we'll have instant – as quick as you can make it,' Jimmy offered, sensing Cleo needed it.

'Come on little bar person, do as you're told. Two coffees,' Cleo said, grinning stupidly at Jimmy and holding on to his arm.

Samantha saw Cleo's hand on Jimmy's arm, and she swallowed back a knot of jealousy. Cleo could touch him, just like that, without any thought, any questions or consideration. She just did it. It seemed so easy. Why did she find it so difficult? When she had to touch him, it was as if she had been asked to take hold of a power cable. There was hesitation and fear of death.

'I was just asking Sam where the happening places were round here,' Jimmy spoke.

'Not here, that's for sure. Dump of a place this is. Look at it, dowdy furnishings, not a shot glass in sight and the snacks – hang on, is that Worcester sauce flavour?' Cleo asked, screwing up her eyes to look at the crisps.

Samantha didn't respond but tried to concentrate on the boiling kettle and not her sister gripping on to Jimmy.

'Gimme some. Two packets, no three,' Cleo spoke.

'Cleo…' Samantha started, about to protest.

'Here, whatever she wants, apart from alcohol,' Jimmy said, handing a note across the bar.

'You don't have to do this,' Samantha spoke quietly to him, feeling highly embarrassed by her sister.

'It's fine.'

Samantha handed Cleo the crisps and started to make the coffees.

'It's no use asking *her* the best places to go. She doesn't go anywhere,' Cleo said, opening the first packet of crisps and greedily eating them.

'I do go places, I...' Samantha protested.

'Bookshops don't count and neither does the supermarket.'

'I go out, when I'm not working I...'

'You what? Read a book? Go to Tesco? WOW! How happening is that eh, Jimmy? What are you doing here on your own anyway? Shouldn't you be somewhere rock 'n' roll with some really cool people?' Cleo asked, squeezing herself into him.

'I was just here practising with...' Jimmy began.

'Dana. He was practising with Dana. There was a mishap tonight on the ice and he was practising. At least I think that was what he was doing, I don't really know – I'm just the little bar person,' Samantha babbled, unable to look at anything but her sister's arm on Jimmy.

'But...' Jimmy began, looking at Samantha quizzically.

'Two strong coffees, drink up,' Samantha urged, hurriedly putting the cups down on the bar.

'Mmm, smells gorgeous doesn't it? Gorgeous smelling coffee with a gorgeous man. That's got to be a perfect end to an evening, hasn't it?' Cleo asked, licking her lips and looking up at Jimmy.

'Where's Jeremy?' Samantha asked her again.

'Getting a takeaway, he'll be here in a minute. So, Jimmy, you want to know where all the happening places are do you? I could show you, give you the grand tour. I'm sure we could keep each other entertained,' Cleo purred, stroking Jimmy's hand.

'Cleo, I don't think Mr Lloyd wants you to...' Samantha

started the hairs on the back of her neck bristling as she watched Cleo toying with Jimmy's jacket.

'Shut up, Staff, who asked you? Don't you have some cleaning to do?' Cleo snapped, moving closer to Jimmy.

Samantha swallowed and just watched as her sister giggled and ran her hand down Jimmy's arm. She could never be like that. So confident, so brazen, so... Katie Price.

There was hammering on the front doors.

'Oh, that'll be Jeremy, but don't let him in yet. We've barely got to know each other, you and me,' Cleo said, smiling at Jimmy and then putting her finger to her lips and sucking it suggestively.

Samantha hurried to the door and saw Jeremy, red in the face, holding two takeaway bags. He smiled in at her like a demented, drunk clown. She unlocked the door and he staggered through it.

'Hello, Sam. Cleo here? She ran off in a strop when she heard they were out of poppadoms.'

'Over there at the bar, she needs taking home. I'll call you a taxi,' Samantha spoke, leading the way.

'So, are you seeing anyone? Dating?' Samantha heard Cleo ask Jimmy.

'No, not at the moment.'

'Jeremy's here,' Samantha announced loudly, wishing her sister would untangle herself from the ice skater.

'I've got food. Curry, rice, naan, Bombay potatoes. Oh, is that coffee? I could murder a coffee,' Jeremy said, looking at Cleo and Jimmy's mugs.

'You can have mine. I'd better get going,' Jimmy said, getting off the stool and looking at his watch.

'Oh, so soon? We could go to a club. There's one just up

the street that's open 'til four,' Cleo announced, slurping her coffee and then bouncing up and down on her stool waving her hands in the air like she was watching centre stage at Glastonbury.

'Maybe another time,' Jimmy spoke kindly, smiling at her.

'I'll see you out,' Samantha said, accompanying him down the foyer.

As soon as Cleo and Jeremy were out of earshot Samantha spoke.

'I'm so sorry about Cleo. I haven't seen her that bad for ages. I'll be having words with Jeremy when they've both sobered up.'

'It's fine, she's nice. Very different to you though, are you quite sure you're sisters?' Jimmy enquired.

'My mother isn't like that! She married my dad at seventeen,' Samantha answered, unlocking the door.

Jimmy laughed and smiled at her.

'Just for the record, I'm a fan of bookstores too,' Jimmy replied.

'Oh,' Samantha said not knowing what else to say.

'I'll see you tomorrow.'

'Yes, see you tomorrow,' Samantha answered, watching him leave.

'Sam! Get some plates! This'll be cold by the time we get home!' Cleo yelled, tearing off some naan bread and wedging it into her mouth.

11

Samantha was ironing her Civic Hall jumper when Cleo entered the kitchen. It was morning and 7.30 am. After their heated discussion the evening before and Cleo's drunken performance at the hall, Samantha hadn't dared to take her herbal tea. However, she'd known Cleo was awake because she'd heard her stomping around her bedroom and emptying her wardrobe of clothes. It was a morning ritual.

'I disinfected the table,' Cleo greeted as she whisked past her sister and headed for the kettle.

'Me too,' Samantha replied not looking up from her ironing.

'D'you want a cup of tea?' Cleo offered her voice softening a little.

'No thanks,' Samantha responded, still not looking up.

'Look, I hate it when you're like this. I'm sorry about yesterday, about Jeremy and the table and all that – and about what I said about the Civic Hall,' Cleo spoke hurriedly, standing right in front of her sister so she was unable to ignore her.

'That's OK. I'm more concerned about the being drunk and embarrassing last night,' Samantha replied, putting the iron down and switching it off at the wall.

'I know how much your job means to you. I should have been more supportive. I shouldn't have shouted and gone off on one,' Cleo carried on not really listening to Samantha's responses.

'It's OK. The letching last night was far worse than anything you said,' Samantha answered again as she slipped her jumper over her head and started to pack away the ironing board.

Cleo just stared at her blankly.

'What are you talking about? Letching? Drunk? I'm trying to apologise for slagging off the Civic Hall.'

'Don't you remember anything about last night?'

'I went out with Jeremy last night, to the pub.'

'Hmm, and you obviously don't remember anything that happened after that. Don't you have a headache?'

'Well a bit, I suppose.'

'Never mind. I made your lunch, it's in the fridge, usual place,' Samantha spoke, preparing to leave the kitchen.

'Hang on a minute, I'm lost. We had a row yesterday, you said the hall might close, I called it a flea pit and now you say that's OK. And you're trying to change the conversation, making up stuff. Ah ha! It's Darren, isn't it? You met up with Darren last night, didn't you?' Cleo exclaimed and let out a scream of excitement.

'Yes!' Samantha replied, putting a hand to her throat as she swallowed.

Faking excitement was killing her.

'That's great! So, you phoned him yesterday and you met up after the show – where did you go? What did you do? First base? Second? Not third? Tell me you didn't!' Cleo continued, bouncing up and down and tugging at

Samantha's freshly ironed jumper.

'I didn't and you'll be the first to know if I do. Look, I've got to go, I'll see you later,' Samantha said, relieving her sister from her clothes and heading out of the room and into the hallway.

'So, where did you go? Some expensive restaurant I bet! Was it Godiva's?' Cleo interrogated, speaking of the costliest restaurant in the district.

'I'll see you later. If you remember the last part of your evening then give me a ring,' Samantha spoke hurriedly, picking up her coat and bag from the peg in the hallway and rushing toward the front door.

'Don't think you can avoid giving me the details. I will get them, you know I always do. Resistance is futile! Hang on! Sam! Did I have curry last night? I've got a horrible brown mark on my new skirt and I'm really hoping it's curry,' Cleo yelled as she watched her younger sister leave the house.

Samantha smiled to herself as she began her walk to the hall. She never got the Tube, too many people far too close and she wasn't keen on being underground. It didn't help that their mother had been mugged once on the Tube by a man posing as a nun. Samantha had never looked at any member of the clergy in the same light again after that.

After the awful day yesterday, last night had been really good. She had spent an hour in Jimmy's company learning how to skate properly. He had even taught her some of the easier moves of one of his routines from the show. He had been nice, down to earth and a patient instructor when she had wobbled about and fallen over. He kept encouraging her and praising her and picking her up when she hit the floor. He didn't seem anything like the person *Star Life* magazine had been depicting. And he was single. He had told Cleo as much when she was practically sat on his lap. He liked Cleo, he was nice to her and he bought her crisps. But he did say he liked books too.

Today everything felt a bit strange. She didn't know what it was, but it just felt different – *she* felt different. Her nose was still red and sore, her legs were aching from the skating, but she felt almost invigorated at the thought of the day ahead. There was hard work to do, there were spreadsheets and accounts to look through. She needed to ensure everything was up together – the Civic Hall needed her.

However, as the entrance came into sight she stopped in her tracks and a cloud appeared on her bright mental horizon. Felicity and Jane were stood outside the Civic Hall holding aloft placards. They bore the slogans 'Council Cop Out of Community' and 'Civic Hall R.I.P'. Both signs displayed a wobbly drawing of a skull and crossbones. She saw Gobby loitering by one of the bins, ducking behind it whenever Jane stomped past brandishing her sign.

'Felicity, what are you doing?' Samantha asked as she reached her two colleagues and tried to ignore the looks they were all receiving from passers-by.

'What does it look like? We're protesting,' she responded, waving her banner in the air.

'Put the placards down before too many people see you,' Samantha told her, and she took hold of Felicity's sign and attempted to take it out of her hands.

'We want people to see us, don't we, Jane? That's why we're standing here, protesting. There's no point protesting if no one sees you. Anyway, the local paper will be here in a minute. My boyfriend Tony works on the switchboard and he's going to get one of the reporters down here,' Felicity informed Samantha.

Tony sounded like another good choice of man with excellent prospects. At least this one had a job. Where did she meet them? If this was the type of man you met when you actively looked for dating opportunities, then Samantha was glad she didn't bother.

'We have a banner for you too,' Jane announced and held out a sign to Samantha that read 'Bollocks to Borough Council'.

'I don't want a banner and you two shouldn't be standing out here with them either. You'll scare away the customers and it's OAP day in the restaurant. We don't want to make Mrs Nelmes pee herself again, she smells bad enough as it is,' Samantha exclaimed, stepping back from the offending sign.

'Customers have been signing the petition,' Jane continued.

'A petition! A petition for what?' Samantha asked them.

'To stop the council closing the Civic Hall of course,' Felicity retorted.

'They aren't closing the Civic Hall, not yet anyway. The council has to look into things first. So, displaying banners with derogatory slogans isn't going to aid our cause is it?' Samantha spoke forcefully.

It didn't sound like her voice. It was full of authority and power. It was Margaret Thatcher organising her cabinet. It was Hillary Clinton berating her philandering husband. It was her mother telling her father not to leave the electric blanket on. She opened her mouth again and coughed.

'Dave said that…' Jane began, looking at Felicity for confirmation.

'It doesn't matter what Dave said – Dave's leaving – and I bet he didn't tell you that,' Samantha continued.

She seized the opportunity while Jane was distracted and grabbed hold of the banner she was holding and wrestled it from her colleague's grasp.

'Leaving!' Felicity and Jane exclaimed in unison, the tone of their voices giving away their shock at the news.

'Yes, leaving. So, none of us will ever have to listen to any more of his lame pearls of wisdom. Now, let's go inside and get on with our jobs – while we still have them,' Samantha told them and, before she could stop herself, she was putting out an arm and gesturing them towards the door, like she was in charge.

Still taken aback by the news of Dave's departure the two women, rather meekly, did as they had been instructed and trooped back into the building. Samantha picked up the signs, folded them in half as best she could and stuffed them into the bin outside the hall.

'Morning, Gobby, cod fillets on the menu today, back door about one,' Samantha spoke as the cat dared to stick his nose out from his hiding place.

He mewed and licked his lips and Samantha followed her colleagues into the hall.

⋆

Lunchtime came and Dave hadn't made an appearance. There had been no phone call stating sickness, no appointment in his diary – although Samantha had never really thought he kept it up to date – and the bun lady had left disappointed because her best customer had failed to show.

Samantha had been flat out all morning. She'd been on the front desk for the majority of the time, but the rest she had spent doing something unheard of and completely out of character. She had rifled through Dave's office. She needed to find out everything she possibly could about the council's plan. She was certain Dave must have received more than a phone call a few days before the visit and the more she thought about it, the more she was convinced there had to be a letter.

She was supposed to be at lunch, but her stomach hadn't felt right since she had received the news about the hall, and she couldn't even face opening her lunchbox.

The bottom right hand drawer of Dave's filing cabinet wouldn't open. At first Samantha thought it was just stuck, as nothing else in Dave's room was locked and he wasn't really a great one for confidentiality. Then, after some gratuitous pulling, she came to the conclusion that it really must be locked. She was searching through the pot of paperclips and elastic bands on the desk looking for the key when all of a sudden, the office door burst open.

She immediately panicked, shot backwards in Dave's executive chair and, after it had banged against the wall, she only managed to avoid falling onto the floor by gripping the desk tightly with both hands and holding on.

'Hey, you need a hand there?' Jimmy's voice asked as he appeared in the room.

'No! No, I'm fine, thank you. I thought you were Dave – close the door,' Samantha whispered hurriedly as she hauled herself up and indicated the open entrance.

He was wearing blue again. A tight blue t-shirt and

figure-hugging trackers. Blue suited him, well everything suited him, but blue was the best. When she imagined him he was usually in blue. Not that she imagined him often.

'Why are we whispering?' Jimmy asked her in hushed tones.

'Because I don't want the others to hear. How are you with picking locks?' Samantha enquired, tugging again at the drawer.

'Picking locks. Hmm, can't say I've much cause to do that in my line of work. But I'm ashamed to admit I did break into the odd high school locker in my time – purely for prank purposes obviously. I wouldn't want you to get the wrong idea about me,' Jimmy spoke as he joined Samantha behind the desk to see what she was doing.

'Can you open this drawer? I can't find the key and I just know the evidence is in there,' Samantha said still pulling at the drawer with all her might.

'I don't think it's locked, I think it's just jammed,' Jimmy told her.

'No, it's definitely locked. I've been trying to open it for at least ten minutes and believe me, it's locked,' Samantha insisted, going red in the face as she carried on tugging.

'Humour me and let me try?' Jimmy suggested, taking hold of the drawer's handle.

'Well, you can try but I'm telling you, it's…' Samantha began, standing back and letting Jimmy take up her position.

In one quick motion Jimmy fiercely jerked the drawer handle and it opened, revealing the contents.

'I was sure it was locked,' Samantha said her face red with embarrassment.

'Beginners luck. You loosened it I'm sure. So, what are

we looking for?' Jimmy enquired, taking out some files and beginning to flick through them.

'Goodness! No! You mustn't look at this. It's Civic Hall property, highly confidential – give the files to me!' Samantha exclaimed in horror and snatched the paperwork out of Jimmy's hands.

'Just trying to help. I hope you haven't forgotten our deal,' Jimmy reminded her.

'No, I haven't forgotten it. I'll be on the ice, after the show, being your useless pupil, putting my feet in the wrong position and not holding my arms out,' Samantha spoke as she leafed through the correspondence.

'That makes it sound like you didn't enjoy last night. And I know that isn't true because you were practically skipping round the ice at the end,' Jimmy spoke.

'I think it was actually more like tripping than skipping. I'm really sorry about Cleo, being drunk and mauling you and everything.'

'It was fine. I had hoped for a quiet drink, but it was very entertaining. I admire Jeremy, he must have his work cut out.'

'Something like that. He had to hold her head out of the taxi window so she could puke, but not a trace of a hangover this morning though. Apart from the memory loss.'

'Why didn't you want Cleo to know you'd been learning to improve your skating?' Jimmy enquired.

'Didn't I? Well, I…'

'You told her I'd been practising with Dana.'

'Well, er, she was drunk, it was just easier – ah ha! I knew it!' Samantha exclaimed, pulling some pieces of correspondence out of one of the files and ignoring Jimmy's comments.

'What exactly are you looking for?' Jimmy wanted to know.

He leaned closer to Samantha to try and get a glimpse at the paperwork she was perusing.

'This! And this! And this! He's had at least three letters telling him what was happening with the council's amenities budget and saying that there would be someone coming to talk to him about the matter. At least *three* letters and he said nothing to any of us!' Samantha exclaimed in horror at Dave's lack of consideration.

'I don't know why you're surprised. Look at the guy's desk. I'm shocked your acts arrive in the right place at the right time. It doesn't look like anyone could coordinate anything from here,' Jimmy commented, pushing aside a packet of biscuits and two men's magazines.

'This is it on a good day. Oh my goodness! There's a meeting, about the halls, it's on the twenty fourth, that's next...' Samantha began as she read the letter she was holding.

'Next week. Yes, that's what I came to tell you,' Jimmy butted in.

'How do you know about it?' Samantha asked, looking at him suspiciously.

'I phoned the council this morning and spoke to a Mrs Randall. She's a colleague of Mr Radcliffe's in the amenities section. She was really helpful, and we had a good talk. She said that of the two amenities in question they would prefer not to close the Civic Hall, because of the history, because of its size, just like you said. But she said that the other hall did seem on the whole to be more efficiently run.'

'Why did she tell you all this? Who did you pretend to be? Barack Obama?'

'No, Dave.'

'What?! You can't go around impersonating people!'

'Should I have pretended to be Barack Obama?'

'Maybe, at least there's less chance she's met him, and you might have been able to do a more convincing accent.'

'I can do Northern, Duck.'

'That wasn't very good.'

'Well, moving on, Mrs Randall told me about the meeting, and she said the council would be more than happy to hear any proposals you had to make on improvements and future potential of the hall at that meeting. It would all be taken on board when the decision-making process is in progress,' Jimmy informed her.

'Hear my proposals? I don't *have* any proposals. What have you done? I'm not the manager here, I'm just a box office assistant,' Samantha exclaimed in horror.

'I think that will be changing soon. I suggested you as my replacement, me as in me being Dave and Mrs Randall said she would be giving you a call about becoming the temporary manager,' Jimmy continued.

'Temporary manager,' Samantha repeated her eyes glazing over as she considered the job title.

'Yes, but temporary doesn't mean temporary. I'm sure it will become permanent, it's just a formality,' Jimmy responded.

'Manager of the Civic Hall,' Samantha spoke, the words almost taking away her breath.

Her, Samantha Smith, in charge, running things, managing. She would be able to ensure that the Berry Fruits situation never arose again!

And then the excitement she felt was suddenly swamped with a feeling of terror. Being in charge meant the buck stopped with her. There would be no one to confer with, no one to advise her, no one to fall back on and no one else to blame for mistakes. And what if the hall *did* close and she had been the manager in charge of the failing amenity? She would be to blame for the job losses. Felicity, Jane, Karen, Aaron, Milo and Margaret and Mabel in the restaurant.

'I know what you're thinking, but I know you can do this,' Jimmy stated hurriedly as if able to read her mind.

'I don't have any ideas or proposals. I can't speak in front of a council meeting, I can't do it. I cannot do it!' Samantha exclaimed in almost a scream.

'And you said that last night about the spiral and what happened? By the end of the session you really had it,' Jimmy reminded her.

'That isn't the same,' Samantha replied.

'It's exactly the same. It's all about you not having any confidence in yourself and what you're capable of,' Jimmy spoke, and he held both her arms and looked at her sincerely.

'I don't know the first thing about proposals, or public speaking, I…' Samantha began.

'We can work on it. I said I'd help you and now we know what we need to do. We need to find out what the other hall has that the Civic Hall doesn't. We need to implement some new schemes to get more people through the door and I've given a friend of mine a call about developing the web page for doing on-line booking,' Jimmy informed.

'But I shouldn't spend money. We need to save money and…' Samantha spoke as she again began to worry, fear pummelling her chest.

'Relax, it won't cost the hall anything. He owes me a favour,' Jimmy insisted.

'Why are you doing this? Why do you want to help me?'

'Well, for one I'm getting a very capable and improving student ice dancer to work with and secondly – I think you're genuine and loyal and you need a bit of a break. There aren't many genuine people in my world right now,' Jimmy told her sincerely.

Samantha took a deep breath and then she realised he was holding her arms. She caught sight of the Minstrel eyes and quickly stepped backwards in a sudden and awkward motion, knocking Dave's packet of biscuits off the desk and onto the floor.

There was a knock on the door and Felicity appeared.

'Sorry to interrupt but there's a phone call for you and I thought it sounded important,' Felicity spoke as she watched Samantha's face turn red as she picked the biscuit packet up.

'It can't be for me, I don't get personal calls here,' Samantha retorted nervously pushing her hair back behind her ears.

'It isn't a personal call. It's Mrs Randall from the council – she asked for you specifically,' Felicity continued.

'Hey, see! I told you, go and take the call,' Jimmy said encouragingly.

Samantha's cheeks reddened even more, and she hurried from Dave's office to the front desk where the call awaited.

12

The temporary manager. She was the temporary manager of Woolston Civic Hall. They were even going to provide her with a new name badge. Samantha Smith, Manager. Dave had left. He had phoned the council from the airport. He was joining his cruise ship, setting sail on his new career journey pissing off holidaymakers and probably arranging COCKS (Cruise Operatives Certificate for Keen Service). It would no doubt involve a large meal onboard and a grope behind the lifeboats. His reign had ended, and Samantha was now in charge.

She hadn't known what to say to Mrs Randall and when the call finished, she couldn't remember exactly what she *had* said. Fortunately, Mrs Randall had done a lot of talking so Samantha's stunned silence had probably just come across as attentive listening, or so she hoped. She did remember that she had had a lump in her throat when Mrs Randall told her of her appointment. That, she decided, was probably a good thing as it partially blocked her urge to hyperventilate. She was sure she had managed a 'yes', a 'thank you' and a 'goodbye', although she couldn't really be sure.

Even now, as she watched the ice show going on in front

of her, she still couldn't believe she was in charge of the hall and all its functions. It was both terrifying and exciting. A bit like ice skating really.

Samantha was so engrossed in her thoughts, trying to determine how she was going to convince the council the Civic Hall was a local necessity that she didn't see Cleo approaching.

'Is Darren here?' Cleo whispered as she sidled up to Samantha's shoulder.

'What? No, no he isn't. What are you doing out of your seat? There's fifteen minutes before the interval,' Samantha remarked, checking her watch.

'Well I've seen the show haven't I, I know what's coming. This is the boring bit – that skinny Russian chick being flung around on a chair,' Cleo spoke and indicated the performers taking to the ice.

'Sshh, keep your voice down. It's very difficult to use a prop on the ice you know – they're very unpredictable,' Samantha informed her.

'So, when are you going out with Darren again?' Cleo questioned.

'Sshh,' Samantha hissed as a woman in a row near to them looked around at their chatting.

'Sorry! So, when are you seeing him again?' Cleo asked, lowering her voice a notch.

'I don't know. Go back to your seat, you're causing a fire hazard by standing here,' Samantha informed her sister.

'Two women in the toilets were saying that Jimmy Lloyd must be back on the booze. Apparently he dropped his partner the other night, almost blood on the rink. You never mentioned it,' Cleo continued in hushed tones.

'That's a complete exaggeration. He didn't drop her, and it was her fault actually,' Samantha replied hurriedly and rather more loudly than she had anticipated.

The woman who had looked at them before turned around again and glared.

'Well the women in the loos said they saw him after the show and he had a really ruddy complexion and stare-y eyes – you know – like he'd been downing scotch in the interval,' Cleo carried on.

'I've never heard anything so ridiculous. That's how gossip starts. You shouldn't listen to it and you definitely shouldn't be passing it on,' Samantha exclaimed angrily.

'Sshh, Sam, you're shouting,' Cleo told her as the woman looked around again and this time gave a loud tut of disgust.

'Well, fancy starting a rumour like that! Especially spreading it around in a public place,' Samantha continued, beginning to perspire.

'Calm down, Sam, and keep your voice down. God, I wish I hadn't told you now. I didn't think you were going to go all crazy on me,' Cleo replied.

'I'm not going crazy I just don't think people should spread gossip like that, particularly when there's not an ounce of truth in it,' Samantha told her sister.

'Whoa! OK, don't shoot the messenger. I'm sorry I relayed the awful, untrue gossip and I won't repeat it to anyone else. Will that do?' Cleo asked her.

'What are you doing here anyway? You only saw the show a few nights ago,' Samantha commented as she tried to gather her composure.

'Well, I gave some tickets to these clients I met when I showed them round a house the other day, but Sarah, the girl, had to go and visit a sick aunt or something. So, Jeremy and I have Paul as our gooseberry. He insisted we accompany him. I think he thinks he can get us to knock ten grand off the house he likes,' Cleo explained.

'Well perhaps you ought to go back to your seat and help Jeremy. It's only ten minutes until the interval and I have to get my skates on before I get weighed down with ice creams,' Samantha spoke, wanting to get rid of her sister.

'Yeah OK, I get the hint. But I will wait up with hot chocolate and I expect all the information on Darren. By the way I know what happened last night, Jeremy told me. We had coffees, Worcester sauce crisps and curry here – bless you,' Cleo spoke with a smile, backing away from Samantha.

Samantha smiled back at Cleo, glad Jeremy hadn't noticed her outrageous flirting with Jimmy and also glad he hadn't mentioned the puking down the side of the taxi.

When she was sure Cleo was completely gone and not returning, her smile dropped. She had defended Jimmy rather too fiercely and again without thinking before opening her mouth. What did she really know about him and his problems? All she knew was that he had perfect eyes, perfect hair and a perfect smile. He was kind and funny and, although she knew she shouldn't, she liked the way he held her when they skated. And this morning she had managed a whole conversation with him without having a panic attack. That had to be a good thing didn't it?

*

'Miss Smith, Civic Hall manager! How was your first evening in charge?' Jimmy asked her as she skated onto the rink to join him after the show.

'Uneventful, which is good. Down to less than two thousand Berry Fruits which is even better,' Samantha spoke.

'What?'

'Oh, sorry, just stock control on the ice creams.'

'Stock control – you're talking like a true leader,' Jimmy told her, taking hold of her hand and smiling.

'But it's just ice cream. It isn't standing up in front of Woolston Borough Council trying to save the hall. Maybe dealing with an ice cream situation is my limit,' Samantha suggested as they began to skate around the rink to warm up.

'Well I don't think anything much has changed. Dave may have had the fancy job title, but I think you know you ran the hall,' Jimmy stated.

'No offence but you've only been here just over a week, how can you…' Samantha began.

'I'm a terrific judge of character! Ask anyone. So, shall we skate? Try the routine again? Learn a little more?' Jimmy suggested to her.

Samantha nodded. At the moment, with Cleo on her back about the imaginary Darren and the hall in crisis with her at the helm, meeting Jimmy in the solitude of the auditorium was what she looked forward to more than anything. And when she skated, she somehow changed from Samantha Smith Miss Self-Conscious to Samantha Smith Ice Queen. Well, maybe not quite worthy of the title of Ice Queen yet, but she was definitely improving.

The routine Jimmy was teaching her wasn't one from the show, but one he had performed in a previous ice tour, 'Pop on the Ice'. Although not very technical it did include some overhead lifts, some tricky footwork and spins. So far, they had only got a quarter of the way through learning it.

'Are you ready to learn a lift?' Jimmy enquired as they stopped skating at the end of the section they had learned.

'No, no thanks,' Samantha answered straightaway and she hurriedly skated away from him.

'Come on, it isn't really all that hard. We could just start with a roll up into a crucifix hold or something. It's simple really, once you learn how to position your body,' Jimmy spoke as he followed her across the ice.

'It's fine, I'd rather not. I'm a keeping my feet on the ground kind of girl,' Samantha answered, upping her pace to try and shake him off.

'Now hang on, you promised me you'd let me teach you – let me teach you this,' Jimmy spoke, skating in front of her so she couldn't avoid him.

'Yes, and you said skating, not lifting. I didn't sign up for being thrown in the air. Besides I'm sure the crucifix position was what did for Jesus,' Samantha spoke as she attempted to swerve out of his way.

'Maybe, but no one *I* lifted ever died that way I promise,' Jimmy replied.

'I'd rather not take the risk, thanks all the same. Argh! Argh! Goodness! What are you doing? Arrgghh!' Samantha shrieked as Jimmy lifted her up, rolled her up over his shoulder until she was held high on his back, with her arms outstretched – hence the name of the position.

'Just hold the position, keep still and keep a smile on that face. Eyes and teeth remember,' Jimmy spoke as he carried on skating holding her over his head.

'Eyes and teeth?! Just get me down!' Samantha shrieked hysterically, seeing the hall from a whole different angle than she ever had before.

'Ready? Same way you came up. Whoa! There you go – put your feet down on the ice. Sam, put your feet down!' Jimmy ordered as he rolled her back down towards the floor.

She didn't put her feet down and landed with a bump, bottom first, on the ice. She let out a gasp as the cold, hard, landing shocked her.

'Always be ready to land the lift,' Jimmy reminded as he leant over her.

'Thanks, but I wasn't actually ready to be lifted sky high in the first place,' Samantha answered.

'Are you OK?' Jimmy asked, offering her a hand up.

'Another bruise to add to the dozens I have already,' she replied, accepting his hand and hauling herself up from the floor in as ladylike a fashion as possible.

'Listen, why don't we take a break and start thinking about that proposal for the council – brainstorm some ideas. Say, wanna go to a club?' Jimmy suggested.

'A club?' Samantha exclaimed as if the very words were alien to her.

'Yeah, didn't Cleo say there's a club just down the street? It sounds good. Wanna try it?'

'Oh no, I don't think so.'

'I wasn't thinking about the rave room or anything, they have quieter chill out areas where you can talk.'

'It's quiet here.'

Jimmy laughed out loud and nodded. He skated towards the edge of the rink and sat down on one of the seats, taking a drink from his bottle.

'What's funny?' Samantha asked, following his lead.

'Cleo was right – you really don't go out, do you?' he remarked.

'Don't be ridiculous, of course I do. Just because I don't want to go to a silly club doesn't mean I don't go out.'

'OK so where?'

'Well, there's a pub just round the corner and there's a couple of nice restaurants and Cleo says that...'

'Where do *you* go out round here?' Jimmy continued, looking at her.

'I work most days,' Samantha admitted, 'and there's always stuff to do round the house.'

'God Sam, you really do need to get out more.'

Samantha couldn't help but blush. She knew he was probably right. Cleo was always telling her exactly the same thing, but she didn't like hearing it.

'Look, I wasn't trying to sound patronising, just suggesting it might be an idea to broaden your horizons.'

'My horizons are the exact width I like them thank you.'

Jimmy laughed.

'Anyway, I would have thought you were avoiding nightclubs. Aren't you barred from most of the ones in America?' Samantha snapped defensively.

'Who told you that?' he enquired.

'*Star Life* magazine,' Samantha replied with an air of authority.

Jimmy laughed again, his brown eyes crinkling at the edges in that sexy way.

'Sorry, that's funny. I can't believe you read *Star Life* magazine.'

'Why not?'

'It isn't something I'd expect you to read.'

'So, what would you expect someone like me to read?'

'The instruction manual on anything you ever bought?'

Samantha felt her cheeks heat up and tears sprang to her eyes. He thought she was boring.

And he was right, just like Cleo was always right. She didn't do anything outside the hall, and she didn't have many interests. She was a nobody, insignificant.

'Hey, it was a joke. Sam, it was just a joke. You're always so organised and it was just a joke about that, I didn't mean…' Jimmy began, seeing he had upset her.

'I've got to go,' Samantha spoke, swallowing down a boulder of tears.

'No, don't go. Please, I apologise, unreservedly. I apologise for what I said, it was stupid and *I'm* stupid. It was jealousy that made me say it.'

'Jealousy?'

'Yeah, I'm the least organised person I know. I can't pack a suitcase. I never show up anywhere on time and I have trouble remembering my schedule for the next week let alone any further ahead. I wish I was more like you.'

'What, a non-nightclub goer, an ice cream seller with nothing better to do than read instruction manuals?'

'You shouldn't be ashamed of who you are, but you shouldn't be afraid to try new things either.'

Samantha didn't reply. It would be so easy to forgive what he said when he was looking at her like that. The large puppy dog eyes, the warm expression, the sincere lips and not forgetting the lovely hair.

'Look, I won't mention another word about nightclubs.

Just don't go. We need to brainstorm, don't we?'

'I'm not sure I want to now.'

'Please. Do I have to beg? If I have to beg I will. I'll get right down on my knees and beg, over there on the ice if you want so I'm wet and everything,' Jimmy told her.

Samantha let out a laugh.

'I'm sorry,' Jimmy spoke, taking hold of her hand.

Samantha felt the warmth of his fingers in hers and she had never wished she was Cleo more than she did now. Cleo would make the most of the opportunity of holding his hand. She would pounce on him, suction her lips to his and have him vowing eternal love in a matter of minutes. But that was exciting, vibrant, flighty Cleo, not plain, boring, Samantha Smith who only got excited by filing systems and seating plans.

'Come on let's go wild and brainstorm here. Take a seat – d'you want some water?' Jimmy asked, offering her his bottle.

Samantha shook her head but sat down next to him.

'Come on, let's hear your ideas,' he encouraged.

Samantha let out a sigh.

'Well I've been having a think today and the first thing that needs to be decided is who I choose to deliver the speech. It can't be Jane, she gets more tongue tied than me, if that's actually humanly possible, and Felicity is really...' Samantha began to talk.

'Whoa! Hold on, *you* have to give the speech,' Jimmy told her.

'Who says? I've thought about it and it doesn't have to be me,' Samantha carried on.

'You're the manager,' Jimmy reminded her.

'Which means I can delegate. Dave always delegated.'

'And I thought we agreed Dave was a God-awful manager.'

'Well, maybe, but...' Samantha started.

'There are no buts or maybes about it. You have to be the one to give the speech. Not only are you the manager, but you're the one person who's truly passionate about this place,' Jimmy told her.

'I can't stand up in front of all those people,' Samantha stated seriously.

'Sure you can,' Jimmy responded, producing a pen and some paper from his bag.

'I can't.'

'You can.'

'This isn't panto you know! I can't do it, I cannot do it!' Samantha yelled, her voice echoing around the empty auditorium.

Jimmy looked away from her and began to write, ignoring her hysterics.

Samantha took a deep breath, the thought of public speaking made her feel sick. Her heart was racing now, just contemplating the idea of it. The future of the Civic Hall could not hang on her ability to stand up and sell its merits to an audience of councillors.

Jimmy had written half an A4 page before Samantha found the courage to speak again.

'I'm not like you. Performing to a crowd is way out of my comfort zone,' Samantha stated.

'I get it,' Jimmy replied, not lifting his eyes from the paper.

'I'm just not very good at talking – in crowds – well, at all really – basically talking in general,' Samantha continued.

'I said I get it,' Jimmy answered.

'I mean it isn't that I don't want to do it, I just can't. It would be an impossibility for me to do anything, like even breathe, in front of anyone,' Samantha carried on, making excuses for herself.

'And I thought you really cared about this hall,' Jimmy said, still not lifting his gaze from the paper he was writing on.

'I do! Of course, I do, the hall means everything to me,' Samantha answered immediately.

'But obviously not enough to break out of that comfort zone,' Jimmy retorted this time raising his eyes to look at her.

'That isn't fair,' Samantha said straightaway, swallowing a knot in her throat.

'If you don't start believing in yourself, you're never going to be able to achieve anything in your life – let alone be able to save the hall,' Jimmy stated firmly.

Samantha felt the urge to weep creeping over her again. She could feel the tears forming in her eyes and her lip was trembling. She bit the inside her mouth and attempted to quell the emotion that was threatening to take over and embarrass her.

'Every so often I have to walk into a room full of strangers and stand up at the very front of that room, looking at each and every one of them. I have to tell them my name, the fact that I am an alcoholic and how many days it's been since my last drink. Believe me, there's nothing in this world more embarrassing than that,' Jimmy told her with a heavy sigh.

'You didn't have to tell me that. I know how pathetic I am,' Samantha answered, feeling smaller than she had ever felt in her life.

'You aren't pathetic, and I wanted to tell you. Although I'm embarrassed by it and ashamed of it, it's also really liberating to get it out there. Sometimes in life you get given this amazing opportunity to try and make something good happen out of something bad. In your case, although you know it could spell the closure of the hall, you've a chance to get across to that council everything you feel about the place and its importance to the area. And, even if it doesn't work, you'll know you had the courage to stand up for something you believe in and you'll know you gave it everything you had to give. Things like that, they can't be delegated,' Jimmy told her.

Samantha just stared at him. His handsome face, the sincerity in his dark brown eyes, his full lips. Before she could stop herself, she was conjuring up thoughts of what those lips would feel like on hers. It would be a movie moment kiss. It would be Richard Gere and Julia Roberts in *Pretty Woman*, Patrick Swayze and Jennifer Grey in *Dirty Dancing*. If only she were blonde and slim…

She was brought out of her daydream when a mobile phone began to ring. Jimmy reached into his bag, pulled out his phone and accepted the call.

'Hey, Giles,' he greeted and stood up to move away from Samantha to talk.

She was a first-class bird brain. Why couldn't she just be more like Cleo? Cleo always knew exactly what to say and do in any situation. Samantha couldn't even bring herself to go clubbing. She'd never been clubbing, again, like the Tube, it was a case of too many people and too little space. If she were Cleo, she would've not only written the speech by now, she would have had Jimmy undressed and on top of her by now.

Just as Samantha was thinking back to the nosebleed and seeing Jimmy's bare torso, he turned back towards her and came to retake his seat.

'Are you free tomorrow night?' Jimmy asked, turning to face Samantha.

'Free?' Samantha asked stupidly not understanding the question she was being asked.

'Yeah, you know, not doing anything. There's no ice show tomorrow, are you busy?' Jimmy enquired.

'Well, I don't know, I…' Samantha began, trying to digest exactly what it was she was being asked.

'No clubs I promise. That was a friend of mine, Giles Palmer. He's a singer in a band called Air Patrol and they're playing at the Presbook Centre tomorrow night – he's given me two tickets,' Jimmy informed her matter of factly.

'That's nice, I've heard some of their records, at least I think I have, or perhaps it was Air Supply,' Samantha questioned herself.

'I looked into the type of acts the Presbook Centre get, saw they were playing and gave him a call. I thought if we went, we could have a look round at the competition – see what the Presbook Centre has that the Civic Hall doesn't,' Jimmy carried on.

'Me and you,' Samantha stated before she could stop herself.

'Can you come? I think it would be really useful for you to see first-hand what you're up against,' Jimmy repeated, ignoring her remark.

Samantha was panicking. She didn't know what to do or

say and she could feel her chest start to tighten. She couldn't spend an evening with him, going out at night, to a concert, it would be like a date. A date with Jimmy Lloyd and not an ice skate in sight. He would want to talk, and she wouldn't know what to say. Although she could talk about Cleo, she could talk endlessly about Cleo. Well, perhaps not endlessly. What if she couldn't talk endlessly? What if she ran out of things to say? Even about her sister…

She began to cough loudly and struggle to breathe. She needed a focus. She stared at his chest. It only made things worse.

'Here, have some water,' Jimmy said to her and he passed his bottle of water to her.

Samantha took a large gulp and regained control of her breath.

'If you give me your address, I could pick you up about seven,' Jimmy spoke no longer waiting for her to reply.

'No!' Samantha shrieked, her voice reverberating around the hall for the second time that night.

Jimmy didn't react but just kept looking at her, waiting for a response.

'No, no don't pick me up. I'll, I'll meet you there,' Samantha spoke hurriedly.

'Good, about seven thirty then. Now, shall we work out what you're going to say to the council at the meeting?' Jimmy suggested, putting his pen back to the paper.

'I'm not sure, but I think I might rather attempt the crucifix lift thing again,' Samantha responded with a sigh.

'Well perhaps we'll have time for both,' Jimmy replied with a smile.

Samantha managed a weak smile back, but inside she felt

sick. It was almost a date. It was the closest thing she had had to a date in almost a year, since the nipple ring incident. And it was with Jimmy Lloyd, who'd probably dated a hundred women and never had any of them take so long to accept an evening out as she had. But it wasn't a date, not really and she mustn't think of it as a date. In fact, why was she so worried? It wasn't a date at all. It was intelligence gathering for the greater good of the Civic Hall. Although thinking of it like that didn't stop Samantha from starting to panic about what she was going to wear.

13

The following day Samantha printed off flyers advertising up and coming events, together with a 'meal deal' voucher. She sent Karen up town to distribute some of the vouchers in shops and also to hand them out to passers-by. By lunchtime Karen had got rid of all the leaflets and the restaurant was full to capacity. In the end Samantha deployed Milo to help serve and clear and she also took her turn on the till.

In the afternoon, as soon as she had finished helping Mabel and Margaret clean up the restaurant, Tyrone arrived. Tyrone was Jimmy's friend who was going to improve the hall's website. He had taken charge of the computer in the office and by the end of the day he said he had all he needed to include the on-line booking section. He was going to come back to the hall when the site was ready to go live and give the employees training.

'It's alright for you, Gobby, all you have to worry about is avoiding the traffic and the sharp ended boot of Andre from the kebab shop. You don't have to worry about talking to a load of official people, all looking at you – all waiting for you to faint,' Samantha spoke as Gobby polished off a leftover portion of cod, chips and peas.

She was outside the back door of the hall, behind the

kitchens, hiding from Jane. Jane had accosted her that morning asking for annual leave. Apparently the infirm, chain-smoking mother had won an all-inclusive holiday to Bulgaria in one of her women's magazines, but the prize had to be taken within four weeks. She'd asked for two weeks off starting the week after next. Samantha had coughed and gasped at the thought of being shorthanded when the hall was in crisis and Jane, fearing she was going to perform another theatrical collapse, had suggested Samantha think on it for the rest of the day and let her know that evening. She'd been grateful for the breathing space, but she still didn't know what to say. OK, Jane was no linchpin, but she was good on the phones and it relieved Samantha from that role and allowed her to focus on managerial matters.

'What shall I do, Gobby? Be one of those heartless bosses and say no, you can't have the time off, tell your mother she'll have to share her holiday with someone else or forfeit the prize? No, she would probably just resign. But if I say yes, I'll be putting the hall under strain and we need all the help we can get right now.'

Gobby raised his head and looked at her, as if thinking about her question.

'I'm going to have to say yes. She is due the holiday and maybe I could ask Aaron to do some more hours. He's OK on the phone, well apart from when he kept ending up ringing the Australian government whenever he leaned on the keyboard. Perhaps I could lower his chair and keep his elbows under the desk,' Samantha said, sitting down on the step with a sigh.

Gobby mewed and went back to eating.

'And then there's tonight. What am I going to do about

that? It's going out at night – with Jimmy Lloyd,' Samantha spoke.

It had been on her mind all day, despite being busy. She'd hidden in the freezer for ten minutes at one point, in the hope that the cool air would somehow expunge the panic. It hadn't worked. All it had done was remind her she still had thousands of tubs of sodding ice cream to shift.

'The thing is, Gobby, I like him, and I know I shouldn't. He's different to me. He's confident and brilliant and totally gorgeous and I'm just – not any of those things. I'm just me, boring and routine driven. I don't like clubbing or crowds, or clothes shopping. I'm not slim, or blonde or interested in fashion. I don't get goose bumps when I buy a new pair of shoes. I'm not like other people, I'm different. But I'm not sure it's different good, I think it might be different weird. Goodness is it different weird? Am I weird?'

Gobby raised his face and licked his lips.

'I'm not sure I want to be different weird,' Samantha said, a frown filling her features.

Gobby munched noisily, chomping on a chip.

'What am I going to wear tonight? I can't get out of it and I do need to see what the Presbook Centre is doing that we aren't. And do I tell Cleo? If I tell her she'll try to help and then she'll suggest wearing something very, very small and very, very short.'

Gobby suddenly looked up from his bowl of food and stared at the door to the kitchen. He arched his back and hissed.

'What is it, Gobby?'

He just continued to look unsettled and backed away from the door.

The door opened and Jimmy appeared, almost hitting Samantha on the back with the door as he came through.

'Whoa! Sorry!' Jimmy said quickly as he grabbed the door and Samantha hurriedly stood up from her seat on the step to avoid getting bashed.

She could feel her cheeks turning crimson. Had he heard her talking to Gobby? Asking a feline what she should wear for the date that wasn't really a date? She'd been talking to a cat! He would need no further evidence of her weirdness.

'Hey, a cat! Aww, hello, boy. Is it a boy?' Jimmy asked, coming out into the alleyway and crouching down.

'I think so, I mean I haven't looked. He looks like a boy – well, his face I mean,' she replied.

'Hey, boy, come here. You're not scared of me, are you? Come on,' Jimmy encouraged, stretching out his hand and rubbing his thumb and forefinger towards Gobby who had taken refuge under an empty catering sized box of peas.

Samantha watched as Jimmy whistled quietly at Gobby, coaxing him out of hiding and towards his hand.

He knelt down on the concrete ground, getting the knees of his designer jeans dirty, and called for the cat. Gobby looked first to Samantha and then at Jimmy, or the other way round maybe, because of his eye. Then sensing there was nothing to be afraid of, he crept out from under the box and slunk up to the ice skater.

'What's his name?' Jimmy asked as Gobby rubbed his face against his hands as he stroked him.

'Gobby,' Samantha answered, watching Jimmy's affection with the cat.

She swallowed and tried to get some saliva into her dry mouth as she wondered what it felt like to have your body stroked by his hands.

'What?' Jimmy queried, turning to look at her.

'Um, it's Gobbolino. Well that's what I call him. He doesn't belong to anyone. I checked, no collar and no electronic chip, so the vet said. I think he's got fleas again, but he doesn't like the powder and he won't take worm tablets either. I tried crushing them up in his food, but he just sniffs them out. And he won't eat normal cat food, I tried, even the expensive stuff. He only eats leftovers, which I know isn't good for him, but I just thought it was probably better than Andre's kebab meat – especially when it's covered in chilli sauce,' Samantha rambled, watching Jimmy continue to rub Gobby up and down.

'Gobbolino, the witch's cat,' Jimmy remarked, picking the cat up and sitting him on his lap.

'Have you read the book?' Samantha enquired wide-eyed.

'Of course! It's one of the greatest books ever. Although I haven't actually read it – it was serialised in a storytelling magazine with an audio cassette I used to get when I was about eight,' Jimmy replied with a smile.

Samantha smiled back at him.

'He's an affectionate little fella, isn't he?' Jimmy remarked as he stood up, holding Gobby in his arms.

'He didn't like Dave,' Samantha commented.

'A good judge of character too then.'

There was silence apart from Gobby's energetic purring and Samantha began to perspire as she desperately thought of something to say.

'Oh, I almost forgot why I was looking for you. There's been a slight collapse in one of the dressing rooms,' Jimmy informed her, putting Gobby on the floor.

'A collapse! Who's collapsed? Have you called an ambulance? Is it Mrs Nelmes? I've told her countless times not to go into restricted areas but her mind wanders and...' Samantha began, opening the door and preparing to rush off.

'No Sam, wait, not a collapse like that. One of the make-up stations has come away from the wall. No blood spilt just a bit of foundation and eye liner,' he explained.

'Oh goodness, that's awful. Well, not as awful as if Mrs Nelmes had collapsed obviously, but awful enough. I'll see to it, I'll ring the repair man,' Samantha said, slipping through the door and heading back into the kitchen at full pace.

'Thanks, that would be great. I'll tell Andrei and Mark you've – got it under control,' Jimmy spoke as he watched Samantha hurry away from him.

Mind focussed on the task in hand she rushed off through the kitchen, out into the restaurant and back towards her office. It was a relief to have an excuse to evade him, particularly now she knew he liked animals.

*

It was almost 6.00 pm when she got home, and she still didn't have a clue what she was going to wear. Gobby had been no help at all. When she had gone back to check on him after calling the carpenter, he had finished the portion of food she'd given him and fallen asleep under the pea box.

The rest of the day, in between rushing about the hall multitasking to the max, she had tried to envisage the clothes in her wardrobe. It wasn't all that hard given she had so few outfits and an excellent memory. Having said that, her wardrobe was actually fit to burst because it was jam packed with Cleo's clothes. High fashion items and contemporary classics Cleo couldn't live without one minute and hated the next. So, although Samantha always protested, Cleo used her wardrobe as a dumping ground. Think every item from the Next sale from 2003–2009.

Should she wear jeans? Or was that too casual? It was business after all. Perhaps she should wear a suit. She only had one that she wore for interviews and funerals and little else in between. She'd last worn it to a ridiculous time share appointment full of aggressive, hard-nosed salespeople trying to sell her two weeks in Florida on the proviso that the American family would like to stay on a barge in the Norfolk Broads. That was one of Cleo's worst jobs ever and supporting her by attending one of the 'information days' had been awful. By the time the so-called silver service lunch had been served up Samantha's mind was befuddled with pyramid schemes and week sharing.

Cleo hadn't been cut out for the hard sell and Samantha had heard her glossing over the holiday properties and discussing the merits of Rimmel make-up with the female invitees. Unlike Wayne, who had spoken to Samantha, and done everything but screw her thumbs to the table in order to get her to sign up.

Perhaps she should be really casual and wear a tracksuit. She only had one of those, the pastel pink one she had met Nipple Ring Boy in, and now that was faded from another of Cleo's washing accidents.

Cleo's room was displaying the amber crystal when Samantha reached it. She knocked cautiously and waited for a response.

'Sam is that you? If Jeremy's here already I'm going to be at least half an hour. I'm in the middle of waxing,' Cleo called out.

Samantha opened the door and put her head round it. Cleo was sat on her bed, wearing nothing but some rather tiny red underwear, applying warm wax to one of her legs.

'Can I come in?' Samantha asked in a rather subdued voice.

'God, yes, you can help me with this. I seem to be making a right mess of it,' Cleo spoke, ushering her sister into the room.

Samantha came in and sat down on the bed next to Cleo.

'Why the long face? Ah ha, I see they've made up your new name badge. Surely that was a highlight of your day – something to smile about? By the way, what on earth time did you get in last night? Jeremy left at eleven and I waited up until almost one with hot chocolate at the ready, but there was no sign of you,' Cleo spoke as she put some waxing strips on her leg.

'I had paperwork to do, at the office – you know – what with being manager,' Samantha replied quickly.

'So, you didn't go out with Darren last night?' Cleo quizzed.

'No,' Samantha answered.

Cleo let out a blood curdling scream as she ripped the strip from her leg.

'God! This flaming kills! The things we have to do to be hair free! I thought epilating was painful but that has nothing on this,' Cleo remarked, smoothing another strip of paper on her leg.

'I didn't go out with Darren last night – but I'm going

out with him tonight,' Samantha stated with a deep breath.

'Wow! Great! Where? When? Is he coming here?' Cleo babbled excitedly.

'We're going to see a band, Air Patrol at the Presbook Centre. I…' Samantha started.

'Air Patrol! How the Hell did he get tickets for that? When those tickets went on sale, must have been a few months ago now, they sold out in four minutes or something stupid – I heard it on the news,' Cleo exclaimed impressed.

'Have I heard any of their records? "I'm All Out of Love?" Is that one of theirs?' Samantha enquired.

'No, Muppet, that was Air *Supply* in the 1980s. Air Patrol is a rock band. They've had loads of hits, you'd know some of them for sure. God, I can't believe you're going to see them,' Cleo carried on.

'I don't know what to wear,' Samantha told her sister bluntly.

Cleo let out another shriek as she ripped more hair from her leg.

'Is your skin supposed to go that red?' Samantha enquired as she scrutinised her sister's shin.

'Yes, at least I think so. Anyway, I'm done now and hopefully, by the time Jeremy arrives, it'll be back to somewhere near flesh colour. Either that or I'll have to wear stockings or something. Right, outfits, come on, let's have a look, I am, after all, the fashion expert of the house,' Cleo spoke.

She grabbed her dressing gown, wrapped it round her and got to her feet. Then she led the way to Samantha's bedroom.

'I was thinking maybe a suit. My black one or maybe

I could borrow one of yours. There's that grey one you bought that was too big,' Samantha suggested as Cleo marched straight up to her wardrobe and threw open the doors.

'A suit! To a rock concert! Are you insane?' Cleo exclaimed in horror.

'Well, I'll be having a look at the facility too, in a professional capacity. They are our rivals for the council's cash,' Samantha told her as Cleo began to remove articles from the cupboard. Blouses, tops and skirts were parted, taken out, scrutinised and then either put back or held on to.

'But it's a date isn't it? We have to dress you for a date. Try on this, this and this,' Cleo said, handing Samantha some items of clothing.

'I can't wear this, you wore it to that party where the hostess was sick all over your boyfriend,' Samantha said and she held the green top away from herself with two fingers, as if it were soiled.

'Oh God, yeah it was. But she wasn't sick on *me*, just him. What was his name?' Cleo asked her mind wandering.

'Well, whatever it was I can't wear that top. I wouldn't be able to think about anything else all night. He was called Gareth, I think,' Samantha said, and she dropped the offending item to the floor.

'Alright, well try this top instead,' Cleo spoke, and she handed her sister a replacement.

'Oh no, I can't wear that one. That one you wore when you went on that date with – erm, I think his name was Mark. He took you horse riding. It wasn't very supportive, and you basically cantered out of your cups. What was the silly name of the horse?' Samantha told her.

'Jesus, Sam! Do you know where I wore every item of clothing I ever had?' Cleo wanted to know.

'No. Well, OK, probably. Doughnut, that was what the horse was called. Hang on, how about, this top?' Samantha asked and she pulled out a plain black, long-sleeved top.

'Hmm,' Cleo said, surveying the item of clothing.

'What does "hmm" mean?' Samantha asked her.

'It means the top is plain and boring and it will say "Hello, Darren, I'm Samantha Smith and I'm as plain and boring as this top I'm wearing",' Cleo stated bluntly.

'Well, if I wear something of yours it'll say "Hello, I'm Cleo, let's cut to the chase and go to bed",' Samantha told her.

'Cheek! No, it won't. It'll say "Hello, Darren, I really like you, so much so I've made a real effort to dress nicely",' Cleo insisted.

'Oh, I don't know – maybe I shouldn't go,' Samantha spoke with a heavy sigh.

'Don't be ridiculous, of course you're going. What time is he coming?' Cleo asked, checking her watch.

'He's not. I'm meeting him there at seven thirty. My goodness, it's half six, I haven't showered, I've got nothing to wear and I need to catch the bus at ten past,' Samantha exclaimed hysterically.

'You're not getting a bus, get the Tube.'

'You know I don't like the Tube and what if there's a priest on there or something? I'll probably end up sat next to him and then I won't be able to relax, and I'll be clutching my bag to my chest the whole way,' Samantha explained.

'Mum's mugger wasn't a real nun you know.'

'Yes, I know that, but can you tell a real priest from a fake one?'

'Right, well, so we avoid everyone from the church, imposters or not, by calling a taxi. Now calm down or you'll make yourself red and blotchy. Go and have a shower now, I'll find you something to wear that's a compromise between understated and a come-on and then I'll do your hair and make-up,' Cleo spoke and she began shooing Samantha towards the door of her bedroom.

'But what about your date with Jeremy? Won't he be here any minute?' Samantha asked, stopping in the doorway.

'I'll call him, tell him I won't be ready until half past. He's usually here too early anyway and I'm never ready on time,' Cleo spoke with a grin.

'Thanks, Cleo,' Samantha answered, smiling back at her sister.

'Well. don't just stand there, shoo! Get in the shower!' Cleo ordered and she pushed Samantha out onto the landing and closed the door behind her.

14

The taxi arrived at 7.15 pm and Samantha began the five-mile journey to the Presbook Centre.

Cleo hadn't done too bad a job with her outfit. She was wearing jeans, some designer ones Cleo had bought in a size twelve instead of a ten in some sale or other. Usually a twelve wasn't big enough but Samantha could only assume they were a big cut, because they hugged her in all the right places, and she could sit down without feeling her stomach was rolling up towards her chin.

With the jeans she was wearing a red long-sleeved top that had two bits to tie around the neck that Cleo had done up in what she called a 'nonchalant bow'. On her feet were a pair of shoes she had long since forgotten she owned. They were black wedged sandals she had bought on impulse in Simpkin's Shoes. Lydia, the bitchiest of the band of The Witches of Woolston, had been standing by her at the time, looking over her shoulder when Samantha had been contemplating buying them for Cleo. Lydia knew Samantha would never wear anything like it and suggested loudly that Cleo might prefer them in yellow. She had then cackled, bringing Samantha to the attention of the other witches. Riled by the comment Samantha had picked another pair up in her size, taken them to the counter and bought them with her ten percent discount, loudly announcing they were just the right pair to go with the new Miss Selfridge dress she had bought to attend her cute cousin's wedding. It had been worth the nineteen pounds ninety-nine just to see the smarmy looks wiped from the witches' faces for five minutes.

The red top was a bit brave for her though. She was very much a black/brown kind of girl, but, having limited time, and Cleo being so desperate to help, Samantha didn't have the heart to protest. Cleo had toned and moisturised her, put on foundation and a small amount of eye shadow but Samantha had drawn the line at the pillar box red lipstick. She had hung her head upside down and blasted her hair with the dryer too, so now it had some volume and the finishing touch had been the red handbag Cleo insisted she took. It was tiny, like a Barbie doll bag, but it did fit in her money and door key and was really all she needed. She had flatly refused the packet of Durex Cleo had offered.

As soon as the taxi pulled up outside the Presbook Centre, Samantha saw Jimmy. He was standing just outside the main doors where there were throngs of people flooding into the building. He was wearing jeans and a three-quarter length khaki jacket with, what looked like, a blue top underneath. His hair was freshly styled, and he looked amazing.

As the taxi prepared to come to a halt, Samantha saw a woman approach him. They began to talk, and Jimmy was smiling at her, showing his perfect white teeth. The woman was attractive, blonde and slim. Samantha let out a sigh and watched them out of the window. The woman produced some paper and Jimmy began to write on it. Samantha's heart lurched. They were so obviously exchanging phone numbers. And why shouldn't they? He was single, he was completely gorgeous and funny and nice, and the woman was slim and blonde and probably had white teeth too. She probably also liked clubbing.

'Is here OK, love?' the taxi driver asked as he stopped the car and looked at Samantha in his rear-view mirror.

'Oh yes, yes, here is fine. How much is it?' Samantha asked as she struggled to get her wallet out of the tiny bag.

'Call it seven quid,' the cabbie spoke.

'Keep the change and could I have one of your cards for later?' Samantha spoke, handing him a ten-pound note.

'Sure, here you go,' the taxi driver replied, passing a business card back to her.

The door of the taxi was suddenly swung open and Samantha found herself looking at Jimmy.

'Hey! You made it! D'you want me to pay the guy?' Jimmy asked her.

'No! No, I've paid. It's fine, thanks – thank you,' Samantha called to the driver as she hurriedly scrambled out of the taxi.

Jimmy took hold of her arm to help her out and Samantha felt her cheeks burning. She really had to get over herself and stop thinking that this night was a date in the ordinary sense of the word. This was nothing but business. She needed to find business mode. She needed to think of the Civic Hall where she was in complete control and felt comfortable – she needed to focus. The very idea that someone like Jimmy would ask her out on a date was utterly laughable. She wasn't his type at all. She wasn't an actress with cosmetic enhancements and a collagen smile.

She didn't know her waist size or how many Ryvitas you had to eat to call it a main meal.

'You look really nice,' Jimmy commented as they walked towards the entrance.

Oh, why had he said that? Business, business, business.

'Oh, ho, ho,' Samantha replied involuntarily, sounding like a petrified Father Christmas.

'Sorry, I didn't mean to make that sound how it came out. I just haven't actually seen you dressed in anything but your uniform. I was beginning to think you didn't have any other clothes,' Jimmy continued.

'No, ho, ho, hee,' Samantha responded nervously.

She quickly clamped her mouth shut, pressing her teeth together hard before she could deliver any other ridiculous noises.

'I actually got here early, but so many people came up to me wanting autographs I had to go inside for a bit to look around – just to escape,' Jimmy informed her.

'Oh, so the pretty woman wanted an autograph,' Samantha commented again not thinking before she spoke.

'Pretty woman?' Jimmy queried as they entered the centre.

'Oh wow, look. They've got a really open plan box office. The desk is low and there are – goodness, look at their leaflet holders,' Samantha exclaimed excitedly, walking up to the plastic mounts and touching them fondly.

'Should I be writing all this down? Low desk and cool leaflet holders?' Jimmy spoke, putting his hand in his jacket pocket.

'You've brought a notebook?' Samantha asked, turning to look at him and feeling secretly impressed by his organisation.

She had wanted to bring a notebook but there was no way anything other than one the size of a matchbox would have fitted in the petite bag.

'No! Of course not! I was just kidding. Besides, Felicity tells me you have a photographic memory,' Jimmy replied with a smile.

Samantha smiled, hiding her disappointment and wondering why Felicity seemed to have time to chat to Jimmy when she could never find time to audit the stationery cupboard.

'Their bar is absolutely full,' Samantha remarked, seeing a large gathering of people at the end of the room.

'Yeah and they have tables in there too so you can eat there if you don't want to go to the restaurant. Shall we go and get a drink?' Jimmy suggested.

'A drink? Well, I don't know, it does seem very busy and…' Samantha started nervously.

'Get used to it. This could be what the Civic Hall is like if its future is secured – come on,' Jimmy encouraged, and he linked his arm with hers before she had a chance to say any more.

'What would you like?' Jimmy spoke above the noise of the crowd as they jostled their way towards the bar.

'Oh, erm, just a glass of water will be fine,' Samantha told him.

'Listen, don't feel you have to abstain from alcohol on account of me. I won't start dribbling and shaking if you have some – I promise,' Jimmy remarked with half a smile.

'Oh no, no, I didn't even think of that. I don't really drink very much. I'll have a Coke, a diet Coke,' Samantha said, quickly making her mind up.

'OK. Well, why don't you go and get us some seats. There's a table over there. Have you eaten?' Jimmy enquired.

'Eaten? No, no, but I'm not really...' Samantha began nervously.

'Neither have I and I'm starved. Why don't you go and look at the menus and check out their range and prices – see if we can't borrow some of their ideas for the hall. This is kind of cool isn't it? Spying on the enemy!' Jimmy said, grinning.

Samantha managed a weak smile of agreement and then left him, making her way over to the table he had pointed out.

She needed to get a grip. She could hardly talk. She had ordered a diet Coke when she really did need something alcoholic – like a litre of wine all to herself. Now, to top it all off, she had the tallest stool in the world to get up on.

She had to get on it gracefully and she had to do it without anyone seeing in case she didn't quite pull graceful off. She looked around the bar, waiting for the perfect opportunity. The half a dozen men dressed in Air Patrol tour t-shirts at the table nearest her all looked towards the merchandise stand in unison as someone started to cause a scene by trying to queue jump. Samantha took her chance. She leapt up onto the stool, slid along the seat and fell down the other side of it, landing in a heap on the floor.

Cheeks ablaze, she hurriedly stood up, cautiously looking around to see if anyone had noticed.

A group of mainly blonde, attractive women, at the table next to the men in Air Patrol t-shirts, laughed out loud and looked over in her direction. Samantha's cheeks continued to glow as red as the top she was wearing, but she managed to get up onto the stool on the second attempt, using the table as an aid. The top had been a mistake. She stood out like a sore thumb. Like an Arsenal fan in the Spurs end.

Samantha looked over to where Jimmy was positioned at the bar and was glad his back was towards her. It might just have been possible he hadn't seen her fall or seen her scrambling onto the stool in such an undignified manner.

*

'One diet Coke,' Jimmy spoke when he came back. He put the drink down in front of her and with one hop, hoisted himself effortlessly onto the seat.

'Thank you,' Samantha answered.

It was the first normal sentence she had managed that evening.

'So, how's the menu?' Jimmy enquired, picking up a copy of his own.

'Just like McDonald's really – except there's no Happy Meal,' Samantha responded.

'Probably because it's cheap, quick to make and all people really expect before they watch a show,' Jimmy commented.

'But there's little variation, hardly any vegetarian options and you're stuck if you don't like potatoes. We've got curly fries, crinkle fries, wedges, Cajun twists and jackets,' Samantha said, finding herself becoming defensive.

'Hey, I know I'm just a humble ice skater and I really know nothing about running a facility like the Civic Hall but, if I was you, I'd take a leaf out of their book. I'd decrease the size of the menu and put cheaper, quicker options on there. That's what's gonna get you a higher turnover on those tables,' Jimmy told her.

'Not exactly an eating experience though is it?' Samantha said with a sigh, putting her glass back on the table.

'You aren't selling the experience in the restaurant – the experience should be the show. Everything else should just complement that,' Jimmy spoke and he took a sip of his mineral water.

'I guess so,' Samantha replied.

'Listen, let's try one of the cheaply made meals and see what they're like. If they're really all that bad then I'll take it all back,' Jimmy suggested.

'Goodness, must we?' Samantha asked, looking again at the menu.

'Come on, Sam, live a little,' Jimmy said with a smile.

'I suppose I ought to live a little quickly before I eat here – these might be the very last moments I have. I'll have the chicken burger with Cajun sauce and curly chips and hurry up before I change my mind,' Samantha ordered him, and she put the menu back down on the table.

'I'll be right back,' Jimmy said, jumping down from the stool and heading back to the bar.

*

Twenty minutes later they had not only had the food brought to the table, but they had also eaten it. They both had empty plates.

'Well?' Jimmy asked her as he wiped his mouth with the paper napkin.

'Actually, it wasn't bad for something that had obviously been chargrilled at speed,' Samantha admitted.

'I agree,' Jimmy responded, putting his napkin down on

the plate.

'But it's so different to what we do now.'

'I'm thinking burgers and fries, a vegetarian option and a kid's portion on all meals. I think you were right when you said "Happy Meal" earlier. Kids portion in a box with a drink and a plastic toy,' Jimmy told her.

'But maybe we could keep OAP discount day and put traditional meals on the menu for that. Just two or three easy options. I really need to keep shepherd's pie,' Samantha spoke almost excitedly.

'Perfect,' Jimmy agreed, smiling back at her.

'It wouldn't take a lot to make those changes. We could get in the supplies, have some new menus printed...' Samantha mused her mind working overtime.

'Sure, and I have a friend who runs a printing company. He could probably do a good price,' Jimmy told her, finishing up his drink.

'Do you have friends in every position imaginable?' Samantha enquired.

'I know a lot of people, what can I say? Hey, it's almost nine, the band will be on soon. Shall we go and sit down?' Jimmy suggested, checking his watch.

'Sit down? Oh, I presumed it was a standing concert, Cleo said that...' Samantha began.

'Sorry, the tickets Giles got me are for the VIP section. Allegedly everything was sold out in four minutes or something,' Jimmy remarked.

'Oh, VIP section,' Samantha repeated her mind flashing her images of Cleo's face when she told her later.

'Is that OK?' Jimmy checked.

'Yes, of course. To be honest it's probably a good thing

– it's been a while since I wore these shoes,' Samantha admitted.

'Cool, well let's go,' Jimmy said, and he led the way.

★

Air Patrol were very loud but very good and there were several songs Samantha recognised. Margaret and Mabel had a radio in the Civic Hall kitchen that could only get Radio One, so they knew all the latest hits and could often be heard humming Eminem as they served up lunch. Thankfully neither of them had attempted rapping as yet.

She couldn't quite believe she was sat at a concert on a 'kind of but not quite' date with Jimmy Lloyd. She tried not to, but she kept sneaking a sideways glance at him every now and then to check he was still next to her, to check that he was real. He seemed to be enjoying the concert. He'd stood up and danced and waved his arms with the rest of the crowd and, in the end, he had pulled her to her feet to do the same. She had cautiously moved from one foot to the other, trying to keep in time, but she had to draw the line at arm waving – she didn't feel comfortable doing it. And she found she couldn't wave her arms and move her feet at the same time.

By the end of the gig both her and Jimmy were applauding the band's efforts along with a few thousand other people.

'So, what did you think? Was it your thing?' Jimmy enquired as they made their way down from the balcony area.

'They were very good,' Samantha answered brightly.

'But very loud! I must be getting old, I'm starting to sound like my father,' Jimmy remarked with a laugh.

Samantha reached up to her ear and pulled out a plug of cotton wool.

'No! You're kidding me! You could have shared!' Jimmy exclaimed.

'I didn't bring any more,' Samantha told him.

Jimmy smiled and the Minstrel eyes were looking at her. Samantha felt her cheeks reddening again and the urge to cough rising in her throat. Hurriedly she unzipped the tiny red bag and pulled out the taxi card.

'I'd better call my taxi driver,' she spoke, holding the card aloft as if it were some sort of prize.

'I can take you home. My car's parked just behind the venue,' Jimmy told her.

'Oh no, no, I couldn't let you do that. You got the tickets and everything and you paid for the food, which I'm happy to pay my share of, I do have some…' Samantha started already trembling at the thought of getting into a car with him.

'I insist. You live near the hall, right? Well, it's on the way back to my hotel,' Jimmy told her.

'It's fine, honestly. I'll get a taxi, they're very reliable and I'll feel like I've let them down if I don't. I mean I did say I'd use their service later and…' Samantha babbled, feeling more and more flushed by the second.

'Sam, it's just a ride,' Jimmy told her.

'I know, of course. I mean, what else would it be? Ha, ho, hee,' Samantha spoke as she lost control of her vocal cords.

'Come on, I'm not taking no for an answer,' Jimmy insisted, and he linked arms with her for the second time that night and led the way out of the Presbook Centre.

What was she doing? Inside the concert hall it had been

safe. There were people, there was a concert going on, she was able to wax lyrical about the Civic Hall and how she could improve things. Now she was about to get into a car with the object of her affection and nothing but a gear stick between them. He would want to talk, and she wouldn't know what to say. She could feel herself starting to perspire already. Thank God for Sure! roll on. She'd given herself a double dose earlier.

'See, here we are. Told you it was nothing fancy, just a hire car,' Jimmy announced as he indicated the Volkswagen Golf they were approaching.

'I don't know anything about cars,' Samantha admitted her chest becoming tight.

'Do you drive?' Jimmy asked as he unlocked the door and opened it for her.

'No,' Samantha replied bluntly.

'And Cleo? Does she drive?' Jimmy questioned.

'No, she took her test five times and failed. They, called her "erratic and vulnerable",' Samantha responded, trying to breathe properly.

'Are you going to get in?' Jimmy enquired, indicating the open door and the seat inside.

'Well, I – d'you know what? Let's go to a club!' Samantha announced at the top of her voice.

'What?' Jimmy replied in shock.

'Let's go to a club! Come on, there's one just opposite the centre, it's called Revolution. Cleo goes there all the time – let's go!' Samantha spoke excitedly, backing away from the car and turning towards the main street.

What was she saying? Anything to avoid getting into such a confined space with him. She couldn't get in the car, it was so small, and the seats were so close together they would practically be touching the whole way back to her house – no, she couldn't do that. A club was terrifying too, but at least there would be hundreds of other people there and toilets to hide in if necessary.

'Let me get this straight – you want to go to a club?' Jimmy spoke, looking at her in amusement.

'Yes, I mean, you were saying earlier I ought to live a little and Cleo is always raving about clubs and saying what fun they are – I want to try it, let's go,' Samantha said her heart threatening to break free from her chest as she talked her escape route.

'Well, OK, if that's what you want to do,' Jimmy answered, closing the door and relocking the car.

'Yes, it is. That's exactly what I want to do – it will be – fun,' Samantha responded with an unconvincing smile.

15

Revolution had a queue of at least fifty people outside and three burly bouncers on the door. Two of them were bald and looked like Ross Kemp and the third had stringy, black hair tied back in a ponytail. He was taller than the Ross Kemp twins and looked like a cross between Francis Rossi from Status Quo and Steven Seagal.

Even from the back of the queue, Samantha could hear the *thump thump* of the drum and bass music that she knew was likely to bring on a migraine. But she smiled at Jimmy and did a ridiculous jig like something from *Lord of the Dance* in appreciation of the song that was playing and hoped she would be able to lose him in the crowd once they were inside. Then she could call a taxi and go home. That way there would be no awkward lifts touching knees in the teeny tiny car, clutching her teeny tiny handbag to her chest.

'So, what sort of music are you in to? This sort of stuff? Or stuff more like Air Patrol?' Jimmy enquired as they moved up the queue.

Oh God, he wanted to interrogate her before they got inside. She hadn't bargained on there being a queue to get in, and a quiet queue at that. She could vaguely hear a stag party near the front singing 'the bouncer is a wanker', which surely wasn't going to do them any favours, and there were two women behind them puking up into the gutter. Apart from that it was basically silent.

'Sorry, what did you say? The music's quite loud,' Samantha spoke, holding her ears.

What was she saying? The music wasn't loud, she could hear him perfectly well. He would now think she was deranged.

'I like all sorts of music, anything from Madonna to The Carpenters,' Jimmy informed her.

'Oh – I think I got some of that – still a bit fuzzy though, because of the music,' Samantha shouted loudly.

'Oi, you alright love or you got some mental problem? What's with all the shouting? I can hear what he's saying back here. He said he likes The Carpenters,' spoke a huge man in his forties wearing a checked shirt with sweat under each arm pit and a horrible brown stain on the front.

Samantha swallowed, realising her ridiculous game was up and tried to stop the laughter from spilling out as nerves threatened to overwhelm her.

'Hey, give the lady a break,' Jimmy suggested to the man who had spoken.

'Wooo! We've got a tetchy one here, boys. One with an attitude that likes The Carpenters,' the man said in a confrontational manner.

Samantha grabbed at her chest, feeling the feeling, knowing what was going to come next. She couldn't stop it.

'Ah ha ha ha ha!' she laughed in the highest pitch her vocal cords would allow.

'What the fuck? She on day release, mate?' the man questioned, nudging the club goers stood next to him and encouraging them to look at Samantha.

'Ahhhhhhhh ha ha ha ha!' Samantha continued, knowing the coughing and shortness of breath was going to follow rapidly afterwards.

'Come on, let's get in the club and get you a drink of water,' Jimmy urged, and he put his arm around Samantha, directing her out of the queue and towards the bouncers.

The Francis Rossi/Steven Seagal lookalike was busily checking the ID of very young-looking girls in very short skirts and making the best use of the opportunity by looking down their tops. The Ross Kemp twins glared in unison as Jimmy and Samantha approached them.

'Hi guys, could we go in? My friend needs to sit down and have a glass of water,' Jimmy said, holding Samantha up as she gasped for breath and started to cough like a walrus.

'Pissed, is she? I don't think so, mate,' Kemp number one spoke, looking Samantha up and down.

'She isn't drunk, she's having an anxiety attack. She just needs to sit and have a glass of water.'

'Yeah right, that's what they all say. Hang on a minute, you look familiar. Oi, Trev, who does he look like to you? Is it someone off the box? That detective from *The Bill* innit?'

'Nah, he's taller and his hair ain't right.'

'Look, please, can you get the management? If she doesn't take a seat in a minute she's probably going to pass out,' Jimmy told the duo.

'Nah it ain't *The Bill,* I know you. You're that ice skater. Me and the wife came and saw the show last week – tasty bird that partner of yours. You're Jimmy, ain't ya. It's Jimmy, Trev. Now, what's your last name again? George? James? James, innit?'

'It's Jimmy Lloyd – now we're coming in,' Jimmy said seriously as Samantha's eyes began to roll.

'Yeah, course, mate, course. VIP section's to the right. Oi! You! Guy with half his gut hanging out! See the sign up there – it's smart casual not fancy dress,' Kemp number one spoke, pointing at someone in the queue.

Jimmy hurried into the club and headed for the nearest table. He put Samantha onto a seat where she landed with a bump and surprised a couple who were furiously necking as if the world was going to end.

Samantha led her head on the table in front of her and tried to regain some control of her bodily functions. She felt dreadful. She was damp and clammy and overheating. Her head began to pound even more as the table vibrated to the loud house music that was being played by the DJ.

Where was she? What had happened? Why did she remember seeing Ross Kemp? Was she out on a night with Cleo? Had she made her drink red wine? She sluggishly pulled her head from the table and looked around her. There were people, hundreds of people, everywhere. They were occupying every corner as far as her eyes could see and there was a couple next to her trying to perform a tonsillectomy on each other. She was in a nightclub! What was she doing in a nightclub! Panic gripped her heart and then a glass of water was put down on the table in front of her.

'Are you OK?' Jimmy asked above the music.

Oh goodness she was with him! They'd been to the Presbook Centre to see the concert, she remembered that now. She'd had curly chips, but how did they get here? The tiny car! His tiny car and her avoidance plan to get out of him giving her a lift home. Oh, why was she so stupid?

'I got you some water,' Jimmy said, indicating the glass.

Samantha picked it up and hastily drank the contents in the hope it would make her feel better.

'Do you want to go somewhere quieter?' Jimmy asked.

No! No, despite the music hurting even the inside of her head, quiet meant less people, less noise and more chance of him asking the questions she didn't want to answer.

'No! No, here is good. I like it,' Samantha replied, and she made an attempt at bopping up and down on her seat and nodding her head in time to the music.

Jimmy came and sat down next to her.

'So, if you like this type of music how come you haven't been here before?' he enquired.

'Well – you know – it's having the time really,' Samantha said her voice wavering.

He was sat really close to her, as close as they would have been had she braved the car. His leg was almost touching hers. She would have been able to feel the rise and fall of his chest as he breathed if it hadn't been for the loud repetitive music and the DJ yelling 'Wave your hands in the air, whoop, whoop'.

'To be honest with you clubs don't do a lot for me anymore. They used to be somewhere to go when the bars shut but, well I don't do that anymore either,' Jimmy said over the din.

She didn't know what to say to him. Just having him sit so close to her was disabling her. There was only one thing she could say, and the words were out before she had thought it through.

'Let's go and dance!'

The minute she said it she wanted to be sick. What was she thinking of? She didn't do dancing – she *couldn't* dance. It had taken all her effort at the concert to move her feet in time to the music and that had been in a narrow aisle where no one could see her feet. Here there was a dance floor, filled with energetic people all unafraid of waving their arms and shaking their booty. Oh, why had she suggested dancing?

'You want to dance?' Jimmy asked, checking he had heard correctly.

'Well, I – yes! Why not?' Samantha answered feeling stupider than ever.

'If that's what you really want to do? Come on,' Jimmy said, standing up and offering her his hand.

Samantha gulped as she looked at the hand he was offering and then she looked at the dance floor. Hundreds of sweaty revellers, glassy-eyed and drunk, arms flailing, feet pounding. It reminded her of her leaver's party at school. She had ended up staying behind to help Mrs Coles, her form tutor, clean up all the vomit.

But this situation was completely her fault. If she hadn't been so pathetic and just got in his car she could be home now, safe in her bed. She took hold of his hand and let him lead her to the dance floor.

The music was horrendously loud, the beat was thumping through her body making her internal organs rattle and Jimmy was in front of her, completely at home in the surroundings, dancing wonderfully and looking gorgeous.

Samantha bent her knees like she was ice skating and her bottom stuck out. She tried to move her feet in time, but it was hard to figure out what 'in time' was when her insides were being pummelled by the bass line. She couldn't concentrate. Jimmy was smiling at her and Samantha smiled back, grimacing as she trod on the open-toed shoe of a female dancer next to her.

'Oh, I'm sorry,' Samantha said immediately, embarrassed.

The woman didn't hear her over the music and seemed not to have noticed. She threw her arms into the air and started yelling 'Whoop, whoop!'.

This was truly horrendous. How long did one song last? She didn't know how long she would be able to carry on sucking in her stomach, pulling in her bum and keeping her top half stiff so her boobs didn't bounce about. And, as well as doing all that, she then had to move from one foot to the other and pretend she was enjoying herself. It was painful and the black wedges were starting to rub her toes.

She looked around the dance floor to see if anyone else was having as much difficulty as she was. There were a group of women, dressed in neon colours wearing novelty sunglasses and veils who seemed to be doing a properly choreographed routine. There were a group of lads in polo shirts in circle formation, arms around each other's shoulders, bouncing up and down and shouting. And there was a lone club-goer, dressed as John Travolta from *Saturday Night Fever*, pointing his finger up in the air and then sweeping it across his body to point at his shoe in a frenzied fashion. And then she saw someone she knew. Felicity.

Felicity was wearing tight, black, wet-look leggings and a geometric print top. She was shaking her body in all sorts of directions and occasionally clasped hands with the man dancing opposite her. He was a sight to behold. He was wearing bottle green skinny-fit cords, a flowery shirt, open at the neck and pixie boots. He shook his head a lot, flicking his floppy fringe across his face. Samantha assumed this was the new boyfriend who worked on the switchboard of the local paper. He looked more like he should be in a band with Jarvis Cocker.

Felicity stopped gyrating and looked over in Samantha's direction. Oh goodness, she couldn't be seen, not here, in a club – or with Jimmy. Staff and performers didn't interact, it was one of the main Civic Hall rules. She grabbed hold of Jimmy's hands and pulled him closer to her, using him as a human shield.

'Oh, well, this is really, really fantastic but I'm so tired. Do you mind if we go?' Samantha shouted to him above the music, analysing her footwork so she moved behind Jimmy in time to his steps and avoided getting into Felicity's line of vision.

'No, of course not, let's go,' Jimmy agreed with a nod.

Samantha smiled and waited for him to move off first before she moved in close behind him and tried to hide herself from anyone who might be looking.

She didn't breathe until they were back outside. The Kemp twins had two men up against the wall of the club while the Francis Rossi/Steven Seagal lookalike radioed for assistance.

'Ooo, a taxi, I'll get in it. May as well, seeing as it's here,' Samantha spoke, suddenly taking off towards the waiting cab.

'Sam, I'll give you a ride,' Jimmy insisted.

'No, ho, he, that's OK. There's a cab just here – hello, Woolston please,' Samantha said through the open window to the driver as she prepared to open the door of the taxi.

'Sorry love, I'm booked.'

'Oh, oh well. I expect there will be another one along in a minute,' Samantha said.

'You'll be lucky love – an hour wait at this time of night,' the cab driver answered.

Samantha swallowed, not daring to face Jimmy.

'Come on, I'll take you home,' Jimmy told her.

Samantha reluctantly let go of the handle of the taxi, her very last form of escape, and trooped after Jimmy as he led the way back to his car.

And then there it was. The tiny car she had tried so hard to avoid, still there, in the same place it had been an hour ago and she still had to get in it.

Jimmy opened the door for her and she gulped. Was it possible it had shrunk in an hour? It definitely looked smaller and narrower. She knew Jimmy was watching her, so she hurriedly hopped into the car and closed the door behind her. She closed her eyes and took a deep breath.

Jimmy got into the driver's seat and started the engine.

Samantha clutched the small red bag to herself and looked out of the passenger window, trying to focus on anything other than the fact she was alone with him in the very small car.

'So, how did you like the club? Was it what you expected?' Jimmy asked as he started to drive.

'I – I think probably it was,' Samantha answered.

'I was thinking earlier, how little I know about you. I mean, I probably know more about Cleo than I do about you. That's kind of weird seeing as we've spent so much time together,' Jimmy continued.

'Well, Cleo's the interesting one,' Samantha responded and then wished she hadn't.

'You don't think you're interesting?' Jimmy asked her.

'Did you know, they used to hang people from that tree there on the green? It's hundreds of years old,' Samantha blurted out pointing out of her window at a protected oak.

'I know virtually nothing about you,' Jimmy stated.

'No? Ho, he, well...' Samantha began as she started to cough.

'I know you don't really like going to clubs, I know you like books – but are concerts like tonight your thing?' Jimmy continued to question.

'Yes, no, maybe. I don't know,' Samantha replied, and she barked a cough like a seal.

'Do you like the movies?' he carried on.

'Sometimes, I don't know. Well I guess black and white ones on the TV – you know, Deanna Durbin or Judy Garland. Cleo likes anything with Brad Pitt or Tom Cruise...' Samantha spoke, taking a deep breath.

'How about sports?'

'Cleo likes rugby, not that she knows the rules. I think...' Samantha began, putting her hand over her mouth as she coughed again.

'Not Cleo, Sam, *you*. What do *you* like?' Jimmy asked again, taking short glances at her as he drove.

'Me? Well, I like – hmm, I like – I don't know – just books and old films I guess,' Samantha said, her cheeks bright red and her chest bursting with nerves.

She wanted the floor of the car to open up and for her to sink down out of it and onto the road. Anything to get herself out of this situation.

Jimmy didn't ask any more questions and the silence was worse than anything he had asked her. Infinitely worse.

'My house is here,' she muttered as she saw her home coming up a few houses away.

'Here?' Jimmy checked as he pulled the car over to the kerb.

'Here will be fine, thanks,' Samantha spoke, ensuring that he hadn't stopped directly outside the house. She didn't want to give Cleo any chance of seeing Jimmy rather than 'Darren'.

'I had a really good time tonight,' Jimmy stated his brown eyes looking at her.

'It was – very – productive,' Samantha spoke hurriedly as she fumbled around for the door handle.

'I'll take that as meaning you enjoyed yourself,' Jimmy replied with a smile as Samantha opened the door.

'I'm sorry about the coughing and the...' Samantha began awkwardly.

'It's OK.'

'See you tomorrow,' Samantha said as she prepared to get out of the car.

'Sam,' Jimmy called, making her stop and turn back to face him.

She saw the perfect hair, the full lips, the dark brown eyes and swallowed.

'You dropped your bag,' Jimmy said, and he held out the red Barbie bag to her.

'Oh, oh thanks. Wouldn't have been able to get in the house without that – not the bag – I mean you can't get into a house with a bag, especially one that small – I mean it has my key in it,' Samantha babbled.

'See you tomorrow,' Jimmy spoke, re-starting the car.

Samantha closed the car door and watched Jimmy drive

up the street.

When she was sure he was out of sight and not coming back she let out a heavy sigh of frustration. She had acted like an idiot. Firstly, all she had talked about was the Civic Hall and menus and Happy Meals and then she had coughed and hyperventilated and somehow ended up at a nightclub dancing and almost bumping into Felicity. She'd been with Jimmy, all night, on a date that wasn't a date. She had been with him, out of the Civic Hall, not ice skating, for hours and nothing had really happened. She realised then that she was disappointed. Stupid! Stupid! He wasn't for her. He was too good looking, too outgoing, too nice. She was pathetic indulging her fantasies, imagining his lips on hers, looking into the chocolate eyes. She was turning into Cleo, finding all that superficial stuff attractive – except there was more to him than that. He was kind and generous and he made her laugh and he looked after her.

Samantha walked up to the front door of the house and before she had a chance to put her key in the lock the door was swung fiercely open. Cleo grabbed her by the shoulders and pulled her into the house.

'I heard you coming up the path, I've made Horlicks. Come in here, sit down and tell me everything!' Cleo ordered excitedly.

16

The following morning when Samantha came downstairs, she was amazed to see Cleo already in the kitchen. It was only 6.30 am and Cleo being up before her was practically unheard of. It had only happened a few times when a dark-haired twenty-something had started doing the street's milk round. The fact that she was also cooking made Samantha immediately suspicious.

'Morning! I thought I was going to have to come up and wake you for a change. Come on, come and sit down – I'm making scrambled eggs,' Cleo announced, pulling a chair out for her sister.

'What d'you want?' Samantha asked her.

'Oh Sam, you don't mean that. Does there have to be a reason for your big sister to cook you breakfast?' Cleo enquired as she rapidly stirred the eggs.

'Well, you've never done breakfast before and the last time you tried to poison me with an impromptu dinner you wanted me out of the house for a whole weekend,' Samantha reminded her.

Cleo went quiet and turned her body towards the cooker, hiding her face behind her hair.

'I could tell you were keeping something back last night.

You listened to me telling you all about Darren and the concert, but there was something else on your mind wasn't there? Well, just get it over with. What do you want? I have an office I can sleep in now if you need me away for a night,' Samantha reminded her as she took a sip from the mug of tea that was on the table.

'Jeremy and I had a talk last night, before you came home, about our relationship and other things,' Cleo stated.

'That's nice. Was that before, after, or during the shagging? I didn't realise you talked *and* had sex – this is something new for you,' Samantha spoke sarcastically.

'Sam! Stop it!' Cleo exclaimed, plugging her ears with her fingers as Samantha mentioned the 'S' word.

'Sorry, go on. What was this earth-shattering pillow talk you need to share with me?' Samantha asked her.

'We want to live together,' Cleo said hurriedly.

The tea she'd just put in her mouth caught in her throat before she had a chance to swallow it. She began to cough violently, leaning over the table and gasping for air.

'Sam! Are you OK? Breathe! Here, have some more tea,' Cleo ordered, hurrying over to the table, picking up the mug and offering it to her sister.

Samantha caught her breath and took hold of the mug, gulping down the tea as fast as she could. When she had recovered enough, she took a deep breath and looked at her sister with a serious expression.

'Did I really hear what I thought I heard? Or are my ears still ringing from the concert?' Samantha asked her.

'What did you think you heard?' Cleo enquired sheepishly.

'I thought you said you and Jeremy want to live together. But I couldn't have heard that, could I? Because you've known him like five minutes!' Samantha spoke, her voice high pitched.

'It's two weeks actually and I know it seems fast, but he really is different from any other guy I've dated before,' Cleo told her.

'And do you know how many times I've heard you say that?' Samantha exclaimed.

'It's different this time,' Cleo replied.

'Oh, I see! OK, so where's this living together going to take place? Has Jeremy got a pad? Or were you thinking of having him move in here?' Samantha questioned frantically.

'Well, I'm not sure. We need to talk about it and consider the options,' Cleo stated.

'Well, I'll make it easy for you. I'm not having a guy you've only known a week living here,' Samantha told her firmly and she got to her feet.

'It's two weeks,' Cleo reminded.

'Whatever.'

'But you wouldn't be able to afford the bills here on your own,' Cleo exclaimed concerned.

'No, I wouldn't. But don't let me stand in the way of your plans. By the way, your eggs are burning,' Samantha said as she turned away from her sister and left the room.

Cleo ran over to the cooker and hurriedly took the pan of blackened scrambled eggs off the heat.

★

At the hall Samantha couldn't concentrate on her work. Everything in her life was just falling apart. For years her life had been settled, routine, comfortable and safe. Now in such a short space of time every area of it was breaking down. She might lose her job and her beloved Civic Hall, and she might also lose her sister and her home to a brogue-wearing estate agent. And then there was Jimmy. An infatuation she just couldn't seem to ignore. He was being so nice to her and helping her more than anyone had ever helped her, but it was turning into torture. She was starting to like him more and more and the longer she spent with him the worse it got. She held his hand and he touched her every night when they skated, but that was all it was – it was just skating. And that fact hurt, because she knew, even though she shouldn't, she desperately wanted it to be more.

She had been devising the new menus all morning and she had called a staff meeting for the afternoon to let everyone know about the changes. Tyrone, the computer expert, had called earlier and he was coming back the following day to implement the online booking. Now she was chewing her pen and looking at the piece of paper in front of her. It was a mixture of writing, starting off with Jimmy's erratic scrawling and ending with her small, neat and ordered writing. It was supposed to be notes for her speech at the council meeting, except she hadn't added to it in over an hour. She didn't know what to say, her mind was full of stuff it shouldn't be full of. She put pen to paper and wrote 'menus'. Oh, who was she trying to kid? There was no way she was going to pull this off. Most of the ideas came from an ice skater. If she was capable, if she was destined to be the manager, she should be able to handle this on her own. But she couldn't, she was useless.

There was a knock on the door of the office.

'Come in,' Samantha called with a heavy sigh.

The door opened and Jimmy appeared, shaking a brown

bag at her. Great, that was all she needed, someone kind, considerate and fit to distract her.

'I've brought some lunch. Have you got time? I thought we could go through the speech,' he suggested, stepping into the room.

'I haven't really got time, I...' Samantha began to protest.

'I bought it all in the restaurant. I've got baguettes - tuna mayo - I'm told that's your favourite. I've got diet Coke and I've got cheesecake,' Jimmy told her, and he got out all the food and lined it up on Samantha's desk.

'Is that *chocolate* cheesecake?' Samantha queried, leaning forward to sniff the food.

'The very same. Mabel tells me on one particularly bad day, involving a bust up with the conductor of a children's choir and one of the judges of a dog show, you had three pieces of this stuff. On that recommendation, I can't wait to taste it,' Jimmy spoke, opening the lid of the box and letting the aroma escape.

'Goodness, let me have it. I missed breakfast,' Samantha said, reaching for the pudding.

'I take it you're not having a good day,' Jimmy remarked.

'I've been busy. I've sorted out the new menus and ordered the stock, I've dealt with some of the backlog of administration that Dave left behind, Tyrone's been on the phone and he's almost finished updating the website and then I've been staring at this piece of paper. This is supposed to sum up everything the council needs to know to make them save the hall and all it represents is what desperate trouble I'm in,' Samantha remarked as she spooned cheesecake into her mouth.

'It's still two days away,' Jimmy spoke, sinking his teeth

into a baguette.

'Two days! Exactly! Only two days and look at it – look at me!' Samantha exclaimed.

'Relax, it'll be fine,' Jimmy stated.

'Relax! Yes, I have plenty of time to do that! I'm trying to run the hall, change the hall, save the hall and on top of the hall stuff, my sister wants a guy she's only known a week to move in with us,' Samantha told him, her breathing becoming erratic. Or was it two weeks? She wasn't sure and she was the one who lived by timelines!

'Whoa! Go Jeremy,' Jimmy commented, putting down his food.

'Yes, Jeremy. Jeremy she has known for five minutes. It isn't about him being very irritating and leaving his shoes in the middle of the hallway, it's about her and how she always jumps headlong into things without thinking about them,' Samantha continued.

'And what would be the alternative? That she moves out?'

'Yes. And she knows that I couldn't afford all the bills and expenses on my own – even more so when I make a complete pig's ear of this speech, the council close down the hall and I lose my job,' Samantha informed him as she finished off the cheesecake.

'Well, from what you've told me about Cleo, which is quite a lot, the whole idea will probably have been forgotten by next week. She'll probably even be with a new guy,' Jimmy suggested.

'I don't know why I'm telling you all this,' Samantha said, and she picked up Jimmy's portion of cheesecake and began to eat it.

'Because I'm a good listener? Come on, put the cake down. Let's go and do some skating,' Jimmy spoke, and he took the pudding from one hand and grabbed the fork from the other.

'I can't, I have a tonne of things to do. Besides, won't the other skaters be practising on the rink?' Samantha asked, checking her watch.

'Rehearsal's at three and I think you need to do something to take your mind off things. By the way, I've fed Gobby. He sniffed me out and came scratching at my dressing room door earlier. Mabel let me have cottage pie,' Jimmy told her.

'Oh no, not cottage pie. He doesn't like cottage pie. He doesn't like anything with mince in,' Samantha exclaimed, standing up.

'Really? Well, he wolfed it down, licked the bowl clean and then had seconds,' Jimmy informed.

'He'll probably be sick, and he'll probably do it outside the front doors. He always does it there, and I'll have to clean it up because Jane's allergic to other people's vomit and Felicity has a no vomit clause in her contract and then it will smell, probably for a week and…' Samantha began.

'He'll be fine, Sam. Come on, take a break, come and skate,' Jimmy urged.

Samantha let out a sigh, picked up the portion of cheesecake from the desk and spooned the remainder into her mouth.

*

Twenty minutes later the two of them were skating round the ice rink, practising the routine Jimmy had taught her.

'You really are a good skater you know and a real quick

learner,' Jimmy remarked as they moved around the ice.

'I'm not good, not like Dana. She's a wonderful skater, I never get bored of watching her in the show,' Samantha remarked.

'She could have been very successful. I mean we were successful as a partnership for a while, but after the world championships and the fall, she's never really trusted me again, not one hundred percent,' Jimmy answered.

'What happened?' Samantha wanted to know.

'Well, we had a difficult move at the end of our routine and she just didn't get her feet in the right position. I picked her up, her blade cut my chin open and she fell and hit her head on the ice. She had ten stitches, I had six,' Jimmy explained, pointing to his scar.

'Oh, dear,' Samantha stated.

'She refuses to do any lifts or spins with me where there's an ankle hold now. Anyone else partnering her and she'll do anything – she just doesn't trust me,' Jimmy spoke.

'Then why does she skate with you at all?' Samantha queried as they changed direction on the ice.

'Because we were famous as a couple and that was where our success was. People expect to see us together. I know if it was down to her, she'd never skate with me again,' Jimmy explained.

Samantha span around on one leg and then came to a halt, slightly out of breath.

'That was really good! But the way to really find out if you know the steps is to do it blindfolded,' Jimmy informed her.

'Yeah OK, very funny,' Samantha replied.

'I'm serious,' Jimmy told her.

'I can barely stay on my feet. I can't skate with a blindfold on,' Samantha told him.

'Do you trust me?' Jimmy asked her.

'What sort of a question is that?' Samantha responded a cough rising in her chest.

'A straight one. Come on, I won't let you injure yourself,' Jimmy assured her, and he took off his sweater, leaving his top half covered by a tight t-shirt.

It was blue! Oh goodness it was blue again! It was a nice, light blue colour that really complemented the lovely hair and clung to his body perfectly, emphasising its perfection.

'I trust that you wouldn't deliberately injure me, but you don't have any control over me injuring myself,' Samantha told him, trying not to stare at his chest through the very thin material.

'I know you can do this,' Jimmy told her, and he put the sweatshirt over her eyes and tied it together at the back of her head.

'I can't do it. Are you crazy?! Where've you gone? Don't leave me here like this,' Samantha shrieked suddenly realising Jimmy was being serious when the sweatshirt was tied across her eyes.

She was back feeling five years old again, playing Blind Man's Buff. She hated that game, once she had fallen over and stuck the pin in Cleo's arm at Lucy Jackson's party.

'I'm just going to restart the music,' Jimmy said as he skated over to the edge of the rink and skipped off it towards the show's mixing desk.

Samantha felt stupid. She was standing in the middle of an ice rink with a sweatshirt over her face, she had a hundred and one things she should be doing, a speech she had to deliver to the council in two days and the realistic prospect that she could lose both her job and her home. Not to mention the one thousand eight hundred Berry Fruits tubs in the freezer. She was hopeful of selling a good batch tonight though, as there were a couple of coach parties in and coach parties never failed to have ice cream. Something to do with the effect of the throat drying air conditioning on the journey there.

Jimmy returned to her and took hold of her hands as the music began. Skating and not having a clue where you were in relation to your surroundings was the oddest sensation. Samantha was sure that, at any moment, she was going to collide with the hoarding around the edge of the rink. But she was concentrating so hard to remember the steps and how to position herself for the lifts and turns, she hardly had time to panic. Jimmy was true to his word. He held her firmly, and when they were apart, she could sense he was still close, and she knew he wouldn't let her fall.

The routine seemed to be a lot longer than two and a half minutes when you couldn't see. Her face was starting to feel hot as she breathed heavily onto the fleecy, sweatshirt material and she couldn't tell at all whether she was in the middle or at the edge of the rink. She held Jimmy's hand and they changed direction and then she held his arms as he lifted her up for a spin. She landed the move, turned around and stopped in her end position leaning back into Jimmy's arms, thankful he really was there to catch her.

And then, as he held her, she began to laugh. It had been the most ridiculous, yet exhilarating thrill she had ever experienced. She was completely out of breath when she stood up straight, still laughing happily, amazed that she had done it without breaking any bones.

'Take your blindfold off,' Jimmy instructed her.

'That was actually fun, very scary, but fun, I...'

Samantha stopped talking the second she removed the blindfold. Jimmy was stood beside her, bare-chested. The t-shirt he'd been wearing was covering his eyes. He had blindfolded himself too.

'Oh, my goodness! No! You did not just do that! Are you totally mad? You picked me up and threw me in the air and you couldn't see?!' Samantha exclaimed, clamping her hands to her mouth as she watched him take the top from his eyes.

'I told you you could do it,' Jimmy spoke softly, smiling at her shock.

'That must have been contravening every rule in the ice-skating code of conduct,' Samantha said to him.

'You trusted me,' Jimmy stated.

He reached out his hand and took hold of hers. A shiver ran through Samantha's whole body as he touched her. What was he doing? He had taken her hand so many times when they skated, but this felt different. She couldn't explain why. He was looking at her with the Minstrel eyes, his body unmoving.

'Nice to see you practising. You never want to when I suggest it.'

The loud comment from Dana, as she appeared on the ice, startled Samantha. She stepped backwards, forgot she was on skates and fell to the ice with a bump.

Jimmy hurriedly bent down to help her up, as one by one, the show's skaters came onto the rink for their rehearsal.

'Are you OK?' Jimmy queried as he helped her to her

feet.

'Yes, yes I'm fine. I'd better get back, I'll see you,' Samantha spoke hurriedly, and she sped off across the ice as rapidly as she could, her heart hammering in her chest.

17

When Samantha opened up the front door that evening, she immediately fell over Jeremy's brogues.

'Oh hello, Sam. Sorry, I shouldn't have left those there – I was just going,' Jeremy spoke as he greeted her in the hallway and removed the shoes from the floor.

'No sex on the table today, that's good,' Samantha retorted as she brushed past him and continued up the hall towards the kitchen.

She heard the front door close as Jeremy left and she went over to the kettle.

'Jeremy's gone,' Cleo announced as she entered the kitchen from upstairs.

'I know, I almost twisted my ankle again trying to avoid the shoes,' Samantha responded as she filled the kettle with water.

'He isn't going to be moving in,' Cleo stated rather sombrely.

'So, you're going to be moving in with him? Fine, you'd better tell him, or one of your estate agent friends, to put the house on the market,' Samantha snapped.

'No, I'm not moving in with him either,' Cleo replied.

Samantha put down the kettle and turned to face her

sister.

'Is everything OK? You haven't broken up, have you?' Samantha asked, changing her tone as she saw that Cleo was upset.

'No, everything's fine. You were right that's all. You're always right. It's too soon,' Cleo said, sitting down at the kitchen table.

'Do you want an herbal tea?' Samantha offered.

'Thanks,' Cleo accepted.

'Listen, I'm sorry if I went a bit over the top this morning. I'm just panicking a bit about the Civic Hall. I do like Jeremy, yes, his shoes are big and irritating, but he's certainly not the worst you've brought home. That accolade most definitely goes to Byron, the ZZ Top loving librarian,' Samantha stated.

Cleo couldn't help but laugh at her sister.

'And, I didn't want you to rush into anything and get yourself hurt,' Samantha added seriously.

'I know, and you were right. I mean, what do you really learn about someone in a week? He could be an axe murderer or someone who likes S Club 7 for all I know,' Cleo remarked.

'I don't think he's an axe murderer, but you're going to have to ask him about S Club 7. You know the rules of the house, he simply can't be allowed to have ever owned or downloaded an S Club 7 song,' Samantha replied.

Cleo smiled and then her face clouded over again.

'I just really like him, Sam, and he really likes me. I don't think I've felt like this about anyone before. I know you've heard me say that loads of times but honestly, this time I really mean it. He just accepts me as I am you know – he seems to love my eccentricities. I don't have to put on any airs and graces, I can just be myself. Like, I was supposed to go out for bagels at lunchtime the other day and I kind of got side-tracked and ended up buying this cute handbag in Dorothy Perkins. Well Jeremy just got that. He smiled and said it was nice and I'd completely forgotten about everyone's lunch,' Cleo spoke, her eyes misting over.

'That's nice,' Samantha replied, thinking about Jimmy.

'But we've talked again about it and we both agree it would be too soon. And, if it's really going to be a long-term relationship, then there isn't any point in rushing things,' Cleo said as Samantha brought over her tea.

'Well, I'm sorry I reacted like I did this morning. I've just got a lot going on at the moment, with the hall,' Samantha spoke as she sat down opposite her sister at the table.

'And Darren? Have you heard from him today?' Cleo enquired.

'No, no, not today. He'll probably call me later,' Samantha spoke rapidly, burying her face in her cup.

'So, how do you feel about him? Could he be 'the one'?' Cleo continued.

'Oh, I don't know. I'm not sure I'd really know what I was looking for – apart from no wives, no nipple ring, and definitely no body odours,' Samantha admitted.

'Well, how does it make you feel when you see him?' Cleo asked, sipping her tea.

'Sick usually because I never know what's going to come out of my mouth next. I go to say one thing and something else comes out,' Samantha told her.

'And your stomach turns over and your heart races and all you want to do is rip his clothes off?' Cleo guessed.

'Well, I'm not sure I'd go that far. I mean, I haven't known him very long,' Samantha answered, flushing as she thought of Jimmy's chest.

'But you've thought about it? Considered that you might?' Cleo assumed.

'Maybe,' Samantha admitted, thoughts of what Jimmy would look like naked springing to mind.

Cleo shrieked excitedly.

'But how do you really know if a guy likes you? I mean, if they haven't made it obvious – you know, not just likes you as a friend but *likes* you,' Samantha wanted to know.

'How old are you, Sam? Twelve?! What d'you mean how do you know? He snogged you last night, didn't he? When he brought you home,' Cleo asked.

'Well no, but I don't think I stayed in the car long enough to find out if he wanted to. I didn't really sit still from the moment he put the brakes on. And the journey home was awful, he started asking me questions and I didn't know what to say – he makes me nervous,' Samantha admitted, recalling the previous night.

'God! What did you do? Run away?' Cleo enquired.

'No, well, not really. But he has touched my hand and…' Samantha began.

'He touched your hand,' Cleo repeated.

'Yes, and it felt strange – you know – different, not platonic – like he *liked* me,' Samantha attempted to explain.

'And that's all he did? Touch your hand? Bloody Hell, Sam! I mean, I know you like to take things slowly, but Christ!' Cleo spoke, gulping her tea back.

'Well, like I said, I don't really know if he likes me in that way and you can't just leap on someone and hope for the best,' Samantha responded in frustration.

'But he gave you his number, he invited you on a date – surely that means he likes you,' Cleo told her.

It was impossible for her to understand – she didn't know the real situation. Samantha knew her sister was picturing the six foot reasonably-faced executive with the expensive house and a wardrobe full of beige trousers and red shirts – not the gorgeous, toned, intelligent, humorous celebrity ice dancer.

'I suppose so,' Samantha mumbled, hiding her face in her mug again.

'I'd make the first move if I was you, before he starts to think you're a lesbo,' Cleo told her.

'I have trouble talking to him about anything that matters, except the Civic Hall. I can talk to him about that, but there's no way I could make a move on him without hyperventilating,' Samantha admitted honestly.

'Then be prepared to have him stolen away by someone who *can* talk to him and *will* make a move. Good blokes don't hang around forever and I really wouldn't spend all your dates talking about the Civic Hall – it bores me rigid and I only listen because we're related,' Cleo informed her.

Samantha knew that her sister was right, but it was an impossible situation. She just didn't have the nerve and she wasn't sure she ever would. Not with anyone. She was destined to be a virgin forever and it wouldn't be long before Cleo started offering her use of her Rampant Rabbit. She could think of nothing worse than ten inches of rubber your sister had already used.

★

That evening, while the skating show was going on in front of her, Samantha was jotting things down on her notepad. It was still just rough notes and she had to turn it into a formal presentation by the following night. It was driving her mad. She knew she had all the ideas, she knew what she needed to say, it was just how to get it in order and then to deliver it eloquently and effortlessly when the time came. She had only ever spoken in public once before. She had to say a four-line prayer at a school assembly when she was eight. She had said 'Our Father' in a voice that resembled Mickey Mouse and Douglas Davies, the school bad boy, had snorted with laughter, leading everyone else to follow suit. She had heard Mary Kennedy and her cronies giggling too and she had clammed up. She stood on the stage, open mouthed, with glazed eyes for what felt like hours but was really only seconds. Then Cleo had run up the steps, hair flying behind her, skirt six inches above regulation, and gently moved her aside to take over. Cleo made the four-line prayer sound like the Martin Luther King speech. Everyone applauded and Samantha felt smaller than she had ever felt before. She had never put herself in that position again, until now.

She wrote down 'history', 'OAPs', '21st century' and chewed the end of her pen. One of the songs from *Miss Saigon* ended and it was time for Jimmy and Dana to take to the ice to perform to 'Don't Cry For Me Argentina' from *Evita*. Jimmy and Dana always got the best reception from the crowd because they were the most well-known skaters of the ensemble. Dana always looked amazing and tonight was no exception. Samantha envied the way she looked, the hair, the make-up, the beautiful outfits, how they fitted her, and her perfect poise. Samantha watched intently as they began to dance. There was no way she could ever be as elegant on the ice as Dana.

Samantha continued to watch as Jimmy held his partner, twirled her around, lifted her skywards and held on to her hand. Cleo was right, a touched hand was no indication of someone's feelings. He held hands with Dana every night and he didn't even like her. It was part of what he did, and she needed to get realistic about things. There was something far more important at stake than her feelings for Jimmy – something that could affect her whole future. She needed to keep her concentration on the hall, her hall.

*

'I can't skate tonight,' Samantha called later.

She was sitting on the front row of seats when Jimmy arrived back in the auditorium well after the audience had left. Hearing her call, he walked over to her, his skates slung over one shoulder.

'How's it going?' he asked, sitting down in the seat next to her.

'It isn't. That's why I can't skate tonight. I need to get home and finish this,' Samantha informed, and she put the lid back on her pen and stood up.

'Let me see what you've got so far,' Jimmy said, indicating the pad.

'Oh no, thanks, it's very rough. I only just got started trying to put it in some sort of order,' Samantha spoke, clutching the pad to her chest.

'Come on, this is no time to get possessive of it – show me,' Jimmy said, and he stood up, took the pad from her and began to read.

Immediately Samantha's face began to flush as she watched him read. It was awful, it was basic. It wasn't awe-inspiring or Shakespearean – it was just her thoughts and feelings and her ideas about the future of the hall.

'It isn't very good, not yet. I need to spend the rest of tonight on it and probably all day tomorrow and then maybe it might make some sense. Well, it still might not be perfect then, but it will definitely be better than it is, because it isn't very good now, I mean...' Samantha started, feeling she had to defend the text.

Jimmy looked up from the pad, the Minstrel eyes staring directly at her.

'Goodness, you think the hall's doomed, don't you? Despite all the help you've given me, and all the favours you've called in with Air Patrol and Tyrone the internet guru, I'm going to blow it all because I can't write anything remotely good enough,' Samantha spoke, her voice rising in pitch.

Jimmy shook his head at her.

'This is the story of my sad little life you know. Nothing I ever do is going to be good enough. I'm just pathetic, weak, useless Samantha Smith,' Samantha exclaimed louder than she had anticipated.

She was on the very edge of gushing her real feelings about who she was. The fears she had were set to tumble out of her at any minute.

'That isn't true,' Jimmy responded.

'Oh, yes it is, I'm a *nightmare*! I don't know why I'm even bothering writing this speech, because no one has ever listened to me before – why should they start listening now?

People look at me like I'm weird and when I speak, I prove them right. I stumble over my words, I feel sick and I get breathless, and that's just on a good day. Standing up in front of the council I will probably have a freaking heart attack. I'm not up to this, I can't do it! I cannot do it!' Samantha shrieked hysterically, dropping the notepad on the floor and getting out of breath with panic.

Jimmy grabbed hold of her and forcefully pulled her towards him, shocking her and relieving her of breath. Before she had any chance to react, she felt his lips on hers, firm, passionate, and definitely not platonic. She couldn't breathe at all now. She could feel his mouth on hers and it felt magical. She felt his hands on her cheeks, holding her face to his and she tried desperately to savour every moment in case it never happened again.

Then he let her go, stood back from her and she was left stood opposite him, her mouth hanging open like a guppy fish. She hurriedly closed it up and swallowed nervously.

'I-I-I...' Samantha attempted to speak as she looked up at him.

'Do you find me attractive?' he asked directly.

'I-I-I...'

'Don't try and talk, just gimme a nod if you do.'

Samantha vigorously nodded her head up and down like the Churchill bulldog.

'Good, because I find you so attractive, Sam, you just wouldn't believe. When I'm not with you I can't stop thinking about you. Don't ask me why, because you hardly speak and I've no idea what stuff you like, but, I've been trying to decipher how you feel about things in between the panic attacks and I've come to the conclusion that I like you – a lot.'

'I…'

'Sshh, you don't have to say anything,' Jimmy spoke softly, and he put a finger to her lips, gently rubbing the skin.

Samantha desperately tried to suppress the urge to cough that was rising in her. Just feeling his finger brush her lips was almost too much.

'I don't want you to say anything yet. I know you're panicking right now thinking you're probably going to throw up or laugh or cough and say something stupid, but I want you to know that's OK. That's you and it's those kitschy, skitzy things you do that I find kind of endearing. Well, maybe not the fainting because that's a bit worrying, but the overreaction to things is kind of cute,' Jimmy told her.

Samantha didn't respond, couldn't respond. All she could do was look at him and wonder if she really was hearing what she thought she was hearing.

'I really like you, Sam, and the more time I've spent with you the more feelings I've had for you. Which is pretty crazy seeing as I only really know about your sister – but I'm hoping that may come in useful,' he continued.

This had to be a dream. She had had a similar dream two nights ago except she hadn't been herself, she'd been Sandra Bullock. It had seemed much more believable seeing Jimmy kissing Sandra Bullock.

'Sam, you're bright and honest and genuine and you care about things. You're funny and you're real and I like that. I really like that,' Jimmy said.

Samantha started to feel very hot. What he was saying

couldn't be true. He couldn't like her like she liked him, that only happened in films. Sandra Bullock films actually.

'And I want to know about you, if you want me to. I kind of took advantage a minute ago, didn't I?' Jimmy spoke, running his hand through his hair.

'No, you didn't,' Samantha responded, surprised at the strength of her own voice and the fact that she had managed to say anything.

'No?' Jimmy enquired.

'No, you didn't take advantage. Cleo would probably have slapped me for getting hysterical, you kissed me – it was infinitely better,' Samantha found herself speaking.

'I'm not out of the woods with the alcohol, Sam, I want you to know that. That's my baggage. Every day's a minor battle, it's getting better but it's always going to be there,' Jimmy told her honestly.

Samantha nodded, cleared her throat and took a deep breath, crossing her fingers behind her back.

'I do suffer from panic attacks and sometimes, well a lot of the time, I wish I was my sister,' Samantha replied, not believing her own ability to get the words out.

'What a couple huh!' Jimmy remarked with a smile.

'A couple,' Samantha repeated not really meaning to.

'Yeah, if you want to see how it goes. If you'll have me,' Jimmy replied quietly, looking at Samantha.

'You and me,' Samantha spoke, drowning in the Minstrel eyes as they looked at her.

'Yeah, you and me,' Jimmy repeated, edging nearer to her.

He cupped Samantha's face in his hands again and she felt the full lips for the second time, so soft on hers. This time it was like being kissed by the lightest, most sensual of feathers. Her head was spinning with excitement and arousal and she clung to him, holding his muscular shoulders, touching his hair with her fingers. She felt out of control, her deep emotion for him overriding any impulsive tendencies she might normally have had.

Jimmy kissed her mouth gently and then held her away from him to look at her. He smoothed her hair back behind her ears and held her hands.

'I've-I've never been kissed in the Civic Hall before,' Samantha admitted and then she blushed at the stupidity of the remark.

'I'm glad. Besides, I had to kiss you here. It's the only place we've ever really talked properly and the only place you really feel comfortable. My God, we have to save it!' Jimmy responded with a smile.

'I don't know if I can change,' Samantha admitted almost sadly.

'Change? I don't want you to change,' Jimmy insisted, and he gently stroked her fingers.

'Not even the gasping for breath and coughing,' Samantha replied.

'We can work on that,' Jimmy responded with a smile.

Samantha smiled back at him and then she let out a gasp and put her hands to her mouth.

'The speech! You made me forget the speech! I don't have a speech for tomorrow! It's all just notes and ramblings and you hated it – even though you were too polite to say, and I need to feed Gobby and…' Samantha exclaimed in panic, looking for her notepad which was lying on the floor.

'Come on, let's go feed Gobby and I'll take you home.

You can get a good night's sleep and tomorrow morning we can look at it together,' Jimmy told her, putting an arm around her shoulders.

'Together'. The word sounded so unfamiliar to her in the way he had spoken it, but it wasn't frightening or unwelcome and the weight of his arm around her wasn't worrying or repellent. It was comfortable and she liked it.

18

'Sam, are you OK? Are you sick?'

Samantha opened her eyes to see Cleo's face extremely close to hers, so close she could smell...

'Worcester sauce,' Samantha said out loud.

'What?' Cleo queried, retracting slightly.

'You've had Worcester sauce on toast again – I can smell it. You'll need to clean your teeth again,' Samantha spoke, yawning and sitting herself up in bed.

'It's gone seven,' Cleo stated, still eyeing her sister with suspicion.

'Oh, is it?' Samantha stated, checking her watch.

Then she smiled, remembering the previous night. Jimmy had driven her home, in the small car she had actually ended up wishing was smaller. Who would have thought it? And he kissed her again, right outside the house – for ages. And she hadn't cared. Usually she would have worried about Mr Peterson at number twelve twitching his curtains, but she hadn't given him a second thought.

'"Oh, is it?" Something's happened hasn't it? Something happened last night with Darren! Tell me!' Cleo exclaimed, ruffling up Samantha's duvet.

Samantha just carried on smiling, reliving in her mind

what had happened between her and Jimmy. She had had her hands in the gorgeous hair, on the firm chest, and she had felt his lips on hers.

'Sam! You're scaring me! What happened?!' Cleo said, almost screaming.

'We kissed!' Samantha admitted proudly, still wearing a mile-wide smile.

Cleo did scream this time and grabbed hold of Samantha, embracing her in a bear hug and breathing more Worcester sauce fumes in her face.

'Oh, tell all! When? Where?' Cleo interrogated.

'It was really romantic. I'd started to hyperventilate because I was worried about the council meeting and losing the Civic Hall and he just grabbed me and kissed me – right on row AA,' Samantha spoke, starry eyed.

'In the Civic Hall, on row AA. I think I need to meet this Darren sooner rather than later if that's his idea of romance,' Cleo said with a tut.

'And he told me how he felt. He told me he really liked me,' Samantha stated, feeling gleeful.

'*Liked* you. Hmm, not exactly a fast mover, is he? So, did you – you know – go back to his place?' Cleo wanted to know, winking at her sister.

'No! No, of course not! We only just kissed. I mean, I couldn't do that yet, I…' Samantha started immediately feeling uncomfortable.

OK, Jimmy was the first guy she had ever really mentally undressed, but that didn't mean she was actually ready to undress him. Although, she had seen most of his body because he did tend to wear his trousers quite low on his hips. And when he had his top off there wasn't much left to the imagination. Well, the important procreation part obviously, but she hadn't thought about that. Well, only so far as thinking she hoped it wasn't pierced.

'Now, I don't want you to take this the wrong way, but losing your virginity is kind of sweet and resembling a fairy-tale when you're sixteen – but at your age it's just going to be a case of going with the flow and getting it over and done with,' Cleo told her.

'Why?' Samantha queried.

'Well, I think it's highly commendable and all that, not that I pretend to understand it, but I don't know any man who would relish the prospect of a virgin – not one of your age anyway. I think you should just do it ASAP and whatever you do, don't tell him, or he'll run for the hills,' Cleo advised.

Samantha let out a laugh, drew back the duvet cover and got out of bed.

'What's funny?' Cleo wanted to know.

'You are, Cleo. Who did you lose your virginity to? Michael Rudman wasn't it? Michael "Spotty" Rudman who you only liked because his dad was rich and he did motocross. In fact, it was lucky he did a sport that needed a helmet because there were more craters on his face than on the motocross track. And where did he take you to lose your virginity? The cricket pavilion. The same cricket pavilion that everyone we knew from school had thrown up on or urinated against. You were sixteen and you did it behind a dirty, cricket pavilion on a pile of crash mats the playgroup used for gymnastics. How romantic – how fairy-tale,' Samantha spoke as she got her Civic Hall uniform out of the cupboard.

'OK, Michael Rudman was a mistake, but what I'm trying to say is...' Cleo began her cheeks red with embarrassment.

'I know you're doing the elder sister routine and trying to advise and protect me but I'm fine and I can make my own decisions – even about sex,' Samantha assured her.

'Argh! Stop it! You know I hate it when you say that word,' Cleo exclaimed, clamping her hands over her ears.

'Thanks for waking me though, hectic day ahead. You'll have to make your own lunch, oh and don't forget to clean your teeth again, unless you want Jeremy tasting your breakfast,' Samantha spoke as she headed out of her bedroom towards the shower.

Cleo pulled a face at her sister but ran her tongue across her teeth to see if she was right.

*

By the time Samantha arrived at the Civic Hall the speech was coming along. She had written some after her shower, went through things mentally on her walk to work and now she was furiously typing on the computer, trying to compile it all. Her head was strangely focussed and clear, she was smiling and happy and earlier she had made time to make coffee for Felicity and Jane. It had shocked them because she hated coffee herself and hated using the temperamental machine. She hadn't even got annoyed with it when it started to make stupid noises and spat at her.

By 10.00 am she couldn't wait any longer to share the results of her hard efforts on the speech with Jimmy. She knew they had had early rehearsals that morning, but she hoped he would be in his dressing room by now. She practically skipped up the corridor, excited about seeing him. She reached the door of his room, knocked and waited. There was no reply. Looking at her watch and, certain he wouldn't be long, she opened the door, intending to wait for him.

Being the principal male skater, Jimmy had his own dressing room, as did Dana. The other skaters had to share the other five rooms designated for performers. Samantha smiled as she stepped in and noticed one of Jimmy's t-shirts draped over the arm of the sofa. She was just about to pick it up and put it to her nose to smell the scent of him when she was aware of someone else in the room.

'Goodness, sorry! I didn't think anyone was in here,' Samantha exclaimed as she was greeted by the sight of Dana stood by the dressing table.

The Canadian woman was dressed in full *Evita* costume, still wearing her skates. Her red hair was tied back from her face and her complexion was flawless. Samantha suspected this was due more to Maybelline than it was to youthful skin.

'No need to apologise, honey, I was just leaving. Although, while you're here, I did notice my room isn't as clean as it has been. Could you organise a more thorough going over and perhaps have a word with the offending member of staff,' Dana spoke, putting a plastic bottle back down on the dressing table and moving towards Samantha and the exit.

'Of course, I'll speak to the cleaners,' Samantha replied professionally.

'Great, I wouldn't want to have to make up with an inch of dust on my dresser,' Dana retorted, and she smiled her Hollywood smile at Samantha before leaving the room.

It was only a few seconds before the door opened again and Jimmy walked in. He was sweating and looked hot from the practice, but he smiled as soon as he saw Samantha.

'Hey, I was just coming to see you,' he announced.

'Well, here I am,' Samantha replied her heart already racing just at the sight of him.

'No regrets?'

'Regrets?' Samantha queried.

'You didn't get home and think what a mistake you'd made kissing me?'

'No, oh, did you think it was…' Samantha started her heart jumping into her mouth.

'No! Of course not! Don't be crazy, come here.'

He kissed her tenderly and then he held her hands, smiling down at her.

'I have no regrets whatsoever,' Jimmy insisted.

'Me neither,' Samantha answered with a smile.

'So, how's your day been? Has Gobby visited yet?' he asked her.

'Not yet, but once he gets the whiff of macaroni cheese he'll be here. Today's been really, really good. Look, come and see this,' Samantha encouraged, and she let go of his hands and beckoned him over to the coffee table where she had placed her print out.

'Is this what I think it is?' Jimmy enquired hopefully.

'It is. I've been working on it since last night really. I couldn't sleep when I got in, so I wrote some then and, after that, there was no stopping me – ideas just kept coming,' Samantha announced, handing him the pieces of paper.

'This is really good. I like the tone, authoritative yet not pushy, stating the facts and not embellishing things. I like the comparisons. Sam, this is great,' Jimmy told her as he speed-read the script.

'Really? I mean I've read it several times and I think it's good, but I wrote it. Do you honestly think it's good? Good enough?' Samantha enquired, looking to him for approval.

'I think it's awesome and why shouldn't it be? You've worked so hard on this,' Jimmy reminded her.

'*We've* worked so hard on it, I couldn't have done any of this without you,' Samantha spoke sincerely, and she nervously took hold of his hand.

'You could have, I just pushed you in the right direction that's all. That leads me into what happened in my morning,' Jimmy remarked with a sigh and he sat down on the sofa.

'What happened?' Samantha asked, sitting down next to him.

'More a case of *who* rather than *what* really. Dana ran off the ice again, screaming and shouting, claiming I hadn't put her down properly after a lift. She ended up facing the wrong way and skating in the opposite direction to me. I mean this is simple stuff, Sam. She's a professional ice skater and she's making these basic, basic errors. But, apparently only when she's skating with me,' Jimmy informed her.

'So, what happened?' Samantha wanted to know.

'She starts yelling at Nigel, he's the show director, telling him I'm a liability and she can't trust me, and I make her look stupid. All this is going on while the whole ensemble is trying to practice one of the group dances. Everyone can hear her, and I just wanted the ground to open up,' Jimmy explained with a sigh.

'But it isn't your fault, it's her. She keeps making the mistakes. She left a lift out of one of the dances the other night. I don't think the audience noticed, but I did. What did the director say?' Samantha asked him.

'He didn't say much, but I know he sides with her. He wasn't sure about having me on the tour, and I don't blame him. I was fresh out of rehab, this was my first skating gig since that and he was bound to have reservations – anyone would,' Jimmy spoke.

'But it's not fair, to blame you for her mistakes just because you're dealing with other things in your life. Your skating is perfect, and I know how hard you work at that,' Samantha said firmly.

'Thanks, Sam, I know. I'm not going to let it get to me. She has issues, lots of them, probably more than me – in a way I feel a little sorry for her,' Jimmy told her.

There was a knock on the dressing room door.

'Come in,' Jimmy called.

It was Felicity who appeared at the door.

'Oh good, you're here. Mr Radcliffe from the council has come to see you,' she announced, looking at Samantha.

'What?!' Samantha exclaimed, leaping up and clutching her print out of pages to her chest.

'Hey, relax. Take a breath,' Jimmy suggested, getting to his feet and taking one of her hands.

'But what's he doing here? I thought he was on sick leave. It must be serious – oh goodness,' Samantha continued to panic, her mind working overtime.

'Listen, you don't want to keep him waiting. Go and see what he has to say – it might be good news,' Jimmy encouraged, squeezing her hand.

'You think so?' Samantha asked looking at him like a frightened rabbit caught in the headlights.

'Go and see. You won't find out anything unless you go and speak to him,' Jimmy urged her.

'You're right.'

'I'm just going to chill here for a bit. Come and see me when he's gone and tell me what he said,' Jimmy said.

'OK, I will. Where is he?' Samantha questioned of Felicity as they headed for the door.

'I put him in your office,' Felicity replied.

Samantha nodded and followed Felicity out of the dressing room into the corridor.

'What did he say when he arrived? Did he say anything? How does he look? Does he look like he would look if he had good news or bad?' Samantha asked, firing the questions at her colleague.

'I don't know, he just looked normal really. Well, a bit peaky, but then he has been ill,' Felicity replied as they walked into the foyer.

'Did he have paperwork with him? A briefcase? What's he wearing? A suit?' Samantha carried on questioning.

'I don't know, I didn't really notice. Are you dating Jimmy Lloyd?' Felicity asked her as they reached the box office.

'No! No, don't be so absurd! He's a performer, it's against regulations. I was just taking something he asked for, some water and some of those little plastic cups, to his dressing room. It has to be chilled and – with ice. You know how fussy these celebrities are,' Samantha remarked, going red in the face.

'He was holding your hand,' Felicity remarked with a smirk.

'We were exchanging the water and he, er, missed the jug. Do I look OK? Is my hair tidy?' Samantha asked, smoothing her hair behind her ears and then straightening her Civic Hall jumper.

'Fine and don't worry, your secret's safe with me. I dated one of the guitarists from the Eagles tribute band last summer,' Felicity informed her.

'I wish you hadn't told me that,' Samantha replied, and she marched as confidently as she could toward her office.

★

When she opened the door, Mr Radcliffe got up from his seat to greet her. He did look peaky. He was even greyer than she remembered him, if that was possible.

'Hello, Miss Smith,' he greeted.

'Mr Radcliffe, I'm so sorry I wasn't here when you arrived, I was attending to some important business. Have you been offered a drink? May I get you one?' Samantha babbled as she knocked a lever arch file onto the floor with her elbow as she attempted to get behind her desk.

'No, no thank you, I'm fine. I will sit back down if that's OK with you. It doesn't do to stand for too long,' Mr Radcliffe said, and he gingerly lowered himself into the chair again.

'Perhaps a glass of water? Or a fruit juice? It isn't any trouble,' Samantha insisted.

'I'm fine, thank you. Why don't *you* have a seat?' Mr Radcliffe suggested to her.

There was something in the tone of his voice that made Samantha do as she was asked. Goodness, he sounded like the Grim Reaper with the worst of news, or perhaps that was just his way. He had sounded like that the first time he visited.

'I thought that Mrs Randall was looking after things in your absence,' Samantha said, picking up her pen and tapping it on the desk.

'Yes, Mrs Randall has been dealing with the majority of my workload while I've been away, but I thought it only courteous to come here in person today to tell you the outcome of last night's meeting,' Mr Radcliffe continued.

Samantha felt her chest lurch and her insides turn over. She couldn't have heard correctly. She thought he had said 'the outcome of *last night's* meeting', but that couldn't be what he said because the meeting was tonight.

'I'm sorry, what did you just say? I think, I think, I must have misheard,' Samantha spoke hurriedly, trying desperately to keep herself calm.

'We had the meeting last night to decide the fates of the Civic Hall and the Presbook Centre and–' Mr Radcliffe started.

'No, no you couldn't have, because the meeting's tonight. I spoke to Mrs Randall, I even emailed her yesterday, the meeting is tonight. I've spent a week putting a proposal together for the meeting – tonight,' Samantha stated, standing up and picking up her calendar, as if to clarify the date.

She would not have got the date wrong. She had never, ever, in her whole life got a date wrong. She bought family birthday cards at least six months in advance, every year. She even memorised the Queen's birthdays and all the bank holidays.

'Tonight is the regular council meeting but there was so much on the agenda a special meeting was convened last night to discuss this one issue,' Mr Radcliffe informed her.

'No, you can't have, because you need to hear what I have to say. I have everything all worked out,' Samantha spoke quickly, locating her files and papers for Mr Radcliffe to see.

'Miss Smith, there's no easy way to say this. The council has decided to close the Civic Hall and put the building up for sale,' Mr Radcliffe spoke sombrely.

Samantha dropped the file on her desk as she stood frozen to the spot by the news he had just delivered. Her lip began to tremble, and tears immediately pricked her eyes. This couldn't be happening, this was all wrong. It had started as a preliminary investigation a short time ago and now he was saying everything had been decided?! In this short a time?! Without telling anyone?!

'Miss Smith, this in no way reflects on you. Everyone agreed that you have been a first-class employee and during your short time in charge Mrs Randall was very impressed with the improvements you implemented at no cost. I can only admire your enthusiasm and commitment,' Mr Radcliffe continued.

'But the decision was going to take weeks, months even – everyone said so. And we have a better website now, with on-line booking and a new menu with those children's meals that come with a plastic toy. I have lots of ideas to utilise all the rooms in the week. Jane's friend, Sonya, she teaches yoga and the sports centre is getting expensive to hire and...' Samantha started, pulling out some more paperwork.

'It all came down to expansion really. The Presbook Centre has room to increase its capacity to rival the Civic Hall's and to incorporate a leisure pool. One of the most well-known supermarkets is sponsoring the improvements,'

Mr Radcliffe informed her.

'We could get sponsorship, I'm sure of it. You have to think of the history here. The Beatles performed here and T Rex. We could get one of those blue plaques put on the wall, do tours of the building with a special lunch or something. I've managed to book Air Patrol to play here next summer. Do you know Air Patrol? They've had two platinum selling albums,' Samantha gabbled as she tried to get as much information out of her mouth as quickly as possible.

'I really appreciate your efforts and of course you and your staff will be fairly remunerated in accordance with your contracts,' Mr Radcliffe told her.

'No! I don't want to be fairly remunerated! I want this hall open – I want its history protected,' Samantha spoke firmly, her whole body shaking with emotion.

'We had to look at the bigger picture. The Presbook Centre can provide a host of amenities that the Civic Hall just can't,' Mr Radcliffe attempted to explain.

'It couldn't provide an ice rink when it was needed – it wasn't big enough. I was planning public ice skating here around Christmas time,' Samantha told him.

'I'm sorry, Miss Smith, I don't really know what else I can say,' Mr Radcliffe said with an uneasy sigh.

'And what about the OAPs? How will the extended Presbook Centre cater for them? They don't do anything at discounted rates there – they don't even do shepherd's pie!' Samantha exclaimed in a shriek.

'A lot of older members of the community have expressed an interest in water aerobics,' Mr Radcliffe told her.

'Water aerobics! They chose water aerobics over the half price meals I've been serving them for years? No wonder half of them can't afford to heat their homes if they fritter their money away on water aerobics,' Samantha continued tears rolling down her face.

'Miss Smith, would you like a glass of water?' Mr Radcliffe offered.

'No! No, I don't want a glass of water. I want you to go back to the council office and tell them they've made the wrong decision. You tell them how much history there is here, you tell them about the on-line booking, the new menu and Air Patrol, tell them about Air Patrol. No, on second thoughts, you stay there. You stay right there, *I* will tell them!' Samantha spoke hysterically.

She couldn't breathe. Everything was closing in on her. Mr Radcliffe's grey face, the Wheat Dream walls of her office, the grey carpeted floor. She began gathering up files from her desk, knocking things over and hunting for things she couldn't immediately see.

'Miss Smith, I know this wasn't the news you wanted to hear, and I realise you're upset, but there really isn't anything you can do,' Mr Radcliffe spoke as kindly as he could, getting to his feet.

'I can go and see Mrs Randall and I can ask her why she didn't tell me in her email yesterday that she was about to stab me in the back!' Samantha exclaimed her breathing rapid and her emotions high.

'Miss Smith, please, I–' Mr Radcliffe began.

'Do *not* stand in my way! Not unless you want another ambulance ride to the General,' Samantha screamed, moving toward the office door.

Mr Radcliffe stepped aside and Samantha bowled out of the office, carrying half a dozen lever arch files.

'I'll be popping out for a while, Felicity – hold the fort. Oh, then again, you needn't bother,' Samantha spoke as she marched past her colleague and moved out into the main lobby.

'Samantha? Is everything OK?' Felicity called as she watched her superior moving towards the door.

Samantha didn't reply, but when she saw Jimmy entering the foyer from the corridor to the dressing rooms her resolve weakened, and she just dissolved into tears. She stood in the middle of the foyer sobbing, trying hard to keep hold of the lever arch files in her arms.

'Sam? What's happened?' Jimmy questioned as he reached her and saw her reddened eyes and tear-streaked face.

Samantha looked up at him, her mouth opening and shutting like a goldfish. Her heart was bursting, and she couldn't breathe.

'The hall – they're closing the hall,' Samantha blurted out.

And then the tears became hysterical, the sobs coming over her in waves. Her shoulders shook and she felt like someone was stamping all over her insides.

'What? I don't understand, the meeting...' Jimmy began, putting his arms around her and enveloping her away from the onlookers as she cried out loud.

'It's over, it's all over,' Samantha sobbed, burying her face into Jimmy's chest and not caring who saw her.

'Sshh, it's OK. Everything's going to be OK, I promise. Come on, let's go and get some tea,' Jimmy spoke, shepherding her over towards the restaurant.

19

Samantha sat at one of the corner tables in the restaurant. It was Mrs Machin's table. Mrs Machin and her eighty-year-old friend Miss Fipps ate toasted teacakes at that table every morning at 11.00 am. Or at least they had. Now they truly had had their last cake and eaten it. Samantha stared into space, not really seeing anything or anyone as she went over in her mind what Mr Radcliffe had told her. It was like an awful dream. It had been pretty awful before, worrying about how she was going to try and save the hall, fretting about giving the speech and how she was going to compose herself. None of that compared to how she felt now, she was just numb.

'Here, it's blackberry. It'll make you feel better,' Jimmy spoke as he joined her at the table.

He put one cup in front of Samantha and then sat down opposite her.

She was still unmoving. She felt weak, devoid of feeling, apart from the numbness, she could feel the numbness. Was it possible to feel numbness?

'What happened, Sam? What exactly did Mr Radcliffe say? What happened to tonight's meeting? Why did they reschedule without telling anyone?' Jimmy queried, trying to make sense of the situation.

'We ate there, we watched a concert there – we contributed to the decision,' Samantha muttered, thinking about the Presbook Centre.

'They chose the Presbook Centre over the Civic Hall. Well when? What about tonight?' Jimmy spoke, trying to unravel her vague sentences.

'There was another meeting, last night – a sneakily especially convened meeting. They want a leisure pool and OAPs doing synchronised swimming. They don't care about the history, they don't care about the central location – they didn't give it a chance,' Samantha stated, picking up her teacup and almost spilling the hot water over herself.

'I don't know what to say, they're wrong,' Jimmy said firmly.

'Do you know, I don't know who I was trying to kid thinking I could make a difference. After all, I'm just a box office assistant who has no life apart from this hall. Perhaps I'm going mad, perhaps no one wanted the hall saved, except me,' Samantha spoke her eyes again filling with tears.

'I don't think that's true, I really don't. I think it's got great potential,' Jimmy replied.

'Don't you mean it *had* great potential? Because that's what we should use now – the past tense,' Samantha answered.

'You can't give up,' Jimmy said immediately.

'Look, I know I'm pretty unintelligible right now, but you did hear what I said, didn't you? They are closing the hall and selling it off. In less than a year it will probably be flats,' Samantha spoke, trying to swallow the knot of emotion in her throat.

'I don't believe they can make a decision just like that. I'm sure that's not how it works,' Jimmy told her.

'You obviously don't know much about the council system around here. This is exactly how it works. One of the big supermarkets is probably getting a plot of land for a superstore in exchange for paying for the improvements to the Presbook Centre. I don't know why I even thought there was a chance of keeping the hall open,' Samantha continued.

'Because you were led to believe there *was* a chance. I think what they've done is wrong on so many levels,' Jimmy spoke with a shake of his head.

'Well, wrong or not, they've done it,' Samantha told him.

'Is there still a meeting tonight?' Jimmy asked her.

'Yes, but apparently just a routine monthly meeting. Probably to discuss their big, fat bonuses now they don't have the Civic Hall to fund,' Samantha spoke, sipping at her tea.

'Then you're going to go and you're going to tell them what a huge mistake they're making, and they are going to listen to your proposals, just like they promised they would,' Jimmy said seriously.

'What's the point? I'm half-expecting the estate agent to arrive at any second and start measuring up,' Samantha replied her emotions moving from distraught to angry.

'The point is they didn't give you a fair chance. You're probably right, all this was a foregone conclusion and that's wrong. You need to go to that meeting, and you need to tell them everything you were going to tell them before today,' Jimmy told her.

'But they've made their decision,' Samantha reminded.

'Then they need to be made to realise they made the wrong one,' Jimmy answered her.

He reached across the table and took hold of her hands, squeezing them supportively.

'How can you be so positive? This is just about the end of my life,' Samantha stated with a sigh of despondency.

'Don't say that. This isn't the end of anything. It's just a setback that's all,' Jimmy insisted, holding onto her hands.

*

They had been given two weeks. Two weeks until the ice show came to an end and the Civic Hall closed its doors for the very last time. Acts would have to be cancelled, refunds would have to be sent and before all of that, Samantha had to tell the staff. She shivered when she thought about that, most of the employees were the main wage earners in their households, they would struggle and have to find alternative employment in a difficult time. She would be as popular as a mobile fish and chip van outside a Slimming World meeting.

She had read and re-read the letter Mr Radcliffe had left on her desk confirming what he had told her and countless times of reading it did nothing to change its contents.

How could she cope without the Civic Hall? It was everything to her. It was where she felt close to normal and it was where Jimmy had kissed her…

Now all she faced was complete uncertainty in every area of her life. In a fortnight the ice show would move on to the other end of the country and what would happen then? She hadn't even thought about the fact she was getting involved with someone who had his home in America and was currently travelling around Britain, staying at a different place every few weeks.

And then there was Cleo. She actually believed her about Jeremy being the love of her life no matter how implausible it sounded. She was therefore on borrowed time with the house too, unless she gave in and could cope with another housemate. Could she put up with falling over his brogues every five minutes and having them shagging in every room of the house whenever the urge took them? She didn't want to think about that, but she would definitely have to double her dose of Domestos on the surfaces.

*

That evening the Civic Hall seemed ironically busier than ever. The majority of the tables in the restaurant were full and there were scores of people in the bar area and more heading that way from the foyer.

She gazed around the room, letting each and every piece of décor, and every nook and cranny, sink into her, knowing it was all a matter of a few short weeks before she would never set eyes on any of it again. And there were the posters, the one advertising Jethro, the pantomime that would never happen, *Ballet for All Seasons*. It brought a lump to her throat again and she swallowed it down.

She had only been home briefly to change. Cleo had been having telephone sex in the kitchen when Samantha came in and was still having it when she popped her head around the door to announce she was going again. Her sister had just nodded and turned her back on her, continuing to whisper suggestive things into the mouthpiece. There had been no opportunity to tell her about the hall and Samantha was glad really. She had cried so much already her eyes were swollen like a boxer who had managed ten rounds against someone much better.

She had dripped hot, wet tears into Gobby's fur when she had served him up more macaroni cheese before the doors opened for the evening performance. Where would he go? Who would ensure he got his unorthodox, but balanced diet of meat, vegetables and carbohydrates? She couldn't have him at the house, Cleo hated animals. Their parents had a budgie and it used to whistle whenever Cleo walked into the room. She hated it, said it smelt and refused to take a turn feeding it or cleaning the cage. Their next pet was Bodie, a Yorkshire terrier and for a while Cleo enjoyed putting bows and bobbles in its hair, but the Alice band was one step too far and it bit her. Needless to say, she made such a fuss about the little nip on her hand and accused the animal of being somehow related to the Rottweiler line and an accident waiting to happen. He was quickly dispatched to the vets to be put down. They didn't have any more pets after that.

She clutched the file she was holding to her chest. She was dressed in her funeral suit, under the circumstances it was entirely appropriate.

It was almost 7.00 pm and her taxi was late. She checked her watch again and then looked back towards the bar area. People were having a wonderful time, unaware that the entertainment centre they were laughing and joking in was set to close forever.

Then the doors at the side of the room swung open and Jimmy came rushing out of them. He was wearing costume and skates and he hurried over to her.

'I'm so glad you're still here, I thought I'd miss you. I got held up, another row with Dana,' Jimmy stated, taking her hands as she stood up to greet him.

'My taxi's late and I'm starting to have second thoughts about doing this,' Samantha admitted with a sigh.

'No, don't do that. You're doing the right thing, the only thing. You mustn't give up without a fight,' Jimmy told her.

'But I know what's going to happen. I'm going to get there, I'm going to either back out before I've begun or I'm going to begin, throw up all over someone and be escorted from the building,' Samantha told him.

'And looking on the positive side, if that happens then make sure you barf all over Mrs Randall, the sly witch,' Jimmy suggested with a grin.

'This isn't funny,' Samantha reminded him.

'Excuse me, could we have an autograph and a picture?' a woman asked as a group of them sidled up to Jimmy and Samantha.

'Yes, sure, just give me a minute, Sam...' Jimmy began.

'It's OK, I'll go and wait outside. I'm sure the taxi won't be long, I did pre-book,' Samantha said, still clutching her folder.

'Well, come back here straight after the meeting and let me know how it goes. I'll be thinking about you,' Jimmy told her, and he kissed her softly on the lips.

The group of women made a *woo-ing* noise at his show of affection and Samantha turned crimson with embarrassment and hastened towards the exit.

★

The taxi arrived, almost fifteen minutes late. Thankfully Samantha had planned for any eventuality. All through the ten-minute ride to the council offices she went through every emotion possible. She went from sad, feeling like someone had died, to mad, feeling like the Incredible Hulk with rage that would burst the sleeves of her suit. She kept telling herself she was going to make this stand for the community of the borough, but was that really why she was doing it? Or was it just to save her job and her safe haven? She didn't have time to worry about that now.

Before she knew it, she had arrived.

The Borough Council offices were in a rather shabby 1970s building squeezed in between Bridal Fantasies, a low price wedding dress shop specialising in alternative gowns, including the red leather PVC gown on the mannequin in the window and an oriental food shop that sold all manner of dried things, most of them a really bizarre shape.

Samantha took a deep breath and pushed on the front door. To her horror it was locked! She hadn't considered that possibility. She had just assumed it would be open. The lights were on in the building, obviously because of the meeting, but she had no way of getting to it. That was it, it was over, just like that. All that build up and nothing. It was a stupid idea anyway, they wouldn't be interested in listening to her, they had made their decision.

'*Miaow!*'

It was a familiar sound, instantly recognisable. Samantha turned around and there was Gobby sat behind her on the street, looking at her.

'Gobby, what are you doing here? This is too far from the hall. It's miles – how did you get here?' Samantha asked him, bending down as the cat ran towards her.

Gobby licked her hand and rubbed his face against her knee, purring and nuzzling.

'You should go back to the hall or to wherever you sleep at night. There's nothing for you here – there's nothing for me here either,' Samantha responded with a sigh.

Gobby miaowed loudly and ran up to the council offices, pawing at the front door.

'It's locked, I can't get in,' Samantha said, cuddling her file to her body.

Gobby continued scratching and started to make an insistent howling type noise.

'Gobby, stop it,' Samantha told him.

He mewed louder and scratched even more, and Samantha wondered what she should do. Perhaps Gobby was as perceptive as she always thought he was. Maybe he knew what was going on and couldn't face losing his favourite feeding spot. Perhaps this was his protest, or maybe it was a wake-up call for her.

Jimmy wouldn't let a locked door stop him making his voice heard. She had to make a stand. She had to try no matter what the final outcome.

She walked over to the alleyway between the offices and the wedding dress shop and found the biggest thing she could.

★

She charged at the glass door with the naked, armless mannequin. The first two attempts had no effect. On the third attempt one of the legs fell off, but on the fourth try the head impacted on the glass at exactly the right point and it finally shattered. She dropped the plastic woman, picked up her lever arch file and opened the door.

Once inside, she followed the trail of lights until she stood outside the room where the council meeting was being held. It was like being outside the head teacher's office at school. She had only been there on one occasion when she had hit Mary Kennedy in the eye with a conker. It had been a perfectly executed manoeuvre, although she had never admitted to that.

She could hear the discussions, people talking in turns and then she heard laughter. Loud laughter, like a hundred clowns guffawing all at once. It set her teeth on edge, especially when she recognised it was Mrs Randall's laughter. The posh, fake-sounding laugh she probably practiced at coffee mornings with the bridge club. Samantha felt the hairs on the back of her neck stand up and a furious feeling deep in her gut propelled her forward.

She opened the door forcefully and stepped into the room, her head held high. There were fourteen people present, including Mrs Randall and Mr Radcliffe, sat in a semi-circle formation, behind desks. At the sound of the door banging open, all discussion halted, and all eyes turned to face Samantha.

'Good evening everyone, my name's Samantha Smith. I am the manager of Woolston Civic Hall and I was invited here tonight to tell you about my proposals for the hall's future,' she spoke loudly and clearly, moving towards the group and removing a sheaf of paper from her folder.

Every one of the councillors was staring at her, as if wondering what was going on.

'Er, Miss Smith, I was under the impression that Mr

Radcliffe came to see you today to tell you we held the decision-making meeting last night and that...' Mrs Randall began.

She looked like a typical 'retirement isn't enough for me and I want to serve my local community' councillor. She had blue/grey hair carefully rollered into position and huge silver glasses on her face. She was wearing a tweed jacket and a set of pearls around her wrinkled neck. She looked like a cross between someone's mad old aunt and a judge at a gymkhana.

'Here is a five-year plan for the Civic Hall that details how we can make several fundamental changes to its operation that will increase profit. And this will be achieved with no initial outlay,' Samantha continued.

She completely ignored the fact that Mrs Randall had spoken and started handing out individual copies of her proposal.

'Miss Smith, please – I did discuss the decision with you today and I left you a letter explaining why that conclusion was reached. I think...' Mr Radcliffe began, rising to his feet.

'Mrs Randall kindly invited me here, *tonight*, to tell you all a little about the improvements I've made at the Civic Hall, since I took on the role of manager, and to put forward my suggestions for the future. So, where do I start? Perhaps with the restaurant? Yes, let's start with the restaurant,' Samantha carried on, pacing up and down in front of the councillors, looking at her file every now and then to ensure she got her speech in the right order.

'Miss Smith, this is pointless. A decision has been made. I'm sorry it wasn't in your favour, but this was a decision agreed and passed unanimously,' Mrs Randall told her, removing her big spectacles.

'We have scaled the restaurant down. We are now providing fast food at reasonable prices with two healthier options, two vegetarian alternatives and children's meals. This should ensure a quicker turnover on tables and more customers through the door. However, we are keeping traditional meals and light bites on the menu for lunchtimes when the restaurant usually does well with the senior members of the community,' Samantha carried on, her heart thumping in her chest.

'Mike, she needs to be removed,' Mrs Randall spoke to one of her fellow councillors, putting her glasses down onto the table.

'On-line booking. We have introduced a comprehensive website that's very informative and on-line booking has already proved extremely popular,' Samantha carried on, as the largest, most burly of the male councillors stood up and motioned towards her.

He had a beard and a beer gut and looked like he should play professional darts. He also looked like he could probably lift her up with one hand.

'It's time to go, Miss Smith. I'm sure your proposals would have been of interest, if the decision hadn't already been made – as I keep stating,' Mrs Randall repeated herself sternly.

'Don't you dare touch me! I'm not finished, and you will sit here, and you will listen to what I've got to say!' Samantha exclaimed as she shrugged off the advances of the bearded official.

'Miss Smith, I do realise how you feel, but all this is only making the situation worse,' Mr Radcliffe spoke calmly, and he gave her a creepy little smile from his grey face.

'I don't think you understand – any of you. The situation couldn't get any worse, not just for me, but for the all the other Civic Hall employees too. I have to tell them all about this, I have to tell them they are going to be out of a job. Jane with her dependent mother, Karen whose husband got made redundant last year, Felicity with her string of useless, weird boyfriends, I'm asking you, I am *begging* you to reconsider. Look at my proposal, go onto the website, come down and visit the hall – you'll see how much it's changed in only a week – just imagine what could change in a month or two,' Samantha said hurriedly, rattling the words out as fast as she could as Mike descended on her.

'I say again, I am sure the proposal is excellent, but the provision will be given to the Presbook Centre. Go home, Miss Smith, there's nothing more you can do here,' Mrs Randall spoke, narrowing her eyes at Samantha.

'I don't believe that's true! I *won't* believe that's true! Read my proposal, change your mind. You have the power to change the decision,' Samantha told them.

'Mike! Will you please remove her! We've wasted too much time on this already, she needs to go now!' Mrs Randall yelled, rising to her feet.

'I've told you, I'm not going anywhere! Not until you've read my proposal. No decision is so etched in stone that you can't go back on it! Please, give the hall a chance, give *me* a chance!' Samantha exclaimed, backing towards the door as the burly councillor again attempted to close in on her.

'Miss Smith, if you do not leave, we will have you removed! I won't have this behaviour at a council meeting!'

Mrs Randall barked.

'How many times do I have to say this?! I am not going anywhere – and if it's really come to this, *you're* not going anywhere either,' Samantha announced as she got to the door, holding off Mike with her left arm.

In one quick move, Samantha turned around, locked the door, took out the key and theatrically put it into her mouth and swallowed.

'Now, are you all sitting comfortably? Has everyone got a copy of the proposal?' Samantha asked, looking at the councillors calmly and trying to ignore the feeling of hard metal slithering down her throat.

'Oh, good God! Call the police! Someone call the police!' Mrs Randall screamed hysterically.

20

Strangely, it wasn't the first time Samantha had been in a police car. In year eight her class had been shown around the local police station, locked in a cell and been allowed to sit in a patrol car with the siren on. It had made such a terrible noise it had made her sick.

There was no siren tonight, just Samantha, Gobby and PCs Dunbar and Davis. Samantha didn't feel quite herself. It hadn't really gone to plan. Perhaps naively she had thought they would listen to her and realise their error. Swallowing the door key hadn't really been on her agenda either and it meant she now had two repair bills to settle – thanks to CCTV outside the offices that caught her determined entrance, and the police battering ram on the door inside. Still, the good news was she hadn't been formally arrested, just removed from the council offices and given a ride.

Gobby was purring contentedly on her lap. He had been waiting outside the offices when the officers had escorted Samantha to the patrol car. He had hissed and howled and snagged PC Davis' trousers.

'Are you sure you wouldn't rather go home, Miss Smith?' PC Dunbar asked her as the patrol car pulled up outside the Civic Hall.

'No, thank you – this is kind of home for me. At least it was,' Samantha remarked with a sigh.

'Cheer up, the councillor said they wouldn't press charges providing the damage is paid for,' PC Dunbar reminded her.

'That'll be two new doors and keys I guess,' Samantha spoke her stomach contracting as if it could feel the alien metal swimming around.

'I would have thought so,' PC Davis remarked.

'Well, sorry about all the trouble and everything. And your trousers – Gobby isn't usually like that. He's just been under a lot of stress lately,' Samantha spoke, opening the door of the car with one hand and cradling Gobby with the other.

'Goodnight,' PC Dunbar called as Samantha left the car.

She stood outside the hall, Gobby in her arms and looked up at the sign, the coat of arms on either side of the lettering. What cruel irony that while she and Jimmy were sharing their first kiss in the place she loved so much, the council had been putting the final nail in its coffin.

She put Gobby down and ruffled the fur on top of his head.

'Thanks for trying to help, Gobby. I'm sorry I couldn't save it,' Samantha spoke, tears welling in her eyes as the cat looked back at her with his large eyes and all-knowing expression.

'But you promise me you'll go and hang out at Charlotte's Bistro now. She has fish on the menu, three different types and all the other things you like,' Samantha said, swallowing a lump in her throat.

Gobby let out a mew of appreciation and licked his lips.

She took a deep breath and pushed open the front doors.

The bar and restaurant were virtually empty. She checked her watch and realised the ice show must still be going on, well into its second half. She entered the auditorium and saw Felicity by the nearest fire exit. She hurried over to join her.

'Hello, is everything OK? Any problems?' Samantha asked her in whispered tones.

'No, everything's fine, sold out of Berry Fruits tonight so we must be under the thousand mark. Things not so good on the ice though,' Felicity remarked.

'Oh no, not another fall! Who was it? Not Dana,' Samantha enquired.

'No, no fall – more like a falling out. Your Jimmy has quit the show, minutes before curtain up,' Felicity informed her.

'What? No, that can't be right. I mean I saw him, tonight, right before I left. He was in costume and everything,' Samantha spoke hurriedly, panic in her chest as she tried to digest the information.

'Mmm, he was in costume when he was shouting and bawling at the show director that Nigel Fancy Pants or whatever his name is – the one who walks around thinking he owns the place, wearing cashmere cardigans. I was taking the refreshments to the dressing rooms when it all kicked off,' Felicity carried on.

'Well, what was said? What was the argument about? And where is he? Is he really not skating? Who's dancing with Dana?' Samantha babbled desperate for answers to all her questions.

'Some Russian bloke, Andrei someone. I don't think the audience were too happy Jimmy wasn't performing tonight.

I don't know what the row was about, I came in in the middle of it, but they were definitely not happy bunnies. In the end, before I even had a chance to put the juice cups down, Jimmy left – stormed out – nearly took the door off its hinges,' Felicity informed her.

'Well, where is he? Did he leave the hall?' Samantha questioned.

'I don't know, I've been seeing to things here. I'm glad you're back, we could really do with an extra pair of hands,' Felicity spoke.

There was no reply and when Felicity turned around it was to see Samantha fleeing the auditorium at breakneck pace.

She ran out onto the main thoroughfare, traffic flashing past her as she jumped up and down waving her hands in the air. What had the row been about? Why wasn't Jimmy skating? Had Dana been stirring things again?

She managed to hail a taxi and directed it to the Metropole Hotel. She knew that was where the skaters were staying, and she even knew Jimmy's room number. Being able to remember everything you had ever seen and everything you had ever been told definitely came in handy sometimes.

She paid the driver, dropped her bag on the floor, and fell up the steps of the hotel. Ignoring the scrape on her leg, she hurried into the lobby and scanned the signs for directions to the rooms. It was four flights up and there was an 'out of order' notice on the lift.

By the time she got outside the door of his room she was gasping for breath, exhausted by both exertion and emotion.

She took a deep breath and tried to compose herself. She

pushed her hair back behind her ears and straightened her jacket. She then knocked on the door and waited. There was no response.

'Jimmy! It's Sam, open the door,' she called.

There was sound of movement inside the room, someone getting to their feet and moving across the floor, and then the door opened. Samantha let out a gasp.

Jimmy looked like she had never seen him before. He was pale, his eyes looked red and sore and his whole demeanour was of someone who had been wrung out and stamped all over. His hair was tousled, his shoulders were hunched, and he barely acknowledged her.

She didn't know what to say. He looked dreadful. He stepped back into the room without a word and she followed him, closing the door behind her. She immediately noticed a half-packed suitcase on the bed and a vodka bottle on the coffee table.

'What's happened, Jimmy? And what is *this*?' Samantha exclaimed and she picked up the bottle of vodka.

'I haven't drunk any of it,' Jimmy stated straightaway as he sat down on the edge of the bed and put his head in his hands with a sigh.

'Then what's it doing here? Where did it come from? They don't have them that size in a mini-bar,' Samantha questioned frantically.

'I bought it,' he admitted.

'Why?'

'Because I thought I wanted to drink it – I don't,' Jimmy responded, still not looking at her.

'Well, good, that's really good, because that means there's all the more for me. Cheers! Bottoms up!' Samantha spoke and she undid the lid of the bottle, put it to her lips and took a large swig.

'Sam, what are you doing? Put the bottle down,' Jimmy said as he looked up to watch her downing the neat alcohol.

'Why? I've nothing left to lose, may as well have a commiseration drink to help wash the misery down. Maybe it will make it easier to swallow, maybe it will numb the pain. Is that what it does, Jimmy? Does it numb things? Make them go away for a little bit?' Samantha asked him, glugging back the clear fluid.

'Yes, for a bit, but it doesn't work, the pain comes back. Come on Sam, you don't need that. Give it here, I'll pour it away,' Jimmy told her, standing up and going over to her.

'Going somewhere?' Samantha questioned, pointing at the suitcase and then again putting the vodka bottle to her mouth.

This was good, the alcohol was making her feel nice and warm.

'I don't know, maybe. I quit the show,' Jimmy told her as he watched her pace up and down the room gorging on the booze.

'Yes! So I hear! Want to fill me in on that, do you? Before you pack up and ship off?' Samantha asked the alcohol and despondency mixing lethally as she talked. She pulled at one of the velvet curtains and picked up a room service menu.

'Please put the bottle down,' Jimmy urged her.

'I want to know what happened at the show. So far, I only have Felicity's version and she told me you almost broke a dressing room door. If only you knew how significant doors were for me tonight,' Samantha spoke hysterically.

Her eyes were wide, and she was holding onto the bottle

as if it were the most precious object she owned.

'Oh, it's all bullshit! I try and change, I try and make things better and I just get shit from everyone,' Jimmy exclaimed angrily.

'And a proper explanation?' Samantha asked, drinking more and feeling super confident.

'Someone set me up. After I met you in the foyer, I went back to my dressing room and Dana and Nigel were in there, looking at my drink bottle. I ask them what's going on and Nigel says he has reason to believe there's alcohol in my drink. I say "no way it's just an energy drink, nothing more" but when I tell him to taste it and he does, it's laced with whiskey,' Jimmy told her.

'Keep going,' Samantha spoke, sitting down on the bed and drinking more vodka.

'Well, before I even say anything to explain, not that I have an explanation because I have no idea how it got in there, he starts yelling, sounding off that I've broken the terms of our agreement. He tells me how disappointed he is in me and how when everyone in the industry was telling him not to take a chance on me, he put his reputation on the line for me. I try and interrupt, I manage to get out that there must be a mistake, that the drink isn't mine, well not the alcohol part anyway, and he just doesn't listen. He stands there and he shakes his head and says I'm out,' Jimmy explained.

'So, what did you do?' Samantha enquired still sucking the vodka as if it were life dependent fluid.

'I left. He didn't want to hear what I had to say, he didn't believe me, and he'd already made up his mind and condemned me,' Jimmy told her.

'What?! So you didn't fight? You didn't stand there and make him listen?' Samantha exclaimed, passing the vodka bottle from hand to hand as if it were a rugby ball.

'What's the point? I knew this show was my last chance. He believed I'd been drinking, I could see it in his face, he *really* believed it. And to be honest I don't blame him. I mean why should he consider the word of an alcoholic who's been lying about things for most of his life?' Jimmy continued.

'A *reformed* alcoholic! Someone who doesn't deny the things he did in the past but someone who's trying hard to move on from it. That's the person I thought you were, but then what would I know? I'm the sort of person who fails at everything she tries – that's when she plucks up the courage to bother to try at all,' Samantha spoke as she downed more vodka.

'With some people you just run out of chances and that's that,' Jimmy told her.

'So, if that's how you feel, what was that pep talk you gave me tonight all about? You said I mustn't give up without a fight and you've done exactly that. You know it wasn't your drink and yet you've shrugged your shoulders and walked away, leaving everyone to think the worst of you. Is that what you want?' Samantha blasted at him.

'Of course it isn't,' Jimmy answered.

'Then fight! Take some of your own advice. Go back to the hall, tell Nigel it wasn't your drink and keep on telling him until he believes it!' Samantha ordered him, gulping down more of the bottle.

'I don't know. I don't know if I can face him again. I don't know if I can face anyone again,' Jimmy spoke quietly.

'No, I don't know either really. I'm talking rubbish, aren't I?! And talking a lot! Perhaps the most I've ever talked, maybe alcohol really works for me. I'm not gasping for breath, I'm not laughing or coughing. In fact, this is great!' Samantha slurred with a tipsy smile.

'I think maybe you've had enough,' Jimmy said, attempting to take the bottle from her as he came to sit next to her.

'Enough of what? Vodka or life? Do you know what I did tonight? Thanks for asking by the way. While you were throwing away your skating career, I was holding the members of Woolston Borough Council hostage. Yes! Me! Holding people hostage like an Al-Qaeda operative! Can you believe it? I broke a door down with a bridal mannequin and then I locked us all in and swallowed the key so they'd have to listen to my proposal. And did they? Well not really, they briefly paid me lip service and then the police turned up. I had a ride back to the Civic Hall in a patrol car,' Samantha informed him.

'Sam, I'm sorry, I didn't even ask, I...' Jimmy started about to put his arm around her.

Samantha stood up and walked away from him.

'No, you didn't ask. So, let me tell you, if you think you've had it rough tonight then think again, because I have had it infinitely worse. And, after all that Jim, after the failed attempt to change their minds, the key and the cops, I get here and find you staring at a bottle of booze with your bags packed. Last night you told me you liked me and tonight you're ready to leave – I must be some kisser,' Samantha continued to babble.

'Sam, this has nothing to do with you,' Jimmy insisted.

'Nothing to do with me! Well, that's just great, that makes me feel really special,' Samantha replied, finally loosening her grip on the vodka and putting it down on the table with a bang.

'I didn't mean that how it sounded. What I meant was, that how I feel right now isn't to do with you or with us. You're my only reason to stick around right now,' Jimmy spoke.

'You don't want me! Look at me! I'm a mess! I've got no job, I've got no personality, I've got a crazy sister who got all of the good genes and at the moment I'm seriously wondering whether it was entirely sensible to swallow a door key,' Samantha announced, clutching at her stomach.

'I do want you, Sam, I just don't want to hurt you. Although that alcohol in my drink wasn't mine, what was the first thing I did when I was hurt and angry? I went and bought a bottle of vodka and, OK I didn't drink it, but for a few moments I really wanted to. If anyone's a mess here then it's me,' Jimmy spoke.

'But you're trying and you're moving on,' Samantha spoke, her stomach making her shift uncomfortably on the spot.

'I want to make it work. I want to make it work with us,' Jimmy stated sincerely.

'I want to be sick,' Samantha exclaimed, and she rushed from the bedroom into the en suite bathroom.

She vomited. All the vodka and everything she had eaten that day. And then she began to wretch again and cough and choke, holding her throat and gasping for air. Jimmy rushed to her aid and thumped her hard on the back. The council office key shot out of her mouth, hit the sink and landed with a clatter on the tiled floor.

Samantha took a deep breath and looked up at Jimmy who was standing over her, holding her shoulders and rubbing her back.

'Sorry,' she spoke weakly and then passed out.

*

The next thing she knew a large tub of Berry Fruits ice cream was on stage, presenting Mr Radcliffe to the applauding audience. But it wasn't Mr Radcliffe as he normally appeared, thin and grey, it was Mr Radcliffe's head on Dave's rotund body with Mrs Randall's coiffured crop. And then the image changed, and it wasn't Mrs Randall's hair she could see, but the lovely tawny brown, spiky hair that complemented the chocolate eyes so perfectly. Samantha opened her eyes and quickly saw that it wasn't a dream. The owner of the hair and eyes was looking down at her and she was led on a bed.

'Hey,' Jimmy greeted.

'My throat's sore,' Samantha croaked as she tried to sit up.

'I think that was probably the key. It might be a good idea to go to the emergency room, there might be damage,' Jimmy spoke, helping her to sit up and prop herself up on the pillows.

'The key! Oh no, the key,' Samantha remarked, suddenly remembering the events of the evening.

'Yeah, the key. We should get you checked out,' Jimmy spoke.

'No, I'm fine, I don't want to make a fuss and I...' Samantha began.

'You're scared of hospitals,' Jimmy finished off for her.

'Yes,' Samantha admitted with a sniff.

'Well, let's try the king of all cures. I've made some tea,' Jimmy told her, and he got off the bed to go to the table.

'What happened to my hair, it's damp and it smells,' Samantha said, trying to look at it and smelling.

'You were sick, your throat is sore – the key,' Jimmy recapped for her as he brought the tea over.

'Oh goodness, I was sick? Oh no, I'm sorry, I...' Samantha began as she flushed with embarrassment.

'It's OK, you apologised already. Just before you passed out,' Jimmy said, handing her a cup of tea.

'Oh no, the vodka – I drank the vodka. Where *is* the vodka?' Samantha said, clamping her hands to her mouth in shame.

'I poured it away,' Jimmy assured her.

'You poured it away?' She wanted to believe him.

'I swear,' Jimmy told her. 'It's gone.'

'Goodness, what was I thinking of?' Samantha asked him as she accepted the cup.

'You've been under a lot of pressure,' Jimmy stated.

'Oh no, the hall! They're closing the hall and they're building a swimming pool at the Presbook Centre,' Samantha spoke as a feeling of panic and upset suddenly overwhelmed her like a wave breaking at the height of the crest.

'Yeah, the hall,' Jimmy said with a shake of his head.

'And the skating show, you're leaving the show and – hold on, you were packing – there was a suitcase,' Samantha remembered, and she looked around the room for evidence to back up her memory.

'I've put it away and everything is back in the closet,' Jimmy informed her.

'You're not going to leave?' Samantha queried.

'Not before I've had a chance to speak to Nigel and put my case forward. You were right, I've gone through too much to carry on running away. Yes, I'm an alcoholic but I am recovering, and I don't deserve people jumping to assumptions without proof,' Jimmy told her.

'And I said all that? Goodness, I must have drunk a lot of vodka,' Samantha said with a sigh.

'So, tomorrow, I'm going to speak to Nigel and I'm going to make him listen to me,' Jimmy spoke.

'What about tonight? Can't you speak to him tonight? You could call him and...' Samantha began.

'Sam it's two thirty in the morning,' Jimmy informed her.

'What?! It can't be! I mean, I got here before ten I'm sure I did. The show was still going on and...' Samantha exclaimed, checking her watch.

'You slept for quite a while after the being sick thing,' Jimmy spoke.

'Oh,' Samantha remarked, again flushing with the shame of it.

What must he think of her? Getting pissed and puking everywhere was something Cleo did, not her.

Jimmy took hold of her hand and softly stroked each finger as if it were the most delicate thing he had ever held. Samantha swallowed, his touch disturbing her in the most enjoyable of ways. She was barely able to breathe.

'But you should know that I didn't put away the luggage because of Nigel or for the ice show. I unpacked it for you,' Jimmy told her.

Samantha looked at him, watching him take a nervous breath.

'I put it all away again because I'm falling in love with you,' Jimmy told her.

He was holding her hand so softly and Samantha watched the rapid rise and fall of his chest. She looked up at him, taking in the sincerity of his expression and all she wanted to do was hold him. Slowly, with a trembling hand, she reached out to touch his face, caressing his cheek and running the tips of her fingers over his lips and the scar below. She saw him close his eyes and felt him kiss her fingers gently, slowly, sensually. Her heart was hammering like it was ready to burst but, despite everything that had happened that night, despite feeling really unwell and probably having a Yale imprint on the inside of her throat, there was no doubt in her mind that this was her moment. She couldn't quantify what she felt for him and she had difficulty speaking it. She would just have to try to express it. She kissed him firmly, passionately, not wanting to leave time to think or analyse. He kissed her back and ran his hands through her hair, full of desire, yet lovingly, full of consideration. Carefully, he lowered her down onto the bed and sat astride her, looking at her as if he was drinking in every part of her. Samantha reached up and pulled his sweatshirt up and over his head. He helped her take it off and discarded it. She admired his torso, ran her hand across his smooth chest, his stomach and then stopped at the belt of his jeans.

Jimmy took hold of her hand and moved it back onto his chest. She could feel his heart racing.

Samantha put her hand back onto the buckle of his belt and tugged at the leather strap.

'Sam,' Jimmy began his voice faltering.

'Sshh,' Samantha ordered as she began to slowly unbutton his jeans.

Needing no further persuasion, he removed her top and began to kiss her every part. Samantha shivered at the sensation of his mouth and held him tightly to her. She was about to lose her virginity to Jimmy Lloyd, an alcoholic ice skater, with vodka on her breath and sick in her hair. Yet somehow it couldn't have been more perfect.

21

'I like black and white films, the really cheesy ones with singing and dancing and pretty actresses with operatic voices,' Samantha stated with a laugh and she leaned over on her side and kissed Jimmy on the mouth.

'No way! Like Fred Astaire and Ginger Rogers doing all those corny routines,' Jimmy said, rolling his eyes.

'Yes! Exactly like that and I'll thank you not to mock or I won't tell you anything else,' Samantha replied, moving a little away from him.

'OK, OK, I'm sorry, come back,' Jimmy urged, and he put a strong arm around her and pulled her back towards him.

'It's your turn,' Samantha told him.

'OK, I like action movies and I'm ever so slightly scared of spiders, but don't tell anyone. That's two things, two kisses, right here,' Jimmy said pointing at his mouth.

'Well I like tuna and mayo sandwiches and I can only use one particular brand of toothpaste because the others bring me out in a rash. Now that has to be worth three at least,' Samantha told him.

'Uh huh, I knew about the tuna mayo but as this game is win/win, go ahead,' Jimmy replied, waiting for her to kiss him.

Samantha smiled and kissed his lips, brushing his hair off his face as she did so. She looked at him, his eyes closed, looking so perfect. She wondered if she should…

'I was a virgin,' she blurted out.

'So was I once,' he answered, opening his eyes and taking hold of her hands.

'No, I mean I was a virgin, until now – until tonight – with you,' Samantha spoke nervously her face reddening all the time.

'I know what you meant,' Jimmy replied, giving her hand a squeeze.

'Does it matter to you? I mean, I don't know what you – well the thing is – Cleo says that…' Samantha began to gabble.

Jimmy put a finger over her lips.

'Sshh, I really don't want to hear Cleo's philosophy on virgins, I think it would probably scare me,' Jimmy told her.

Samantha didn't respond.

'Does it matter to you that I can't remember some of the women I've slept with?' Jimmy enquired.

'I expect you were drinking. I mean if you hadn't been drinking you would've remembered – wouldn't you?' Samantha asked him.

'I'd like to think so,' he replied.

'Well, I just thought I would tell you,' Samantha responded nervously.

'Hey, I'm glad you did. *And* you told me without having a panic attack – things are getting better already,' Jimmy answered, pulling her closer to him and wrapping his arms around her.

Samantha smiled and closed her eyes, enjoying the feeling

of security. She felt safe and comfortable and looked after. She wanted to feel that way forever.

'I don't want tonight to end or tomorrow to start,' Samantha admitted, enjoying having his naked body next to hers.

'Tomorrow will be OK,' Jimmy told her.

'I have to tell the staff they're going to be out of a job. I have to apologise to the council for holding them hostage and pay the repair bill for the doors. Then I have to face the prospect of living my life without the Civic Hall,' Samantha spoke with a sigh.

'Don't give up hope just yet,' Jimmy replied, stroking her hair.

'They aren't going to change their minds. Believe me, they made that very clear,' Samantha spoke.

She immediately began having a flashback to earlier when Mrs Randall was baring her teeth at her and Mike, the burly, bearded councillor she had kneed in the balls when he had got too close, had ceremoniously ripped up his copy of her proposal.

'Stranger things have happened,' Jimmy said.

'I'm way ahead of you. I've already thought about torching the Presbook Centre but talked myself out of it. I don't want a reputation with the local police, it would kill my mother,' Samantha answered.

'I just hope I get to talk to Nigel before Dana or someone else from the show sells me out to the press,' Jimmy told her with a heavy sigh.

Samantha felt for his hand and interlinked it with hers.

'I used to lie about being able to do long division and I own a Barry Manilow record,' she spoke and she turned to kiss him again.

'Barry Manilow! Now, that bothers me way more than the black and white films!' Jimmy exclaimed, moving away from her slightly.

'Well, when you told me you eat lemons, I did think it was a bit freaky, but I was kind and smiled and pretended that was normal. You don't have an S Club 7 CD, do you?' Samantha enquired.

'S Club 7?' Jimmy questioned, as if not knowing what she was talking about.

'Good answer,' Samantha replied with a smile.

'I want to know everything about you Samantha Smith,' Jimmy told her as he rolled over on top of her.

'Well, we'll see. You know I'm not much of a sharer,' Samantha replied, reaching up and putting her hands on his shoulders.

'But you're willing to try?'

'Put it this way, you know more about me than anyone else on the planet – even Cleo,' Samantha spoke.

'That's some accolade,' Jimmy said, smiling down at her.

'Oh! Oh, my goodness! I've just remembered something,' Samantha exclaimed, removing her hands from his body and putting them to her mouth.

'What is it?' Jimmy asked.

'Yesterday, before Mr Radcliffe arrived, when I came to see you in your dressing room, Dana was in there. She had hold of one of your bottles, I'm sure of it,' Samantha told him as she thought back.

'Well, I had kind of figured it was her. She's the only one who hates me enough to want to do this. That and the fact she witnessed the whole argument with Nigel and couldn't keep the smug look off her face,' Jimmy answered.

'But if I tell Nigel I saw her with the bottle then he'll believe you and you can go back to the show and *she'll* be kicked out,' Samantha spoke cheerily.

'It might help, but you have to understand that there's no one better than Dana at getting her own way,' Jimmy replied.

'But he'll have to listen to you now. I mean, it's obvious, I saw her with one of your drinks – it was her,' Samantha said hopefully.

'Let's not worry about it now, it's five a.m. Let's try and get a few hours' sleep,' Jimmy suggested, kissing her.

'And when we wake up the nightmare of last night will all be over,' Samantha said, curling herself around him and getting comfortable.

'Hey, it wasn't all bad,' Jimmy responded, holding her close to him as he shut his eyes.

Samantha smiled and closed her eyes too, feeling content and deliciously happy. Lying beside him, feeling the motion of his breath and the warmth of his skin on hers and knowing how he felt about her, made facing the prospect of life without the Civic Hall more of a dull ache rather than a fatal blow.

*

The next time she opened her eyes her head ached with every blink. She coughed and put her hand to her sore throat. And then it hit her where she was. She was naked, in bed, in Jimmy's hotel room. She pulled the covers up to her neck as Jimmy came out of the bathroom, fully clothed.

'Hey, you're awake,' Jimmy remarked, smiling at her.

'My head hurts and my throat's sore,' Samantha spoke with a cough.

'Vodka, council office key – haven't we been over this already?' Jimmy asked as he slipped on his jacket.

'Yes, I know. It seems like days ago all that happened, not hours. What time is it?' Samantha enquired, still keeping the covers high.

'Almost nine,' Jimmy told her.

'What?! Nine?! I have to be at the hall! Felicity and Milo and Jane will be there, but I need my uniform! I'll have to go home for it! Goodness! Where are my clothes?' Samantha exclaimed as her eyes desperately scrutinised every corner of the room.

'Here,' Jimmy said, and he brought them over to her.

'Thanks,' Samantha replied, flushing.

'Listen, I'm going to the hall now, Nigel's left the hotel already. I'm going to try and speak to him. I'll tell Felicity you're going to be late. I've ordered you breakfast, it'll be here in a matter of minutes and I've put some headache tablets on the table. I think you should have something to eat, take a shower and let someone else worry about the hall for once,' Jimmy spoke, sitting on the edge of the bed next to her and running his hand through her hair.

'I only have two weeks left to worry about it then it'll be closed. Although, I'll still worry about it obviously, wondering what it's going to be turned into – you know – a car park, a department store, housing association flats,' Samantha said, the images coming to mind.

'Take the pills, have a shower and take your time. There's cable TV here, might be some old films on, Judy Garland or Frank Sinatra or something equally appalling,' Jimmy said with a smile.

'Oh, I don't have time for TV or breakfast, but I do need a shower,' Samantha said, remembering she had vomited the night before.

'Well, just take your time – for me,' Jimmy urged, stroking her cheek with his finger.

'It sounds like you want to keep me here,' Samantha remarked with a smile.

'If only,' Jimmy replied, and he kissed her lips.

'You're going now?' Samantha queried, holding his hand.

'Yeah, I thought I'd try to speak to Nigel before any of the others get there,' Jimmy spoke.

'Well, wait for me, I'll be two minutes in the shower,' Samantha spoke, preparing to get out from under the covers.

'No, it's fine, you stay – have some breakfast,' Jimmy urged her.

'Why don't you want me to leave? Something's happened, hasn't it? You don't want me to come with you for a reason. What's happened? Tell me,' Samantha begged, sensing something wasn't right.

Jimmy let out a sigh and stood up.

'What is it, Jimmy?' Samantha wanted to know.

'The press is outside the hotel. They know about last night and they're asking questions. They know alcohol was found in my drink and that I'm out of the show. I don't know how they know but they do and they're here,' Jimmy told her, looking at her and watching for her reaction.

'Dana,' Samantha said simply.

'Probably. But it could have been any one of the other skaters. I'm sure the press pays quite highly for a rumour like this,' Jimmy continued.

'So, what does that mean?' Samantha asked him.

'Well, firstly it means they want to get a picture of me red-faced, red-eyed and inebriated. Secondly, it means by the time the day is over the story will be all over the news and thirdly, it means I don't want to put you through that. That's why I'm leaving now, and I want you to stay here until I'm gone. They don't know you, they don't know you're here with me and I want it to stay that way,' Jimmy told her.

'But you haven't done anything wrong. How can they print something that you haven't done?' Samantha queried.

'You must have read stuff like this, they print unconfirmed information all the time. I'm used to it, I don't like it, but I'm hardened to it. But the last thing I want is them finding out about you, trailing you, asking you questions,' Jimmy said protectively.

'They wouldn't get any comment, I would probably hyperventilate and pass out,' Samantha replied her chest contracting at the thought of it.

'It isn't usually like this, Sam. I'm not so well known that paparazzi tail me around. It's just gossip like this sells and people love to read about people making mistakes,' Jimmy explained to her.

'Will you be alright? I mean...' Samantha began, feeling for him.

'I'll be fine, I've nothing to be ashamed of, nothing's happened. I'll just smile and be polite, get in my car and that will be that,' Jimmy assured her.

Samantha nodded.

'So, have some breakfast, take a shower and I'll see you at the hall in that sexy uniform,' Jimmy said, smiling at her.

'OK,' Samantha replied meekly, smiling back at him.

'See you,' Jimmy spoke and he kissed her mouth tenderly before heading to the door.

'Jimmy,' Samantha called to him.

He turned around to look at her.

'It will be alright, won't it?' she asked.

'Everything's going to be fine – I promise,' he responded cheerfully, and he smiled again before leaving her alone in the room.

Samantha hugged the duvet cover to her and then brought it to her nose to see if she could smell the scent of him. Her uneventful life had just become as eventful as anyone could handle. She smoothed her hand across the sheets as if she could feel the impression of him. She had spent the night with him, they had made love, they were *in* love. She had a boyfriend, someone who made her feel weak, someone who loved her for her, someone who hadn't yet freaked out when she had a panic attack, someone who hadn't run away when she had almost vomited all over him. It was real. The hall may have slipped out of her grasp, but she had Jimmy and she was going to hang on tight to him.

She had the breakfast Jimmy ordered for her and it made her smile. Blackberry tea and a tuna and mayonnaise bagel. She then took a long, hot shower, using all the free products there were and washing her hair twice to remove the smell of sick. As perfect as her night with Jimmy had been, she would much rather have had clean hair. And she'd been wearing her comfy pants. They had been white in a previous life but were now verging on grey. So much for fancy lingerie! It was no good when you'd had no warning that you might require it.

An hour after Jimmy left her, she arrived outside her front door. She had phoned Felicity from the hotel and told her she was going to be late. Her colleague wasn't surprised at all as she had already seen Jimmy. Felicity's voice had gone all silly and schoolgirl-like and Samantha could tell, although she didn't know how, that she was winking. She kept asking if Samantha had had 'an interesting evening' and in the end it was all she could do to get her off the phone and back to picking up the box office calls that were going unanswered in the background.

Samantha put her key in the front door and was just about to turn it and let herself in when it was flung open and Cleo appeared at the threshold, her hair wild, her face red and tears streaming from her eyes.

She screamed out loud and grabbed Samantha roughly by the shoulders, pulling her into her embrace and squeezing her so hard that all the air was almost forced from her lungs.

'She's here, Jeremy! She's alive!' Cleo yelled at the top of her voice, right into Samantha's ear.

Jeremy appeared from behind Cleo and smiled at Samantha.

'See, I said she'd be fine. Been clubbing?' Jeremy questioned cheerily.

'What?' Samantha asked as Cleo temporarily loosened her grip and she was able to take in some much-needed oxygen.

'God, I'm so angry with you! I've been out of my mind with worry, get inside! I have to phone Mum and Dad or they're going to be getting on a train,' Cleo exclaimed, rushing into the house and dragging Samantha behind her.

'I don't understand, what's happened?' Samantha

questioned oblivious to the reason for the fuss.

'Did you hear that, Jeremy? What's happened?! She appears on the local news breaking into the council offices, she doesn't come home all night and she asks what's happened! I think you'd better start making some tea because I know I need one. I'll be wanting brandy in mine – lots of it,' Cleo spoke as she rushed into the lounge and picked up the phone.

Samantha looked at Jeremy, bewildered by her sister's reaction.

'She's been up all night. Well, we both have. She started ringing the hospitals just after one. I did tell her not to panic, but well, you know Cleo,' Jeremy said, heading towards the kitchen.

'Yeah, I know Cleo. Did she say I was on the local news?' Samantha enquired as she followed him down the hallway.

'Mmm, that's what worried her more than anything. We were just about to put on a DVD, and we caught the tail end of the local news and there you were, breaking into the council offices and then being bundled into a police car,' Jeremy spoke as he put the kettle on to boil.

'Oh,' Samantha stated, thinking CCTV was a 21st century curse.

'So, you can imagine, when you didn't turn up, Cleo was concerned,' Jeremy continued.

'And she phoned our parents, probably worrying them half to death,' Samantha spoke.

'Well, she was running out of people to phone. She called the police station, she called the Civic Hall and she phoned the council – not that anyone was there and as I said, she'd already phoned the hospitals,' Jeremy explained.

'Honestly! Anyone would think that I hadn't spent a night away from home before,' Samantha exclaimed.

'Well, Cleo said you hadn't,' Jeremy replied.

'Well, Cleo doesn't remember everything,' Samantha remarked.

Not wanting to hear any more she hurried out of the kitchen, back down the hall and started to climb the stairs.

'And where d'you think you're going?' Cleo questioned, bounding out of the lounge and catching her sister halfway up the stairs.

'To my bedroom, to get changed into my uniform. Have you seen the time? I'm late,' Samantha answered, continuing on her way.

'You're not going anywhere until I've had an explanation,' Cleo retorted, and she began to mount the stairs in pursuit.

'Have you turned into Mother? I've only been away one night. Don't tell me you've taken up knitting too,' Samantha asked, risking sarcasm.

'I'm glad you think this is a joke, Sam. I've been sat up all night, going out of my mind with worry. What's been going on? You were arrested, it was on the tele for Christ's sake. I want answers!' Cleo yelled.

'I wasn't arrested, not really. I was just assisted in leaving the council offices that's all,' Samantha told her, opening her wardrobe door and getting out her uniform.

'You smashed the front door with a mannequin for God's sake! What were you doing there? Sam, this isn't you! Mum and Dad had a fit when I told them, they were all for dashing down here last night,' Cleo spoke, following Samantha around the room.

'I can't believe you called them! They are serial worriers

at the best of times, and you know Mum has high blood pressure. I'm twenty-four years old remember, not twelve,' Samantha said as she began to unbutton her top.

'I was worried! You never stay out all night! Where have you been?' Cleo demanded to know.

'I spent the night with…' Samantha began.

'Oh my God! No! No, no, no! Please do not tell me that I've been sat up all night tearing my hair out, worrying you're lying in a gutter somewhere, cold and unconscious and you've been, you've been – what have you been doing?' Cleo questioned hysterically her hands waving about as if she were directing traffic.

'Having sex,' Samantha yelled at the top of her voice.

Cleo yelped and put her hands to her ears to attempt to block out the words.

'So, I wasn't cold, or unconscious – well not unconscious the whole of the time – and I definitely wasn't alone. So, you can ring Mum and Dad again and tell them exactly where I've been if you like,' Samantha replied as she put her polo shirt over her head.

'Oh my God!' Cleo stated, looking at her sister with wide eyes.

'What?' Samantha questioned, stepping into her A-line work skirt and doing up the zip.

'You're not joking, are you? You've really done it, with Darren. Oh my God!' Cleo exclaimed as if suddenly feeling the need to sit down.

'Oh Cleo, you sound completely shocked. Did you really think I never would?' Samantha enquired.

'No, of course not. I just didn't think it would be so soon. I mean, you said the other day that it was too soon. Christ!

He didn't force himself on you, did he?' Cleo questioned as she watched Samantha put her sweatshirt on over the top of her polo shirt.

'No! Don't be ridiculous! If anything, it was actually the other way round. I'd been drinking vodka, it seems to do wonders for your confidence,' Samantha spoke.

'What?! But you don't drink. Functions and Christmas or maybe a glass of wine at a restaurant that's all. Did you go to a restaurant?' Cleo wanted to know.

'No, half a bottle of vodka and some vomiting and it just happened,' Samantha responded as she shut the wardrobe door.

'Sam, what's happened to you? Why are you being like this?' Cleo quizzed not liking the answers she was getting to her questions.

'Being like what?' Samantha asked, looking at her sister.

'Like this! All weird, like it's you on the outside but someone else has taken over the inside. Like someone out of *Alien*,' Cleo remarked.

'A bit like you turning into Mum before my very eyes. I have to get to work,' Samantha said, heading towards her bedroom door and escape.

'You're not going anywhere in this state,' Cleo ordered, getting up and running to the door to block her sister's exit.

'I'm not in a state. So, I've lost my job, I've been escorted off council premises by the police and I've had sex. For you that would be nothing more than a run-of-the-mill weekend,' Samantha replied, pulling the door handle and making Cleo have to move out of the way.

'But not for *you*! That's the whole point! That's why I'm so worried, I need to know that you're OK, that everything's

OK,' Cleo spoke, chasing after her sister as Samantha prepared to go down the stairs.

'If you mean did we use a condom, then the answer is yes,' Samantha replied.

Cleo put her hands over her ears and continued to pursue her sister down the stairs.

'Tea's ready. And the Civic Hall's on the news again. Apparently, Jimmy Lloyd's been booted off the ice show – fallen off the wagon again,' Jeremy remarked as the women appeared in the hallway.

'Let Cleo have my cup. She looks like she could do with two,' Samantha stated as she walked toward the front door.

'Sam! Please, don't go like this, perhaps I overreacted a bit, but the concern is genuine. I worry about you and...' Cleo began, hurrying down the hallway with her.

'I'm fine, honestly. I'll see you later, probably teatime, but don't go calling the emergency services if I'm a bit late. Oh, and perhaps no shagging on the kitchen table either just in case I'm early,' Samantha remarked as she opened the front door.

'Sam!' Cleo called.

'See you later,' Samantha replied, and she left the house, banging the door behind her.

Once outside Samantha took a deep breath. There was so much going on in her mind she just didn't have the capacity to deal with her sister's anxieties. She really hadn't considered Cleo might worry when she hadn't come home. But then again, she hadn't really thought about anything normal since the council meeting. Events had taken over and all she had been able to do was react to them. And yesterday she was just virginal Samantha Smith, today she was Jimmy Lloyd's girlfriend.

22

As she approached the Civic Hall the first thing Samantha saw were half a dozen reporters and photographers stood outside. They were talking amongst themselves, cameras slung around their necks and to her horror, Civic Hall cups and saucers in their hands.

She hurriedly walked past them and entered the hall, heading for the box office. She was immediately relieved to see Felicity manning the desk and obviously busy on a call.

Samantha gave her a smile and then went behind the counter to hang up her coat. However, before she could even get her arms out of the sleeves, Felicity appeared at her shoulder.

'Is it true?' she asked almost angrily.

'Sorry?' Samantha queried, turning to face her colleague.

'Is it true the Civic Hall's going to close in two weeks' time?' Felicity questioned.

'Oh,' Samantha stated her cheeks flaming.

'So, it *is* true! How long have you known? Why haven't you told any of us?' Felicity asked her.

'I only found out yesterday. I was hoping to get the council to change their minds. That's where I was last night – at the council meeting,' Samantha replied hurriedly removing her coat and hanging it up.

'You should have said something. Jane's been in tears since she heard. I've had to assign her to the kitchen, so she isn't weeping all over the customers,' Felicity spoke as Samantha turned to go into her office.

'But she hates working in the kitchen.'

'I didn't give her a choice. I told her I'd tell her mother where she goes on her day off and I said you'd cancel her holiday.'

'Who told you?' Samantha enquired.

'One of those reporters out there. Most of them are here to take pictures of Jimmy, but not the reporter from the local paper, he was there to take pictures of the hall and he asked me to comment on the closure. It was embarrassing, I didn't know what to say. Then Tony rings me up and tells me he's heard the news, so it's gone from reporting room to switchboard in a matter of minutes and I don't know a thing,' Felicity continued.

'Well, I'm sorry. I was trying to see if there was any way I could salvage things. I didn't want to tell anyone until I'd exhausted all the options,' Samantha spoke, realising that she sounded like a politician and not in a particularly good way.

'And have you? Exhausted all the options?' Felicity continued to question as she followed Samantha into her office.

'I don't know, probably. Have you seen Jimmy?' Samantha wanted to know, picking up the papers in her tray.

'He was in the auditorium on the ice rink about twenty minutes ago when I went to check how the repair man was doing with the broken seat in row M. I found that this morning too,' Felicity explained.

'Look, Felicity, I'm doing my best here. I don't want the hall to close any more than you do and I'm trying to think of a way round all this. I didn't tell you because I thought I might be able to do something about the council's decision. I couldn't, I'm sorry,' Samantha spoke a lump forming in her throat and tears springing to her eyes.

'Well, perhaps I could help,' Felicity suggested, as if realising she had upset Samantha.

'Thanks, but I'm not sure anyone can help now. I'll call a meeting, probably tomorrow,' Samantha said with a sigh as she headed out of her office.

'Would you like a cup of tea?' Felicity offered kindly.

'No thanks, I need to get on. There's a lot of stuff to get organised,' Samantha spoke with a swallow as she walked back out from behind the counter into the foyer.

'Well, perhaps I'll tell Jane that the press got it wrong – just for now – until the meeting,' Felicity called out after her.

'Thanks,' Samantha responded, not really caring what was said any more.

'By the way, she does ballroom dancing on her day off – at the Grand with a fishmonger called Leslie,' Felicity informed as Samantha departed.

*

She walked through the foyer, heading for the auditorium. She had to see Jimmy. He was the only thing that made sense from the night before and she wanted to be sure that it hadn't been imagined. More than that, she needed to know he had made things right with Nigel and was back in the show.

The arena was deserted when she got there, except for Jimmy who was powering around the ice. He looked up when he saw Samantha enter the room and immediately skated over to that side of the rink.

'Hey,' he greeted as he stepped off the ice to meet her.

'Hello,' Samantha responded.

She felt a little bit awkward, realising that the last time she had seen him she'd been completely naked.

He kissed her deeply and then held one of her hands in his.

'Good shower? Get time for an old movie?' he asked.

'No, I had to get home and get changed and then I endured an anti-terrorist inquisition from Cleo. Have you spoken to Nigel?' Samantha asked quickly.

'Why don't you go and get your skates? No one will be here for at least an hour,' Jimmy told her, holding onto both her hands.

'Have you spoken to Nigel? Are you back in the show?' Samantha repeated.

'Go get your skates,' Jimmy urged.

'Tell me what he said, Jimmy. I'm starting to panic, and you know that isn't good for me. See, I'm getting wheezy already,' Samantha spoke as she coughed.

'I'm not going back in the show,' Jimmy stated, looking at her seriously.

'No!' Samantha exclaimed, her voice coming out in a wail.

'Sam, it isn't like you think,' Jimmy spoke.

'No! This isn't fair! You haven't done anything wrong! Didn't he listen to you?' Samantha asked as she started to tremble.

'Yes, he listened – for a while at least, but...' Jimmy started.

'But he *has* to listen! You haven't done what he thinks. Dana put alcohol in your drink – did you tell him that? I saw her with your bottle, did you tell him I saw her?' Samantha questioned as her breathing quickened and she struggled to maintain control.

'Hey, Sam, calm down. This isn't the end of the world,' Jimmy spoke, trying to get her to focus on him as he held her hands tightly.

'It is! It *is* the end of the world! There are reporters outside, people think you've done this. People think you're drinking again, and it isn't true,' Samantha carried on tears filling her eyes.

'It doesn't matter what *people* think, they can think what they like. *I* know the truth, *you* know the truth, that's all that's important,' Jimmy spoke still holding on to her and trying to get her to look at him.

'I won't let this happen to you! I can't let you lose your place in the show. I'm already losing this hall, I won't let Dana do this to you,' Samantha told him her voice loud and out of control.

'She's insignificant, Sam, don't let this get to you. This is a positive thing, maybe I need to have a break. Let me explain what was said,' Jimmy begged, as he tried to calm her down.

'No! I won't let things go! I've got nothing to lose now! Nothing! I can say what I want to who I want because, to be honest, I don't care anymore. Is she here?' Samantha questioned, taking her hands from Jimmy's and beginning to walk in the direction of the dressing rooms.

'Sam! Wait! Sam!' Jimmy called as he hurried after her, teetering along on his skates.

Tears threatening to spill from her eyes at any moment, Samantha raced down the corridor from the auditorium towards the dressing rooms. She felt hurt and let down by everything and everyone. It was like the whole world was conspiring against her. But the emotion overriding all the others, and the one winning the battle to appear at the forefront of whatever was coming next, was anger. She was furious like she had never been before.

She pushed open the door to Dana's dressing room with force and it slammed against the inner wall as she stormed through it.

There was a loud, ear-splitting scream and Samantha put her fingers to her ears as she tried to digest the scene before her. What she saw stopped her in her tracks momentarily and made her gasp aloud.

Dana was completely naked, led over the sofa, and Nigel, the show producer was also minus his clothes, down on his knees, performing an intimate sex act on her. Both catapulted from their position and began rooting around on the floor for articles to cover themselves with.

'I should have guessed,' Samantha spoke when she had recovered her power of speech.

Dana was scrabbling for her clothes and Nigel, who had turned beetroot red at being caught in such a compromising position, desperately tried to hide his 'embarrassment' with a cushion.

'What the Hell is going on here?! You can't just barge into a private dressing room!' Dana yelled at Samantha as she tried to cover herself up.

'Yes, I agree entirely! And you should have thought about that before you intruded into Jimmy's dressing room and laced his drink,' Samantha spoke with authority, hoping that her trembling legs wouldn't give away her fear.

'What are you talking about? Get out of here!' Dana screamed, able to stand up now that she was loosely clothed.

'No. Not until you admit what you did. I want Loverboy here to hear it. I saw you in Jimmy's dressing room with his sports drink,' Samantha continued, trying to ignore her racing heartbeat.

'She's crazy, Nigel! Will you leave?' Dana repeated, approaching Samantha, an angry expression on her heavily made up face.

'I told you I'm not going anywhere until you admit what you've done,' Samantha ordered, standing her ground.

'Sam – whoa! What's going on?' Jimmy remarked as he entered the room and saw Nigel cowering on the sofa behind a very small cushion.

'I told you to get out of my dressing room, now get out or I'll call security,' Dana warned, and she pushed Samantha's shoulder.

Samantha let out a loud nervous guffaw of laughter that echoed around the dressing room and then, quick as a flash, she grabbed Dana by the hair, pulling it tight into her fist.

'In this hall I *am* the security! I'm the manager here, so you tell your naked friend over there what you did to Jimmy's drink,' Samantha ordered, and she dragged Dana over to where Nigel was still hiding his manhood under the Civic Hall furnishings.

'You're deranged! Get her off me! Nigel!' Dana screamed

as Samantha tugged harder at her hair.

'Sam! Let her go,' Jimmy ordered.

'I'm not letting her go until she's admitted it! Admit it or I swear I will pull out every hair in your head. Let's see what make-up can do for you then,' Samantha yelled, pulling again at Dana's hair.

'Nigel! Don't just sit there! Do something!' Dana shouted almost in tears as her scalp started to smart.

Nigel had turned the colour of a radish and, needing to hang on to the cushion that seemed to be shrinking by the second, he was in no position to help anyone.

'Sam! Come on, just let her go, she isn't worth it,' Jimmy urged, taking hold of Samantha's free arm.

'Admit it!' Samantha continued, hissing the words into Dana's ear.

'Alright! Alright! I did it!' Dana shouted her voice hoarse.

'You did what?' Samantha asked, keeping a hold on the skater's hair.

'I put scotch in Jimmy's drink. Now please, let me go, you're hurting,' Dana begged, crying out loud.

Samantha let go of Dana's hair and shoved her hard away causing her to fall into the sofa and knock Nigel's cushion on the floor.

'There! The truth! At last! Did you hear it? Did you hear her admit it?' Samantha questioned, staring wide-eyed at Nigel who was scrabbling on the floor for something to salvage his dignity.

'Yes, I heard,' he replied.

'Good, that's good. Well, Jimmy seems to think you're a fair man, so now you know the truth he can be back in the show regardless of who you wish to pleasure during your spare time – yes?' Samantha spoke her voice verging on sounding triumphant.

'Sam, let's go and get a drink,' Jimmy suggested, taking her arm.

'No, not yet. Not until he says you're back in the show. That's what we're here for, to see justice done. I couldn't save the hall but at least I can get you back in the show where you belong,' Samantha spoke, staying where she was, looking at Nigel and Dana.

'Sam, come on, let's just go and get a drink. We can talk about it,' Jimmy suggested, holding her hand.

'I don't want a drink. I want him to say you're back in the show. Why haven't you said it yet?' Samantha asked him.

'He won't be telling me I'm back in the show,' Jimmy told her bluntly.

Samantha turned to look at Jimmy, a bewildered expression on her face. She waited for an explanation, her mouth dry and her stomach contracting in anticipation of whatever she was about to hear.

'You should have done your homework, Ms Manager, before you came storming in here. You don't get back into the show when you're an alcoholic who's purchased a bottle of vodka. In the end Jimmy dug his own hole,' Dana retorted a smug look on her face.

'Sam, come with me and let me explain,' Jimmy spoke still holding her hand.

'I don't understand. What's happening here? She spiked your drink, you did nothing wrong and you're not going to be reinstated in the show? Doesn't he care about what she did? Did he know about it? Are they in this together?'

Samantha questioned as Jimmy led her to the door of the dressing room.

'Come on, I'll get us some tea,' Jimmy said, gently nudging Samantha towards the door as she began to cough violently.

*

A few minutes later Samantha found herself sat in the sound booth, looking down at the ice rink. It was beautiful and pure, white and glistening, and as empty as it had been the first time she had set eyes on it a few weeks ago. So much had happened since then, so much was still happening. She felt exhausted. She wasn't used to change, and she wasn't sure she liked even the idea of it. Anyway, change was what happened to other people.

The door opened and Jimmy entered, carrying two cups of tea. He had removed his skates and now had trainers on his feet. He handed Samantha one of the cups and sat down on the chair opposite her.

'It's camomile – apparently they're all out of blackberry,' Jimmy remarked to her as he took a sip of his drink.

'What?! Out of blackberry?! They can't be! We had a delivery yesterday – unless it was missed off the order. Who served you? Margaret or Mabel?' Samantha questioned, becoming agitated.

'Sam, it doesn't matter does it? Not for now,' Jimmy spoke.

'No, it doesn't matter. Let the place go to the dogs, it will all be rubble in a few months anyway,' Samantha stated, placing her cup on the desk with a shaking hand.

'Don't say that, you never know what might happen,' Jimmy told her.

'No, I don't anymore, do I? I used to know, you know. I used to know exactly what would happen at every minute of every day and now I don't. Now all I know is that nothing in life is fair. You think you can win, you think you know what's right, you try your best and you don't ask for much, just a fair chance. And then one day you wake up and you realise that life just isn't like that! It's hard and cold and mean and people lie and cheat and stamp all over you! And to top it all off, they get rewarded for it!' Samantha exclaimed.

'It isn't like that, I don't want you to think like that. The council's decision is wrong, Dana is evil, but those things aren't a true reflection of life as a whole. If we all thought like that then there'd be no hope for anyone or anything,' Jimmy replied.

'Hooray! You get it! You're catching on! That's exactly what I'm saying. Everyone's a liar and a cheat and people like that always seem to win. And me, plain old Samantha Smith, someone who's done the right thing all her life has to watch everything she ever had and everything she ever wanted get trampled on,' Samantha shrieked as she became hysterical.

'No, stop this. I don't want you thinking like that. Leaving the show wasn't about what Dana did or what Nigel said, or about how unfair life is – it's about me,' Jimmy stated, taking hold of Samantha's hand and making her look at him.

'I don't understand,' Samantha replied, taking deep breaths.

'I told Nigel everything when I saw him earlier. There was no point telling him anything else. Despite the conclusion he jumped to yesterday he did give me a chance on this tour, and I owed him the truth,' Jimmy started.

'What truth? That witch spiked your drink,' Samantha reminded him.

'I told him about buying the vodka. I told him I was angry because he didn't believe me and my first thought was to have a drink to suppress that anger with alcohol,' Jimmy explained.

'But why did you tell him? You didn't drink it! *I* did,' Samantha exclaimed.

'I told him because it proved that essentially his decision was right. I'm not strong enough yet if I can't deal with things without my first thought being alcohol,' Jimmy told her.

'But, the only reason you thought about it was because he didn't believe you, because he didn't trust you. *He* caused that reaction, the unfairness of his reaction caused you to think about drinking,' Samantha told him with a sniff.

'Maybe, but the thoughts were mine and the action was mine. I bought the drink and I shouldn't have,' Jimmy responded.

'So, what are you going to do now? Without the show? Are there other ice shows? There must be others, I mean, what are Torvill & Dean doing these days?' Samantha asked him.

'I was going to talk to you about this tonight, but I guess it can't wait,' Jimmy admitted a serious tone to his voice.

Samantha's heart began to beat almost incessantly detecting his tone, frightened about what he was going to say next. She could feel the uncontrollable laughter rising up in her already.

'I'm going back to rehab,' Jimmy told her.

Samantha laughed out loud and then coughed, her face turning almost purple such was the ferocity of the attack. She felt sick and panicked and she clutched at her chest, the pain like a thousand heavy duty kitchen knives.

'Hey, come on, there's no need for that. It's all going to be OK,' Jimmy spoke, wrapping his arms around her as Samantha bent double, coughed and tried to keep breathing.

'OK? No, I don't think so. I don't think things are going to be OK, ever again,' Samantha managed to speak.

'I need to go back, Sam and see my counsellor. I need to go through the process again, I need to reaffirm my intentions and come out feeling one hundred percent able to get through it,' Jimmy told her as he held her.

'But you are getting through it. You've been doing it – you didn't drink,' Samantha reminded him.

'No, but I was so close to drinking it's scared me. I need reassurance. I need to know that I'm going to be strong enough to keep resisting it,' Jimmy tried to explain.

'But I can – I can help you – here,' Samantha said still struggling for breath.

'Oh, Sam, you've already helped me, more than you realise. You've been like a breath of fresh air in my life,' Jimmy told her, holding her face in his hands and gazing at her.

'But now you're leaving. We spent the night together, just last night and you're going. Didn't it mean anything to you?' Samantha asked desperately.

'Of course it did. It meant everything to me, I thought you knew that,' Jimmy responded, smoothing down her hair with his hand.

Samantha just looked at him, tears threatening to spill from her eyes at any moment. She didn't know what to say.

'Sam, I'm doing this for us – so we have the best chance,' Jimmy told her sincerely his brown eyes looking into hers.

'I really don't know how much more I can take,' Samantha admitted, her shoulders beginning to heave with emotion.

'I know, but it's going to be OK, I promise. We haven't had the most conventional beginning, but it can only get better and it will,' Jimmy spoke as he took her in his arms and held her tightly to him.

He stroked her hair as she cried and then suddenly, she moved out of his embrace and looked up at him again. She had had a flash of inspiration, a thought of pure genius. She could go with him. Yes, that's what she would do. She didn't wholly feel safe with the whole concept of flying, too many people, too flimsy a construction, but millions of other people did it all the time. If they could do it so could she! They would step out together in public, she would let Cleo dye her hair, she would go on an 'eat nothing but your own body weight in lettuce' diet and they would be a celebrity couple. She could be there supporting him while he did what he had to do. OK, so there would be a few cameras and reporters and people wanting to know every intimate thing about her. But she could cope with that, couldn't she? Just because she didn't usually like her photo taken and hated talking about herself to anyone, didn't mean that she couldn't actually really do it if she put her mind to it. And she could put her mind to it for Jimmy.

'I could come with you,' Samantha blurted out, swallowing a knot of fear as she conjured up images of her and Jimmy on Oprah talking about his alcohol issues and her panic attacks. She tried to envisage her newly-dyed hair and matching luggage, carefully packed, and could almost see Cleo waving her off at the airport, wearing sunglasses and a new Topshop dress, pouting for the paparazzi.

'Oh Sam, it doesn't work like that. Rehab is something you have to do on your own – completely on your own. You have no contact with the outside world at all – I won't even be able to call you,' Jimmy explained.

'But I could go to America with you. I could wait for you, in a hotel or something,' Samantha told him, remembering an article she had once read about how many millions of viruses you could catch from air travel. She tried to erase it from her mind.

'America's a big place, Sam. You told me you get panicky when you go to another part of London. Let me tell you London has nothing on the vastness of the cities in the States,' Jimmy responded.

Multi-storey buildings rising up in front of her, hundreds of people all rushing somewhere, barking into their mobiles or walking tiny little dogs, and hundreds of yellow taxis all heading towards her beeping their horns. OK, now the Oprah show was sounding positively tranquil.

'Well, when are you going? I mean in two weeks I won't have anything to keep me here and I could go with you. I have to step outside of my box sometime, Cleo's always telling me that,' Samantha spoke banishing all imaginings from her mind.

And the taxis and little dogs were just New York. He wasn't going to New York. America was a big place, there was bound to be quiet there somewhere. Perhaps she could go to rehab too, she could certainly do with the rest.

'I've got a flight in the morning,' Jimmy answered.

This time Samantha felt like her heart had actually stopped beating entirely. She could feel the colour draining away from her face, her hands felt icy cold and she knew she was trembling again. This was it. He was leaving her. He didn't want her. He had spent one night with her and that was enough.

'You're leaving tomorrow,' Samantha said as best as she was able.

'Yeah,' Jimmy replied.

'Tomorrow,' Samantha said again, moving backwards on her wheeled chair, away from him.

She couldn't be near him. What had she done? She thought he cared about her, she thought he found her liking black and white films cute and kooky. He so obviously hadn't.

'Yes, but I'm coming back. As soon as I've sorted myself out, the minute I know I'm ready, I'll be back,' Jimmy told her.

'And how long will that take? Weeks? Months?' Samantha questioned bitterly.

'I really don't know. If I did, I'd tell you, but you just can't put a timescale on it,' Jimmy spoke.

'You don't know,' Samantha repeated, getting off her chair and standing up.

'Sam, I *am* coming back,' Jimmy reassured her.

'I don't believe you,' Samantha stated, her voice faltering as she avoided looking at him.

She couldn't look at him anymore, it was tearing her up. She had to pretend he was someone else, to strengthen her resolve and save face.

'What? Why?' Jimmy asked.

'You haven't got any intention of coming back here – I mean what have you got to come back for?' Samantha questioned, looking at the floor.

Think of someone unattractive, swap their faces, don't cry.

'For you! For us!' Jimmy insisted.

'I don't believe you. I think I've just been some sort of project for you, a distraction – something to take your mind off your own problems. All this was just a hobby for you. A guinea pig to teach how to skate, a freak who has panic attacks to feel sorry for and a mediocre entertainments centre to try and rescue,' Samantha yelled at him her whole body quaking.

'I know what you're doing, Sam, and it won't work. You think it's easier to put up that brick wall again than to believe that something good might happen between us,' Jimmy replied.

'Well, you had me fooled, for a while at least,' Samantha carried on her heart crumbling.

Johnny Vegas. It wasn't Jimmy, it was Johnny Vegas.

'Don't do this, Sam, don't turn what we have into nothing because that isn't how it is. I'm in love with you,' Jimmy stated, watching her moving anxiously from one foot to the other and playing with her fingers.

'Don't you have packing to do? Hair gel? Ice skates? Lemons?' Samantha replied, still unable to meet his eyes.

'I'm not leaving you like this,' Jimmy told her.

'Well, how would you like me to be when you leave me? You tell me, I have a wide range of reactions, I'm sure I can be accommodating,' Samantha babbled.

'Sam, listen to me. I'm going back to America, I'm going

to see my counsellor and then I'm getting the first plane back here – to be with you,' Jimmy told her sincerely.

'"Counsellor" was a very bad choice of word given the current hall closure scenario, I think perhaps you should have said "therapist",' Samantha replied, staring into space as if he wasn't there at all.

The monkey and the tea bags. *Benidorm*. Think *Benidorm*.

'No matter what you say I'm going to come back for you because I know how you really feel. I know you, Sam, and I know what's going on in there and in there,' he said tapping his head and then his chest.

She swallowed and tried to think of anything else other than the fact that she hadn't actually ever felt pain like it. She had fantasised about him, admired him, longed for him and fallen in love with him and just when she thought she had him, he was going away.

'You're hurting and I appreciate that but I'm doing this for the future, for *our* future,' Jimmy insisted.

'Yeah? Well don't bother. Drink. Don't drink. I don't care,' Samantha answered before she could stop herself.

Jimmy was still looking at her, unmoving and Samantha started to feel very uncomfortable. She was beginning to feel like she was going to faint. His image was starting to blur round the edges, and she had black spots appearing in her line of vision.

'Could you go now please?' Samantha asked him as beads of perspiration appeared on her forehead.

'I'll go, but I'm coming back,' Jimmy insisted.

Samantha didn't look at him, couldn't look at him.

'Here, I got you this the other day. I was hoping to find

a right time – I guess that's about now,' Jimmy said, and he placed a gift-wrapped package on the mixing desk. The present lay between them like a bundle of unspoken thoughts.

Samantha swallowed and watched him as he went to the door. He took one last look at her and then left. The door swung shut and Samantha just watched it close. It wasn't until the last crack of light from the corridor disappeared and the door was completely shut that she let go. The breath caught in her throat and she started to cry. The tears rolled down her face like a torrent. What had she done?

She wiped at her eyes with her fingers and caught sight of the package. She picked it up and with a sniff she began to unwrap it. It was a book. She discarded the paper and pulled it out.

It was a first edition of *Gobbolino the Witch's Cat*.

23

When Samantha arrived home that evening, she was greeted by the strong scent of Worcester sauce as soon as she opened the door. The smell shook her already delicate disposition and she gagged.

After Jimmy had left, the day had just got worse. News had got out about the hall closure and she had been ganged up on by all the staff working that day. Milo and Aaron had done a lot of shouting and finger pointing and Jane had sobbed and wailed. She had had no choice but to confirm the news and apologise they hadn't heard it from her. She told them the proposed date of closure and then she burst into tears and fled the angry employees for the walk-in freezer. She would usually have hot-footed it to the sound booth, but she couldn't bear to go back there. It was where Jimmy had last been and it probably still smelt of his aftershave.

When she had straightened the boxes of ice cream to her satisfaction and her fingers had turned so red and numb she almost couldn't open the door to get out, she hid in the alleyway behind the kitchen. She spoiled Gobby with fresh fish, not leftovers, and she stroked and held him. It made her cry all over again as she had thought about the way Jimmy had been with him... and the book. The beautiful book.

'Sam?' Cleo's voice called from the kitchen.

'Yes, I'm home. No need to call any of the emergency services,' Samantha replied half-heartedly as she took off her coat and hung it up on the peg in the hall.

'Quick! Come in here! I need help before I have a culinary disaster,' Cleo yelled.

Samantha entered the kitchen to see Cleo, wearing the cooking apron over a leopard print cat suit. Her hair was tied up and she had splashes of sauce on her face.

'It's all sticking to the pan! How do I make it stop?' Cleo asked as Samantha came up to the cooker.

'What stock did you have in there?' Samantha asked as she leaned over the pan.

'It's chopped tomatoes and garlic and…' Cleo began.

'Worcester sauce, I know. We'll just put some olive oil in to stop it sticking and we'll see what happens,' Samantha informed, and she took hold of the spoon and made a grab for the oil.

'It's for Jeremy. According to the recipe, it's good with pasta,' Cleo spoke.

'Is it lamb?' Samantha queried, looking at the meat in the pan.

'No, beef. Does it look alright?' Cleo queried, concerned.

'It looks fine,' Samantha replied with a heavy sigh.

'Are you OK?' Cleo asked her.

'No,' Samantha replied, suddenly feeling giddy and needing to sit down.

She was starting to feel like she had spent the last couple of weeks behaving like an extra on *Holby City*.

'What's happened?' Cleo queried, turning off the hob

and going to sit opposite her sister at the table.

'Everything's just gone wrong,' Samantha stated her voice wobbling as her composure began to slip.

'Oh God, what's happened? Is it Darren? What's he done? If he's done something to you, I will kill him,' Cleo exclaimed immediately.

'He's leaving,' Samantha blurted out as tears began to spill out of her eyes.

'What? Leaving? Leaving where? London?' Cleo enquired, not completely understanding.

'Leaving the country, tomorrow,' Samantha said as her crying escalated.

'What?! Well, where's he going? What's he doing?' Cleo queried desperately.

'He needs to go back to America for a while. He, er – has some unfinished business there,' Samantha managed to get out.

'Shit! He isn't married, is he?' Cleo asked, putting her hands to her mouth.

'No, not married. Just going away,' Samantha restated, the words sticking in her throat.

'Well, is he coming back?' Cleo wanted to know.

'That's the thing, he says he is. He says he's coming back for me, but I just can't believe him,' Samantha continued, taking a deep breath.

'I don't understand.'

'He doesn't have anything to make him come back here *except* me and I can't be enough, can I? Not when there isn't anything else. I mean, look at me! Dowdy uniform, crap hair, personality disorder,' Samantha spoke, still crying.

'Hang on, now I'm really confused. I thought his mother,

the ice skating fanatic lived here,' Cleo replied, quoting from the Darren Jacobs profile Samantha had created.

'She does, but – you know – she's elderly and she has a sister who dotes on her. She doesn't really rely on him,' Samantha lied quickly.

'Well, when did all this happen? I mean, you spent the night with him last night. Didn't he mention this trip then? Or might it have killed the moment? What a bastard! He took advantage,' Cleo spoke angrily, beating her dinner with the wooden spoon.

'No, no it wasn't like that. He didn't know last night, not really. It was sudden and that isn't a line he's fed me, I know it's true,' Samantha told her sister as she wiped her nose with the sleeve of her Civic Hall sweatshirt.

'And how long has he said he's going for?' Cleo questioned, tasting the food.

'He doesn't know,' Samantha stated sadly.

'Bastard,' Cleo spat.

'No, no he isn't. He's wonderful and handsome and he's been there for me and helped me with so many things. I'm just terrified that I'm in love with him and what if I'm in love with him and he isn't going to come back? What do I do then? I mean what happens then?' Samantha asked, thinking only of Jimmy.

'I think you're right to be cautious. It all sounds like a tall story to me,' Cleo replied.

'And then on the other hand, what if he's telling the truth? What if he really does love me? Like properly, like in the Sandra Bullock films. What if he really has to go to make things work between us and he *is* coming back?' Samantha enquired.

'Then he'll come back when his business is sorted, and you'll know. It's called having a bit of faith and some patience. OK, I've never been good with either, but you have more willpower than me,' Cleo told her.

'But I can't wait, I need to know. I should trust him. Trust is so important to him. I was so horrible to him, I acted like I didn't care because I was scared to let him know how I really feel,' Samantha spoke.

'Well, I think it was right to be guarded. I mean, men are deceptive little shits when they want to be. I should know, I've dated most of them,' Cleo told her.

'But if Jeremy told you he was going away but that he loved you and he'd be back would you believe him?' Samantha asked her.

'Yes, I think I would,' Cleo answered.

'Oh goodness, I've been so stupid. How could I have said what I said to him? I have to see him, I have to make it right. I have to tell him how I feel,' Samantha exclaimed, checking her watch.

'Jeremy's a terrible liar though, he wouldn't be able to get a fib past me. And he'd be putting himself in line for some serious below the belt injury if he tried,' Cleo told her, eating some of the meal

'I've got to get ready for work. Listen, don't wait up, or call the hospitals or Mum and Dad. I probably won't be home tonight,' Samantha spoke, getting up from the table.

'Sam, just be careful,' Cleo called after her, as Samantha disappeared out of the room.

'I've been careful all my life and look where that's got me,' Samantha replied as she ran up the stairs.

That evening she hardly watched the show. Dana was skating with Andrei Olapov as her partner and although she appeared more relaxed on the ice than she had been when partnered with Jimmy, Andrei didn't have any of Jimmy's charisma or showmanship. It was like comparing caviar with Shipman's fish paste.

When Jimmy skated, there was an air of anticipation that fell over the audience as if they expected nothing less than brilliance. Jimmy was skilful, graceful and strong, and all three of those things she'd experienced at close quarters. She looked at her watch for the fourth time in as many minutes. She had a plan.

She had tried to call the hotel earlier but every time she had got halfway through the number she had rung off. She didn't know what to say, she would get tongue tied and it would all come out wrong. She needed to see him, his face, his smile, the Minstrel eyes.

She wasn't sure, but she hoped Jimmy would come back to the hall after the show. If he was feeling half as dissatisfied with their farewell as she was, he would *have* to come back. The hall was where they had spent so much time together. It was where they had got to know each other, and it was where they had fallen in love.

And when he came back, she would be there waiting for him. She would apologise and say she understood and make things right between them. For the first time ever, she couldn't wait for the show to finish.

However, the audience called for two encores and due to having a party of disabled guests from Kent, getting everyone to leave promptly took longer than ever. Eventually, the auditorium was empty, and Samantha hurried to lace up her boots and get onto the ice.

She began to skate around, practising all that Jimmy had taught her, twists and turns and spins. She looked around the auditorium, searching for signs of someone entering but there were none. Perhaps he wasn't coming, after all she had said to him. The horrible, horrible things. And what if he had believed the horrible things? She hadn't meant it, she had been upset, she had been trying to deal with the situation the only way she knew how. He had to realise that.

She carried on skating, imagining the music, performing the moves as best as she could without a partner. She turned around on one foot and then looked again towards the entrance Jimmy usually arrived from. The door was unmoving, there was silence, apart from the sound of her blades on the ice.

She looked at her watch and tried to concentrate on her skating. He had to come here, she had to have the chance to say she was sorry and tell him how she felt. After everything she had been through, life couldn't be that cruel.

She performed the fast step section of the routine, span around too quickly and fell with a bump onto the ice just as the door to the auditorium opened. Samantha looked up expectantly and scrabbled to her feet, brushing the ice from her jumper.

'Bar's all cashed up, is it OK if I go? My mate's got a party,' Milo's voice called as he entered the arena.

Samantha felt tears spring to her eyes as she looked at her colleague. She could barely bring herself to speak, disappointed that he wasn't Jimmy.

'Yes, you go. I'll lock up,' Samantha managed to speak

as she skated towards the edge of the rink to leave the ice.

'Sorry about today, Boss – you know – having a go at you about the hall closing and that. We know you did your best to keep it open. Aaron saw the news report, you breaking into the council offices with that plastic doll. Genius,' Milo said with a grin.

'I've been under a lot of pressure,' Samantha answered.

'Yeah, well, see you in the morning.'

'Yes, see you in the morning.'

'Your skating's great by the way. My cousin skates a bit and not even she can lift her leg up like that,' Milo remarked as he prepared to leave.

'Oh, I can't really skate, not properly – not anymore,' Samantha responded, swallowing the lump that was forming in her throat.

Jimmy wasn't coming.

As soon as Milo left the auditorium Samantha sat down and practically ripped the ice skates from her feet. She slipped her shoes back on, ran around the arena turning all the lights off and hurried from the hall to begin checking all the other rooms.

*

Twenty minutes later she was in the repaired elevator of the Metropole, waiting for it to stop at the appropriate floor. Her heart was beating so hard she almost couldn't breathe. She had run all the way there, it was almost a mile. A hundred different thoughts were going through her head. She didn't know what she was going to say to him, perhaps he wouldn't even want to see her, but she needed to see him. She had to look into the Minstrel-coloured eyes, even if it was for the last time and tell him how much he meant to her.

The elevator doors opened, and she hurriedly walked down the corridor until she got to Jimmy's room. She stood outside, just looking at the room number, trying to compose herself and wondering what was going to come out of her mouth when she saw him. She raised her hand and knocked firmly on the door. Holding her breath, she waited. There was the sound of movement inside and then the door opened.

Samantha opened her mouth to speak and then stopped herself. Her mouth was left hanging open like a jowly hound.

'Can I help you?' the woman asked.

She was about forty-five, had curlers in her hair and was dressed in a Metropole Hotel dressing gown. Samantha had worn one only that morning after her shower. It had been Jimmy's and far too big for her, but it had felt nice being wrapped up in something of his. She had sat on the sofa, curled her legs up under her, eaten the tuna bagel and drank the blackberry tea. For a second all her worries about the hall and reporters had evaporated. It seemed like a lifetime ago.

'I, er, um, I'm looking for Jimmy Lloyd, is he there?' Samantha spoke, the words only just escaping.

Who was this woman? What was she doing in Jimmy's room? Why did she look like Robin Williams in *Mrs Doubtfire*?

'I'm sorry, you must have the wrong room,' the woman responded.

'No, this is his room. It's definitely this room. I was here, only this morning, it was this room. I don't forget anything, you see I have a great memory. It's a curse but there you go, and it was this room. Is he there?' Samantha questioned as she tried to look past the woman into the room.

'No! There's no one here, except me, trying to get some sleep. Do you know what time it is?' the woman enquired.

'Yes, I do, I know. Could I just come in and look? I mean, he should be here, this is *his* room,' Samantha said, still straining to see if she could look around the woman and into the room.

She couldn't see anything. She could see the edge of the bed and that was all. She had been in that bed – with Jimmy.

'I've told you, there's no one in this room but me, now please leave,' the woman spoke, stepping back into the room and preparing to close the door.

'Please, I'm sorry, you don't understand… I have to see him. I have to tell him…' Samantha began as she started getting emotional.

She could feel the laughter coming and she tried to breathe out to stop it escaping. She puffed out long breaths of air and the woman looked at her in horror, wondering what was going to happen next.

'Are you alright?' the woman enquired as Samantha breathed out and then let out a laugh she was unable to stop.

'Yes, I'm fine. I just need to see Jimmy. Are you sure he isn't in there? Could I look? Please, just to make sure,' Samantha asked as she coughed.

'If I let you look will you leave?' the woman enquired, sounding very irritated.

'Yes, of course – absolutely,' Samantha responded

gratefully.

The woman stepped aside and Samantha hurried into the bedroom.

It looked different somehow. Bare. There was nothing of Jimmy's there. The dressing table was full of face creams and make-up products and there were three wigs on stands. Samantha turned around and looked at the bed. She had been in that bed, just last night – with Jimmy. Now it had an extra blanket on and there were more face creams on the nightstand. How many face products did one person need?

'See, I told you. No one here but me,' the woman spoke, folding her arms across her chest and staring at Samantha with an 'I told you so' look on her face.

'Could I just check the bathroom?' Samantha asked.

'No, you can't! Come on, out!' the woman ordered, and she shooed Samantha towards the door.

'But you don't understand! This is important. He must have had to change rooms, could you…' Samantha began as the woman ushered her out into the corridor.

The room door was shut in her face and Samantha didn't know what to do. For a moment she just stared at the door, remembering standing there the previous night, recalling how Jimmy had come to the door looking worn down. Then she had drunk the vodka, then they had talked and then they'd made love.

There had to be some mistake. He must have switched rooms, he had to be here somewhere.

She ran. She ran down the corridor, and down the stairs. He had to be here. He couldn't be gone – it was just a case of finding him. The receptionist would know.

By the time she got into the reception area she was crying,

she was sweating, and she was gasping for air. She rang the bell on the reception desk, and no one came. She banged it up and down, over and over, until it came apart. A piece fell onto the marble floor making a loud clatter.

Finally, hearing the commotion, a dark-haired woman in her twenties wearing a maroon Metropole hotel uniform approached the desk.

'Can I help you?' the receptionist asked politely.

'I need to see Jimmy Lloyd. He's staying here, he was here last night. I went to his room, but he isn't there and I need to see him. So, could you tell me which room he's moved to please,' Samantha babbled, becoming more agitated by the moment.

'I'm sorry, Madam, I'm not at liberty to give out that information,' the receptionist responded with a smile that was somewhat smug.

'But I know him, he knows me – we know each other. I need to see him, and he would want you to tell me which room he's in,' Samantha tried to explain.

'I'm sorry but we have strict privacy rules,' the receptionist told her.

'Um, er, OK, yes. OK, hang on, I know his code word. I know the code word he used to book in here. It's "Toronto". "Toronto", because that's where he's from – "Toronto",' Samantha stated loudly, banging her hands on the desk as enthusiastically as if she had just successfully answered the final question on *Who Wants To Be A Millionaire*.

'In that case, Madam, I can tell you he checked out this afternoon,' the receptionist informed, looking at the computer screen.

'Checked out,' Samantha said in no more than a whisper.

'Yes, Madam,' the receptionist affirmed.

'No, there must be some mistake. He can't have checked out, he isn't leaving until tomorrow,' Samantha spoke as she began to sway, feeling dizzy.

'I can assure you he checked out, this afternoon at three twenty. Now is that all, Madam? Or can I help you with anything else?' the receptionist wanted to know.

'He can't have checked out. He can't have. I need to see him, I need to – I need to…' Samantha said, her words slowing up as her body began to shut down.

She gasped for air and she looked for something to hold on to as the coughing started.

The chandelier on the ceiling above her head began to spin around as she looked up at it and the last thing she saw before she hit the marble floor was the receptionist's name badge. 'Tiffany'.

24

Tiffany had called an ambulance. The ambulance had taken Samantha to the hospital despite her gasped protestations. Then, such was her incoherent speech about trying to find someone who had to be at the Metropole hotel and her relentless repetition that there was a conspiracy to keep him hidden from her, they had called the psychiatric doctor. He had phoned Cleo and she and Jeremy had turned up within minutes. Cleo didn't even have make-up on, and she was wearing her Hello Kitty pyjamas.

On the drive home in Jeremy's Jaguar, Cleo had bombarded Samantha with questions, none of which she had answered. She had completely lost the power of speech. She just sat in the back of the car, looking out the window, feeling like her life was over. She didn't want to talk, what was the point? Talking wasn't going to bring Jimmy back. She couldn't do any more, he had gone, and she had no way of contacting him. His last memories of her would be her telling him 'Drink. Don't drink. I don't care'.

Now she was lying in bed, listening to Cleo and Jeremy discussing their action plan for dealing with her, right outside her bedroom door.

'No, she hasn't been like this before. I don't know what's

happened. When she left here tonight, she wasn't in this state. She was going to meet this Darren and sort things out. He's going away or something,' Samantha heard Cleo speak.

'They said she had some sort of panic attack and blacked out. Has she done that before?' she heard Jeremy inquire.

'She does that sometimes. She's a bit nervy, a bit cautious about things. Sometimes situations get on top of her,' Cleo responded.

'Isn't there medication for it?' Jeremy asked.

'Jeremy! It isn't an illness like that. She just doesn't have much confidence, particularly with men. I don't know why, I mean, she's not ugly or anything. But it's worse this time, I think she really fell for this Darren,' Cleo spoke.

'What are you going to do?' Jeremy asked.

'I'm going to talk to her and see if I can find out exactly what's happened and exactly what she was doing at that hotel,' Cleo told him.

Cleo knocked on Samantha's bedroom door and Samantha immediately snapped her eyes shut and pulled the duvet up around her neck. Cleo didn't wait to be invited in before she entered the room and walked up to the bed. Samantha could feel her sister looking at her and a reflex reaction made her swallow.

'I know you're not asleep, so there's no use pretending. We need to talk,' Cleo spoke, plonking herself down on the edge of the bed.

Samantha didn't respond, keeping her eyes as tightly shut as she could.

'Sam, come on, we're worried about you. What happened?' Cleo questioned and she stroked Samantha's hair gently and tucked it behind her ear in a motherly fashion.

Samantha snapped her eyes open, sat up and moved away from Cleo's touching, pulling the duvet cover right up to her neck defensively.

'What happened with Darren?' Cleo continued.

'Nothing,' Samantha replied with a sniff.

'Well, something must have happened. You don't go from leaving here telling me you probably wouldn't be home, to passing out in the Metropole hotel without something having happened,' Cleo stated.

'I don't want to talk about it,' Samantha answered, and she lay back down and closed her eyes again.

'Maybe you don't want to talk about it, but *I* do! Your behaviour these last couple of days has been completely out of character. You've been like a different person and that's got to be down to this Darren. I'd like to meet him and give him a piece of my mind. He's turned my predictable sister into…' Cleo began, the volume of her voice rising.

'Into what?' Samantha wanted to know.

'Into someone out of control! Someone who gets arrested, someone who passes out in the best hotel in the borough – someone who's stopped telling me the whole story,' Cleo shrieked.

'I'm really tired,' Samantha responded, turning her face away from Cleo.

'I'm not going to go away just because you don't want to talk,' Cleo carried on, unmoving.

'There's nothing to say,' Samantha replied sadly.

'Well, did you see Darren? What did he say to you to upset you so much?' Cleo enquired.

'He's gone,' Samantha muttered under her breath, not letting her sister see her devastated expression.

'What? I thought he wasn't going until tomorrow,' Cleo replied.

'Well, he probably had a change of plan when I stood there and told him I didn't care what he did,' Samantha spoke as she replayed the scene in her head.

'Drink. Don't drink. I don't care'. It was the worst possible thing she could have said.

'But I thought you went to see him to make up,' Cleo said a puzzled look on her face.

'I thought he would be there after the show, like he's always been. But he wasn't, it was just Milo. So, I went to find him, at his hotel,' Samantha began to babble as the emotion she felt welled up in her chest.

'I think I'm losing the thread of this. His hotel? I thought he lived in one of those posh houses up West,' Cleo remarked not understanding.

'And I went to his room and a woman answered the door. She looked like Robin Williams and she said he wasn't there, that it was *her* room. But it couldn't be her room because I was there with him, last night. So, then I went to reception and I asked Tiffany where he was and eventually, after going on a power trip about privacy laws, she told me he'd checked out that afternoon. He left, after we spoke, after I was so horrible to him – after I said I didn't care,' Samantha carried on, talking at full speed and becoming distressed as she recounted the tale.

'He was living at the hotel?' Cleo questioned.

'And now he won't be coming back. He thinks I don't care. He left and I didn't get a chance to tell him properly how I feel, to let him know that I support what he's doing and that I understand,' Samantha spoke as she began to cry.

'Well, won't his mother have a contact number for him?' Cleo asked her sister.

'What?' Samantha queried as she reached for a tissue from the box beside her bed.

'Darren's mother, the one he took to the skating show – you could get his number from her,' Cleo suggested helpfully.

'You don't understand. He doesn't have a mother. Well, I mean, he probably does have a mother but not like you think. He doesn't have a posh house up West either,' Samantha stated with a sigh.

'What? But I thought…' Cleo began, looking even more bewildered.

'There isn't a Darren Jacobs, Cleo, I made him up – along with his mother, the posh house and the camp red shirt and chinos,' Samantha admitted, trying to stop the tears spilling from her eyes.

'What? Well, why would you do that?' Cleo wanted to know.

'Because you wouldn't have believed the truth,' Samantha answered, looking at her sister.

'For God's sake, Sam, stop talking in riddles. What's been going on with you? Are you dating someone or not?' Cleo wanted to know.

'Yes, I was dating someone and I'm in love with him,' Samantha spoke her heart breaking as she thought about the last few weeks.

'But it isn't Darren,' Cleo spoke.

'Aren't you listening?! Darren doesn't exist! It's Jimmy! Jimmy Lloyd! I'm in love with Jimmy Lloyd!' Samantha exclaimed her voice breaking as she spoke his name.

'Good God,' Cleo remarked, putting her hands to her mouth in shock.

'And he's gone now, and he won't be coming back,' Samantha added the lump in her throat almost choking her.

Cleo took a deep breath and spoke.

'Oh Sam, stop with the theatrics. I don't believe you're doing this! I thought this was something you'd grown out of!'

'What?' Samantha questioned as she wiped the tears away from her eyes with her fingers.

'Making up stories. I mean Sam, how farfetched is this?! This outdoes anything else you've ever told me – even the story about Michael Jackson being booked for the Civic Hall,' Cleo spoke, sounding annoyed.

'He *was* booked for the Civic Hall! Not the real one, obviously, it was a joke. I didn't think you'd take it seriously,' Samantha responded.

'Just like *this* is a joke. You and Jimmy Lloyd. Am I really supposed to believe this? I mean, Jimmy Lloyd, who's been out with models and film stars and could basically have any woman he wanted! Do you remember when you told me Aaron Watkins had asked you out on a date? Aaron Watkins, the head boy, the best-looking boy at school. I believed you, I don't know why really, but I believed you. And, lo and behold, of course it wasn't true. He was dating Caroline Rodgers, the carnival queen and that is how the pecking order works,' Cleo said accusingly.

'I was fourteen then, I'm not fourteen now. And he did speak to me at the tuck shop. Anyway *this*, *this* reaction is exactly why I didn't tell you. I knew how you would be and that's why I invented Darren,' Samantha told her.

'Rather good at inventing things, aren't you? Well, now I don't know what to believe. Yesterday you told me you lost your virginity. Am I supposed to believe that was to Jimmy Lloyd! Ha! Jimmy Lloyd the serial womaniser, bedding my sister the virgin! I have to say Sam, it's a sensational storyline and completely and utterly unbelievable!' Cleo exclaimed with a laugh.

'Leave me alone,' Samantha spoke as the tears welled up in her eyes again.

'With pleasure. I was feeling sorry for you, I really thought you'd found someone you cared about but no, now you come out with this phoney story about a famous ice skater. Someone who just happened to have a conversation with you when you were working the bar one time. I'm not saying another word to you until you're ready to tell the truth about whatever's made you like this,' Cleo told her, and she pointed her finger in an accusing way.

Samantha just pulled the duvet cover up around her again and stared blankly at the wall. Cleo let out a loud sigh of displeasure and left the room, banging the door behind her.

Samantha sniffed and wiped at her nose with the back of her hand. And then, suddenly, she whipped the duvet cover off, leapt out of bed and bent down on the floor on her hands and knees. She pulled out the copies of *Star Life* magazine from under the bed and started leafing through them manically. She looked at one after another until she found what she was looking for. It was the picture of Jimmy, taken six months ago, coming out of rehab, looking how he had looked the day they had met. She ran her fingers over the photo, touching his cheek, his hair, his mouth.

She would give anything to turn back the clock and say something different.

She hugged the magazine to her chest and began to cry all over again. In the very same week, she had lost her beloved Civic Hall and the only man she had ever loved.

25

They were putting sold signs across the estate agent's boards. The boards had only been up for a week and already someone had purchased the hall. Samantha felt queasy as she watched the 'SOLD' banner being plastered across the board. She knew there was more than a strong possibility that a developer had bought it and within weeks the Civic Hall would be demolished to make way for flats for people on benefits. She shivered with the realisation that the very place she was sitting would soon be nothing but a pile of bricks. All that history and nostalgia gone.

The phone rang loudly, diverting Samantha's attention away from the man fiddling with the estate agent's board outside and back to the box office.

'Good afternoon, Woolston Civic Hall, Samantha speaking.'

Her greeting was lifeless, cold and uncaring. It was pointless, she may as well have been a robotic voice on an answering machine. To begin with, after the news of the closure had broken, the phone lines had been buzzing with customers demanding refunds. Then, there were those who hadn't heard the news who rang up to book tickets for events Samantha had already cancelled. And finally, the calls went down to approximately a dozen a day that were from those who wanted last minute tickets to the ice show and 'to drink in the nostalgia'.

The ice show, the wonderful ice show that Samantha had so enjoyed she could now hardly bear to watch. Every night she stood by the fire exit, eyes facing the ice yet unseeing. She didn't see Dana and Andrei or the rest of the company, all she saw in her mind was Jimmy. The visions replayed in her memory over and over again. The way he had lit up the ice with his grace, his speed and his skill, how the crowd had reacted to him, the smile on his face as he saw the joy in theirs. But most of all she remembered how they had skated together, in the empty arena. They'd been all alone, sometimes laughing, sometimes bickering, holding each other, learning from each other – being with each other. Tears sprang to her eyes now as the woman caller asked about *Skating on Broadway*. She had to clear the lump in her throat before she could speak.

'Yes, erm, we do have some tickets left for the ice show, but they are quite near the back. Do you like Berry Fruits ice cream by the way? We're doing a special offer – buy two get four free,' Samantha spoke, wiping at her eyes with the sleeve of her Civic Hall jumper.

She hadn't spoken to Cleo for a week. Not one word. For the most part she had managed to avoid her completely. She went to her bedroom when Cleo was home and only came downstairs when she was sure the coast was clear. It was easy to know when to disappear again as it was impossible to miss the sound of Jeremy's car when he pulled up outside the house.

While sitting in her room, avoiding Cleo, reading was all

there was to occupy herself. Reading and thinking, thinking while reading, thinking and sleeping, sleeping while thinking and reading. She had read *Gobbolino the Witch's Cat* about five times a day since he had left. She had even brought it into the hall and read it to Gobby.

It was a hopeless situation. She couldn't stop thinking about him. In a few days the hall was going to close, and she was going to be unemployed. But this prospect, the most awful prospect she could ever have imagined, just didn't register with her anymore. She felt numb about everything that had happened over the past month, it was if it had all been a dream which had turned into a full-on nightmare, and now she didn't even feel involved in that. It was like she was separated from everything, a spectator as life went on around her.

'Yes, Madam, that's fine. Call back when you've spoken to your friend,' Samantha replied to her customer and ended the call.

She looked up at her monitor and realised she had been pressing the 'J' key over and over again. She pulled off her headset and put it down on the desk.

The cruel irony of the situation was the restaurant was doing really well. The simple, cheaper, more quickly prepared range of food had been well received. Takings had almost doubled in the evenings and lunchtimes were still popular with the OAPs. It made Samantha feel sick knowing that their ideas were working so well but that it had all been a fruitless exercise.

She began to leaf through one of the five newspapers she had bought en route to work that morning. She had bought newspapers every day since just after Jimmy left, scouring them for news. She needed to check for any articles about Jimmy, no matter how small. She simply needed a reminder that he existed, that he hadn't been a figment of her imagination. Samantha didn't know what she wanted to read, she didn't know why she expected to see anything but every day she hoped. She read everything, from cover to cover, every paragraph of every column. It passed the time between telephone calls and signing letters of apology to accompany the refund cheques.

'You gave me your lunch.'

Hearing her sister's voice so close to her Samantha immediately raised her head from the desk and knocked the newspaper off and onto the floor.

Cleo was stood in front of her looking bedraggled. Her hair was wet and had turned into a wiry fuzz. She looked less than happy.

'I just had to size up the shittiest one bed flat I've ever been in. I get outside, gasp for air, shake the fleas off me and think I'll have a bite to eat to take away the taint of tat from the back of my throat. So, I get the sandwich out of my bag and the smell makes me feel sicker than I did when I set foot in the dump in Fosters Gardens. It's tuna, it's yours,' Cleo continued, and she took the offending item out of her bag and placed it on the desk in front of her sister.

'Oh, sorry, I...' Samantha began, finding the situation awkward and beginning to blush.

'Where's mine?' Cleo demanded.

'Oh yes, sorry it'll be in my bag, I'll just get it,' Samantha spoke, and she hurriedly scrambled off her chair and headed towards the pegs.

She rifled through her bag, dropping things on the floor

as she did so, but then finally produced a neatly wrapped package and rushed back to her desk to hand it to Cleo.

'Sorry, I must have taken the wrong one this morning and...' Samantha began, stumbling over her words and not able to look her sister in the eye.

'This is stupid,' Cleo stated.

'I'm sorry, I should have checked the packets. I mean, usually I do but...' Samantha started.

'Not the sandwich Sam – *this* – *us* – *not speaking* – you going to your bedroom all the time,' Cleo told her seriously as she dropped the cream cheese and Worcester sauce sandwich into her bag.

'Oh,' Samantha answered not knowing what else to say.

'We live in the same house, it isn't practical,' Cleo continued.

'No, I guess not,' Samantha replied, her cheeks reddening as she still tried to avoid her sister's gaze.

'Jeremy says that underneath it all you and I are too alike,' Cleo stated.

'Oh, I don't really think...' Samantha began unsure of Jeremy's analogy.

'I don't believe him! I mean, it's probably the most stupid thing he's ever said but I know why he said it. He wants us to make up. I haven't been myself since all this happened and I'm always on edge when we're not speaking and Jeremy's wearing it and I don't want him to go off me. He's a good one, you know – one worth hanging on to,' Cleo gabbled, pulling at a tendril of hair that was dripping water onto her face.

'Well I...' Samantha started.

'Look, I don't know what happened with you last week.

I know you've been under pressure here, with the council and everything and I know how much this place means to you, no matter how bizarre I think that is – but I want to call a truce. I want to get back to how things were. You know, you slagging off my cooking and knocking on my door at inopportune moments. I don't like the awkward silences, I'm just no good with quiet, you know that,' Cleo continued.

'Yes,' Samantha responded.

'Jeremy says that if we make up, he'll foot the bill for a slap-up Indian meal. Poppadoms, bhajis, main course and one of those funny ice creams you like – or another meal – it doesn't have to be Indian. Did you say yes? As in, yes we're calling a truce?' Cleo questioned finally pausing for breath.

'Yes,' Samantha answered, smiling at her sister.

'Oh good! I'm so glad that's all done and dusted. I'm not very good with making up. So, shall I tell Jeremy to book a table at the Taj Mahal? Next week sometime? Which night is best for you?' Cleo questioned.

'Well, I won't be free for a couple of weeks, not until – the hall closes,' Samantha told her a lump forming in her throat as she said the words.

'Oh, yes, I saw the men outside. Wonder who's bought the place and what it's going to be? I think they should turn it into a multi-screen cinema. Perhaps you could get a job there, I could see you as usherette,' Cleo remarked.

'It'll be houses, I'm certain of it. Or housing association flats – blocks of them, all filled with pregnant fifteen-year-olds,' Samantha commented angrily.

'Well, actually, on the job front, I've been asking around and I might just have found you something already. They're interviewing for staff at the tourist information centre! Chantelle from the office saw the advert in the paper and I thought it would be absolutely perfect for you. I mean what you don't know about this area could be written on a – cocktail stick,' Cleo announced excitedly.

'Oh, wow, well, that's – great,' Samantha responded completely unenthused by the idea.

'Anyway, we can talk about it later, now we are talking again – just promise me one thing,' Cleo spoke, smiling at her sister as she prepared to leave.

'What?' Samantha asked.

'No more fantasies! No more made up stories about people like Jimmy Lloyd! If you want a date Sam, I can get you a date. Maybe we can invite Connor to the Indian,' Cleo said cheerily.

'Well, I…' Samantha began, not knowing what to say.

'I'll see you later, probably annoy you by burning my dinner,' Cleo called as she headed towards the exit.

'Yeah, bye,' Samantha answered, putting on a false smile as she watched her sister leave.

As soon as Cleo and her oversized floral handbag were out of sight Samantha's face dropped. No more fantasies about Jimmy Lloyd. She only wished it was that easy.

*

'Are you sick of answering these phones because I am,' Felicity remarked to Samantha later that afternoon.

'Yes,' Samantha replied, not looking up from her newspaper.

'Why don't people know the hall's closing? I mean, it's been on the radio and in the local paper and on that stupid

Tonight with Carol Greaves show. I don't like that Carol Greaves. She's always got a smirk on her face and she wears leather too much. It was the tan leather skirt the other night – a woman her age shouldn't wear leather,' Felicity remarked, taking a swig of her tea.

Samantha didn't respond. She was still scouring the newspapers for any mention of Jimmy. There had been such a fuss in the papers about him leaving the ice show and now there was nothing. It was like the scandal was over and nobody cared what he did now. That was good in a way but not ideal when you needed information.

'You heard from Jimmy?' Felicity asked as if reading her mind.

'No. Jimmy who? Why would I? Do you mean Jimmy Lloyd?' Samantha spoke her cheeks glowing as she became flustered.

'God, I wouldn't be hiding away a relationship with him, I mean he's gorgeous. If I was dating him, I would want the whole bloody world knowing about it,' Felicity remarked.

'We aren't dating.'

'Come on Sam, I'm not daft. Word is you had that Dana Williams in a head lock over him,' Felicity informed her.

'Who told you that?'

'Not a great deal gets past Mabel in the restaurant – she heard the screams.'

And then she found it. It was three short paragraphs, on the bottom of page eight of the last paper she had to look at. It was squeezed between a report about a corn snake in Durham escaping from its tank and another article about a Fife woman's fight for compensation when her breast implant exploded at thirty thousand feet over the Pyrenees.

Recovery on ice?

After being dramatically pulled from ice show 'Skating on Broadway' former gold medal winning ice dancer Jimmy Lloyd (30) has gone back to rehab, fuelling speculation that he is back on the booze.

Jimmy spent two months at the Freedom Vale Rehabilitation Centre earlier this year where he is thought to have undergone counselling, hypnosis and group therapy sessions in order to beat his alcohol addiction.

Jimmy joins former girlfriend Hilary Polar at the Centre. She has been in residence for the last month undergoing treatment for her ongoing issues with prescription drugs and anorexia.

Samantha felt herself weaken. Why wasn't there a picture of him? She needed proof he was really there. There should be a photo of him going in or something. Or if they didn't have a picture of him going there, either because he wasn't really there or they didn't have a photographer available that day, they could at least have pulled a picture from the archives. And *she* was there, Hilary Polar, the tarty actress who had whiter teeth than him. They had dated. What if they were in adjoining rooms, or sat next to each other at lunch? Did they have group lunches in rehab? What if Jimmy looked at Hilary Polar, who was bound to be dressed in something designer with all the enhancements money could buy and realised he had been wasting his time with her. How could he possibly want her when Hilary Polar was with him – now – in his hour of need, reeking of Christian Dior and throwing her cleavage in his face. She did do that a lot in most of her films and Cleo did a good impersonation of her when she was wearing her Wonderbra.

'What are you reading?' Felicity asked and she leant over to look down at the paper.

Samantha tried to shut it up quickly so Felicity couldn't see but she wasn't fast enough, and Felicity picked up the paper and read the article herself.

'Ah, I see,' Felicity said, putting the paper back down and nodding at Samantha.

'"Ah you see?" What's that meant to mean? I was just reading about that poor woman whose boobs exploded. I mean, I can't imagine the pain,' Samantha said hurriedly folding the paper up and putting it away.

'Did you know he'd gone back to rehab? It's such a shame, isn't it? I mean, to look at him you wouldn't think he had a care in the world, would you? And what a fantastic skater and an incredible physique too. I mean, you wouldn't think...' Felicity began.

Samantha just looked at her, tears welling up in her eyes.

'Oh dear, have I said the wrong thing? You're not going to have a panic attack, are you? Shall I get you some water?' Felicity offered.

'No, I'm fine. Thanks anyway,' Samantha said quickly, coughing away her tears and sniffing.

'Listen, the trouble with men is, they don't ever really know what they want. I mean, they want you one minute and the next they want every other woman on the entire planet *except* you. That's just the way they're made. It's not really their fault, it's genetic. I mean, take the guitarist from the Eagles tribute band. I mean, he actually thought he'd morphed into one of the Eagles, poor deluded individual. He thought he could have a different woman at every venue. He thought he was God's gift to the female race – so I had to tell him. I said "Cliff, take a look in the mirror, love, you're not Don Henley, you're an overweight strummer from Bridport". That was the beginning of the end really,' Felicity told her.

'I said some really horrible things to Jimmy,' Samantha admitted sadly.

'Forget about it. Don't let it eat you up – he probably deserved it.'

'He didn't.'

'Well, never mind, move on. Look, I got this in the post this morning, preview guide for the Presbook Centre. They've got Seal there next year. Remember Seal? Huge hunk of a man him. Bet he could cheer us both up – probably at the same time. What d'you think?' Felicity asked, passing Samantha the leaflet.

The Presbook Centre's new glossy brochure advertising new acts and introducing the leisure pool that would be built and open in six months' time was impressive. Samantha didn't even want to touch it.

'You seen that scruffy cat around today?' Felicity enquired as she took off her headset and opened a KitKat.

'No, why?' Samantha asked.

'Stupid thing was in the bins yesterday when I lobbed a broken seat into it. Don't know if I hit it but it made a horrible howling noise,' Felicity informed.

'Well, did you check if he was OK?' Samantha asked frantically.

'Didn't have a chance. It took off up the high street,'

Felicity replied.

Samantha left her chair without another word and headed for the restaurant and the kitchen. She needed to find Gobby. She wanted to make sure he was alright. It would be too much, on top of everything else, to have him injured, frightened and alone thinking no one cared about him.

She filled a bowl up with chicken curry, peas and chips and headed out into the alleyway.

'Gobby! Here, boy! Dinner!' Samantha called, banging the side of his bowl with a wooden spoon.

She checked her watch. He was usually hanging around by now.

'Gobby! Dinner time! Come on! It's curry!' Samantha called again, walking further up the alleyway and looking under boxes and any nooks and crannies where a small cat was likely to hide.

'Come on, Gobby. Felicity didn't mean to scare you, come on, come and eat,' Samantha begged, banging the wooden spoon on the bowl again.

There was a faint mew and then he appeared from behind the skip belonging to the furniture shop. He was limping even worse than usual and his coat looked very matted. He slowly skulked towards Samantha and she put the bowl down for him.

'Oh Gobby, I was worried about you,' she spoke as he began to eat slowly, with less conviction than normal.

She stroked his back and he mewed with discomfort, looking at her with sorrowful eyes. She tickled his chin and he began to purr more happily. There was simply only one thing for it.

26

'Ooooo what's that? Is it a delivery? Is it for me? I've been in for ages and no one rang the bell! I was in the bath though, for about an hour. Who's it for?' Cleo exclaimed excitedly as Samantha staggered through the front door carrying a huge cardboard box.

'Well, it's kind of for both of us. But you have to make a promise before I let you see what's inside,' Samantha said as she walked down the hall and put the box on the kitchen table.

'God, is it illegal? You haven't been getting that awful, smelly man in the hall again, have you? You know, the one who tried to sell knock off DVD players. It isn't a games console, is it? Because you know I don't like games like that – too many buttons to press at different times,' Cleo said, following Samantha and looking at the box with intrigue.

'No, it isn't a games console. Now, you have to promise not to scream and not to go mad at me,' Samantha told her, holding tightly onto the lid of the box.

'God, what is it? Was it really expensive? Have you blown the whole week's household bills budget on a treat? That isn't like you, I remember you freaking out when I spent the electric money on a purse.'

'Well, that was kind of ironic. Listen, promise me you won't scream or freak out,' Samantha demanded.

'Alright, alright, I promise. Open the box! It's a flat screen tele isn't it, with Freeview and everything,' Cleo said excitedly, jumping up and down and clapping her hands together.

'No, but it's an entertainment centre of sorts. Cleo, meet Gobbolino – Gobby for short,' Samantha announced as she let go of the box lid.

Gobby popped up like a magician's rabbit from a hat and let out a loud miaow. Then, when he saw Cleo, he hissed and leapt from the box, ran through Cleo's legs and hid behind the pedal bin.

'Arrrrrrrrrrrrrrrrggggggggggggghh!' Cleo shrieked at full volume.

'Cleo! You promised! Don't! You'll frighten him!' Samantha spoke, bending down on her hands and knees and trying to entice the cat out of the corner.

'What the Hell is that?! Who does it belong to and what's it doing here?' Cleo demanded to know, fixing Gobby with one of her Darth Vader stares.

'Well, he's sort of mine, but we can share him. He's very friendly, I think he's house trained, well he's used to the outdoors, but he always pees in a corner and he only eats leftovers, so no expense on cat food,' Samantha explained.

'Oh no! That thing is not living here,' Cleo said as Gobby continued to stare at her from behind the bin.

'But he doesn't have anywhere else to go. He's been living on restaurant leftovers from the hall for the last six months and now the hall's closing he doesn't have anyone to look after him, except me. And Felicity hit him with a chair yesterday and he needs TLC, the vet said,' Samantha said in her best persuading voice.

'You took him to the vet. You paid for the vet to look at him? How much did that cost?' Cleo asked, appalled.

'Nothing. I gave the vet four tickets to the last night of the ice show, back row but he was grateful. Come on Gobby, come and meet Cleo, she's not scary really,' Samantha said as she picked Gobby up, cradled him in her arms and brought him over to her sister.

'I do not want to touch it. Argh, don't bring it any closer – it smells!' Cleo said, creasing up her face and backing away from Gobby.

'So does Jeremy but I don't ban him from the house,' Samantha remarked.

'Is this cat a man substitute? Because if that's what it is, I don't think it's the right route to go down,' Cleo spoke, watching as Samantha rubbed Gobby's chin.

'He isn't a man substitute,' Samantha replied.

'I'm telling you now, if that thing so much as sniffs near my bedroom I'm going to sell it to the Chinese restaurant. It lives in your bedroom and it eats in the kitchen and you get a proper bowl for it and its own fork and you wash the bowl and fork up and not with our stuff, separately. And if it claws anything of mine, and that includes the sofa, it's out the door,' Cleo said firmly, still stepping back from Gobby as if he were a nuclear bomb about to go off.

'Thanks, Cleo,' Samantha replied with a smile as Gobby licked her face.

'I'm only doing this because I think you need company. Personally, I would have chosen Connor, but if you really prefer an animal then so be it,' Cleo answered.

'One more promise,' Samantha said, putting Gobby down and watching as he weaved in and out of the chair legs.

'God! Isn't letting him stay enough?'

'Just promise me you won't kill him like the budgie or make him bite you like the Yorkshire terrier,' Samantha said.

'What? What budgie? Our budgie? Tweety Pie?'

'Yes.'

'I didn't kill him, Sam. Mum left him out in the garden and next door's tabby leapt up at the cage and frightened the life out of him. He died of shock. And as for the dog, well the vicious thing could have had my arm off,' Cleo told her.

'You were trying to put plaits in its hair,' Samantha reminded.

'Dogs like that are supposed to be groomed,' Cleo replied defiantly.

'Well, Gobby doesn't really go in for grooming and he doesn't like mince either, so no trying to poison him,' Samantha said, stroking Gobby's back.

The front door opened and Jeremy entered, kicking off his shoes and striding down the hallway towards the kitchen, briefcase in hand.

'Hello, what's this? Both of you together? Talking?' Jeremy enquired as he dropped his case in the middle of the room and looked at the women.

'Yes, of course we are. The whole situation is forgotten and things are back to normal, so you'd better honour your promise and book that Indian meal,' Cleo told him, wrapping her arms around his neck and planting a wet kiss on his mouth.

'Please, get a room,' Samantha remarked, putting her hand over Gobby's eyes.

'Awww! Is that a cat? Awww, look at the little thing. Awww, look at its funny eye. Is he yours, Sam? Can I hold him?' Jeremy enquired, letting Cleo go as he caught sight of Gobby.

'Yes of course. So, do you like pets Jeremy?' Samantha asked as she passed Gobby over and Jeremy began to rock the cat in his arms like a baby, stroking his tummy and making cooing noises.

'Not pets in general. Not keen on dogs. Had goldfish when I was younger, but they never lasted that long. Cats are a different matter though. I love cats. I had one until a couple of months ago, got run over. Poor Millie, she was Persian,' Jeremy said a tear in his eye.

'Oh Jeremy, that's terrible, you never said,' Cleo remarked, looking at her boyfriend with sympathy.

'Well, I don't like to talk about it, too upsetting. Awww, he's a friendly thing, isn't he? What's his name?' Jeremy enquired as Gobby licked his fingers.

'He's called Gobby, aren't you darling? Yes, little Gobby Wobby Woo,' Cleo spoke quickly before Samantha had a chance and she began tickling Gobby and swooning over him.

'Do you like cats, Cleo?' Jeremy asked.

'Of course! What's not to like?' Cleo replied with a happy smile as she rubbed Gobby's fur.

Samantha smiled and then a sudden thought struck her, and she looked at Jeremy and Cleo with suspicion.

'Hang on a minute, neither of us let you in. Do you have keys?' Samantha questioned Jeremy accusingly.

'Well, er – shall I make us a cup of tea?' Cleo suggested hurriedly.

*

Later that evening Samantha introduced Gobby to her bedroom. He limped up onto the bed, made a nest in her duvet and fell asleep, dribbling on the covers.

Apparently, Jeremy had keys for convenience purposes only and he wasn't intending on moving in. Three times he had called for Cleo when she was still languishing in the bath and according to her, now he had his own keys, this problem could be overcome. He could just let himself in and watch Sky Sports until she was ready. Samantha hadn't even known they had Sky Sports until that moment. Apparently, Jeremy had offered to pay for it as he was spending so much time letting himself into the house with his own set of keys and watching television while he waited for Cleo. Now Samantha knew why there was a box of lager in the fridge and whose slippers were in the shoe cupboard.

Gobby started to snore as he slept and Samantha stopped what she was doing. She had been going through her wardrobe, sorting things into type, colour and size. Most of it was Cleo's but it still needed tidying. It had got completely muddled when they had been looking for an outfit to wear on her date watching Air Patrol with Jimmy.

She let out a sigh and reached into her bag for the newspaper containing the article about him. She spread the paper on the bed and re-read the words.

It was so frustrating. She wanted to know what he was doing. Was he sat alone in a room fighting his demons or was he in a group talking about his fears and listening to the fears of other people? She couldn't stop thinking about him. There were memories of him everywhere at the hall, the blackberry teabags, the temperamental coffee machine, the ice rink, his dressing room, her office, the bench outside the hall, row AA – especially row AA.

But was he thinking about her? Did he care about her? Or had she messed everything up by being too scared to tell him she loved him? Maybe he wasn't in a room alone – maybe he was with Hilary Polar. She was in his league. Beautiful, thin, blonde, famous, and she could definitely speak without laughing and coughing, apart from in the film where she had lung cancer, there had been gratuitous coughing in that.

She ran her fingers over his name until she got ink on them and then her bedroom door burst open and Cleo entered without warning.

'Want Chinese, Sam? Jeremy's just about to order. Chicken chow mein?' Cleo offered.

Her eyes met with the paper and then Samantha's inky fingers. She could see right away from the smudges on the page which article Samantha had been reading.

'Corn snake in Durham escaped,' Samantha said, knowing it was futile.

'What are you doing? Why are you reading articles about Jimmy Lloyd and getting print all over your hands while you're doing it?' Cleo questioned.

'He's gone back to rehab,' Samantha stated miserably.

'Yes, I know. Everyone knows. He's back drinking again, that's why he was kicked off the ice show,' Cleo replied.

'It wasn't like that.'

'And what would you know? Sam, I thought we'd been

through all this. Do you have some weird obsession with Jimmy Lloyd or something? If I look under your bed am I going to find an effigy of him in a makeshift shrine with scented candles and photos cut out of *Star Life* magazine?' Cleo wanted to know.

'No,' Samantha answered.

'Good, because celebrity crushes are what you should have had when you were fifteen and reading my copies of *More!* magazine.'

'I never read your *More!* magazine,' Samantha insisted.

Cleo let out a sigh and sat down on Samantha's bed, running her hand over Gobby's fur and making him dribble even more.

'I'll have chicken chow mein, and get some rice and curry sauce for Gobby,' Samantha said, trying to avoid whatever Cleo was going to say next.

'Sam, do you *want* a boyfriend?' Cleo enquired bluntly.

'Well, I...' Samantha started.

'Because if you don't right now then that's fine. But if you do, then let me help you,' Cleo spoke, patting the bed next to her and encouraging Samantha to join her.

'I don't know what you want me to say, Cleo. Everything I say seems to be wrong or not what you want to hear,' Samantha answered reluctantly sitting next to her sister.

'I just want you to be happy, that's all. And I don't think you're happy at the moment on your own.'

'I'm fine, Cleo, honestly,' Samantha lied.

Images of Jimmy flashed through her mind. The night they had lay in bed together, wrapped in each other's arms – the night she had felt truly content.

'Look, I know I keep saying this, but Connor's a really

nice guy. He's nice looking, he has a good job and he's got his own apartment,' Cleo told her.

'I'm sure he's very nice but I don't find him attractive – sorry,' Samantha said almost feeling guilty that she didn't find him attractive and thinking it might all be easier if she did.

'Well, there are a couple of other guys at my work that are OK. I mean Greg's really good looking, better looking than Jeremy, but don't tell him I said that. He's a bit of a ladies' man though and I don't think he would be into an exclusive relationship. And then there's Brandon. He's OK, has a few large moles on his face, but nothing laser surgery couldn't fix if you could persuade him – he works out,' Cleo continued.

'Cleo, I'm already in love with someone,' Samantha stated matter of factly.

'Jimmy Lloyd,' Cleo said the words almost making her mouth smart.

'Yes,' Samantha replied.

'Right, OK, fine. You go back to your newspaper, make a creepy scrapbook full of cuttings and ask him to send you a lock of his hair and an old toothbrush. I've tried to help you and make suggestions but you're obviously not ready for a relationship in the real world,' Cleo spoke angrily as she stood up and headed for the door.

'Cleo, I don't want to fight,' Samantha said, looking at her sister with water filled eyes.

'Neither do I, but all these silly fantasies are making it very hard. I mean, who's it going to be next? Brad Pitt? Nicholas Kaden?' Cleo enquired.

Samantha didn't know what to say in response. Cleo was

never going to believe her.

'So, chicken chow mein for you and rice and curry sauce for Gobby,' Cleo repeated, standing in the door threshold.

'Please.'

'OK, I'll let you know when it's here. By the way, we've got a DVD to watch if you're interested. Some new flick with Hilary Polar in it. Jeremy chose, so it's probably crap,' Cleo spoke.

'I wouldn't want to be a gooseberry,' Samantha replied, feeling sad again and not wanting to look at Hilary Polar for a millisecond.

'Well, bring the cat down,' Cleo suggested.

'But you said he wasn't allowed to go...' Samantha began.

'I know what I said, but that was before I knew Jeremy was the biggest cat lover on the planet. Maybe I was a bit hasty. He is quite cute if you ignore the whole weird eye thing,' Cleo said, looking at Gobby who now had his tongue hanging out.

27

'Full house tonight,' Felicity remarked as she and Samantha checked tickets at the hall.

It was the last night. The final night of *Skating on Broadway* and the last time the Woolston Civic Hall would hold a performance. Getting ready and putting on her uniform had been sadder than she could ever have imagined. Her life would really never be the same again.

She had almost left the house wearing the Civic Hall jumper she had dropped tuna on at lunchtime. She had been late home and Cleo had waylaid her asking for tickets for the show. As hard as Samantha had tried, Cleo hadn't believed the show was fully booked. Her sister knew full well she always kept six tickets in reserve just in case a VIP, like the Queen and her family, happened to saunter into the Civic Hall wanting to watch a show. By the time she had given in, there had been no time to eat or have a shower. She had been just about to leave when Cleo let out a shriek and pointed a finger at Samantha's offending top. So she was now wearing an un-ironed polo shirt and no name badge. She had creases and for the first time ever, no identity stamped on her chest.

They had held the interviews for the tourist information

centre yesterday. She had applied, got an interview and practiced reciting all the things she could bring to the job. Good organisational skills, excellent telephone manner, intimate knowledge of the area, ability to ice skate with an ice cream tray around her neck – no, that wouldn't be needed. All she would have to do was give directions and hand out maps.

Interview day dawned and she dressed in the funeral suit. She had left early and waited outside half an hour before her appointment watching Japanese couple after Japanese couple enter the office. She could see the women at the desk inside, dressed in matching blue uniforms, trying to understand the broken English and decipher that the tourists wanted to see Buckingham Palace. It looked painful.

The time came round and she was just about to push open the door and go in when she caught sight of a Civic Hall poster advertising the ice show. There was Dana, red hair flying behind her, black catsuit clinging to her and there was Jimmy dressed in the red sequinned Lycra top, looking out at her like a face from long ago. The poster was fading and so was her hope. She hadn't been able to go in after that. It didn't feel right, nothing felt quite right at the moment. So, as of tomorrow, she had no job and no idea what she was going to do with her life.

Samantha didn't respond to Felicity. Her mind wasn't on the job and as it began to wander more and more, thinking about being jobless and single, the harder it was to concentrate on checking the tickets that were being handed to her at speed.

'Are you OK, Samantha?' Felicity enquired as Samantha handed the wrong part of the ticket back to one of her customers.

'Oh, sorry, Sir. Here, turn left, row J and seats forty-nine and fifty are halfway along,' Samantha spoke hurriedly, realising her error and correcting it.

'The estate agent isn't telling anyone who's bought the hall,' Felicity commented as she tore another set of tickets.

'What? You spoke to them?' Samantha asked, coming out of her dream world and looking at her colleague.

'Yes, I phoned them. I didn't think it would do any harm. I know you're worrying about it and I thought if I could find out who'd bought it and what they were planning to do with it, it might not actually be as bad as you're thinking,' Felicity responded.

'Oh Felicity, that's really sweet of you, but I'm in no doubt it'll be turned into flats. We just have to come to terms with it,' Samantha replied with a sigh.

'But someone might have…' Felicity started.

'Can you manage here?' Samantha asked her head beginning to ache.

'Yes, of course,' Felicity replied.

Samantha hurried through to the main auditorium, visually checking that her staff were all occupied and performing their roles adequately. *Her* hall. It was finally *her* hall and it was being taken from her. The realisation of that made tears spring to her eyes. The ice looked nothing short of magnificent tonight. The coloured lights swirling all around it seemed to be brighter than ever and the arena was full of people chatting, laughing and purchasing programmes and souvenirs. The scene was a picture of how she had always wanted the hall to be, but now it had gone and slipped away from her – just like Jimmy.

'Yoo hoo! Sam!' Cleo's voice called, standing up and waving elaborately.

Cleo wasn't alone. Jeremy and the pigeon-chested Connor were seated either side of her. Samantha silently cursed her sister for bringing him and then walked over to the group. If she made an appearance now, hopefully she wouldn't have to do it later.

'Sam! You remember Connor, don't you?' Cleo exclaimed, indicating the man next to her and winking at her sister.

'Yes, hello, nice to see you again,' Samantha replied politely not looking at him but watching as her colleague Jane fell over on the ice and a stack of programmes skidded across the rink.

'And you. We were talking about going for something to eat after the show if you…' Connor began, standing up to face Samantha.

'I'm sorry, I've got to rescue hundreds of pounds worth of merchandise,' Samantha spoke hurriedly as she began rushing down the steps towards the ice.

'Sam! Sam! Connor was…' Cleo called after her.

By the time she reached Jane some customers waiting to be served had helped her to her feet and had begun to bundle up the damp programmes.

'Are you OK?' Samantha asked her colleague.

'Yes, yes I think so. I'm still not getting any better at staying up right I'm afraid. Still, it's the last night,' Jane responded with a heavy sigh.

'Look, why don't you go and help Aaron with the souvenirs. I'll do this. Just give me a second to get my skates on,' Samantha offered kindly as she took the programmes and money belt from Jane.

She had never seen Jane look so happy. She practically ran from the ice and tore the skates from her feet. She would miss her, Felicity and Milo. She hadn't really thought of them as friends before, but perhaps they were. You really had to be friends with someone when you heard all about chain-smoking mothers and the latest exotic illegal immigrant being romantically pursued.

Samantha hurriedly laced up her boots and got onto the ice with the remaining programmes. She checked her watch. There was little more than fifteen minutes before the show started.

'Programmes!' she called, holding one of them aloft in the air as she started to skate along the edge of the ice.

She could see Connor was looking at her and it made her feel uneasy. She wished Cleo hadn't brought him, but her sister never listened to her. She knew she meant well, but things would be a lot easier if Cleo actually believed what she had been trying to tell her for the last fortnight. She didn't want another man, she wanted Jimmy. And even if she had blown it and he wasn't coming back, she just wasn't ready to think about anyone else. Not yet and possibly not ever.

Samantha could see someone motioning to her for a programme, so she turned and moved across the ice towards them. But, as she gained momentum, suddenly all the lights on the ice went out and the rink was plunged into darkness. The crowd wooed and whooped as if the show was about to start and Samantha felt completely disorientated. She had to get off. What was going on? It was too early for the show to start. People wouldn't be in their seats yet and she needed to sort this out. She moved slowly, trying to find her way to the edge of the rink when she heard the sound of another pair of skates, heading in her direction. She looked into the darkness trying to see what was going on. And then the skater appeared before her, took hold of her arm and turned her around.

Samantha looked up, her eyes adjusting to the darkness. She couldn't believe what she was seeing. It was Jimmy!

She blinked and blinked again and put her hands up to her eyes to rub them. She had to be imagining him, just like she had been constantly since he left.

'Hey,' he greeted a smile lighting up his face, his Minstrel eyes creasing at the corners.

'Oh my goodness!' Samantha exclaimed.

Her legs wobbled with emotion as he spoke, and she realised he really *was* standing in front of her.

Her breathing became erratic, catching in her throat and tears welled up in her eyes. She couldn't believe he was back. She just looked and looked at him, trying to take in everything about him. Then, finally, she threw herself into him, holding him tightly, squeezing him hard to make sure the whole moment was real.

Jimmy held her and ran his hand through her hair, kissing the top of her head as she leaned on him and then, he held her away from him.

'Come with me,' Jimmy quickly urged her, and he began to skate off towards the centre of the rink.

'Wait! I need to say some things to you, lots of things I should have said before. I, I didn't think you were coming back, after what I said, I – oh goodness – we have to get off of here, there's a show about to start,' Samantha reminded him, struggling to get out all the words she wanted to.

'I know,' Jimmy answered with a smile.

'But, we need to – oh!' Samantha exclaimed in horror as a bright white spotlight shined down onto her.

As the lights on the ice went up the capacity audience all gasped and exclaimed at the sight of the two of them in the middle of the ice rink, Jimmy in blue Lycra, Samantha in her Civic Hall uniform.

She felt sick. Everyone was looking at her and she was still wearing the money belt and holding a batch of programmes. Her face began to redden, and her heart went into overdrive.

'OH MY GOD!' Cleo shrieked from her seat four rows back from the ice.

Samantha watched her sister clamp her hands over her mouth as she saw her standing on the ice holding Jimmy Lloyd's hand.

★

'Gimme those, and I'll take that,' Jimmy spoke as he swiftly undid her money belt and relieved Samantha of the programmes.

As Jimmy skated to the side of the rink to ditch the money and the souvenir brochures, she was left stranded with thousands of eyes on her and her alone. People were talking amongst themselves, wondering what was going on, pointing and looking slightly confused. Samantha empathised, because she felt exactly the same way.

Jimmy came back to join her, still smiling. He took hold of one of Samantha's hands and used the other one to take something out of his pocket. It was a blindfold.

'What are you doing? Are you back in the show? What

happened with your counsellor? There's so much I want to know – can we go?' Samantha started, moving uneasily on her skates.

'Put this on,' Jimmy told her, handing her the blindfold.

Samantha looked at what he had placed in her hand. She let out a scream and dropped it onto the ice.

'Are you insane?! I can't skate in front of anyone! And certainly not blindfolded! We did that once and it was CRAZY! I can barely skate with you watching without feeling like I'm going to vomit. Let's just go and get some blackberry tea or something and we can talk, and I can...' Samantha started her body beginning to shake.

The crowd began a slow hand clap as they waited for something to happen. A few people shouted 'Come on Jimmy' and others nudged each other and stared at the scene being played out before them.

'Sam, do you trust me?' Jimmy asked her seriously.

He was looking at her intently, his brown eyes fixed on her face, his expression intense.

'I can't do this, in front of everyone,' Samantha responded with a gulp of fear.

'Do you trust me?' Jimmy repeated, holding onto her hand.

Samantha looked away from him to the audience, the thousands of people all waiting for something to happen, waiting for *her* to do something. Her heart was hammering and her legs were turning to jelly. She looked back at Jimmy.

She replied with a definite nod.

Jimmy smiled, picked her blindfold off the floor and put it over her eyes. He then got a second blindfold out of his pocket and put it over his face. The sound from the audience was a combination of delight, horror and surprise. Some gasped, a few actually screamed.

Jimmy took hold of Samantha's hands as they assumed their starting position and Samantha tried to swallow the pure terror that was threatening to consume her.

*

'What's she doing Jeremy? For Christ's sake what is she doing?' Cleo exclaimed hysterically as the music began.

'I think she's going to skate,' Jeremy replied as he moved onto the edge of his seat to get a closer look.

'Does Samantha skate professionally? Isn't that Jimmy Lloyd on the ice with her?' Connor enquired as he too moved to the edge of his seat and stared at the two people on the rink.

'He's holding her hand Jeremy, he's holding her hand,' Cleo stated unable to keep her eyes off her sister.

*

The haunting introduction of the music began, filling the arena with sound and, both blind, Samantha and Jimmy began the routine they had practiced and perfected alone in the small hours of the morning. Now they were performing it in front of thousands.

Samantha couldn't see a thing, not even a glimmer from the spotlights. She was holding her breath so hard her chest was hurting, but despite that, she could sense Jimmy near her, feel his closeness. Her legs felt like lead and jelly all at the same time, yet somehow, she was performing the steps he had taught her more accurately than she ever had before. She could feel the breeze they were creating as they moved around the ice and she could sense the expectation from the audience. They didn't know what was coming next and they were probably still wondering what the manager of the Civic Hall was doing ice skating with Jimmy Lloyd. Then, as the song built to its first crescendo, Samantha knew what was coming. She felt Jimmy take hold of her and then in one swift move he rolled her up onto his shoulder into the crucifix hold. She could feel she was high in the air, being held by her underarms, almost flying, and the crowd were applauding and shouting their appreciation. Despite being blindfolded Samantha could almost see the faces of shock and surprise at someone un-sequinned, wearing a creased Civic Hall polo shirt and uniform trousers, being held aloft by Jimmy Lloyd.

She span around, catching hold of Jimmy's hand, stepped backwards and turned, just as she had learnt. Her breathing was more controlled now and although she still felt fear, it was mixed with excitement and complete exhilaration. She was caught up in the moment, intoxicated by the music, thinking of nothing but Jimmy and how it felt to have him back.

She skated out backwards, balanced carefully and elegantly on one leg, stretching out the other behind her. She took a deep breath and waited. They had only done this move once before, not blindfolded, and Samantha had screamed the whole way through. But she knew this was what Jimmy wanted, this was the way to end the routine. And before she could think any more the waiting was over. She felt Jimmy take hold of her ankle, spin her sideways and she took her other leg off the ice as he began to flip her up and down in the move Dana would no longer perform with him. Her heart was banging against her chest and she could almost smell the ice. She felt air rush past her ear as she passed dangerously close to the rink and then she felt the coldness of the ice as Jimmy put her down onto it. She felt him slide down onto the floor next to her and then, as the music ended, he lifted her hand in the air with his.

The crowd erupted. There was cheering, whistling, screaming and non-stop applause that had Samantha reaching for her ears. She was breathing heavily, still shaking and she felt exhausted. She could feel Jimmy's body close to hers, his breathing also rapid and then he picked her up under her arms and lifted her back into a standing position.

He took off her blindfold and then removed his own. The crowd were roaring their appreciation, people were stamping on the floor, banging anything they could to make the loudest noise possible. It was something Samantha had never experienced at the Civic Hall before and she had been part of it. She was smiling, she felt happier than she ever had, not caring she was standing in the middle of an arena being watched by thousands. She looked up at Jimmy. He was smiling down at her, looking at her like she was the most precious thing he had ever set eyes on.

Neither of them knew what to say. The crowd

continued to clap, but they were oblivious to them now. Jimmy ran his hand down the side of Samantha's face and then drew her towards him, kissing her deeply. A loud cheer went up from the audience as Samantha put her arms around his neck and held him close to her.

★

Tears were rolling down Cleo's face, threatening to wash away every scrap of make-up she had applied earlier.

'God, what do you say to that? Did you know she could do that?' Connor asked both Jeremy and Cleo as in front of them Samantha and Jimmy did a short lap round the ice to acknowledge their applause.

'They were blindfolded. I mean, have you seen anyone do that before? Ever?' Jeremy remarked to Cleo who was just staring at the ice, watching her sister.

'I didn't believe her,' Cleo spoke quietly almost in a trance.

'Did you know she could skate like that? I mean skating up and down selling programmes isn't doing a professional routine with a blindfold on is it?' Jeremy carried on, clapping along with the rest of the enthralled audience.

'She told me about him. She told me she was in love with Jimmy Lloyd and I laughed at her. *Laughed* at her, Jeremy, and got mad and told her not to tell lies and make up stories. Look at them! Look at them together!' Cleo told him tears still rolling down her face.

'You weren't to know – I mean, how could you? She keeps herself to herself, doesn't she?' Jeremy said, breaking from clapping and putting an arm around his girlfriend.

'She felt she couldn't rely on me, she knew I wouldn't believe her. That's why she said it was stupid camp-sounding Darren Jacobs. I've got to go and see her, excuse me,' Cleo announced, and she got up and hurried past Connor and the other people who were standing up in their row.

★

Samantha's face was glowing as she and Jimmy left the ice, still holding hands.

'You were amazing! You did the move Sam! I just sensed you were going to do it, I knew you trusted me!' Jimmy exclaimed excitedly as the pair of them joyfully held on to each other.

'This has been the craziest night of my life! I just performed in front of thousands of people! Me! Samantha Smith, the girl who's scared of her own shadow,' Samantha remarked, trying to control her laughter.

'God, you don't know how good it is to see you again,' Jimmy responded, stopping her and just looking at her as he held her hand.

'I didn't think I would ever see you again, after what I said. I'm such an idiot and I'm so sorry,' Samantha spoke, looking back at him.

'I knew you didn't mean it, you were just scared that's all. I was scared too, but it didn't take me long away to realise that it's OK to be scared and admitting it just makes you even stronger,' Jimmy said sincerely.

'How did things go? In America, in – the place,' Samantha asked him cautiously.

'You can say "rehab" – it isn't a dirty word you know,' Jimmy replied.

'I know, I'm sorry – I just...' Samantha began.

'It went really well, which is why I'm back. And I don't want to waste another minute talking to you in this walkway. Let's go somewhere where we can talk properly – on our own,' Jimmy spoke, noticing that the skating entourage were preparing to begin the show and making their way back and forth along the corridor.

'OK,' Samantha agreed, smiling at him 'but I have to find my shoes!'

'Sam,' Cleo called as she appeared from the door leading to the foyer.

Samantha turned around to face her sister and immediately saw that Cleo's face was awash with tears and her make-up was almost all gone. She had never seen her look so upset. Not since Miles Jones.

'Shall I go and find your shoes?' Jimmy offered.

'Yes, thanks, they're under the spare seat at the end of row B,' Samantha directed not taking her eyes from Cleo.

'OK, I won't be long,' Jimmy replied, and he kissed Samantha's cheek before making his way back towards the auditorium.

They were left alone in the corridor, just looking at each other, neither knowing what to do. Cleo's expression was unreadable, but Samantha could tell the cogs were whirring and her eyes were still full of tears. Samantha didn't know what to say or do, she just stood still, her mouth dry, her stomach contracting. And then, suddenly, Cleo rushed towards her throwing her arms around her and enveloping her in a bear hug. The comforting smell of Joop! and hairspray filled Samantha's nostrils as she hugged Cleo back.

She could feel her sister shaking as she cried openly on her shoulder. And then Cleo pulled herself away to look at Samantha.

'Sam, I don't know what to say – I am so sorry,' Cleo spoke tears running down her face.

'What for?' Samantha asked her.

'For not believing you, about Jimmy,' Cleo said her cheeks reddening with shame as she said the words.

'Oh Cleo, it doesn't matter! I think if you'd told me the same thing, I wouldn't have believed you either. Well no, I would have believed you because you are you and you could get anyone. I mean, if you were me and you had told me, if I was you – if that makes any sense,' Samantha babbled.

'Absolutely none and it's no excuse for letting you down when you really needed someone. I've been preoccupied with myself as usual, I should've taken more notice of you,' Cleo continued.

'I'm not a little girl anymore. And you didn't know what was going on because I hid it from you, not because you didn't take any notice,' Samantha insisted.

'Oh Sam, you looked amazing out there on the ice!' Cleo exclaimed, hugging her sister again.

'Oh, I wouldn't say that. I almost fell on my face and I was terrified,' Samantha responded her eyes bright, her face lit up.

'You look different tonight,' Cleo spoke.

'No name badge,' Samantha said, indicating the bare patch on her top where it should have been.

'No, I don't think it's that. I don't know what it is, but you just look different, all grown up all of a sudden and so – beautiful,' Cleo remarked, smiling at Samantha.

'It's Jimmy. He came back for me. Apparently, I *am* enough,' Samantha replied happily.

28

'I think Dana looks more comfortable with Andrei,' Jimmy remarked as he watched the skating.

He and Samantha had escaped to the solitude of the light and sound booth. It was redundant for the ice show as it controlled its own light and sound from a set up at the side of the rink. Samantha hadn't set foot in it since the day Jimmy left. She had tried, opened the door, and her harsh words and reaction to the news he was returning to America had echoed all around the room.

'She looks even more comfortable with Nigel these days. Their relationship seems to be out in the open,' Samantha responded, taking a sip of her blackberry tea.

'Nigel's a good guy really. I told him what I wanted to do tonight and he let me hijack the show when he didn't have to. I think he thought I was insane, and I didn't even mention the blindfolds,' Jimmy remarked, drinking from his cup.

'So, are you back in the show?' Samantha enquired.

'Nope,' Jimmy responded.

'But why? I don't understand. I thought you went back to rehab so you could come back to the show,' Samantha said.

'I only ever said I was coming back for you. I had no intention of coming back to the show, I think my performing days are over,' Jimmy told her.

'No! You're an amazing performer! There's no one in the ice show like you. Tonight, the audience loved you, they don't react like that for anyone else,' Samantha spoke.

'Tonight, the audience loved *you*, Sam. I was just background. Anyway, I don't need the show, I have a new job,' Jimmy announced proudly.

'Oh goodness! What? Where?' Samantha responded animated out of both happiness and concern.

'In North London, at one of the entertainment complexes there. They've just converted their bowling alley into an ice rink. It's only small, mainly for kids to come and have fun, not for anything competitive. Anyhow, I suggested giving lessons, being an instructor and they agreed. Why they agreed I don't know, but they did,' Jimmy explained with a smile.

'That's brilliant, teaching is what you wanted to do,' Samantha remarked happily.

'Yeah, it's great. I've been very lucky,' Jimmy agreed, taking another sip of his drink.

'Unlike me. Unemployed as from tomorrow. Cleo wanted me to work in the tourist information centre and I even got an interview, but I just couldn't bring myself to go through with it,' Samantha informed him with a sigh.

'Well, why would you want to work there?' Jimmy asked her, putting his drink down on the table.

'Because it's better than working at Simpkin's Shoes or at McDonald's,' Samantha answered.

'But, what about this place? Who would run the hall?'

Jimmy questioned.

'Has rehab erased your memory of the last month? The Civic Hall is closing, it's been sold,' Samantha reminded him.

'Sure, I know. But do you know what plans the buyer has for it?' Jimmy enquired.

'No and Felicity says the estate agent is keeping it close to his chest. That's because he doesn't want the community up in arms when they decide to turn it into a housing development,' Samantha responded.

'What if the buyer wanted to keep it as it is? As a place for entertainment?' Jimmy asked her.

'That won't happen. He or she won't make half as much profit from keeping it going as they would from development,' Samantha answered.

'What if it wasn't just about profit? What if the buyer had a certain amount of personal attachment to the place?' Jimmy enquired, looking at her.

Samantha turned in her chair and looked directly at him.

'Personal attachment? What sort of personal attachment?' Samantha asked her eyes widening.

'What if the Civic Hall was the very place he had first kissed the woman he's in love with,' Jimmy spoke, looking back at her.

Samantha put her hands to her mouth in shock. He couldn't really be saying what she thought he was saying. Her heart was racing as she gazed at him, her eyes begging him to say something else to confirm her hopes.

'What if the Civic Hall had just made the restaurant a success and the new owner had lots of connections in the entertainment industry to entice new and exciting acts to the borough of Woolston?' Jimmy carried on.

'Oh Jimmy!' Samantha exclaimed still holding her hands to her face in surprise and excitement.

'What if the Civic Hall had a manager who the new owner had so much faith in, he had absolutely no doubt the place would be a success,' Jimmy spoke finally, watching Samantha's reaction.

'You've bought the Civic Hall!' Samantha yelled out loud.

'I've bought the Civic Hall,' Jimmy repeated a huge smile spreading over his face.

'Are you mad?! I know how much it was on the market for,' Samantha spoke.

'I negotiated hard. There were a couple of other offers on the table, some from developers. I talked a good talk about preserving the history and the heritage, and then paid over the odds for it,' Jimmy told her with a laugh.

'But how? Why? I mean, it's too much,' Samantha said with a sigh.

'How? Well I sold my houses and my cars. Why? Because there's no point having houses and cars in America when my heart is over here. And besides the smoochy stuff, I do believe it can be profitable. We never got a chance to implement our ideas and frankly that sucked,' Jimmy spoke.

'Oh, Jimmy!' Samantha exclaimed and she got off her chair and threw her arms around him.

'I know it was only ten days, but I missed you like crazy – even the coughing and the hyperventilating,' Jimmy told her as he held her.

'I love you,' Samantha spoke without concern for how the words were going to come out.

Jimmy held her back from him to look at her.

'I love you too,' he responded sincerely.

Samantha smiled and put her arms around him again, holding him tightly.

'Buying the hall does leave me with one problem though,' Jimmy spoke as he stroked her hair.

'What?' Samantha asked, pulling away to look at him.

'I kind of don't have anywhere to live and I know how you and Cleo fight about house guests,' Jimmy responded.

'Oh, don't worry about that, I think Cleo and I can reach an understanding that won't make me the biggest hypocrite on the planet. Be warned though, I do already share my bed with another male,' Samantha replied.

'I think you're going to have to explain,' Jimmy said curiously.

'He's cute and furry, has a wonky eye and only eats leftovers,' Samantha informed with a grin.

'Gobby,' Jimmy said, smiling.

'Yes, but I'm sure he won't mind sharing me.'

'He isn't going to be given a choice,' Jimmy answered, and he kissed her again.

★

It was almost 1.00 am when Cleo and Jeremy returned home, a little worse for wear. Jeremy kicked off his brogues and left them in the middle of the hallway and Cleo had to hold the banister for support.

'Wasn't my sister fantastic tonight? The press was there you know, taking photos of my sister. My sister and *Jimmy Lloyd*. She kissed him, right in the middle of the ice rink, in front of everyone,' Cleo babbled as she and Jeremy mounted the stairs.

'So you've said, at least a hundred times – to everyone in the Indian restaurant,' Jeremy told her as he swayed violently and caught hold of the wall to steady himself.

'I think Connor was very disappointed, that he missed out on a date with Sam. I mean, you could see his face drop when he saw she was with Jimmy Lloyd. I mean, I don't know what I was thinking of. Connor's a midget and not really the right colouring for Sam. I think Jimmy suits her you know. I didn't think I would ever say that, but I think he suits her quite well. Isn't he tall? And he has lovely hair, doesn't he? I always thought he had lovely hair,' Cleo carried on as they reached the top of the stairs and staggered across the landing towards her bedroom.

'Yes, lovely hair. Remind me to ask him for some tips,' Jeremy responded sarcastically.

'Do you think she's back yet? My little sister. Jimmy Lloyd's girlfriend?' Cleo asked as she halted outside Samantha's bedroom door.

'Looks that way,' Jeremy responded, and he indicated the door handle.

Cleo let out a loud shriek that reverberated round the landing and she put her hands to her mouth. Her black coloured crystal was hanging from the door handle of Samantha's bedroom.

'The little minx! I don't believe it! Wait until I speak to her!' Cleo exclaimed, stumbling backwards and falling off one of her high heeled shoes.

'In the morning, Hon, let's go to bed. That sag aloo's really given me indigestion,' Jeremy remarked, heading off towards Cleo's bedroom.

'Are you sure that hasn't been caused by the six pints of lager? I'm surprised you didn't ask if they did it by intravenous drip,' Cleo said, following Jeremy.

*

Inside her room Samantha smiled as she heard Jeremy and her sister close the door of Cleo's bedroom. She pulled the duvet up around her and laid her head on Jimmy's chest. She had just about everything she had ever wished for. She was Samantha Smith, manager of the Woolston Civic Hall, and she had a gorgeous boyfriend. One day though she would definitely want a new name badge. Samantha *Lloyd*, Manager had the same number of letters and certainly had a nice ring to it.

Gobby let out a sleepy miaow of agreement.

She smiled. Two males in her bed at the same time, not even Cleo had managed that. Well, at least she didn't think so. In fact, she sincerely hoped not.

About the Author

MANDY BAGGOT is an international bestselling and award-winning romance writer. The winner of the Innovation in Romantic Fiction award at the UK's Festival of Romance, her romantic comedy novel *One Wish in Manhattan* was also shortlisted for the Romantic Novelists' Association Romantic Comedy Novel of the Year award in 2016. Mandy's books have so far been translated into German, Italian, Czech and Hungarian. Mandy loves the Greek island of Corfu, white wine, country music and handbags. Also a singer, she has taken part in ITV1's *Who Dares Sings* and *The X-Factor*. Mandy is a member of the Romantic Novelists' Association and the Society of Authors and lives near Salisbury, Wiltshire, UK with her husband and two daughters.

Become an Aria addict

Aria is the digital-first fiction imprint from Head of Zeus.

We are Aria, a dynamic digital-first fiction imprint from award-winning independent publishers Head of Zeus. At heart, we're avid readers committed to publishing exactly the kind of books we love to read — from romance and sagas to crime, thrillers and historical adventures. Visit us online and discover a community of like-minded fiction fans!

We're also on the look out for tomorrow's superstar authors. So, if you're a budding writer looking for a publisher, we'd love to hear from you. You can submit your book online at ariafiction.com/we-want-read-your-book

You can find us at:
Email: aria@headofzeus.com
Website: www.ariafiction.com
Twitter: @Aria_Fiction
Facebook: @ariafiction
Instagram: @ariafiction

Printed in Great Britain
by Amazon